D0494947

Aberdeenshire Library and Information Service
www.aberdeenshire.gov.uk/libraries
Renewals Hotline 01224 661511

3 0 NOV 2010

2 5 APR 2012
1 0 JUL 2012   1 9 FEB 2014

1 9 FEB 2014

1 6 MAY 2015

ABERDEENSHIRE
LIBRARIES

WITHDRAWN
FROM LIBRARY

2 6 MAY 2017
2 2 JUN 2017
0 3 MAY 2019

TOULMIN, DAVID

Collected short stories

X6/TOU

151217

151217

Collected Short Stories

BY THE SAME AUTHOR

Hard Shining Corn	Impulse Publications Ltd. 1972
Straw into Gold	Impulse Publications Ltd. 1973
Blown Seed	Paul Harris Publishing 1976
Harvest Home	Paul Harris Publishing 1978
Travels without a Donkey	Gourdas House Publishers 1980
A Chiel Among Them	Gourdas House Publishers 1982
The Tillycorthy Story	Aberdeen University 1986
The Clyack Sheaf	Aberdeen University Press 1986
Buchan Claik (with Peter Buchan)	Gordon Wright Publishing Ltd. 1989

Collected Short Stories

David Toulmin

GORDON WRIGHT PUBLISHING
25 MAYFIELD ROAD, EDINBURGH EH9 2NQ
SCOTLAND

© David Toulmin 1992

No part of this publication may be reproduced, stored in a retrieval system, or transmitted in any form or by any means electronic, mechanical, photocopying, recording or otherwise without the prior permission of the publisher.

British Library Cataloguing in Publication Data

Toulmin, David
Collected Short Stories
I. Title
823.914 [FS]

ISBN 0 903065 74 6

The publisher acknowledges subsidy from the Scottish Arts Council towards the publication of this volume.

X6/TOU·
151217

Typeset by Gordon Wright Publishing Ltd.
Printed and Bound by Butler and Tanner Ltd. Frome, Somerset.

Introduction

With all my forbears coming from Buchan farming stock, I thought I knew most North-East words and phrases. It wasn't until I was talking to David Toulmin many months ago that I learned about yaval broth - second day's soup. I asked him if he was still writing. He said he had one book left in him, and if he ever got around to writing it he knew what he would call it - *Yaval Broth*.

Later, he thought that a more appropriate title might be *Yaval Crap* - a second crop. There was, of course, a subtle difference between the two, but I still liked Yaval Broth, maybe because as a youngster I always thought that second-day's soup tasted better. In *Buchan Claik*, a dictionary of Doric words which Toulmin wrote with the late Peter Buchan, there is an amusing story about yaval broth. It tells of a tinker who knocked at a farmhouse door and asked for a bite to eat. 'Div ye tak yaval broth?' the lady of the house asked. 'Oh, aye,' said the tinker. 'Then come back the morn,' she said, and slammed the door in his face.

For those who have 'come back the morn,' David Toulmin (or John Reid to give him his real name) has dished up a helping of 'yaval broth' that will be sipped with relish by his readers. His *Collected Short Stories* gives us a chance to savour again the fare that took this one-time farm loon from the byres of Buchan into the front rank of Scottish writers.

His work has been compared to that of Lewis Grassic Gibbon, which is not an extravagant claim, but *Scots Quair* had its roots in the Mearns, while Toulmin's work is set firmly in the weet and clorty soil of Buchan. It is a vanished Buchan that he writes about . . . a land of nicky-tams, fee'd loons, kitchie-deems, sharny boots, chaumers and bothy nichts.

Toulmin, incidentally, demolishes our cosy conception of chaumers and bothies. 'All this yammer about the good old bothy days is just a lot of white-wash,' he says. 'Your chaumer was part of the hay-loft above the stable, with only a thin partition between you and the hayseed, and damned if you could have slept for the stamping of iron hoofs on the cobblestones, or for the rattle of manger chains or the scamper of rats at the corn kists.

'You hung your Sunday clothes on to rusty nails hammered into the partition and the hay-worms came wriggling through the seams and lost themselves in the pockets of your best suit.'

He sees the mid-fifties as the time when the old ways finally disappeared. 'The pickiesae hat and the nicky-tams were gone forever,' he declared. Now there were half-days on Saturdays and summer holidays with pay and never a wet sark sitting in their tractor cabs. Maybe it was for the better, for some of the men were old before their time, wracked with work and rheumatism.

The Buchan of Toulmin's youth was often harsh and uncompromising. Those were the days when the daily diet for a farm servant was 'cabbage brose, kale brose, neep brose, melk brose and ordinary brose,' although on Sunday you got porridge instead of brose and a fried preserved egg instead of a boiled one. Luxury was 'a wee bittie o butter about the size o yer thoom-nail' and a tiny spoonful of jam that 'wad hardly stick a flea.'

'I wadna be a loon again,' declares Toulmin. Nevertheless, a golden thread of nostalgia runs through his work. He remembers, for instance, his first visit to the Turriff Show. That was the year that Harry Gordon opened it – 'the wee laird of Inversnecky in his kilt and sporran' – and the tug-o'-war Bells of Tyrie were at their peak, 'pulling everything in sight, from Alness to Strathdon, Wartle and Tarland.'

He remembers, too, the great days of Aikey Fair, when there were 'acres of bicycles' parked in a field near the Brae and Old Briggie, the farmer of Bridge-end, said it was the best paying field he ever had, though he never planted anything in it but bicycles. It cost you a tanner (sixpence) to park your bike.

The Aikey Fair of to-day is a pale shadow of the old horse market that Toulmin knew. There were penny arcades and fortune-tellers, coconut shies and shooting galleries, a Fat Woman and a Midget, and 'a pirate-looking lad throwing knives at a quine nearly naked.' You could walk about and listen to Curly Mackay and his melodeon or Jimmy Macbeath singing Cornkisters. The evangelists trumpeted a different kind of tune, preaching repentance to the sinners 'till they had your poor quine nearly scared to death listening to all that stite.'

The sights and sounds of Aikey Brae are a thing of the past for David Toulmin. He has lived in Aberdeen for twenty years now (he and his wife Margaret stay out Linksfield way), so he has become a 'toonser,' but there was a time when going to the city was an unforgettable event. In 'Moonlight Flitting' he draws a wonderfully evocative picture of a lad who got a day off for his honeymoon and took a trip to Aberdeen with his bride, Gertie. They walked down Union Street hand-in-hand and went on a shopping spree . . . to Raggie Morrison's, at the corner of St Nicholas Street, and the Guinea Shop, where she had bought her wedding frock for twenty-one shillings, and to Cockie Hunter's in the Castlegate, where they got a second-hand dressing table for their bedroom for a fiver.

This is a pre-war Aberdeen that has changed beyond recognition, and Toulmin brings it vividly alive. The New Market in his tale is the *old* New Market, where Low's bookstall had books piled up to the roof and cheap enough for even a hard-up farm servant. The only thing that made them hesitate about going upstairs were the shabby booths where dubious ladies sat at their stalls 'like a spider at a web, waiting for the unwary fly.' The farmers and country chiels - 'a bit canned and careless with their money' - offered to buy stockings if the 'quines' bared a leg to let them try them on.

Woolworth's 3d & 6d stores, selling the latest hit record, 'Little Grey Home in the West'; Stead & Simpson, where Gertie bought a pair of shoes and a handbag; the Fifty-Shilling Tailors in St Nicholas Street, 'which you had always regarded as Jews' Corner' . . . they were names that everyone knew in the years before the war. Out on Union Street the Rover and Bydand buses rumbled past and bicycles threaded their way among the cars of the gentry.

'Moonlight Flitting' appeared in *Straw into Gold*, which Toulmin once told me was his favourite book. 'It was part of my life,' he said. There are a number of stories from the book in this latest collection. Although they are presented as fiction, there is little doubt that they are drawn from the author's own experience. 'I might have been a Walt Disney, a Beaverbrook, a Sam Goldwyn, a Bernard Shaw,' he writes, 'but the old man had never heard of these men. They were only shadows, he said; they had no substance, they existed only on paper - never make a living that way lad.'

Well, maybe the 'old man' was right. Whatever distinction he has won for himself, John Reid has never made a fortune out of his writing. He occasionally reminds me with a knowing look that I once turned down one of his articles when I was Editor of the *Evening Express*, so I was intrigued by a paragraph in 'Lang Breeks' which recalled that when he 'started sending stories to an editor they came right back.' 'Nivver mak money that wye ma loon, nae wi a pincil ahin yer lug,' said the old man.

It wasn't John's talent that I doubted. I wondered then, and for a long time after, if a city readership was interested in a way of life that had all but disappeared, or in a language that was either dead or dying. Now, looking back, I marvel at what this former Buchan ploughman has done, if not to save the Doric, at least to place it in trust for future generations – 'between book covers,' as he himself puts it.

Another Buchan loon, David Murison, former Editor of the Scottish National Dictionary, now living in his native Fraserburgh, once told me of the alarming rate at which Doric words and phrases were disappearing. I had the impression that most of them would be gone by the end of the century. Here, in Toulmin's book, they spring from the pages like beacons lighting up the past . . . 'a bit o a claik' . . . 'dinna bigg stibble ruckies in yon park' . . . 'a muckle gype' . . . 'taking a tig' . . . 'foostie strae' . . . 'a doll in her oxter' . . . 'yoked to the tattie roguin.' Claik, ruckies, gype, foostie . . . what 'proper' words could possibly replace them?

The characters in Toulmin's stories step straight out of the barns and bothies of Buchan; some of them, you might think, from the very middens themselves (auld Knowie built *his* chaumer over his midden). There are people like auld Snorlie frae Swineden, who tethered his horse at the roadside because there was no grass in the parks, or Rab Imray, the grieve at the Barnyards, a 'tearin brute,' a big chiel who could have been a bobby; or Elsie Wabster, who was mistress at the Dookit Farm – 'Elsie wore the breeks, oh aye, ye could see that.'

David Toulmin, who is now in his eightieth year and among the oldest of the living Doric writers, has had 'a pincil ahin his lug' all his life. His first book, *Hard Shining Corn*, was published exactly twenty years ago, but he points out that he was writing twenty-five years before that – it took him a quarter of a century to get 'into book covers.' He has had nine books published. One of them was called *The Clyack Sheaf*, which means the last bound sheaf, but not the end of the harvest.

So perhaps there is still a yaval crop to come from this great chronicler of North-East life. Meanwhile, we can content ourselves with this rich taste of yaval broth.

Robert Smith

To my Wife
Margaret Jane

Hard Shining Corn.

Shinbrae was a fine hill farm, well set up on the brae above its neighbours. The farmhouse squared its shoulders to the four winds with a sullen dignity, and the steading stood out boldly behind it in brazen austerity. Looking from the road Shinbrae had a dour 'wha daur meddle wi me?' aspect which intimidated the Seedsman's agent and prospective employee alike. It brought them wheedling to the back kitchie door with a respect which Shinnie played up well when it came to a chinwag.

Shinnie's black nowt could be seen for miles, the admiration and the envy of the countryside, fat and sleek as moles, and the sheep crawled like lice on the wide green slopes of Wild White clover. Wild White wasna lang in the go, and it fair took a hold on the hard, sun-drenched knowes at Shinbrae. Shinnies sometimes ploughed down a sole of tassled clover that mony a crofter lad would have been glad tae graze on. Auld Snorlie frae Swineden had tae tether his horse at the roadside, and sometimes herd a coo or twa, on 'the lang acre' as he called it, 'cause there was nae grass in his parks, naething but steens and thistles, and there was only a stone dyke atween him and Shinnies. But Shinnies held on the herrin guts and bone meal no end, and even dulce from the seaside, and though it rotted a corn crap or twa it fair put heart in the grun.

There was an avenue of beech and plane trees leading to the main road and the cottar houses at the entrance. Half down the hill, in the middle of a park was a windmill, 'cause there was no drinking water on the place, and it had to be pumped up to a cistern by the kitchen door, which also supplied the cottars. Surface water that came down the hill was caught in the mill-dam, close by the steading and the stackyard. And man, Shinnies stackyard was worth looking at - every ruck shaved with a scythe and thatched with green rushes from the peatbog, and diced over in diamond squares of golden straw-rapes, each rick as trim as a giant beeruskie, with a wee pirn on top like an ornament.

Shinnies thrashed out well, hard shining corn that had a fine reeshle aboot it, grown on those hard flinty braes where you couldn't put a foot down without standing on a pebble. To a stranger Shinbrae was just a litter of stones and silly folk said they should all be gathered off. But Shinnies predecessors had all been as wise as Solomon and left the flintstones alone. Man they fair kept the moisture in a dry summer and filtered it through in a wet season. Almost every sprouted grain had to push a stone aside before it saw the light, and then the sun was caught on the brae and polished it on the stalk. No wonder that Shinnie put

13

his thumbs in the armholes of his waistcoat on threshing days, when he showed his gold dust to the neighbours.

But if a man was to be judged by the appearance of his farm-buildings maybe Shinnie wasn't all that bad. 'Damned bigsy thing' folk said, a gentleman farmer his wye o't, always respectably dressed in a suit of brownish grey coarse tweed, a watch-chain across his waistcoat, collar and tie and jaunty cap. His shoes were the squeaky type, brown like peasemeal, and always betrayed his silent, thief-like approach. His moustache was always neatly trimmed and the way he curled his lip over his scented pipe you could say there was a quirk in the man somewhere. His eyes were blue and clear but beady as a fox, and when he looked at you you felt he was wondering how he could wheedle a copper out of you more than he was bargained for.

Furthermore Shinnie had the first motor car in the district, a big Chevrolet with a canvas hood that fair gaed tearin bye the ither lads still in their gigs. It stood mostly at the front door as a sort of ornament to impress folks that came in bye. Almost every winter evening Shinnie went to the byre, handling his fat stots to see if they were ready for the butcher. You could always tell if Shinnie was about in the dark because you could feel the scented smell of his tobacco. It sort of charmed the air and though you didn't see the man you sort of liked him in spite of yourself.

But Shinnie was good enough to his cottars and they stayed on with him from year to year if there was nothing better in the market. Shinnie just let them know from the start that he would stand no nonsense and usually he had little bother with his workers. But he had been watchin yon foreman chiel 'cause folk said he was a bit tarry-fingered and couldn't let go of anything he got hold of in the dark. And yon second-horseman's wife was a bit of a claik and had abody's character in the district, and folk she didna like she gaed oot and cried at them on the road. Faith aye, Shinnie was sometimes black-affronted at the limmer but put up wi her 'cause her man was sic a sober, hard-workin stock.

And Shinnie aye had a kind word for yon Charlie Stoddart, him that sortit Shinnie's nowt and pulled his neeps though the rain was running down his chin. Folk said Charlie was a bittie simple but he tore on at his work and pleased Shinnie fine whatever they said. And there was yon scrat o a loon o Charlie's that threw stones on the slates and broke the skylichts and tore doon the dykes lookin for rabbits. He would be a problem to Charlie yon loon yet, him that wore his father's breeks and kissed the quines on the sly. A big loon like that fleein aboot wi a gird or his father's bicycle when he should be helpin the old man in the byre.

But for all that Shinnie never said much to Charlie's loon, just curled his forefinger over the stem of his pipe and spat out a few hints ahin Charlie's back. 'Dinna throw steens on the slates loon, ye could brak the skylichts', or 'that dyke ye knockit doon lookin for rabbits - d'ye hear? Ye'll bigg it up again!' And the loon would behave himself for a fortnight, never a stain in his life, and he would square up beside Shinnie in the byre like he had a share in the place, and Shinnie would wait or Charlie's back was turned and then spit out at the loon:

14

'Dinna bigg stibble ruckies in yon park min, ye'll ruin my new grass!' Dash it, there was no pleasin the man, so the loon would wipe his slate real clean and live like a quine for weeks on end, never striking a match about the place, nor even taking a drag at the old man's pipe, and then in the byre when the lanterns were lit he'd stand real close to Shinnie, his face shining with innocence and Shinnie would blame him for taking the prop out of a leaning haystack. 'Can't ye let things alane, man?'

When Charlie's loon thrashed the foreman's loon coming home from school he never let on at home. But by byre time Shinnie had wind of it. 'Ye thrashed the foreman's loon the day man!' 'Oh aye,' says the loon, 'but he deserved it, even his ain brither said so, and he saw us fechtin. He's been giein me the coordie lick for a lang time, and stickin his nieve in my face every day or I could stand it nae langer, so I let flist at him when he least expected it. He was a bloody mess by the time I finished wi him but his brither never interfered. Maybe it'll teach 'im a lesson.'

Shinnie looked at Charlie's loon almost in sympathy, then he removed his pipe and spat in the urine channel. 'Aye laddie, but he's a bit younger than you, and so is his brother, and likely their father will have his ain back on you for that yet. He's a spiteful mannie the foreman once his birse is up.'

Now Charlie's loon kept a pair of tame rabbits, a white Jack Rabbit and his blue-coated wife. A pair of cannibals they were and between them they had eaten seven litters of young. When the young were littered the loon put the Jack Rabbit in quarantine, but it made no difference, the mother merely dined more sumptuously and one by one the young disappeared. And it wasn't that he neglected them for the nickum took great pride in his rabbits. Almost any day you could see the cratur miles from home with his little hand-cart searching for some delicacy for the hutch, a milky thistle, dandelions, big red clovers that waved in the wind like pom-poms.

Shinnie came to hear of the laddie's rabbits and in the byre one evening at supperin time he said: 'Aye lad, and how are the rabbits doin?'

'Oh fine,' said the loon, 'except that they've eaten their young again.'

'Oh man, that's a peety noo.'

There was a brief pause in which you could hear the nowt rattling their neck chains. Shinnie took his pipe from his mouth and spat on the greep.

'But lad,' says he, pipe in hand, 'what dae ye feed yer rabbits on?'

'Neeps', says Charlie's loon, seeing it was winter and no fresh grass in the fields.

'Neeps man!' said Shinnie, in a tone and expression of accusation.

'Aye neeps!' the loon repeated, all innocence, preparing himself for some advice on a change of diet for the carnivorous rabbits.

'And whaur dae ye get the neeps lad?' Pipe back in mouth, his hands in his trouser pockets Shinnie leaned back on his heels awaiting a confession.

The loon was completely unaware of the trap Shinnie had sprung for him.

'Oh, oot o your park,' he stumbled.

Shinnie took a squint at old Charlie at the other end of the byre. He put his forefinger over his pipe stem and removed it from his set teeth. His eyes glittered down on the loon and his moustache bristled into single hairs. 'Weel,' he snarled, his lips curling into speech, 'that wunna dee, ye understand? Lat there be nae mair o't, d'ye hear? Nae mair stealin neeps. I canna be expectit tae grou neeps tae feed your rabbits on!'

Shinnie turned his back on the loon and went to feel his stots, fondling their flanks where the beef rippled under his fingers like a new wallet, and he put his arm under the warm hoch to feel the firm scrotum on each animal, an indication of their prime condition. He scratched the roots of their itching tails till they forgot their food and twisted their mouths in ecstasy.

The loon watched Shinnie with a lump in his throat and choked back the tears. He had thought himself further in with Shinnie than this and disappointment rankled him sorely.

And the beasts never kicked Shinnie, his touch was gentle and smooth as velvet, and they stopped chewing the cud and looked round at him with great liquid eyes, beseeching and full of trust, while he lured them to their deaths with doting care and loving kindness.

But Shinnie never kept heifers; they were restless and noisy before their menstruations and disturbed the whole byre. Nothing like quietness and peace to get a beast fat, and though some said that quaiks or heifers got fat sooner and gave quicker returns Shinnie still preferred a good stot with more weight in the carcass at the kill out.

But the loon wasn't long out of favour with Shinnie, for Charlie his father took the 'flu and went off work. And daggit if Shinnie didn't have the impudence to go and rap on Charlie's door and ask his wife if he could have the loon to help in the byre with Charlie's nowt. The beasts would miss the smell of old Charlie and the tone of his voice. They were fickle with strangers and would lose condition. It was hard work and Shinnie didn't like hard work, but he would get Charlie's loon to help and he would do the job himself.

For nearly six months now the beasts had been chained, coming almost fat from the pastures to hay and swede turnips, bruised corn and oilcake, and it wouldn't do to let them lag and lose money now. Very soon now the chains would be loosed from their necks and the beasts would break in a panic from the stalls, prancing blindly through the byre like mad demons in their new liberty. But Shinnie would give them twenty minutes on the soft sharn midden where they would sink to their bellies and lose their high spirits before going on the road to the railway station. A few hours of precious freedom and the poor devils would have to pay for Shinnie's kindness under the butcher's hatchet.

Charlie's loon ran three miles to school on a dry piece and when he got back he bolted his dinner and went to help Shinnie in the byre.

Shinnie lit the lanterns and put the match to his pipe. He had his jacket off and his sleeves rolled up and the loon had never seen him like this before.

'Man,' says he, 'yer father's a grand worker but he's affa sair on the broom. He's hard on the besom and sair on himsel. He kills himsel, the breet!'

The loon looked up at Shinnie but didn't say anything. He knew he could never sweep the byre to please his father and he knew the old man raxed his guts with the old turnip slicer. Shinnie wasn't the man to thank him for it but at least he noticed it.

'Aye man,' Shinnie continued, 'and how are the rabbits doin?'

'Oh they're starved tae death,' said the loon, telling a lie to shun the devil.

'And what dae ye feed them on nooadays when ye dinna get a neep tae gie them?'

'Tea-leaves and meal', said the loon, wondering what Shinnie would say next.

'Och laddie,' says Shinnie, 'but ye can tak a neep; ye canna hunger the craturs!'

On the Sunday morning, when the loon went to feed his rabbits they were both dead with their throats cut. The murderer hadn't pommelled them in the usual bloodless way but had slit their throats hatefully and thrown them back in the hutch.

After breakfast Charlie's loon got a spade out of the toolshed and went to bury his rabbits in the backyard. And who should appear but the local bobby, followed by Shinnie and the foreman from next door. They went straight to the foreman's coal-shed where they took a sackful of something from the interior. The foreman was made to shoulder it on his back, and then he walked in front of Shinnie and the bobby up the beech avenue to the farm.

What could it mean? The constable about the place on a Sunday morning brought all the cottars to their doors and windows. And what could the foreman have to do with it? Charlie's loon dropped his spade and ran inside to tell his old man. Maybe he could tell the bobby about his rabbits. Maybe he could find out who killed them.

Charlie Stoddart was still in his box-bed in the kitchen. But he wouldn't hear of his loon telling the bobby about his rabbits. 'Na na,' says he, 'better haud yer tongue aboot it; we dinna want tae get enveigled wi the bobby.'

The foreman's wife watched her husband from the cottage door, the bairns around her, like Christian's wife in *Pilgrim's Progress*, when Christian set out with his bundle of sin upon his back.

The trio marched up the avenue, the foreman with his sack, the policeman and Shinnie, past the farmhouse, where the mistress and the kitchie-deem were glowerin from the window, the single lads keekin from the chaumer, right up the close to the loft door at the top of the stone steps.

Up in the loft the foreman dropped his sack. 'Put it there!' said the bobby, indicating the weighing machine. The sack weighed eighty pounds. Shinnie untied the string and lifted a handful of his 'Golden Rain' seed corn and ran it through his fingers.

Now Shinnie had been real cunning to catch the foreman. He looked like a lad who wouldn't have stolen a worm from a hen, yet here he was thievin Shinnie's corn to feed his poultry. Shinnie had seen him going to the loft now and then, usually about dinner-time, but thought maybe it was a pucklie bruised corn for his horse the lad was after. But Shinnie got suspicious and one day he followed the foreman on the sly. So the lad gaed right through the stable with the sack, out at the back door and into the millhouse, where he hid it in the shadows.

The old wheel-house was an excellent place for concealment, damp and secretive, and the fall of the water under the wheel drowned every sound. Even when the wheel was stationary nobody ventured much into the wheel-house; it was slippery and dangerous at all times, and after dark a veritable death-trap. It was at the back of the steading, away from the farmhouse, where even the collie dog couldn't hear anything.

Shinnie watched the foreman but stayed out of sight and never opened his trap. At yokin time he newsed up the foreman as if he was his most trusted disciple. 'Weel weel Wullie, jist haud back tae the ploo again.'

But as soon as the horsemen had pulled out of the stable with their pairs Shinnie gaed roon the back and had a look in the wheel-house. He found the sack of oats in a bucket of the water-wheel, to be lifted after dark, when the foreman came back to supper his horse.

Shinnie 'phoned the bobby to come up to Shinbrae after dark and the two of them hid in the wheel-house and waited for the thief. There wasn't a whiff from Shinnie's pipe, not a squeak from his shoes, and the foreman came and lifted his sack, unaware of the two pairs of eyes and ears lurking in the darkness. But they never molested him, just followed him right home to his coal-shed with the sack.

It must have been about this hour that Charlie Stoddart's loon got his rabbits killed. They were stone cold by morning and their blood congealed. It is a wonder that Shinnie or the bobby didna see the foreman at the rabbit hutch. On the other hand, when Shinnie saw the bobby on to his bike at the head of the avenue it was easy for him to nip back thirty yards or so tae thrapple the craturs, if he had a mind for it.

The foreman was summoned to appear in court. He was fined £5 and got his name in the papers. It was a month's pay and he had five bairns. He was never 'socht tae bide' and his name was on every tongue in the district. For several months until the May term he had to carry on at Shinbrae, taking his orders from Shinnie and facing his work-mates as if nothing had happened, a hard thing in those days when men were jostling each other for a farmer's favours.

But there were some who despised Shinnie for his harsh treatment; dismissal was enough they said, without the fine. But Shinnie wanted to make an example of his victim, and every cottar at Shinbrae had to get rid of his hens.

Charlie Stoddart got over his 'flu and was soon back in the byre again. One evening his loon squared up beside Shinnie and watched his face.

'My rabbits are deid,' he said, 'they wunna need nae mair neeps.'

'Deid man! Whatever happened tae the craturs?'

'Somebody cut their throats!'

'Weel laddie, I tellt ye the foreman wad hae his ain back on ye for thrashin his loon, though it was a damned sleekit wye o takin his revenge. But he's had tae pay for't mair wyes than wan. And laddie,' Shinnie went on, 'never lat on, but when the foreman leaves at the term ye'll a' get yer hens back. I'll buy them at the roups and keep them or the term's by. And maybe ye'll get up early the morn's mornin and gie us a hand tae drive the nowt tae the station, there'll be a gey steer or we get them a' on the road.'

Playing Truant

I sneezed in spite of myself and it almost proved my undoing. I sat very quiet in the drying loft over the kitchen where my father was at his dinner.

'Is that loon at the school the day?' I heard the old man ask.

'Of coorse he's at the school,' mother lied, 'what sorra made ye think that he wasna?'

'Och, I thocht I heard a soun!'

'Ach,' mother scorned, 'Ye're a muckle gipe, it's only the cat sneezin. Sup yer broth man, and if ye are as hungry as ye usually are ye winna listen for ferlies.'

So I sat very quiet, hoping that Flora, my little sister, wouldn't betray me. She was just at the stage when she might blurt out anything, and to warn her against it was like tempting her the more.

The skylight was a fixture, rusted with age and damp and curtained with cobwebs. Dry rot was crumbling the rafters and the floor-boards were porous with woodworm activity. There was dust and grime in every seam of the place, but also an atmosphere of romanticism and adventure which lent an air of bravado to my truancy.

It was in this loft that all my trophies were stored out of Flora's reach: my Hotspurs and Rovers, Sexton Blakes, Buffalo Bills, Nelson Lees, Comic Cuts and Comic Chips; cinema advertisements cut week by week from the newspapers, stacked high and neatly by the hatch where the ladder came up, and all my cardboard cut-outs, soldiers, ships and motor cars. it just wouldn't do to let Flora get her hands on these. And most precious of all was my shoe-box theatre, with its aproned stage and tiny chairs, the props and characters all set for a performance of *Mill o Tifty's Annie*. I had just seen the play performed in the local hall and I was burning to have it done in puppetry.

My old man fell asleep after his heavy meal and my behind grew numb sitting on the hard floor boards. I felt like a Jack on the Bean Stalk awaiting the Giant to awake from his snooze. The old man was a heavy eater and today he had brose after his usual dinner and it had sent him nearly into a coma.

When confronted with a normal meal the old man would storm at mother about its lack of stamina. What would have satisfied the appetite of most working men was no use to the old man. 'Some licht wuman.' he would screech, 'some licht; I canna work a yokins wark on that, I'll need brose!' So mother would set out the oat-meal bowl, salt and pepper, and a jug of milk, and

20

when the kettle came to the boil he made brose. Today had been no exception and I heard him stirring his brose with the handle of his spoon. He always sat bolt upright on the edge of his chair at meal times, and I could picture it all quite plainly while I listened and waited.

And if it wasn't brose for dessert it was 'melk an breid', oat-cakes warmed at the fire and crumbled into a bowl of milk, sometimes with a dash of cream, sprinkled with pepper and supped with a spoon, a tasty and invigorating diet, which I sometimes shared with the old man.

I heard Flora come and rattle the door at the foot of the loft stair. She had remembered for a moment where I was and I held my breath in fear. But she went away again and all was quiet.

Mother got the tea ready. I heard the tinkle of teaspoons going into the cups. The old man had come to life again. I heard the scrape of his chair on the cement floor as he dragged it back to the table. He was preparing to face another hard yokin in the neep park and the coo byre and I knew he did more than he was bargained for.

'Woman,' says he, 'see that the loon comes tae the byre the nicht: he could hash the neeps or cairry a pucklie strae - maybe gie the calves a sook, it's aye a help ye ken.'

Mother was washing the dinner plates in a basin at the other end of the table.

'Oh aye,' says she, 'but ye maun gie the laddie time tae tak his denner. He has tae travle a lang road frae the school. And never a copper does the fairmer gie 'im for his wark.'

'But it's me he's helpin woman, ye canna expect the fairmer tae pey him for that!'

'No no, but sometimes the fairmer trails the laddie awa tae something else and he gets naething for that. He taks the sap oot o you but he's nae gaun tae tak it oot o the loon as weel. He'll hae tae work for a livin when his day comes and surely that's time eneuch!'

'A' richt woman, but I'll be lookin for 'im onywye. It's better than throwin steens on the sklates or fleein aboot wi a gird. The laddie maun learn, woman!'

I heard the old man pushing his chair back from the table. I knew he would be putting on his sweaty cap and stroking mother's crow-black hair: 'Ye're a bonnie cratur though,' he would purr, 'aye are ye though.'

'G'wa tae yer wark ye gock,' I heard her say.

Then I heard the old man say a few silly childish words to Flora as he stepped over her dolls at the door.

I lifted the latch and descended the ladder into the lobby and the kitchen. The bakers van had been in the forenoon and I glanced at the table to see if there were any fancy pastries on the bread-plate. Snatching a pancake, the only thing available, I sneaked to the door to see how far the old man had gone on the road. I had to do this because the water cistern blocked my view from the window. I couldn't see the old man from the door so I crept outside and peeped round the corner of the cistern .

Ah ha! Too soon! The old man was just entering the farm loanin when he looked round and saw me. He shook his fist at me while I stood there like a fool with my mouth full of pancake.

He hadn't time to come back because it was too near yokin time at the farm. Shaking his fist was all the malice he had resource to at the moment, but it was enough for me until nightfall when I could expect heavier punishment.

I ran back into the house and told mother.

'Weel weel,' said she, as she wrung out her dish-cloth, 'Ye'll catch it when he comes home, and ye're supposed tae gyang tae the byre tae hash the neeps and feed the calfies. Ye should hae kept oot o sicht a whilie langer.'

'I wunna gyang tae the byre. He'll stab me wi a fork like he tried the last time he was angered, the time he chased the foreman oot o the byre.'

I should have gone to the byre and softened the old man's wrath. But I cowered behind mother's skirts and hoped that she would stick up for me. And there was always the risk in the byre that the old man would take a fork over my back if he was thoroughly roused. Just the other day I had seen him chase the foreman out of the byre with a graip. Some tittle-tattle of evil gossip the foreman had spread around and it brought the old man into conflict with the other men.

'Spit it out!' I heard the foreman say, but he didn't wait for the old man to spit out anything, but ran like a schoolgirl when the old man charged him with the fork and well he may, for it was like a Highlander's charge at Prestonpans.

So I was in for it, and as the afternoon wore on my feeling of guilt grew stronger. From behind the window curtains I watched some of my classmates trudging home from school, boys and girls from out-lying crofts, and the sight of them made me feel ashamed. It made me realise that I shouldn't play truant; that I should go to school like other respectable kids, and that I shouldn't deceive the old man, though mother let me off with it.

Mother lit the paraffin lamp and pulled down the blinds. She laid the supper plates on the table and took a bowl of meal out of the oak barrel to make the porridge.

I went up to the loft for my shoe-box theatre and arranged it on the dresser. *Mill o Tifty's Annie* must go on at all costs. Flora was already seating her dolls around the stage to witness the performance. I had already done *Jamie Fleeman*, and although the old man had snored through it all mother and Flora thought it was first class.

The old man had never thrashed me although I suppose I deserved it often enough. Once he had smacked my backside in a playful manner, under the bed-clothes, and I had buried my face in the pillow with embarrassment because he could do this to me.

But now I could hear his footsteps outside on the gravel as he approached the door. Then he lifted the sneck and burst in upon us like a hungry bear . . .

'Fut wye was ye nae at the skweel?' His eyes were like hot pin-heads that burned into mine as I retreated before him to the meal-barrel in the corner.

He never even glanced at the table, which he usually did, whenever he opened the door, to see what was there for his ravenous belly. He fixed his searing eyes on my miniature theatre, stanced on the dresser, and with one swipe of his King-Kong arm he scattered the lot on the floor; stage, scenery, puppets, props and tiny chairs for my imaginary audience went flying under the table and over the fireplace.

That single action was symbolic of what he meant to do with my whole life. He seemed determined I should earn my bread the hard way, as he himself had done, and he had no respect whatsoever for any other inclinations I might have.

'D'ye ken I'm on my last warnin for nae sendin ye tae school? D'ye hear?' he roared, while I squeezed myself in behind the meal-barrel.

Frustration brought his anger to fever heat. He danced round the barrel in a frenzy, while little Flora hung on to the tail of his jacket, trying to pull him away. He wrenched her off and sent her spinning into a corner, where she sat on her doup, howling, with hot tears on her cheeks.

'D'ye want me tae stand in jile for ye? Ye damned rascal!' And he lashed out at me with his open hand.

The blow toppled me out from behind the meal barrel and sent me rolling over the floor. He was on me in a moment and I crawled under the table to escape his groping hands.

Now he was thoroughly roused and began chasing me round the table, first one side and then the other, and all the time I dodged him, while he stretched out his arm to prevent me reaching the door.

The table began to rock, rattling the cups in their saucers and spilling the milk from the porridge bowls. This nettled mother and she flew at the old man like a tigress, dragging him away from me by the jacket.

'Ye senseless fool,' she screamed, 'What sort o wye is that tae carry on in the hoose? Folk wad think ye was mad!' And when the old man turned on her I bolted for the door.

He raised his arm to strike her but she grabbed the poker from the fender and dared him to try it. Her eyes gleamed with defiance and her lips quivered on set teeth.

The old man lowered his fist. 'Oh aye,' he yelled, 'Ye'll tak his bluidy pairt will ye, and hae me stand the jile? Ye're spilin 'im as it is. He'll never do a stroke o wark when his day comes. But mind I'm tellin ye he's nae gyan tae lie aboot here in idleness. He'll hae tae work for a livin the same as I did afore his day. I'll see that he does it. You wait and see!'

Mother shook the poker in his face and his eyes wavered confronting her.

'Gyang tae yer supper man and lat the loon alane. You keep yer hands tae yersel and I'll see that he goes tae school.'

'But woman, it wunna dee at a'! Can't ye see I'm on my last warnin? And what wad become o ye a' if I gaed tae jile?'

'Ach, awa man, ye're saft; they'll never send ye tae prison. They jist say that tae scare ye!'

So the old man cooled off and sat down to his porridge, now getting cold with a skin on top, so he didn't have to blow on the spoon, and it humoured him a little.

I sneaked inside from the cold to gather up my theatre. Flora gave me a hand, her great soft eyes swimming in tears and her golden curls glistening on her shoulders. The stage had been buckled in the scuffle and the scenery squashed and scattered, but we managed to arrange it somehow.

After supper Flora rearranged her dolls on a chair in front of the stage. I had painted a fine back-drop in watercolour of the old Mill o Tifty, with a model of the waterwheel in front, and when I brought Bonnie Annie and Andrew Lammie on to the stage Flora gave a little gasp of delight. And then I began my soliloquy:

> 'At Mill o Tifty lived a man
> In the neighbourhood o Fyvie,
> Who had a lovely daughter fair -
> Her name was Bonnie Annie . . .'

But the old man was asleep, bolt upright on a hard chair, his head hanging over the back, his mouth agape, snoring. He never did really understand me.

Rab o the Barnyards

A Character Study of a North-East Worthy

The Barnyards was a muckle sair toon tae work on. Man and beast were chauved on her lang clay rigs. He was a tearin brute Rab Imray that was the grieve, a big chiel that could have been a bobby, but he took a bit wife and cottared at the Barnyards. Rab was in his late thirties, six feet lang, well-built, with black curly hair, tawny complexion, a mouser and brown dancing eyes. He wore a pickiesae hat, a muffler, a sleeved waistcoat, Kersey-tweed trousers, tackety boots and nicky-tams.

It was a modern fairm for the times, with electric light, milking-machines, attested cows in concrete stalls - and even a tractor, a muckle traction-engine o a thing that stinkit the barn and foonert in the neep park and never did any good at all. There were six cottars and two single lads in the bothy. Three of the men were horsemen, two were stockmen, one was an orraman, while another drove the milk lorry and washed the cans and milk bottles. And of course Rab was also a cottar.

It was hard times, no family allowance, no dole; the work was hard, the hours long and labour was cheap. It was a period that bred men like Rab of the Barnyards; rough, hardy, eident chiels, the likes of whom will never be seen on the farms again. They knew nothing of half-holidays, summer holidays or paid overtime. Their work was their lives and they made a song of the grindstone of life.

Rab had full charge, second only to the Barnyards himsel, and he worked the odd pair of horse, off and on, when he wasn't pooin neeps - usually a pair of raw colts that nobody else could handle. But Rab soon had them tamed with his long strides ahin the harras, or in the muckle stone roller that was for crushing the clods, for they were by-ordinar at the Barnyards.

In the spring, when the grun was made, the creatures were as thin they could have loupit through their collars. Their shoulders were blistered with the strain of the yoke and they had to rest in the stable or they healed. Losh aye, Rab was sair on horse, and while the creatures were convalescent he tore at the neeps or the muck himsel like one demented.

When they emptied the dung court with the horse carts the cottar lads had their wives come up with a drop tea through the yokin. But Rab wadna tak tea, 'Na, na,' says he, 'I've heard o a bairn needin a piece, but nae a grown body. I'll easy fill 'er wantin tay.' And he tore at the muck with a shoulder pick and loaded it in graipfuls that nae mortal body was fit for.

Rab and the first horseman lived next door and their wives couldna gree. They spat at each other like cats and were itchin tae get at the ither's hair, each kyardin the ither from the door-jamb. The foreman's wife had sax bairns. She was a thrifty body and made a' their claes hersel, while Rab's wife could hardly thread a needle. But it made Rab's wife jealous and filled her with envy and she couldna stand the look o the woman.

But Rab got on capital with his foreman, a lang teem whaup with freckles and a red heid. They never spoke about their wives or their bairns but kept the peace like decent folk, and never entered the other's door. And the foreman would say to Rab: 'Man, I need a hair-cut,' and Rab would take his clipper to the stable, and the foreman would sit on a box with a saddle-cover round his shoulders, and Rab would shear off his red hair like wool from a ram. 'Fine deen man!' the foreman would say; then Rab sat on the box and the foreman took his turn with the clipper.

The Barnyards himsel was a hard maister folk said. Woe betide a poor cottar if he was fee-ed to go to the Barnyards. 'Rab will tak the sap oot o the breet!' And maybe he did, the slavin brute, but you didn't do it for nothing. Rab saw to that. And if the Barnyards had been a bit grippie wi the bawbees Rab made it up wi merchandise.

But if the Barnyards was a hard master he was also a tolerant one. And sometimes he said nasty things to his servants that Rab didn't hear, and maybe jist as well, or Rab would have him by the lug. But tons of coal went missing at the Barnyards, loads of firewood, gallons of milk and the finest cream - they even took the man's paraffin and diesel oil to light their fires, and a hantle other petty theft that the Barnyards closed his eyes to. He knew all right but he never locked a door, and Rab carried the keys for the loft and the engine-hoose. But if you pleased Rab; if you could keep up with Rab in the neep park, or in the dung court, then you had nothing to fear from the Barnyards. Coal was a perquisite (part of the wages) and if it was exhausted before the winter term Rab would have the foreman yoke a horse-cart before daybreak and they would fill half-a-dozen sacks from the farm coalshed. And while it was still dark the horsemen would cart it round the starving cottars and dump a bag on every doorstep.

One day at the marts a neighbour said to the Barnyards: 'Man, I dinna ken fut wye ye keep Rab Imray yonder as a grieve; he's sic a lad tae steal!'

'Aye, I ken Rab steals,' said the Barnyards, 'but man, he's worth it!'

And so he was, for Rab got more work out of his men than though he had been thoroughly a farmer's man, with no thought for his workers. They slaved behind him in all sorts of weather without complaint. Though other folks were taking in their tattie-boodies from the wet Rab and his squad were still drabbling on at the hoe. 'Has the man no pity,' folk would ask each other from their stable doors: but the neeps were in a blaze of growth and Rab wanted them singled before they got harder to do, for they were shooting up with every blink of sun between the thunder pelts.

26

For nigh on twelve years Rab had farmed the Barnyards. Never had its yields been so high, or its soil in such fertility. 'If ye can grow grass,' said Rab, 'and bury a good sole, you'll farm the Barnyards.'

If it were a sunny evening in the spring you could see Rab in his sark-sleeves striding on ahin the turnip-sower, to catch a favourable break in the weather. The horsemen had set up the drills in the daytime, still with a dry loam to take seed, and Rab meant to have them all sown before dark. And if you looked again before bed-time Rab was still at it, his mare lathered in foam, the drills all flattened behind him like corduroy.

When the Barnyards had his breeks off, ready for bed, he took the curtain aside on the storm window and saw Rab in the neep park. 'Aye Bess,' he said, looking at his wife, 'I ken ye dinna like Rab, and I ken he steals - but whaur wad I get his marra?'

And if you leaned over the dyke and asked Rab the reason for his hurry he would stroke his fusker and his eyes would dance all over your face. 'Man,' he would say, 'there's naething here but clay and watter. Ye've got tae catch 'er in the mood for seed or ye'll never see a neep or the simmer's gaen; a' droont wi watter or hang't wi hard clay.'

And if Rab 'took a tig' in the hairst time he would yoke a binder and cut a whole park of corn on a Sunday and never ask a penny for it. The hairst was sometimes finished at the Barnyards, and the stacks all thatched, first in the district. And at the marts a neighbour would say to the Barnyards: 'Aye man, ye've feenished!'

'Aye,' says the Barnyards, 'we're throu. Rab took a tig, the breet!'

Now the Barnyards had a cow that took the red-water, and when the vet ordered that two crates of stout be given to her, Rab and the dairymen had their daily pint for a fortnight. When the cow died Rab said: 'Ach weel, the cooie was gaun tae dee onywye. It wad hae been a shame tae conach the gweed stuff on a dyin beastie!'

Rab and the dairymen understood each other perfectly, a rare coincidence on most dairy farms. There were few complaints about 'frostit neeps' or 'foostie strae' if Rab could help it, and the only time they ever emptied the barn they came upon an old horse-gig under the straw that even the Barnyards couldn't remember.

And sometimes on a rainy day you would see Rab and his men with the horse-clipper in the byre, taking turns at the handle, helping the bailies to shear their cows. Rab was a dab hand with the clipper, snaking it under a cow's belly from the long tube on the machine, fondling her teats as canny as if it were a woman's breasts. 'It wad be a bittie akward gaen the women had them here!' he would drawl, and the billies would laugh their agreement. But the cottars went home with their flaggons brimming with milk. Even their cats had something to thank Rab for.

Old Bess of the Barnyards didn't like Rab. Maybe she had good reason, for her hens took such a fancy to Rab that sometimes they laid their eggs in his pockets. 'Man,' Rab would joke, 'I can hardly hang my jacket on an aul roostie nail somewye but there's a hennie lays in my pooches!'

Rab's hens never moulted as far as the grocer was concerned; his basket was about the same level all the year round. Nor was he slack to thraw a hen's neck for the Sunday dinner, especially if he saw her blinking her eyes in a corner, standing there as if she were in a trance, and maybe only needing the rooster. Sometimes the creatures sat down at his touch, as a hen will do in such a mood, but if Rab were in need of a dinner it were better for her that she had flown over the steading.

Bess couldn't risk leaving a fish to dry on the hake by the kitchen door or some lousy cottar would be off with it overnight. She had to lock the meat safe and empty the cheese-press if Rab was on the prowl. And the salt herrin barrel was a sore temptation.

She was a great horticulturist was Bess, the mistress of the Barnyards. She had a great notion of trees and shrubs and such like, and took great pride in her lawns and flower gardens. But when she rose one morning she missed a certain tree from the farm avenue. She looked from her oriel window, high on the slated roof, and behold - the tree was gone!

Bess called to the Barnyards, who was still in his bed, and got him over to the window, where she pointed to the gap in the loanin.

'That's Rab done that I'll be damned!' she cried. 'That's yer grieve you are so daft on!'

The Barnyards stood wheezing at the pane; it was a chest complaint that troubled him, off and on, and he shivered in his night-gown. 'Ach woman,' says he, 'what aboot a tree, it couldna been a big ane. Ye'll see the road better withoot it!'

'It was a beech,' she shouted, 'one o the first tae bud in the spring. But I'll search every cottar's coal-house on the place or I find it!'

And so she did, and found the tree in Rab's coalshed, all sawn into slabs, ready for the hack-block, and the branches in a heap at the gable. And Bess gave Rab's wife a tinking, in front of the foreman's wife and the bairns, and the poor woman was in tears, all for Rab's sake at the ploo.

Bess went back to the farmhouse, where she found the Barnyards in the parlour. 'Ye'll sack that man this very day!' she cried.

'Poor Rab,' wheezed the Barnyards, sair chauved for breath. 'But I'll do no such thing woman. Nae for the sake o a blastit tree! Rab is a kleptomaniac; he canna help stealin. Can't ye understand, woman?'

'I can understand a' richt, but that doesna mean that you should be his nursemaid. A merry dance he leads them all, a wonder he doesna have ye oot at the door. The place is hardly yer ain man, they cottars are takin possession!'

'I'll survive woman. Rab's worth every penny he steals, aye and mair. The wages I can affoord tae pay them doesna gie the cottar bairns justice onywye!'

They argued about it for the rest of the day and it ended in a sulk between them.

Because of his complaint the Barnyards wasn't allowed to smoke, doctor's orders, and Bess watched him with a ferret's eye. So about supperin time in the evening he put on his carpets and went down the close to see Rab.

Some of the lads might be brushing harness on the cornkists, or shaking chains in a sack to make them shine; but Rab had no such capers, for anything did with the colts, all the old harness, and some of it was tied together with bits of wire. He had a little stable all by himself, where he was grooming his colts by electric light when the Barnyards wheezed in at the door.

'Aye Rab,' says he. 'Aye man,' says Rab, and banged his steel comb against the travis post. The post was poke-marked with years of banging to knock the dust out of Rab's comb.

A long pause ensued and the Barnyards cleared his throat. 'Man Rab,' says he, 'what aboot a draw o yer pipe?'

'Fairlie man,' says Rab, and he filled his pipe with black twist and lit it and gave it to his master. And the old man puffed and wheezed fair in his element.

'Man Rab,' says he, 'that's grand!'

There was another long silence. The scrape of iron teeth on horse hair. The rattle of a manger chain. The munch and scent of hay. Cosy. A haven of peace for the Barnyards. The tension of the day had left him and he was relaxed; even his breathing was easier and there was less of a heave in his chest.

'It was a beech, Rab?'

'Aye.'

'Grand burnin Rab?'

'Aye.'

The Barnyards sighed and handed back the pipe. 'For God's sake Rab, whatever else ye steal keep it oot o sicht o the mistress!' And when Rab looked out the door he was gone in the darkness.

Somebody said to Rab that he might get disease letting the Barnyards smoke his pipe. 'Fie man,' says Rab, 'the pipe may kill the Barnyards, but there's nae a germ born that wad live in my pipe!' And they said that if you stood beside Rab in a mornin when he smoked it you could believe him.

But there was a change at the Barnyards. One of Rab's men left for a cairter's job in the toon, and a young chiel newly married took his place. Rab put a sod on his lum and smoked his young bride out of the house her first mornin at the Barnyards. 'We had tae get a look at the cratur,' says Rab. 'I thocht it was the best wye tae get 'er ootside. Lucky she was we didna wash her feet as weel. There's nae scarcity o harness blaik and cairt grease.'

But he was a saft stock the new lad; fair scared at the Barnyards and feart at a' the thievin that gaed on. Bein newly married he didn't have to steal. Most of the older cottars had big families. They had to steal to keep them alive. And besides, if you didn't steal something at the Barnyards you was laughed at. If you had offered to pay the Barnyards for a bushel of corn for your hens he would have been dumb-founded. The cottars got their corn when the mill choked on thrashin days. Rab never swept the barn floor, he left that for the cottars. 'Tidy it up at supperin time lads,' he would say, 'it'll do for yer hens. Losh aye, the hennies like forty-twa pun corn, nae neen o yer sma dirt!'

But the new chiel tried hard to be honest. Fegs aye, hardly took a neep for his broth or a bit stick to light his fire. But he couldna buy kindling anywhere, the stock, at ony price, and he was fair stuck for tinder. In the lang run he had to confide in Rab. So one evening in the barn Rab went up to the loft for an old wooden bushel that was falling apart anyway. He threw it down at the man's feet in the barn, where it went all to staves. 'Noo than,' says Rab, with a wink to the other lads, 'that'll be a start for ye. The iron hoops winna burn, but ye can try yer luck wi the timmer bitties!'

So the new lad gathered up his staves in a chorus of ridicule. To leave them would have angered Rab, the last thing he wanted, but he felt he had paid well enough for his honesty.

It was a tonic to watch Rab start the oil-engine when he was going to thrash or bruise corn for the beasts: filling the glass jars with oil over the piston and fly-wheels, topping up the cooling tank with water from the horse-trough, priming and lighting the blow-lamp.

When the nose cone was red-hot Rab twisted the great black fly-wheels this way and that. The engine gave a pech, spat and said 'Ach! Nae the day!'

'Thrawn bitch!' Rab seched.

But he persisted and spun the wheels again. The engine gave a hoast, then a bark and back-fired, and threw Rab nearly out at the door, muckle brute though he was.

'Stand back lads,' cried Rab, his eyes fair dancin, 'there's life in her yet!'

The piston gave a lurch or two and the black greasy thing sprang into vibrating life, spinning the wheels at such a spate ye couldna see the spokes.

Rab liked to have her chookin afore yokin time, to be ready for the lads. He slipped the mill belt on to the pulley and the stripper drum picked up speed till it hummed in its velocity. Rab jumped into the feed box and opened the lid on the drum, gave his knife a bit scrape on the harled wall and fastened it on his wrist, ready for the sheaves from the foreman's fork. Then look out, as he cut the bands on the sheaves to the drum, for if you wasn't smothered in dust you was nearly buried in straw.

Rab was coming home at the gloamin with a pail of water in one hand and a bucket of milk in the other (not a flaggon mind you - which was all he was entitled to) but an open pail, brimming with goodness.

Now at this time the cottars carried their water from the steading. Some of them had a bowie 'neath the spoot at the gable, to catch a suppie rain water from the roof, mostly for washing, but they carried their cooking water in pails from the Barnyards.

And Rab met a lad wi a hat in the avenue, an insurance mannie or something, and he fair glowered at Rab and his twa pails. And when Rab saw that the mannie kent what was in the off-side pail he says, sober like: 'Jod man, the verra taps are runnin melk at the Barnyards. I jist held tee ma pail and that's what I got!' But the mannie jist nodded his heid and passed on.

But the mannie wasna sae blate as Rab thocht he was. He kent fine it was the cooler tap in the dairy that Rab meant, where he'd no business to be, except that the water tap was beside it. Rab could have said that he mistook the taps, just as cool as he would have told you that the sea was on fire, hoping that you would believe it.

But nobody was any the wiser, nobody that mattered. The mannie never lat dab to the Barnyards. He had his custom to collect and maybe he didn't want to give his name an ill taste with the cottars. But in the winter of that year tragedy struck at Rab and his wife. They lost their youngest son of four years, struck down with some rare disease that the doctors couldn't fathom. Rab stood at the graveside with big tears on his cheeks, great glistening drops that slid down his face and hung at his mouser. You could hardly believe that Rab could greet, him that was always so cheerful and made a joke of life. But he had come to it at last and his great shoulders shook with his sobbing. Those who shook hands with Rab that day had never seen him in such a state.

Rab's moustache had a droop after this, and sometimes the dancing eyes were wet with tears. When you came upon him canny like, when his thoughts were deep, you could see it had been a sair day for Rab when his son died.

Old Bess even softened her heart to Rab in his grief. For a time she settled her differences with the Barnyards about Rab the grieve.

But Rab took a thinking, for his wife was sair come at in their sorrow, and when feeing time came round Rab thought a change of scene might help her.

Folks fair thocht that Rab would be leaving the Barnyards 'cause he hadna put a spade to his gairden that spring. And when he lit his pipe there was a shake in his hands that wasn't there before.

But the Barnyards went down the close in his carpets again to Rab's little stable. Between puffs at Rab's pipe he said: 'Ye'll be bidin on again Rab?'

'Na, nae this time,' says Rab, 'the wife's sair come at. She needs a change.'

'Ye're nae wunnin awa onywye. I'll raise ye a fiver for the year and I'll tak yer wife aboot in the car. She'll get a' the change o scenery she wants withoot flittin for't!'

Rab hummed and hawed and twirled his mouser. 'Weel weel,' says he, 'I'll see what the wife says.'

So for a time Rab's wife went everywhere with the Barnyards, and it fair took her out of herself. But now it was the foreman's wife that was jealous and she taunted Rab's wife about taking up with the Barnyards, an old man that could nearly be her father. But when folks saw Rab's wife chase the woman back to her ain door with a sweeping brush they said she was fair cured of her melancholia.

But a day came at last for the Barnyards poor stock and he became really ill. Rab asked for the maister once or twice but was never allowed at his bedside. When he died Rab knew that his ain time would no be lang at the Barnyards. He knew that Bess would be rid of him at the next May Term, so he looked for another place that suited him. Nor was the Barnyards long under the sod or Bess had a great cumbersome stone set up on top of him. 'Jist tae mak sure he doesna interfere in her wyes,' Rab said, with some of his old good humour returning; 'losh aye, yon muckle steen will fairly hud 'im doon.'

So Bess got rid of Rab at the May Term, and all the rabble of cottars that

31

did his every bidding. 'She wants a clean toon lads,' Rab said to his men, 'we'll a' hae tae go!'

'I wadna like a woman boss onywye,' Rab concluded. 'I've ane at hame already; anither ane at my wark wad be hell upon earth.'

Touch and Go!

It was a dark winter's night that Wee Tam's mither and Mrs. Lunan, a neighbour body, planned a raid on a nearbye farmer's hen-house. Mrs. Lunan's man was a cripple, and they lived in an old croft house down in the howe of Glenshinty. They had three or four bairns running barefoot around the place, with hardly a stitch of clothing on their backs, but somehow they managed to scrape along on a mere pittance from the Assistance Board, and once in a while the Inspector of the Poor looked in by to see if the creatures were still alive.

'Ma man's been real poorly lately,' said Mrs. Lunan, warming her hands at the fire, 'and a drappie o chicken bree wad do him a world o good.'

'But whaur are we gaun tae get a hen at this time o nicht?'

'Steal ane,' said Mrs. Lunan, unabashed.

'Steal ane!' cried Tam's mither, and she looked at the woman half in sympathy, half in fear, wondering what she was going to say next.

'Aye, we'll try auld Grimshaw's place; it's fine near the road and naebody wad jalouse us there. Get on yer coat wife and gie us a hand.'

'A' richt wifie, but it's a bit risky,' said Tam's mither, buttoning up her coat; 'and Tam, put on yer bonnet and come and watch the coast is clear for us, and see there's nae ferlies aboot.'

Wee Tam shut his book and shuddered. He had been reading *Robinson Crusoe*, a big book that he had got from the dominie, one of those old-fashioned editions with beautifully stencilled capitals at the beginning of each chapter, and with a short summary of the events therein related. The loon was just getting fully absorbed in this pirate and cutlass masterpiece when the women hatched their plan.

The lamp was lit and the blinds were down and Tam's father snored in the box-bed. He was an early bedder and missed much of the goings on in the hoose, but Tam felt that the old man had one eye open half the time and that he listened between the snores. But he never interfered, mither was boss. Flora, Tam's little sister, lay snugly at her father's back, curled like a buckie, a doll in her oxter, and Tam felt it was a pity he hadn't gone to bed, then perhaps the women wouldn't have bothered him.

It was inky black and bitter cold outside. A mass of stars spangled the sky, and Tam could pick out the Seven Sisters twinkling above the dark smudge of pinewood on the Berry Hill. But apart from the sough and flap of the wind the world was as silent as a graveyard.

Tam shivered in his thin jacket as he trudged on behind the women, trying

33

to identify the adventure with what he had been reading in *Robinson Crusoe*. About a mile along the road they came to Grimshaw's place, a big croft by the roadside, which Tam passed every day going to school. There was a lean-to poultry shed at the gable of the steading, close by the road, but in full view of the kitchen door.

The women first went past the farmhouse, to make sure there were no lights in the windows, walking on the grass to quieten the sound of their footsteps, then came back to where Tam waited at the henhouse.

Tam watched and listened but nobody stirred, nothing but the faint smell of the sharn midden and the scent of stale peat smoke that came to his nostrils on the wind. Everybody was asleep at this hour so the two women crept into the henhouse. They groped for a couple of good plump birds on the roost and wrung their necks before a cackle escaped them. There was some flapping of wings and a flutter of feathers when they came out, but never a squawk from the dead birds. They put the hens in a sack, closed the hen-house door and made off, Wee Tam behind them, still walking on the grass, all as silent as doomsday.

Safely home Tam went back to Robinson Crusoe Island, thinking no more about the affair, glad to be back to the fire and the lamplight, snug in the satisfaction that he could read till his eyes closed without further interruption, for it was just past midnight.

The women set to plucking the hens in the kitchen, while the birds were still warm, which makes it easier to do, and cleaning them, getting them ready for the dinner, maybe with a plate of broth first and the hen to follow, but Mrs. Lunan said she would roast hers because she wanted the bree for her sick man.

Tam got a helping when he got home from school, running all the way at the thought of it, his satchel unstrapped and under his arm, to save the thump of it on his back. And it had been a rare treat, especially the stuffing and the white flesh around the breast-bone, which mither had laid aside for him, and his old man had never asked where the hen came from.

In the evening, after supper, Tam was lighting a cigarette over the lamp glass on the kitchen table, when the local bobby laid his bicycle against the unblinded window. Tam quickly snibbed the fag in the fire, just as the bobby walked in, never waiting for an answer to his knock on the door.

'Aye lad,' says the bobby, as he peeled off his leather gloves, 'I fairly caught ye that time. I suppose ye ken that sixteen is the age for smokin?'

Tam squeezed himself into the corner behind the meal barrel, his surest refuge in times of trouble. He remembered the hen in the dresser and he felt terribly guilty and afraid. His father was seated by the fireside. The policeman turned to him and said: 'Don't ye know it's illegal for the lad tae smoke afore he's sixteen?'

Tam's father scratched his balding head, tired from his day's work in the byres. 'Oh aye,' says he, wearily, 'but the laddie gie's me a hand in the byre, and for that I dinna grudge 'im a bit blaw at a fag.'

But the bobby was indignant. 'It's not a question of whether you can afford it man, but you're breaking the law!' He turned to Tam's mither, who was placing a chair for him. 'Woman,' he said, 'do ye allow this to go on in the hoose: the rascal smokin and him still at school?'

'Oh aye, but the man's boss in the hoose here,' she lied, thankful that the tiny wish-bone from the hen was in the oven, and not on the crook over the range as it might have been. When it became thoroughly brittle Tam would share it with his little sister: each would take a splint of it in the crook of a little finger, make a wish and pull, and whoever had the broken end when the bone snapped would lose the wish.

The constable sat down on a hard chair in the middle of the cement floor, crossed his legs and laid his 'cheese-cutter' cap on his knee. He was so near the hen now he could have smelled it. He only had to reach over to open the dresser door and there was the skeleton of it, on a plate.

He was much nearer Tam's height on the varnished chair and the loon breathed a little more freely behind the meal barrel. Nevertheless he was still a mighty giant in the shabby little kitchen, his red face polished with stern authority and his silver buttons twinkling in the lamplight. Tam focused his attention on the bobby's putteed leg, which he kept swinging up and down over his knee, as if he wished to show off the highly polished boot at the end of it, a boot that would give you a hefty kick in the buttocks if he got near enough.

'Have ye seen ony strange characters in the vicinity?' the bobby asked, looking first at Tam's mither, and then at his father. 'Auld Sandy Grimshaw has missed some hens out of his shed, and says that by the mess of feathers ootside the door, he feels sure they have been stolen.'

Tam's father suddenly recalled his splendid dinner but swallowed the thought. 'No,' he said, trying to look unconcerned 'no, we hinna seen a cratur, not a cratur!'

Tam's mither poured out a glass of Dr. Watson's Tonic Stout for the bobby, and one for her husband. It was the only hop beverage in the house and she excelled in the brewing of it, though she sometimes made broom wine in the summer, with a taste like whisky.

'Ye ken auld Grimshaw's place?' the bobby asked, taking the glass in his fat, beringed fingers.

'Aye,' said Tam's mither, wiping her hands on her apron, 'I ken the fairm: it's at the top o the quarry brae, nae far frae the shop.'

'Aye, ye ken wuman, I'm nae supposed tae drink in uniform, but in this case we'll mak an exception.'

'Ach man, that stuff will never touch ye!' And Tam's mither busied herself wiping the table of what she had spilled, for the bottles were brisk and the froth had hit the roof when she removed the corks.

Tam's wee sister came forward with her biggest doll and laid it on the bobby's knee. He bent the doll forward in his huge hand and it 'Ba-a-a-ed' pitifully, as if it had a tummy ache. He only had to ask little Flora what Dolly had for dinner and he had the case wrapped up.

But the local flat-foot was no Sherlock Holmes, and he believed only what he saw; like loons smoking while still in short breeks, or a poor farm servant

35

chauving home against the wind without a rear-light on his bicycle.

Otherwise there wasn't a feather of evidence in sight. The wing feathers were tied in a bundle in the cubby-hole under the loft stair. Tam's mither would wash them and use them to brush her oat-cakes before she put them on the girdle over the fire. The downs were concealed in a sack; she would stuff them into a pillow after they had been fumigated. The cats had eaten all the offal on the midden. There wasn't a shred of evidence left anywhere in sight.

The bobby licked his lips and set the empty glass on the table. 'Thanks mistress,' he said, wiping his moustache, 'that was capital!'

He got up and put on his peaked cap and gloves, glowering down at wee Tam behind the meal barrel. 'Ye can coont yersel lucky lad,' he said, 'lucky that I'm nae takin ye tae the lock-up. Gin yer mither hadna been sic a gweed-hertit wuman, and yer faither sic an honest decent body, I might hae run ye in for smokin. But if I catch ye at it again I wunna be sae lenient!'

Turning to Tam's mither in the door he said: 'Bye the bye mistress, wha bides in that hoose in the howe, alang the Laich Road?'

'Oh,' says Tam's mither, wondering what the bobby was leading to, 'it's Mrs. Lunan bides there.'

The bobby was now outside on the gravel, his brass buttons shining in the light from the open doorway, for it was now quite dark. 'Mrs. Lunan,' says he, still quizzical, 'and do ye think she wad hae seen onybody suspicious, or could gie us ony information?'

Tam's mither began to tremble with excitement. 'Oh I hardly think so,' she said, trying to seem unconcerned, 'she's a bittie frae the road and disna see mony strangers.'

'Ah weel,' replied the bobby, 'but I'd better look in and see her onywye. Gweed nicht Mistress!'

The policeman was scarcely astride his bicycle when Mrs. Lunan burst in on Tam's folk from the darkness. They had been watching the rear-light on the bobby's bike as he sped down the brae. All had seemed lost but now they crowded round Mrs. Lunan in the lighted doorway, to see what could be done.

'Run wifie,' cried Tam's mither, exasperated, 'fly hame as fast as ye can, the bobby has been here and he's just left, and he's on the road tae your hoose noo. Run wifie, for heaven's sake run!'

'Michty me!' cried the woman, 'I meant tae borrow something, but that doesna matter noo. Michty me! oor hen's still on the table, or what's left o't!' And away she flew, clambering over the dyke like a schoolgirl, lost in the darkness.

It was touch and go: the bobby on his bike round by the road, the woman on her feet across the wet fields. The bobby had a few minutes start ahead of her and she had another dyke to jump, and a deep ditch lay in her path.

Wee Tam could see the bobby's light as he moved along the Laich Road, but he could only guess how the woman fared in the darkness. The bobby had a gate to open at the end of the cart-track that led to the cottage. Tam closed the lobby door to shut in the light and waited. It wouldn't do to let the bobby know they were watching. It was touch and go . . .

It was close on midnight when Mrs. Lunan went panting back to Tam's mither with the news. 'Michty mee,' she gasped, 'I got hame first but just in time. It was a near thing I can tell ye. I was like tae faint and fair oot o breath or I reached the door. I put the hen oot o sight in the dresser, double quick. I just had time tae get my breath back when the bobby rapped on the door. I closed the lobby door so's he couldna see my face in the licht, and he never cam ben the hoose, so he never noticed my weet shoes and stockins. Thank heavens he didna find us oot. We wunna hae tae try that again wifie!'

Tam's mither was relieved. 'Na faith ye,' she said, 'but how's yer man Mrs. Lunan?'

'He's fine,' said the woman, 'but he doesna ken a thing aboot it. He's sound asleep and he thinks I bocht the hen, me that hardly has a copper penny tae clap on anither.'

Tam's mither gave her a brimming glass of Dr. Watson's Tonic Stout: 'Just to cheer you up wifie,' as she said, while the froth flew from the uncorked bottle.

Wee Tam went back to the lamp glass and relit his cigarette. His old man had gone to bed but he stopped snoring immediately and raised himself on his elbow, blinking at the light. 'Ony tay wuman?' says he, looking at his wife. 'No I dinna want the stout, nae at this time o nicht, jist a drap tay. So that was whaur the hen cam frae, auld Grimshaw. Weel weel, she was a tasty bird onywye!'

And then he turned on Wee Tam, now seated on a kitchen chair with *Robinson Crusoe*, the fag reek rising above the open pages. 'But ye'll hae tae watch yer smokin ma loon, and if ye dinna come tae the byre when I want ye I'll tell the bobby ye've been at it again, ye wee rascal!'

The old blackmailer, Tam thought, but it should have taught the women a lesson.

Knowie's Midden Licht

Auld Knowie lived by the clock. He carried a gold watch with a lid on its face, fastened to his waistcoat by a thin chain. In the stable at noon, waiting for yoking time, he took the bit watch out of his pocket and flicked the lid open, watching the hands as they approached the hour. Several times he did this, and if you had been the fee-ed lad at the Knowehead you would have noticed that when he closed the lid with a final snap the hour had come.

And you would wait for Knowie's orders like he was an army captain, and then you would grab a saddle and throw it on your horse's back like you was in the mounted cavalry, for Knowie was a great lad for discipline and he liked to have you lined up at the drinking trough on the stroke of one.

But for all his barking his bite wasn't as sharp as some folk would say, and his line-up at the horses' trough wasn't all that impressive, especially if you had come from a three or four-paired place, for Knowie had only one pair of horse and an orra-beast, worked by his son, young Knowie yonder that was foreman, and a bit nipper of a loon he had fee-ed for the odd beast and to help with the kye.

And if you had never been to jail, six month's in Knowie's chaumer would have given you a fairly good idea of what it would be like. All this yammer about the good old bothy days is just a lot of white-wash and the sooner you was married the better if you wanted a decent kip. Not that Knowie could help this; he wasn't to be blamed for the chaumer being biggit over the midden, and it was no worse and no better than any other you had lived in. But you would get no fire in Knowie's chaumer, except on your Sunday as 'Toon Keeper' every third week-end, looking after the kye and the horse, and maybe it was for fear you set fire to the steading, you being but a cottar bairn and not supposed to have as much wit as decent folk. And while Knowie's kye could lie down in brilliant electric light you had to go to sleep with a leaking paraffin lamp, so they had to trust you with that because there was no light in your bothy, which made you of less importance socially than the nowt in Knowie's byre.

Your chaumer was part of the hay-loft above the stable, with only a thin partition between you and the hay-seed, and damned if you could have slept for the stamping of iron hoofs on the cobblestones, or for the rattle of manger chains or scamper of rats at the corn kists. And there was no such thing as a wardrobe, so you hung your Sunday clothes on to rusty nails hammered into the partition, and the hay-worms came wriggling through the seams and lost themselves in the pockets of your best suit.

How would you like to be standing at the top of the Broadgate, in the Town Square, having a bit crack with some of your cronies and a caterpillar looking through your buttonhole? He had taken a night's lodgings under the lapel of your jacket, and the heat of your body had made him seek a breath of fresh air, so he wriggles to your buttonhole and sticks his head out to see who you are talking to, and if it happened to be your favourite kitchiedeem, and her a bit squeamish, it would maybe be the last you would see of her. So you would seize the 'crawlin ferlie' with thoom and fore-finger and throw him on the pavement and squash him with your heel, while your deem would giggle or look the other way, depending on her mentality. So you would curse Knowie and his hay-worms and wish for the term, especially if it had cost you your best quine.

Knowie's chaumer had the usual wooden bed which looked like part of the building, and it was fitted with bottom boards and a chaff tick. Some folk called them 'tikes', which were merely two sheets of linen sewn together like a great big sack and stuffed with chaff. They were bought in the shops ready to fill, bed-size and mostly white with red or blue stripes, and they served as a mattress for farmer and cottar, a cosy one at that, and when it was newly filled you had to loup on a chair to get into bed. But Knowie himself maybe had a hair mattress by now, or even a feather bed like the gentry; for seeing he was so far ahead with everything else this wasn't likely to be overlooked for his comfort.

Being a young chiel with the blood of youth in your body you had no need of a hot-water bottle, but if you had been an old frail creature and asked for such a thing at the Knowehead you would have been laughed at, for while you was shut out at night with the horses and the nowt beasts all the others were coddled in the farmhouse. So you would have stood a poor chance if you had been an old body at the Knowehead, for more than likely you would have hoasted your hinder-end or died of chronic bronchitis before anyone noticed you was a human being like the rest of them, and that you shouldn't be treated like the beasts that had thick hides to keep out the cold on a howling winter's night. But you was only a cottar loon, and of no great consequence to anyone in particular, except your own mother, and many a night she wondered how you fared in your damp bed, or if a rat had chewed another hole in one of your socks.

The only other pieces of furnishing in your chaumer at Knowies was a chair and your own kist, but as you was never likely to have more than one visitor at a time, and mostly a neighbour loon as lonely and miserable and ill-used as yourself, there was never any scarcity of seats. Most lads just sat on their kists anyway, and you could easily play a melodion or a fiddle sitting on your kist, or take a bit blow at the mouth-organ, if you had an inclination for such things, or you could lie on your bed and read a book, waiting for your mind to take a turn in the direction you was supposed to go.

The lads before your time at Knowie's had their names burnt out with a hot poker on the walls and around the fireplace, and you could see by the list that the place had been well-tenanted. Some of them had started on the floor, even on the seat of your only chair, but you resisted the temptation to add even your initials to this conglomeration of immortality.

The door of Knowie's chaumer was at the back, or rather it had two doors, one on the inside and an outer door on the porch overlooking the sharn midden. This porch was like a prison observatory, and the likeness was strengthened by the long flight of stone steps and the iron hand-rail leading down to the cobblestones and the cart-shed pends.

The stink of the sharn midden would be with you all the time, which made you glad of the skylight at the end of your bed, for by standing on the chair you could open the skylight and gaze out over the farmhouse and the garden, which were completely separate from the steading. On a fine day you could see Knowie's dothers on the bleaching green, where they would be hanging out Knowie's long drawers on the clothes line, and maybe some other bits of things you wasn't supposed to see, and but for this you might have given them a whistle through your fingers. Faith but you liked the twa quines, Sadie and Nora, even though they were a bit older than you. Sadie the eldest was blonde and friendly but the Nora quine was the one that you fancied, her with hair as black and soft as nightfall and a bonnie sparkle in her eyes, and you would have liked fine to be her lad, but you feared that if Knowie got wind of such a thing he would most likely put you in your place.

Knowie was mostly seated at his parlour window, reading his newspaper, and the moment you saw him fold it up and take off his glasses you knew he would be over to the stable with the working orders for the afternoon. Always on the dot Knowie was, and you could set your watch on the minute he folded his newspaper, or your alarm clock from the moment he rapped on your chaumer door for the morning milking.

Knowie was a great lad for *The Times* newspaper. Him bein with the gentry he had to have a newspaper different from the other fairmer lads, who said he sometimes talked over their heads, him bein educated, like.

But by all standards Knowie was a good farmer. He kept his place tidy and worked the land in season. Over the years he had built up a fine herd of Friesian cows, with two or three of the Jersey breed to raise a cream on his milk. He was far ahead of his neighbours for miles around, for while they were content to poke about in the dark with paraffin lanterns he had his place all lit up with electricity from storage batteries, generated by his own dynamo and diesel engine.

There was even a light high up on a pole above the steading to let you see over the midden with a barrow of dung in the dark. Knowie switched it on first thing in the morning, when he came to chap on your chaumer door, so you might have thought it was for fear you fell down the stone steps and broke your neck; but damn the fears, for it was to let his neighbours see that Knowie was up and about on the stroke of five. For there was nae sleepin-in at Knowie's, and the chiel fair prided himsel in the fact that his customers never had to wait for their milk.

And if the neighbours were up b'times they would rub their bleary eyes and stare at this new star in the mirk. But Dod damned when daylight came and the star was sometimes still in the sky they saw it was just one of Knowie's ferlies and they wondered what the hell the chiel would try next.

They didn't have long to wait, for what does the chiel do but off to the toon and comes back with a tractor, a blue Fordson thing with spade-lug wheels on a motor-lorry. Och it was only an iron-wheeled tractor and it couldn't go much on the road, so the billies round about took a bit lauch at Knowie ahin his back and said it was just another of his daft ploys. Some of them said it would even raise his account with Old Brookie the blacksmith, 'cause young Knowie yonder would soon have everything broken with a beast like that about the place.

But it was a different story when the Spring came; when the grun was fair ettlin to be harrowed, hungry for seed, and his neighbours horses dyin of grass-sickness, for Knowie's tractor was careerin over the drying furrows with a set of iron-toothed harrows dancing behind it, and a clamour of white gulls squacking for grub.

And Knowie got a new drill-sower, with the smell of fresh paint still about it, and though it was a narrow thing compared with broadcast sowing it saved him a lot of harrowing-in; so he had his crops all sown and his grass-seed in before the other lads had barely started, and they shook their heads sadly and said the man would soon be growing two crops in one season. And on a quiet morning you could hear the rattle of Knowie's metal rollers away up on the Stonehill, three of them coupled to the tractor thing and raising a cloud of dust, and the lads said he would raise the very devil from his foundry.

But there were some who were envious and even jealous of Knowie and his go-ahead ways, especially with that midden licht shining every morning, and one carle took it so much to heart that he played a prank on Knowie. And what does this carlin do but gets up in the dead of darkest night and opens the sluice at the Knowhead and drains all the water out of the dam. Not once but several times the wretch did this, and Knowie couldna get a thrash, because there was no water to drive his mill-wheel, and when his barn was empty he was in a sore stramash.

Say what you like about Knowie, but he didn't get the polis. The crafty chiel had an answer for this, so away he goes to the millwright and comes back with a length of belting on the milk lorry. Now this tractor thing had a pulley on it, like a traction-engine, so he whirrs it round and into his barn, couples up the belt with a pulley sic-like on the mill and he had the thing bummin in no time at all.

Dyod but the folks thocht he had fair gone clean skite and this tractor thing was sure to set fire to his barn. But it fair garred the mull dirl or it was nearly riven off its trestles and the dust was comin oot at the skylights. Out by in the sun-haze you could hear Knowie's mill snarling at the sheaves and abody slavin wi their sarks aff and spittin stuff like tar.

Daggit now if Knowie doesn't go and gets the millwrights out of the town to put wheels on his threshing mill, and drags it out of the barn with the tractor, over to the stackyard for a thrash. So there was no fear now of Knowie having a fire in his barn, though yon coorse tyke that drained his dam maybe had a mind to go in the night and set fire to it himsel.

Och, but the chiel will never get a thrash on a windy day: athing will be blawn awa, and it will take a hantle of corn to pay for that contraption. Well now, if he doesn't go and gets a trusser thing fixed on to the tail of his mill and not a straw is lost. Havers man! And he gets a wind-blast for the chaff, a long tube that blows the stuff up in the air and the billies out-by couldna see what he was doing for the sture.

And it fair maddened them! Had the man gone clean wud? The orra slipe! Ah well, there was one consolation: he would find it damned expensive to pay for the binder-twine for that trusser thing. Surely it was enough to bind the stuff in hairst without a second time, and serve 'im right if 'is kye tak obstruction eatin the tow among their straw.

Och-on-noo Skirlie! What's this ye tell me? Knowie wi a motor car! Profits winna hide man. That melk's fairly payin but the folk in the toon says he is a bittie scrimp wi the measure joog. But that's whaur the car has come from! Of coorse we kent he had a motor for deliverin his melk; ye canna grudge the man a motor for his melk when Cairnie and the Mulltoon has wan - but a motor car for pleeshure - Gweed preserve a' livin soul!

But thon quines will be a hud doon tae Knowie yet! You mark my words Birkie, they'll be a pair o randies among the lads yet. The vricht was tellin me yon Nora quine's havin a gie carry on wi that coonter-loupin lad from the Howe Shop. I dinna ken what Knowie will say when he kens that his dother is taking up her time wi yon white-faced scrat o a cratur, and him hardly got a brown copper to clap on anither - a' gone on drink.

Ah weel Skirlie, Knowie will likely be the last one to hear aboot that; but when he does most likely he'll go into a sulk; it's the nature o the chiel, but a glaikit breet when he's got a dram in, which isn't often, him bein parsimonious-like; though yon wife o his is maybe at the back o that, and her all dolled up to the nines in a fur coat and as much poother on her face as would bake a scone.

Aye Birkie, and they tell me she has gotten an electric iron for Knowie's Sunday sark, him bein an elder o the kirk, like, and needin a clean sark every Sunday. Ach, but a good old-fashioned box-iron does fine wi my gweedwife, a body canna afford a' that trock. But they will a' cost Knowie a bonnie penny yet. Fegs aye, they're jist gaun some far alength wi their pride!

Dyod aye Skirlie, and yon loon, young Knowie yonder; they say he's fair terrified o his auld man, fleein up and doon the neep dreels in his sark tails, clean gaen gyte, and his horse in a foam o sweat, tryin to raise dreels and the grun nae half made wi yon tractor thing; nae even grubbit, juist scrattit on the tap wi yon disc things. Did e'r ye hear the like o that? And his mither oot after him with tea and fancy biscuits on a tray to try and simmer 'im doon. The fee-ed laddie was drivin oot muck in the dreels and he said it was the only time he had ever gotten a drop tea at his work sin' he gaed to the place.

And Knowie's wife laid off about how they wouldn't get a cup of tea from the twa quines; 'twa spoiled bitches,' she called them, and that they didna ken what it was to do a day's work, or what it was to be hungry. And then she tells the loons to hurry up and drink their tea afore Aleck's father comes home with the melk cairt, 'cause he doesna take a piece himsel in workin hours and he doesna like to see ither folk at it.

Fie man Birkie, but the conceit o some folk is most extraordinar! But young Knowie yonder could maybe go to the drink yet and land in the herbour; the wye he flees aboot in his father's car ye wad think he hadna another minute to live!

Losh aye Skirlie, but they have the telephone now up at the Knowehead, and Knowie's wife has a talk with the minister's wife or the dominie any hour of the day, making arrangements for the kirk social or the bairns concert, and they were sayin at the Rural that the gentry are fair deaved wi Knowie's wife since they got the telephone.

Aye Birkie, but a body might be glad o Knowie's telephone and I think it's a grand thing for the fairmin folk, especially if ye had to get the vet or the houdi in a hurry; it might save ye sendin for the knackery cairt or the hearse in the lang run, nae tae compare beast wi body like, but it canna be helped.

But mair than that, for Knowie was tellin yon lad up in the Reisk (yon futret o a cratur that kens athing) Knowie was tellin him (or so he says - if ye can believe it) that they have the wireless now at the Knowhead. Nae one o they crystal sets with the halter on't for yer lugs - na faith ye, something better than that for Knowie! He calls it 'a loud-speaker radio' a varnished cabinet thing, with a bit horn on it, like a gramophone, and Knowie gets the time o day from yon mannie away in London yonder, 'cause ye know how particular Knowie is about the time o day. But fancy that mannie speakin to Knowie in his parlour all the way from London, and telling him all about the weather a two three days in front, and Knowie knows when to sow his corn or ploo his neep park afore the weather breaks. Forewarned is forearmed, as Knowie says, him bein educated, like.

Aye Skirlie, but he'll be the speak o the Reisk noo if yon claik o a cratur has got hold on't. But I will say this for Knowie, that durin yon big snawstorm last winter he saw that the toonsfolk got their melk. He had Aleck rigged out wi his pair in a snawploo and he made a sledge and loaded it wi cans and followed Aleck wi the orra beast.

Yea man, but speakin o melk reminds me Birkie that ye dinna ken the verra latest, ye're a' ahin wi the news man, for tae croon a' they've got the new melkin machines at Knowie's noo - what say ye tae that? Yon quines are that bigsy and feart tae fule their hands they wunna melk their father's kye, and Knowie has tae spend 'is money on a melkin machine tae save the weemin folk. I'm damned if I'd lat a dother o mine aff wi that, I'd skelp 'er arse first. Dyod man, but the chiel will never melk a coo wi yon thing, for a' the earth like a bloomin octopus wi its hert in its mou - a mass o rubber chubes that wad tie ye in knots. It's like fower calves sookin a coo and a' chawin awa at the same time. Nae beast will stand that. I tell ye man it's cruelty. Next thing ye'll hear they'll hae the Cruelty up at Knowie's, taraneezin the beasts wi yon things. And certain if ye leave they machines on yer coos owre lang ye'll draw bleed, and folk disna like bleedy melk, it's a fair scunner and he'll lose 'is customers in the toon. That'll be the doon come o Knowie yet wi his new-fangled wyes!

Ah well, Skirlie and Birkie had their say, and so had a lot more besides, but it just goes to show what happens when an energetic, enterprising man like Knowie tried to better himself just that little bit above his neighbours; but it was putting that midden licht above his steading that first set their tongues wagging.

But if you had been the fee-ed lad at Knowies you would have seen that some of the things they said were true, though not all of it. For one thing you wasn't hungered at the Knowehead, 'cause Knowie's wife fed you every day with a knife and fork, like you were with the gentry, and that was more than you could say about a lot of places you'd been at.

And you would be fillin muck into a cart at the steading, on a cold morning with a brittle frost and icicles hanging from the spoots all round the roofs, and Knowie comes over the midden plank with a barrowful of cow dung, tips the sharn out of the barrow and then stands looking at you over the stilts. 'Man,' says he, 'Ye've affa little go aboot ye sometimes. Ye're the first man I've seen fillin muck wi his jacket on!' Which was just another way of telling you to take it off! And not a very polite way at that, so you didn't do it. And you thinks that some day Knowie will maybe say that to the wrong lad, for you knew some lads who would have taken their jackets off right quick, but for a different reason, and maybe taught him a lesson. The impudence of the man. But ach, it wasn't worth risking your wages for, and he really wasn't such a bad stock once you got used to his high-mindedness.

But you didn't follow Knowie's destiny for longer than six months, for you were off when the term came, because of the hay-worms. You thought you would be high and mighty with Knowie and went and fee-ed to another place before he asked you to stay on, which he did, and was a real gentleman about it and had no bad feelings, and you was kind of mad at yourself for being so rash, especially when you were just beginning to get to know the quines better and all that.

And Knowie would shake hands with you when you left, which made you feel a real toff, and which was more than any farmer chiel would ever do with you again in your whole life, and his parting words would be: 'Ye hinna been a bad ane!'

So that was Knowie, a most extraordinar man, as Skirlie and Birkie would say, and you would agree with them.

The Dookit Fairm

'An affa big dookit for jist twa doos!' That was the wye that the folk outby spoke aboot the Dookit Fairm. Of coorse they were referrin to the dwellin-hoose, a great big mansion amon the trees, wi' as mony teem rooms as a beehive efter a swarmin, for they had nae bairns at the Dookit Fairm. Elsie Wabster was mistress at the Dookit, and she said she never would have a littlin, and she never had a tooth pulled in her whole life, for she said that raither than thole these tortures she wad dee.

The Dookit himsel was a queer mannie, and folk thocht that this attitude o' Elsie's had something tae do with it, for there seemed tae be something missin in the man's life, and though the folk couldna fathom what it was they were sure it was the want o' a bairn. And when he took a bit dander roon the sheep, wi' the collie doggie at his heels, a body thocht it wad hae made a great difference had it been a bit loonie hoiterin on ahin 'im.

But the maister o' the Dookit was most affa religious, though nae exactly a Catholic, or he'd never hae put up wi' Elsie's spinster wyes. But he was a staunch elder o the Auld Kirk and never said an ill-word in his life, nae even in anger, and he had the patience o' Job himsel in adversity. Strong drink never touched his lips, nor pipe or fags, and his teachin o' the Sunday School was a credit tae the presbytery.

Elsie was much the same, never missed a Sabbath at the kirk, rain or shine, and the twa o' them wad set oot wi' the motorbike and side-car, and if it was rainin Elsie wad hoist her umbrella tae keep aff the draps. And the Dookit wad squeeze his horn 'Pap-pap,' tae put the bairns aff the road, and when the bairns saw them comin they cried, 'Here's Pap-pap!'

Noo the Dookit was a great lad for sheep, and he keepit aboot three-hunder breedin yows wi' lambs at foot. And he coontit 'es yowies in ilka park three times a day in the simmer, fair terrified that a yowie should die on her back afore the shearin. He could spot maggots on a sheepie's back nearly a mile awa, and if he didna like the wye a lambie was waggin its tail he was sure there was maggots on't, and mostly he was richt. And juist gie 'im a yowie's hoof tae scrape at and ye could hardly get 'im awa till 'es denner.

But Elsie wore the breeks, oh aye, ye could see that, 'cause she was aye oot yappin at the back kitchie door when the grieve cam roon tae see the Dookit aboot the wark. Elsie had tae hae her speen in somewye, there was nae doot aboot that!

Noo the Dookit Fairm was a fairly big place as fairms go, three-hunder-

45

and-sixty-five acres arable, leased oot at a pound an acre, which meant three-hunder-and-sixty-five pounds a year, or a pound a day. So come what may, wind or weet, snaw or sleet, every mornin that the Dookit rose and put on his drawers he had tae mak a pound note clear profit afore the sun set. And believe me, that was by no means easy in the days that the Dookit was fairmin.

It gart ye rub yer een in a mornin I tell ye, especially if ye got a yowie lyin deid on 'er back, her legs stickin up like spurtles and her een picket oot wi the craws, 'cause that was yer pound note nearly gone for a start. Ye could pluck the wool aff the cratur afore ye buriet 'er (gin ye could stand the smell) and maybe ye'd get a twa-three shillins back for that frae some rag tink.

And if a coo lost a calf, weel that was anither set-back. And if ye got a horse or a mere lyin deid wi grass-sickness that jist aboot put ye oot at the door. Or maybe the neep-flea wad ravage yer young plants afore ye got them hyowed, for there was nae beetle-dust in those days. The craws could even clean a neep park efter it was singled, lookin for the grub at the roots o the plants. Weel-a-wite, but sometimes ye was gled o the craws, especially if ye saw them turnin ower the sods in yer lea park, lookin for Leatherjackets, itherwise the Tory Worms wad leave yer corn crap as bald as an auld man's heid, and ye wad get a plague o Daddy-lang-legs in the Autumn. But if the craws fell oot on yer tattie dreels that was a different story, and 'cause the Dookit never handled a gun in his life he was fair pestered wi the black deils. They nestit thick in the trees a' roon the big hoose and fair took advantage o his hospitality.

And if the rings fell aff yer cairt wheels in a dry simmer ye couldna get yer peats hame; and if it was a weet simmer the rings bade on but yer peats wadna dry. Dyod man, ye've jist no idea o the things that cam atween the Dookit and that pound note in the coorse o a day.

But Elsie was his guidin star, as ye micht say, and what he couldna mak on the grun she wad save on the hoosehold expenses. Feed the men on what grows on the place, that was Elsie's motto: self-sufficiency, and but for a few triflin thingies, like saut, sugar and treacle, Elsie's scheme was verra nearly fool-proof. Dyod aye, gin there had been troot in the mill-dam as there was hares in the parks Elsie had naething tae learn aboot feedin the five-thoosan.

Speak aboot a Shepherd's Calendar! Elsie had a menu tae beat a'. Ye could nearly tell what season o the year it was by the food ye was eatin, and the days o the week by yer diet. In the simmer when the eggs were cheap she preserved them, and ye ate them in the winter when they were dearer. That left mair fresh eggs tae sell at the richt time. Dyod aye, and when the butter wasna sellin she made saut butter, and ye got that and margarine when the price rose again. Sell butter and buy margarine, sound economics in those days when the price was sae much agley. And Elsie laid the table hersel, tae mak sure the men didna get ower muckle, a wee bittie o butter aboot the size o yer thoom-nail, a wee ballie or twa that wasna near eneuch; and the jam was the same, maistly rhubarb and wild raspberry, with strawberries for Sunday - a wee spoonfae that wad hardly stick a flea.

So ye got cabbage brose, kale brose, neep brose, melk brose and ordinar brose; melk broth and barley broth, leek soup, chappit tatties and skirlie or sise; stovies, hairy tatties (made wi hard fish and mustard sauce) peel-and-ate tatties and saut-herrin, oat-breid and skimmed melk - maistly onything that grew on the fairm, plus peasemeal, and when ye mixed that wi oatmeal ye was still on hame grun.

And gin ye had a fancy for buttermelk ye could get that as weel, or new-cheese when a coo calved. But Elsie never made sowens; the miller kept his sids and his dist and ye was spared the diet o the Prodigal Son. But woe betide if ye got Elsie's lentil soup made wi margarine, for it wad fairly flatten ye, and ye micht come tae yersel again aboot fower o'clock in the efterneen, streekit oot on a grouth midden wi a belly like a bloatit yow.

But bein an auld bothy haun yersel ye didna mind a' this hame-grown whalesome fairin, nae gin Elsie had left the lambs alane. But na faith ye! and gin a wee lambie died o 'ooball in the springtime Elsie had tae get it for the pot. Speak aboot the Blood o the Lamb! There wasna a drap o bleed in the craitur's body, and it was boiled white as a bleached dishcloth. And teuch! Ye could hae chawed till ye was blin and never left a teeth mark on't. But it saved a shillin or twa tae the butcher's van and added that amount tae the Dookit's daily pound.

But a day was comin for Elsie, folks said, or she wadna get men tae bide at the Dookit. And come it did, but nae in a wye that maist folk expectit. It's a wonder they said, that they dinna ate the rats at the Dookit, when they cam up in a plague oot o the mill-dam, and they swore that gin Elsie could get some chiel tae shoot the rats and the craws she wad hae them on the table. A rabbit or a hare was aricht at a time they said, but there was no sayin how far Elsie wad go once she got startet . . .

But ye could aye tell when it was Sunday, 'cause ye got porridge tae yer breakfast instead o brose, and a fried preserved egg instead o a boiled ane. Ye was quite a gentleman on a Sunday, and ye got a denner fit for a lord: stewed steak and onions and chappit tatties, trifle for yer dessert, and even a cuppie o tay and a fancy piece. And all this was got ready on the Saturday, because Sunday was a day o rest and prayer for Elsie, as it was for the Dookit himsel. But there was nae pride wi Elsie, that was wan thing; it wasna pride that ailed 'er on a Sunday - it was her religion. But her sanctimony was a wee bit topsy-turvy, as ye micht say, 'cause ye fastit a' the week and on the Sabbath ye had the Feast o the Passover. Maybe it should hae been the ither wye roon. But it was jist a sham wi Elsie, and a good deal o hypocrisy, for nae sooner was Sunday bye than ye was back tae the kale brose again, slubberin like swine.

And Elsie was sly too, for if a stranger cam in by, a mill-man or a lorry-driver, he got a stoup o cream at his end o the table, so that he wid cairry a good tale abroad aboot the mait at the Dookit. But fan Elsie gaed ben the hoose and ye showed the lad your joog o separatit melk he was fair astonished and it thwarted Elsie's purpose. But there was wan thing that grew on the place that ye never tastit, and that was the honey. Na faith ye! for maist o it gaed tae the Sale of Work in the kirk hall or ben the hoose.

Noo the Dookit had fee'ed a bit haflin tae ca' the fourth pair and sort a puckle nowt. He had tae haggle wi the lad at the market 'cause the lad stak up for big siller. Twenty-three pounds for the sax months the lad had socht, from Whitsun tae Martimass, and the Dookit was only prepared tae gie twenty-one pound. But Elsie the jawd had telt 'im tae fee somebody respectable, and he liked the look o the chiel, and Auld Keelie ower the dyke gaed 'im a gey gweed character, so the Dookit raxed anither pound. So the stock cam doon a pound and they had agreed for twenty-two pounds.

The chiel cam hame at the term on his bicycle and Elsie was waitin at the kitchie door tae welcome him intae his denner. She liked the looks o the loon and maybe in a wye she wished she had ane sic like o her ain. At yokin time the grieve had sent 'im back tae his last place wi a horse and cairt for his kist, and the lad had settled doon fine wi the other lads in the chaumer.

But the fourth pairie didna last lang, and gin the simmer was gane they were pensioned aff on strae and watter and grew lang tails like colts. The blacksmith cam and took aff their sheen tae save expense and they gaed barfit like bairns and never felt kaim or brush on their hides again. Wi corn at twal-and-saxpence a quarter it didna pey tae ploo, so the Dookit laid doon mair girse and gaed in for mair sheep. As for the nowt, man the chiel never saw a stirk yet, for the Dookit was that hard-up he couldna affoord tae buy them. Folk said that the fifty-odd steers he had in the byres were paid lodgers, belangin tae dealers and butchers wha paid for their keep, and of coorse the heid cattleman sortit them.

So the lad had a go at the sheep, lambin yows and sic like, pooed a pucklie neeps, howkit in the gairden, cleaned drains and ditches, mended a hen-coop or twa and helpit wi the thrashin. Man, the chiel had that little tae dee that he got intae an affa easy-ozie kind o wye, and he used to sit and sup his brose in the mornin wi his spare haun in his pooch.

Losh aye, he wad never hae noticed it but the kitchie-deem tellt 'im aboot it when she cam in wi her melk pails frae the byre.

'But lassie,' says he, 'I'm nae a bairn; I dinna need baith hauns tae haud ma speen. Gin it had been ham and eggs I was eatin, and usin a knife and fork, that wad be a different story. Of coorse he should hae been feenisht wi his breakfast afore Jeannie cam in frae the byre, but syne he got rade o his pair o horse he didna hae tae rise sae early in the mornin as the ither lads, so he lay or the last meenit afore sax and was aye slubberin awa at his brose when the rest o the lads were oot in the stable kaimin their horse. And sometimes the Dookit himsel cam ben the hoose and tied his pints at the kitchie fire, but the lad never turned a hair, jist gave the quine a bit wink if he caught her e'e when he left.

But this late risin gave the lad the only chance he had o speakin tae the kitchie quine withoot the ither lads, and in nae time at a' they had taen a fancy tae each ither in secret. But the lassie was that hard ca'd in Elsie's service she hardly had time tae tak a bit mait, lat aleen look at a lad. Fut wi yarkin at yon lang-handled churn, melkin kye, feedin hens and swine, makin maet, bakin breid and scones, washin claes and dishes, cleanin firesides, cairryin peat and hackin sticks, makin up beds, scrubbin fleers, cleanin windaes and dustin ben the hoose, a' that wark, the lassie was that tired or nicht she could hardly rest in her bed. Frae five in the mornin till nearly ten at nicht Jeannie was on her feet; frae cock craw tae owl hoot ye micht say, and sometimes ironin a Sunday sark for the Dookit when she should hae been anaeth the blankets. Elsie fairly held 'er at it, shakin basses and ae thing or anither, and never a nicht aff withoot a thraw, and only half-a-Sunday aince a fortnicht efter kirk time, nae time at a' tae look tae a lad.

So the chiel was hert sorry for the quine, for he likit her fine, and maybe in a year or twa he'd set up hoose o his ain and mairry her. It wadna be much o a hoose, jist a bit butt-and-ben she could tak some interest in and hae mair time tae hersel. But gie Elsie her due she saw the wye the wind was blawin and took an interest in the pair o them. She couldna dee't hersel but she got the Dookit tae melk the kye every second Sunday nicht tae gie the lassie a langer day aff, and she tellt the chiel he could sit langer at the kitchie fire at nichts than the ithers, him and the quine, and she saw that the lassie got a nicht aff aince a week. So under Elsie's smilin protection this love affair grew, and in her ain religious wye she felt she was doin the richt thing by the young couple. She mithered the quine and upbraided the chiel until she had them eatin oot o her haun so tae speak, and a stranger body wad hae thocht they waur her ain bairns.

The Dookit himsel was fair astonished at Elsie's interest in the lad he'd fee'ed and the servant quine, and something o her ain youth seemed tae return in the process. She became a different woman athigither and less interferin in the wyes o the place. She began tae tak mair interest in the hoose than she did in the fairm, and she had been mair o a wife tae the Dookit in these last months than she had been in years before. Even the man himsel felt a change in his ootlook though nae withoot a little annoyance that the young couple should claim sae much o his wife's attention, though he was pleased and gratefae that his wife should seem sae happy and pleased wi hersel in a wye he had never seen her afore.

And it didna seem tae maitter tae Elsie noo whaur the Dookit got his daily pound and she fed the men like lords. Folk couldna believe the change in the woman was natural, and they shook their heids sadly for the day when she wad be locked up, clean gane gyte. And a' withoot the Lord's blessin, for ye never see her at the kirk nooadays, and the Dookit sits in a pew himsel like an oolit in a sauch tree. And the wye she sottered ower that young pair at the Dookit was the clipe o the parish, and they were only the bairns o cottar folk, that were thocht tae be below a woman o Elsie's standin. It was an evil thing she did folk said amon themsels: a loon and quine o that age dinna need encouragement; but the Lord will be avenged they said, and he will send a plague upon Elsie at the Dookit, you wait and see . . .

So the Lord sent a great plague upon Elsie as they had said, and a great swarm o rats cam up oot o the mill-dam and over-ran the Dookit fairm. They were runnin thick in the close, muckle scabby deils that were as tame ye could kick them against the wa's, and the verra strae in the barn was a hobble wi rats. The Dookit wadna lay pooshin for fear o killin the hens. He set traps and cages and took a few, and when the cages were full he got the new lad tae dip them in the dam tae droon the squirmin brutes.

But Elsie had a better idea, so she took a duster and polished the Dookit's silver-mounted double-barrelled gun that stood in the hall beside the grandfather-clock and gave it to the chiel. The Dookit had never fired a shot wi't in his life; it had belonged to his father but the Dookit had always been too tender-hertit tae use it. He hated killin in a' its forms and wadna tramp on a worm or a beetle gin he could help it. But he jumped on his motor-bike and went to the emporium for a big box o cartridges for the chiel tae rid the place o rottans, for surely that was no evil the Dookit thocht.

So the chiel took the gun and hid himsel in odd corners roon the steadin and the big hoose and baitit the rodents wi bruised corn. When about a dizzen rats had gaithered roon the bait the lad let fly wi baith barrels and blew them tae smithereens. And the chiel was weel content wi this amusement, 'cause efter the evenin's shootin he was treatit in the hoose wi tay and fancy pieces and he could while awa the time wi his lass. At nicht when the licht was gettin dim the chiel baitit the rats in the close and hid himsel in the hen-hoose. He was winnin this war on the rats and they were gettin scarcer and he sometimes had tae wait langer for a shoot. The rats were gettin wily as weel, and were sly at comin oot in the full licht o day, so that only nightfall and hunger brocht them tae the bait.

It was gettin rael dark for Elsie had the lamps lichtit in the kitchie and ben the hoose. And when she had the tay ready she tellt the quine tae run and get her lad afore bedtime.

Noo the servant lass was a bittie feart at the clockin hens durin the day and she minded that she hadna gathered in a' the eggs. She wad look for her lad, but in the meantime she wad get the eggs. The hens wad a' be reistit and she could throw the clockers oot o their nests and grab the eggs, for they wadna see tae pick her sae much in the gloom.

Noo the chiel was watchin 'es rats and jist aboot ready tae lat bleeze when his quine cam runnin owre the close. They began tae scatter, and jist when he fired baith barrels his lass bent doon tae enter the hen-hoose. Even as he pulled the triggers he saw her lurch owre his sichts; in the reek and smell o poother he saw her fa; even in the squak o flyin hens ower his heid he heard her simper. The lad got sic a scare his hert nearly stoppit and he flang the gun on the fleer. His een were het wi tears and he grabbed the quine in his oxter, her warm bleed on his face. He laid her doon canny, feart tae look gin she was deid, and ran for Elsie.

Elsie had heard the shot but thocht naething o't; she heard them ilka nicht, but when the chiel cam in soakin in bleed she got a sair fricht. 'It's Jeannie,' he grat. 'I doot I've killed 'er!' And he sat doon on a chair and grat like a bairn. 'Faur aboot laddie?' Elsie cried, shakin the chiel by the shooder, 'faur's Jeannie?'

'In the hen-hoose!' And his voice rose frae his throat nearly like a scream.

Elsie cried on the Dookit frae ben the hoose and the pair o them ran tae the hen hoose. But the lassie was deid and poorin wi bleed, her face and breist shot tae tatters, so the Dookit jumped on his motor-bike and flew for the doctor. And when the doctor and the bobby cam they cairriet the lassie intae the fairm hoose and laid 'er on the fleer, and the loon sabbit and grat in Elsie's oxter as gin he had been a bairn.

Efter the funeral there was an inquest and a lot o awkward questions speirt at the loon, though abody kent fine he had nae intentions o shootin his lass. And Elsie was sair torn wi guilt for giein the loon the gun that did it and she was hert sorry for the loon. She grat mony a day and priggit sair wi the loon tae bide when the term cam roon. Tears were a thing that Elsie had never felt afore, unless they had been tears o rage or jealousy, and the Dookit was sair perplexed at what could ail his wife.

The term day cam and the loon gaed doon the close for the last time. Elsie could thole her guilt nae langer and she ran doon the close efter the loon. She wad hae gi'en 'im the place tae bide on but it was hardly in her pooer, but she grabbed the loon in her oxter and grat in his airms, and then the most affa thing happened tae Elsie, for she fainted in the close and the Dookit and the loon had tae cairry 'er back tae the fairm hoose.

So they got the doctor and he told the Dookit that his wife was in the family way, and the man could hardly control himsel. And neither could the neighbours: Michty me! Elsie wi a bairn at thirty-echt, and anither doo in the Dookit; weel weel, that was what she got for encouragin that young pair aboot the place, though God knows, there was little need tae say mair aboot that; she wad hae her ain thochts aboot it nae doot.

The Beggar Laird

A Legendary Fragment from Buchan History

Lachbeg House, that fairyland palace in the depths of the woods. The sun scarcely reached the avenues in summer because the trees were so dense. And the lovely lake, dark and smooth as glass, where the luxuriant rhododendrons, mauve, purple and white, were reflected on the surface. Swans white and graceful glided around the satin-green islands, arching their long necks to dip their heads in the water. The water-lilies were just out of reach, where they floated in islands of yellow wonderment. Irises protruded their crimson tongues in mockery of our inability even to touch them. Willows dipped their green feathery tresses in the water, while laburnum spangled the banks with its gold. There were two rustic arbours on the banks of the lake, where you could sit and watch the water-hens jerking in and out among their nests in the reeds. There was also a boathouse with a flat-bottomed cobble tied up inside. The wood paths were veined with tree roots where the feet of many travellers had exposed them.

Sometimes on a Sunday, with my Cousins Selby and Teddy Joss, we used to sneak away from our grandfather's farm to spy on the laird's palace. Gleg Handerson was my grandfather's name, and he said that if the head gamekeeper saw us on the laird's policies he would shoot us. And besides there were signs marked PRIVATE all over the place. But we wouldn't be deterred. Fascination overcame fear and we dared every risk to satisfy our curiosity.

A huge mastiff sat at the front door. Folk had heard the factor say he would tear a man to pieces. But we knew better, or thought we did, because we went to school with the head gardener's bairns, and they said that if you went close enough he would lick your face. He was only an ornament they said, and that he could hardly be bothered to scratch the flies from his own ears.

Maybe the factor was only trying to scare us off? It was awfully tempting to try and see who was telling the truth. The trouble was we never got near enough to find out. We were too scared. The great house was so forbidding, and the air of wonderment so entrancing we could only lie in the long grass and watch at a distance.

When we reached the clearing in the woods Lachbeg House was a wonderful sight. It almost took our breath away every time we saw it. It made us gasp with excitement. We just lay down eager to watch, thankful that the gamekeeper hadn't seen us after all.

There it stood on its green, carpet-smooth terraces, high and white and wonderful. The sunlight was trapped in the clearing and shone on the walls like a spotlight. Far out at sea sailors could see those bartizan turrets above the trees in Lachbeg Woods, just as they could see the white stone deer on the Mattock Hill, when the weather was clear.

Folk said there were as many doors and windows in Lachbeg House as there were days in the year, and dungeons deep down in the earth where the old lairds kept their enemies prisoner in days long ago.

The modern part of the house stood in front, an Adams' mansion, folk called it, pillared like a Grecian temple, with baskets of flowers hanging in the arcades. There were steps of marble up to the front entrance and a coat-of-arms above the massive door, varnished and studded with iron. A stone balustrade went round the roof, with a glass domed observatory in the middle, for looking at the stars. The chimneys were also on the roof, but squat and inconspicuous, so that you hardly noticed them. The towers and keep at the back were of an older date, much older, and looked like a fairy castle, with a flagpole high above the trees. Folk said that in the old days, when the laird was a young man, you would have seen a Union Jack flying from the pole. That was when the laird was home from abroad, and wearing his kilt of Fraser tartan, and to let his friends know they could come and visit him. But now the Laird had been at home for such a long time the flag was tattered to bits, and nobody had troubled to renew it. And besides, the laird didn't want visitors anymore, he just wanted to sit and brood over his only son who had shot himself, and to listen to Gleg's pipes at twilight.

Twice a year our grandfather went to Lachbeg House to pay his rent. Folk said the laird was hard-up for siller and that the time would come when the tenants would get a chance to buy their farms; buy or move out for a higher bidder if you couldn't afford the price. But they said a sitting tenant would get the first option to buy his own holding privately. After all it was only fair after what some of them had spent on their places; the drains they had dug and the fences they had put up, the bits of heather they had taken in with the spade and the manure they had put on the land. 'Fegs aye, it was but richt,' Gleg had said. 'It's but a hand-tae-mou existence onywye!'

A day was set aside for the rent, and all the tenants got a high-tea and a dram - 'Forbyes a bit keek at the hoosemaids,' as Skirlie Wullie said.

The room where they paid the rent was awfully grand Gleg said: 'Wi great big picters o the laird's ancestors glowerin doon at ye, a table as lang as an endrig, and a carpet on the fleer as lush as a new-grass park. Man, the ceilin's like an iced-cake and I'll swear the chandileer wad weigh a hunderwecht. Lord aye, and a marble fireplace, as big as ye could coup a load o peats in't.' And while he told us this we sat at his feet wide-eyed and wonder-struck. And what about the mastiff? we asked. Weren't they afraid of the dog? Gleg said that he was tethered on rent days. Maybe, he promised, when we were men we would see this great room for ourselves; then we would see he had been telling the truth.

The laird sat at the head of the table in his kilt. Folk said he was almost imbecilic since his good lady died and that he took little heed of the proceedings. Nowadays the factor was boss.

'He has a face a' roon,' said Skirlie, 'like a toon clock, and he fair thrives on't.'

The factor put the money in a small black and gold band-box and the clerk signed the receipts. The tenants got a chance to lodge any complaints they had to make and the clerk wrote it down in a ledger for future reference. Long Tom Stag might be needin drain pipes for thon weet howe o his, or Hardyards might be needin the roof of his barn repaired, or a new cement floor in his kitchen. Maybe the travises in Cairnie's coo byre needed replacement, and there was a demand for paint, slates, bricks, new doors and windows and sic like. That wasn't saying that everybody got what he wanted. Not unless he asked often enough. And sometimes a body got tired o askin and just paid for the damned thing himsel. 'Ach weel,' as Jeely Pom would say: 'The fairm will maybe be yer ain someday onywye. Sae lang as ye dinna bigg a new neep-shed, or a dung-coort,'cause that wad put up the price o yer ain fairm when it cam tae buyin it.' And the rest o the billies cried 'Here here!' and said that Jeely Pom's heid was fairly screwed on the right way and that all his back teeth were up.

A lease was based on a cropping rotation system which was considered fair to proprietor and farmer. It lasted for fourteen years but a tenant had a break in seven. He could move out if he wasn't satisfied. On the other hand, at the end of seven years, if the laird had a grudge against a tenant (if the tenant was neglecting his land for instance - or fell in arrears with his rent) the laird could refuse to renew his lease. But to show how seldom this happened you only had to go to the old graveyard beside the Parish Kirk at Lachbeg, where you could see that most of Lachbeg's tenants had been born on their farms, and that generations for more than a hundred years back had their names carved on the old leaning gravestones. Indeed these gravestones were a sort of guarantee that you couldn't be far wrong to rent a farm on the Lachbeg estate.

Folk said it would be a sorry day for the tenants when the old laird should die. The estate would go to his daughters, they said, and they were high and mighty, and would put up the rents and wouldn't repair the steadings.

We hadn't seen any of the laird's three daughters, but folk who had said their faces were painted and powdered like they weren't real, and delicate as a butterfly's wings, that wouldn't stand a shower o rain or a nip of frost, and that their hair was dyed and their fingernails varnished, and that it would take a year's rent from the tenantry to pay for the gaudy dresses they wore. That was gentry for you, and folk said they couldn't stand our winters anyway; that they went away to sunny lands at the first hint of snow and didn't come back until the swallows returned. So what could you make of that when your wife hadn't been out of the close for a six-month and you yourself had never been further than the marts in the toon.

Meantime we could see the great dog lying on his paws at the top of the marble steps, like a lion on guard over his master. We daren't make a sound lest he prick his ears. He knew we were there. He could smell us. We knew by the way he turned his big snout and sniffed the air in our direction, but it seemed he just couldn't be bothered to come and look for us. Maybe it was true what the bairns said about this dog: that he was just an ornament; but none of us would dare to stand up and challenge him, we just lay there watching, listening, whispering . . .

Sometimes through the ferns we could see a coach at the front entrance; a grand coach with four white horses, and it was all so Cinderella-like we really thought we were in fairyland. The fact is that the laird wouldn't hear of a motor car and still kept a coach and driver for his daughters and business transactions.

But there was something else about this wonderful place that reminded us of Cinderella. We all knew the story of the Beggar Laird, who had been one of the present laird's ancestors. One night long ago, as this laird lay in his richly curtained bed in Lachbeg House, he had a strange dream of a lovely girl he knew who lived in Rockbulge Castle, about twelve miles ride away, on the seashore. This young lady was an orphan who lived with her aunt and uncle who were her guardians and trustees of the castle and estates until she came of age to look after them herself. And the laird dreamed that her aunt and uncle were trying to poison the heiress with a goblet of wine, so that they could inherit the lands of Rockbulge.

He saw the maiden in her bed, a finely carved four-poster, while her aunt leaned over her with the glass of poisoned wine. She held the goblet in her lace-frilled hand, and each time she proferred it the maiden pushed it away, while her uncle stood by in his shirt-sleeves, anxious and scowling. They were about to man-handle the girl and force her to swallow the wine when the laird woke up.

He tried to sleep again but found he couldn't. Each time he closed his eyes the same graphic picture came before him. The realism of his dream stung him into action, so he arose and attired himself as a tramp, saddled his horse and rode full tilt to Rockbulge Castle.

It was a clear night, with the moon dipping from one fleecy cloud to the next, and the wind whistled in his ears When he reached Rockbulge, high on the cliff-tops, the moon glittered on the sea and the waves boomed against the rocks. There was only one approach to the castle, across a narrow ledge of rock, and if this was guarded he would have to swim the ravine. Meanwhile he hid in the woods and tethered his horse to a tree. He smeared his face with earth, cut himself a staff and hobbled towards the ridge. But there was no one there, so he scrambled across and made for the castle. He rapped on the heavily studded door to summon the guard. When the door creaked open on its rusty hinges the guard looked at him with a spluttering torch held high above his head. Our laird said he was a soothsayer and wanted but a night's shelter in the castle for his aching bones. If they would only give him the warmth of the kitchen faggots it would ease his aches and pains he said, since he had journeyed far, and in return he would read the good lady's fortune on the morrow.

'I come in peace,' he said, 'I carry no sword, nor have I any knife in my doublet. I can do no harm to your household. But I have travelled far; I am weary and footsore, if you will but give me peace to lie down I shall be thankful.'

Now folks were superstitious in those days and loth to turn away a palmister. Perhaps if you turned them away they might leave a curse on your doorstep, and the household might fall on evil times. He looked harmless enough to the guard as he held the torch higher to look at the tramp; a mumbling old fool with tattered clothes, a crooked back and leaning on a stick. He had a good mind to kick him over the precipice. But the tramp had thought of this as well, and with a keen eye he watched the guard from under his hood - just waiting for him to try it.

So the guard admitted the soothsayer, and very soon he pretended to be fast asleep on a rug by the kitchen fire. Several of the guards came and had a look at him, but satisfied that he was harmless they soon retired to the keep. But the laird was soon on his feet, alert as a deer, and by the light of the fire he crept towards the castle door, where he slipped the bar from its sockets to assist his escape.

His shoes were wrapped in sackcloth and he made no noise. He crept up the great staircase to the bed-chambers, high up in the castle, and along the dark corridors, quiet as a cat, until he saw a light under a door; the maiden's door he was sure, for he had been in the castle before and knew it well.

The young laird listened at the door, his heart beating in his ears, but he could hear nothing. But the urgency of his dream was still upon him and he felt he must act quickly. He lifted the hasp gently, noiselessly, and the door opened, and as it widened his dream came alive in the candlelight.

There on the high-posted bed was the maiden, distressed and in tears, and almost convinced by her aunt that she was sick. Over her stood her aunt with the goblet of wine, and by her side was her man in his shirt-sleeves. The girl's hands were reaching out in a tremble for the goblet when the laird shattered the scene. He had caught them in the very act of murder.

But the laird was lightning quick. He dashed the cup from the woman's hand and gave the man a crack on the jaw that bewildered him. The woman attempted to scream but the laird held his hand over her mouth. She bit savagely at his fingers, but with his free hand he ripped a tassled cord from the bed and wrapped it round her body, lacing her hands to her sides. He was about to stick the tassle in her mouth when she fainted in his arms, so he threw her on the bed. Her man revived and rose unsteadily but the laird chopped him down again. An open-hander on the side of the neck crumpled him into a heap.

The maiden was even more surprised but the laird gave her no time to ask questions. 'Wrap yourself in a blanket,' he said, 'and come with me.'

He seized her hand and dragged her from the bed, picked her up and carried her down the stairs, out into the cold night towards the ridge. How she got across there in her nightdress she could never recall. It was like a nightmare, with the laird holding her hand and guiding her bare feet on the hard stone, while on either side the chasm yawned and the water splashed and gurgled in the darkness. Once across this obstacle they made for the woods, where the laird untied his horse and set her on the saddle. He gathered the reins and sprang up behind her. Next moment they were off, her hair in his face, streaking through the fading moonlight. The laird dug his heels into his horse's ribs and rode hard for Lachbeg.

Once in the shelter of Lachbeg Woods he felt they were safe from pursuit. He stopped his horse and slid the lady to the ground. 'Wait here,' he said, 'by this tree, and I'll be back for ye.' For he didn't want her to think that the laird of Lachbeg had hired a tramp to rescue her. He would carry her home in the style that she deserved, worthy of her breeding. So he galloped off into the wood, while the maid waited in her blanket, her teeth chattering in the cold. It was lithe here in the sighing woods but she shivered a little in the darkness.

She wondered why the tramp had left her here so helpless, unless it were to fetch his master, and he was such a long time about it he must have forgotten her. But lo, he was back at last, the young laird in all his finery, and he threw a warm cloak about her shoulders. Morning light was breaking through the woods and when the maiden saw this braw knight before her she would have nothing to do with him. The laird thought she must be joking. But no, she was dead serious. No wonder he had deceived the guard in his errand of mercy.

'Your aunt was trying to poison you,' he said, 'You must never go back to Rockbulge.'

'I believe you, fair cousin,' said the heiress, 'but where is the beggar man who rescued me?'

'Fair damsel,' said the laird, 'believe me, I am the beggar man. I had a dream that you were in danger and I was just in time to spare your life.'

'Your dream may be true, fair sir. Indeed I do not doubt it, since your worthy servant arrived so opportunely. But why didn't you rescue me yourself? Show me the poor beggar man who risked his life to save me. I will share my life with him, rather than be your lady.'

'But you are being childish,' the laird protested, 'believe me, fair lady, I am the beggar man.'

But the maid was adamant. 'Show me the beggar man,' she insisted; 'let him speak for himself. I will not go on your horse until this is so.'

So the laird left her again by the Eildon tree and rode back to Lachbeg House. He took off all his finery and dressed himself in rags, even to smearing his face with earth as he had done before .

He laughed to himself as he rode back to the maiden, and she smiled also when she saw him. When he dismounted she threw her arms about his neck and kissed him. 'I believe you, my lord,' she said, 'you are indeed my beggar man.' So he picked her up and set her on his horse and led her home to be his lady.

They lived happily for many years. Until about the middle of last century the Beggar Tree still stood in Lachbeg Woods. The tree where the lady waited for the laird to return a beggar. During the whole of her life this lady gave orders that food was to be left in a cleft of this tree for passing beggars. And all the days of her life the soothsayers blessed her, and muttered her name in all their prayers, and she had a life of great happiness and raised a family that were the pride of Scotland.

Her husband was beloved by all. Eventually Rockbulge came to his estate but his lady sold it again. She said she had no memories of that old castle; that her life didn't begin until she came to Lachbeg. with the money the two of them made vast improvements on the estate; planting trees, building dykes, draining, housing the poor, and although they didn't leave this lovely mansion house as we were looking at it now, at least they gave us the castle behind it. Since the days of the Beggar Laird and his fair lady no man had ever had to lift his bonnet to Lachbeg, not even a tink with his besoms, for they had left a latin inscription on the family insignia which read: 'All men are equal,' and for many generations the sons of Lachbeg had honoured it.

But now the spell was broken. The shot that dealt the laird's son his self-inflicted wound had shattered it. The old laird was now a dottard and his inheritance was uncertain.

And now the mastiff gave a bark and shook me out of my daydreams. It sent us scurrying back to the wood like frightened rabbits. But now he was on the lawn, bounding towards us with an arched back, the turf flying from his paws. In a moment he was upon us, all three in a heap, rolling over and over, licking our faces in a great frolic. Before long we were sticking our small fists into his great mouth, while he stood gasping with his tongue out and laughing at us with his eyes.

But we were only boys. It was easy to play with us now. But is there not some great Greek philosopher who once said that what a man loves most he must finally destroy. And it made my heart sad to think that some day we might come back as men, with picks and drills and sticks of dynamite, to savage and destroy the glory of this great house.

In reaching for the stars man is destroying his earthly heritage. He must tax the one to finance the other, and thus these iconoclastic tendencies have become fashionable in our time.

Lachbeg House, my palace. Oh my fairyland. How my heart bleeds for thee.

My Uncle Simon

It was sunny in the evening at Kelpieside. After supper old Gleg Handerson went outside to give his pipes a skirl at the kitchen gable.

There was something of the old Norsemen in my grandfather. You could see it in his blonde-grey hair, in the frown of his sand-coloured eyebrows; sometimes in his fierce, startled expression, when his steel blue eyes held you in a hypnotic stare.

There was something of the old Highlander in him too, for a dirk suited his leg well when he wore the kilt, and a sword would have been as a wand in his powerful grasp. He was passionate and morose, sullen and cheerful by turns, moods that long centuries of trampling the heather and tearing at the sod had bred in his ancestry.

You could hear the skirl of Gleg's pipes up on the Mattock Hill, where the Gaels in olden times had dug peat from its slopes. Folks long back had gathered huge white stones and set them in the shape of an antlered deer on the hillside. On a quiet evening you could hear the wail of Gleg's pibroch in the depths of Lachbeg woods, filled with all the sorrow of Flodden, of Culloden and Lucknow, and the laird would listen from his mansion, the crofter from his ingle, and all those who were heavy at heart found solace in the stricken music. Fingers that were clumsy and gnarled with work now took on a grace upon the chanter as they waltzed in ballerina charm upon the reeds that turned a man's breath to soul-filled ecstasy.

But it wasn't every evening that Gleg played the pipes at the gable window. Even though it was sunny he would just sit on the old stone-roller and stare at the ground. Then his brows would curl over his eyes and you could see the devil at work in his brain. He was as dour as the clouds that gathered on the Mattock Hill, and at any moment a glance from his eye would frizzle your soul like lightning.

Gleg was in one of his black moods and sat on his roller on the evening that my uncle Simon wanted to show me the oatcrusher at work. I think he wanted to show off a little of what he could do on one leg.

Uncle Simon had one of his legs sawn off in his closet when he was nine. His brothers and sisters heard the rasp of the doctor's saw on the bones. Sarah my grandmother ran back and forth between the peat fire and the closet with kettles of boiling water. And when it was all over the children saw the two doctors take Simon's leg away in a brown paper parcel, dripping blood to the doorstep. They said they even heard Simon screaming in the chloroform. Now Simon was a man and he felt his infirmity keenly.

The threshing mill and the oat-crusher were driven by water-power, by a long overhead cable that stretched from the water-wheel to a pulley outside the barn wall. The dam was a considerable distance from the barn and we had to walk past the farmhouse to reach it and open the sluice.

The oat-crusher made a fearful din and made the bells ring in my ears. Indeed I suspected Simon of trying to frighten me, so I stood in the barn to prove he was wrong, and I was just about the age when Simon got his leg off.

After the oat-crushing, when we were on our way back from closing the dam sluice, old Gleg was on his roller putting straw in his boots. We were almost abreast of him when his mood snapped. He stood up from the roller with one of the heavy tackety boots in his hand.

'Simon,' says he, 'wha said we was needin corn bruised?'

'Oh naebody,' Simon whined, 'I jist thocht when there was plenty watter in the dam we should tak the good o't.'

'Ye wad run the place yersel eh! Ye think ye're maister here nooadays and I'm naebody, eh? Efter this ye'll wait till ye're tellt tae dae a job, d'ye hear?'

Simon sensed a threat and said nothing, but moved off in the direction of the barn, his wooden leg creaking at every step. Gleg stood for a moment, watching him, the boot in his hand, held by the tab at the back. Simon ignored him and Gleg took it as a challenge to his authority. He raised the iron-studded boot high over his head and sent it hurtling into the air in Simon's direction.

His aim was sure and direct, and the iron heel of the boot struck the retreating Simon smack on the back of the head. He reeled and staggered against the cart-shed pillar and raised his hands to his ears as if he had been stunned.

The hens in the close got such a fright they were flying in all directions. The pigeons flapped up from the ground and alighted on the coping of the red-tiled barn. Sarah, my grandmother came out from the cow byre with a pail of milk in each hand. When she saw her son staggering in the close she dropped her pails and ran to support him. 'Oh Simon,' she cried, 'what has come over ye?' She spilled the milk in the close and the turkey-cock gobbled in alarm as he ran out of her way.

My aunts Nora and Kirsty came out of the kitchen, my cousin Selby behind them, and they all ran towards Simon, who still stood with his hands over his head by the cart-shed wall. He took away his hands and there was blood on his fingers. They all stared at him and all of them questioned him at the same time: 'What has hurt ye Simon?'

Simon pointed a bloody finger at his father. 'He threw a boot at me 'cause I opened the dam sluice withoot his orders!'

Gleg went hopping forward on one foot to get his boot back. When he picked it up he said: 'Aye, and that'll learn ye that I'm still maister here; and if that doesna suit ye ye'd better clear oot and try yer luck somewhaur else on yer fung leg!'

'Think shame o yersel,' cried Sarah, shaking her fists at her husband; 'shame on ye tae strike the crippled loon, efter a' he has gone through already.' She went as near to Gleg as she dared and stamped her foot, like a ewe when a shepherd would take away her lamb, almost spat at him, like a cat.

'Ye've spoiled the devil.' cried Gleg, pulling on his boot, 'and he thinks he'll do what he likes about the place - but nae as lang as I'm maister here! Tak 'im tae the hoose and gie 'im a sook!' And with that he turned away and went back to his roller.

A band of sympathisers circled Simon. They all moved over to the back kitchen door and squeezed inside amid a hubbub of voices.

The collie dog came out of his kennel, to the full length of his chain and began to yap at Gleg where he sat on his roller. Gleg let fly at him with a stone and he disappeared into the barrel with a yelp. When the pigeons thought it safe to descend they flopped down from the byre roof and strutted about the close among the hens, picking up what corn had been left in their absence.

Simon was not badly hurt, only a slight bruise and a smear of blood on the hair at the back of his head. But Sarah and his sisters made such a fuss over it that Simon made up his mind to take full advantage of their sympathies; to rally them all in his favour and have them all eating out of his hand and spitting on old Gleg till he came crawling back for forgiveness.

So Simon pretended to be worse than he was and said he would leave Kelpieside before dark. 'Daw has ordered me frae the place,' he whimpered, 'and I'll go, this verra nicht!'

'But yer Daw didna really mean it Simon,' Sarah remonstrated, 'he was jist angered at the time and didna realise what he was sayin.'

'He meant it a' richt,' Simon asserted, 'and I wunna need anither tellin!'

Sarah began to weep and Nora tried to console her. Kirsty hung the kettle on the crook over the peat fire and set the teacups on the bare scrubbed table. It was getting dark inside so she lit the paraffin lamp that hung from the ceiling.

My uncle Jonas, who was Simon's younger brother, came into the kitchen and asked what was the trouble. He said he had spoken to Daw on his roller but had got no answer. Jonas had a croft of his own across the road and he only came in by to pass the time of day.

The tea was strong at Kelpieside, boiled in the brewing of it in a black enamelled tea-pot that never left the fireside.

'Heather Bree,' folks called it, that came in by, and you got no milk in it, unless you went to the milkhouse yourself for a stoup of cream.

When tea was over Jonas and Simon lit their cigarettes from a cinder which Selby brought to them on the tongs from the peat ash. Then Simon went into his closet to bundle up his clothes for departure. There were more protests from the women but Simon was determined to bring their sympathy to full maturity, and turn them against old Gleg to his utmost.

Now he was ready to go and they all sallied out after him to the darkness.

Sarah looped her hand through Simon's arm and tried to pull him back. But he shook her off vigorously and limped boldly up the avenue. She implored him to stay, even to tears, and promised that all would be well with Daw. She would see to it she said. But Simon took no notice. Someone cried on Gleg, but he was gone from his roller, most likely in a sulk, and nowhere to be found.

Nora and Kirsty said goodbye to Simon at the head of the avenue. They were both in tears but nothing they could say would induce Simon to stay. But Sarah and Jonas wouldn't give up and I followed on behind them with cousin Selby. I felt partly guilty about the whole affair because Simon had wanted to show me the oat-crusher at work. Perhaps if I hadn't been here it might never have happened.

We were nearly a mile from home and Selby whispered to me that Simon must surely be in earnest; that he surely meant to go for good. But Sarah still clung to Simon and Jonas still reasoned with him.

But Simon wouldn't be dissuaded. He was a man now he said and wouldn't be talked to as if he was still a loon. And had not his father told him to clear out. Even though he was a cripple he wasn't going to submit to this sort of treatment.

Another quarter-of-a-mile and Simon stopped. He could go on no further and burst into tears. How he had managed thus far he didn't know. In his rush to get away he had forgotten his best friend. He didn't even know where he was going; or where he could spend the night. Anger and excitement had borne him along until now. But he could prevail no longer; not without his best friend on such a journey. Why hadn't he thought of it? His crutch!

Simon turned to Selby and asked him to run back for his crutch. Sarah wouldn't hear of it, for now she saw a chance to detain her crippled son. But even as they argued the wail of Gleg's pipes brought them to silence. It was faint but audible, every note as clear and distinct as a falling tear-drop - 'Will Ye No Come Back Again?' was brought down on them with the soft evening breeze from Kelpieside; perhaps from the stackyard where Gleg would be piping round the rucks, his heart softened and the tears running down his face.

But Simon was ridiculed and heart-broken and sobbed out his grief in his mother's arms. So we half pushed half carried Simon back to the farm and shoved him into his closet.

Jonas unfastened the leather straps on Simon's shoulder and took off his wooden leg and set it in a corner. The stump was red and inflamed with the ordeal and Jonas tucked Simon in bed.

And Sarah took Simon's crutch and hid it for three days until he promised he would never leave home again.

Aikey Brae

A Great Many Romances have Blossomed Forth on Aikey Brae and No Doubt They Still Do.

In the old days down in the Howe o Buchan hoeing and haymaking were always associated with Aikey Fair. If you were finished with the hyowe and well forrit with the hay you had a good chance of a day off for Aikey. The seasons were late in those days, because the working methods were more primitive, but if you had the hay in the 'trump (trampled) cole' that was good enough, for there it could remain until the start o hairst, maturing in the sun, when you could build it into rucks on dewy mornings, or when the weather was too damp for harvesting.

But of course the peats were another snag, and it was an awful punishment having to rickle peats on Aikey Day, when most other folks were away at the fair, so you did your damntest to have the peats all set up on their ends to dry before Aikey. Aikey Fair was considered a general holiday, and apart from term and market day, and a day off at the New Year, it was about the only holiday you would get.

Wednesday was the recognised day of the Fair, the first Wednesday after the nineteenth of July, but if your boss wasn't a kirk elder you could jump on your bike and take a run up on the Sunday before then, when the fun really started, and if you didn't care a damn you went in any case, but sometimes it was frowned upon in those days.

Aikey used to be a horse-fair, when all the lads would be there with their horses for the market, their manes rolled and their tails tied up with coloured segs (raffia) standing in rows like patient cavalry, waiting a buyer. They must have missed a lot of the fun these lads, standing all day with a horse on a lead; sometimes without a bite of dinner, unless the dealer gave them a tip, and the cottar lads spent most of it on a sweetie for the bairns.

But that there was fun at Aikey in those days there is no doubt; even though you didn't have much to spend, your money went a long way compared with nowadays. For one thing a bicycle was cheaper to park than a car, and if you wanted to save a sixpence on that you could throw your bike into a hedge at Old Deer and walk up the hill for nothing. There used to be acres of bicycles parked at Aikey, and 'Old Briggie,' the farmer of Bridge-end said it was the best paying field he had, though he never planted anything in it but bicycles, and that but once a year, while it lay in grass perennially.

But if you had a new bike it was safe with Briggie, because he stood there and watched them all day. You gave him your tanner and he licked a label and stuck it on your saddle and put your bike in a stall, and he gave you the other half of the ticket so that you'd know your new Raleigh or your Hercules from the hundreds of others that stood in long rows beside it. And if you didn't take the trouble to scrape Briggie's label off your saddle folks would know for weeks to come that you had been to Aikey Fair.

And gin the kitchie-deem was with you you paid for her bike as well, especially if she gave you one of those bewitching smiles that have a sweetness in youth that last you till your old age. Some lads had got the length of a motor-bike and were taking their quines on the back pillion, so maybe you were lucky that this quine had come along with you, because most of them were looking for lads with motor-bikes, to take them away to dances and such like, stride-legs over the pillion in their short skirts. But you didn't care much for hooching and dancing, and maybe the quine just liked your company, so you took her by the hand up the brae and set her down among the heather bells, and you thought she was the finest picture in all the fair.

There was a kind of sparkle in her soft eyes that was maybe worth more than diamonds, especially if you didn't care much for money, and a velvet gloss on her hair as it tumbled about in the sun glint, with maybe a bit coloured ribbon in it, tryin to beguile a daft gowk like yourself that had been looking all the week at a mare's tail tied up with segs.

She had a straw hat with a red band and a checked tweed coat, but as it was a stifling day these lay beside her on the heather; and there she sat with bare arms in a print frock, net stockings and brown brogue shoes, her smiling lips reminding you of comb-dripped honey and a scent about her like carnations, shy and blushing as a sunrise.

You must have looked an awful gowk yourself sitting there in your best blue suit and an open-collar white sark you had borrowed from the third horseman; hand-sewn brown shoes that were far too dear but suited your vanity, even a watch-chain across your waistcoat and your hair oiled and parted in the middle; your Bogie-roll left at home in your kist and smoking a long-stemmed Sunday pipe filled with scented tobacco.

Ah well, when you'd had your fill of looking at the quine and listening to the music of her laugh, and maybe stealing a kiss on the sly, you'd take her hand again and you'd dander down to the fair to see the sights and maybe listen to the pipe bands. She was quiet-like your quine and didn't have much to say, and you liked her all the better for this, so she took her coat on her arm and her hat in her hand and down the brae you'd go, the soft wind playing with her hair and her voice a timid whisper.

But you couldn't hear each other speaking for the din of the carnival, the hurdy-gurdy organ on the chair-o-planes grinding out 'That Ole Black Mammy o Mine', and the chairs loaded with screaming quines swinging out over your heads. But you soon discovered that your quine wouldn't go on any of the whirligigs; she wasn't going to have her legs swinging out in the air above the gaping crowd, she was far too shy for that, so you took her to see the Death Riders on their Wall of Death, clinging to their motor-bikes like flies in a jar, screaming up nearly to the rim of the giant barrel when they were at full speed, their tyres nearly touching your toes where you stared down at them from the railing. Three motor-bikes were on the wall at one time, with a game bit quine on the pillion of one of them, flying round and round like a bool in a brose caup, the roar of their engines like to deafen you and the speed of their machines shaking the wooden structure under your feet, while all the time you were feart that they flew over the top of the wall. But eventually, when they felt you'd had your money's worth they snorted down their bikes and descended to the grass circle, when everybody threw down pennies to the riders, because it was said that no insurance company would take them on at such a risk. This was above your admission money, and maybe it was just a gimmick, but you felt it was worth it and you threw your maik with the others, maybe a tanner if you felt big-hearted.

So you came down the steps from the tower of death and went and had a bit keek at one of Cleopatra's hand-maidens who had been in a trance for two thousand years, though you would have liked to pinch her in the right places to make sure. But you wondered how they had managed to feed the creature all these years, and a lot of other things that entered your head as you looked at her shapely features under her silken veil. She was the colour of faded lilies, attired in beads and lace; smooth as wax, cold as death to your finger touch, not a tremble on her dark eyelids, and her breathing wouldn't have stirred a feather. She was the picture of a living corpse, if such a thing could be, for she certainly wasn't a mummy.

In another tent a pirate-looking lad was throwing knives at a quine nearly naked, standing against a wooden board, just missing her fair skin by the breadth of your finger-nail, shaping out her body in a quiver of blades. But you couldn't spend all your penny-fee on the side-shows: on the penny arcades, the spinning wheel, the fortune-tellers, the fat woman or the midget, on the ghost train or the coconut shies, the shooting galleries or the slot-machines, darts or hoopla, the Chep-Johns or the boxing booths, the cakewalk or the helter-skelter, so after a squint at yourselves in the contorting mirrors you'd buy an ice-cream cone for yourself and one for the quine.

And you'd walk about hand-in-hand listening to the buskers, Curly Mackay with his melodion or Jimmie Macbeath singing Cornkisters, and maybe dropping a penny in their bonnets lying on the grass.

Away from the skirl and drum-beat of the pipe-bands you could hear the evangelists preaching repentance to the sinners, reminding the ill-gotten creatures that the Kingdom of God was at hand; that the end of the world was nigh, with all the fire and brimstone that would have frightened the monks of Deir from their abbey, till they had your poor quine nearly scared to death, listening to all that stite, for you knew fine it wasn't the way religion should be taught, so you took her away.

When you'd finished licking your cone you took a swing with the mallet to see if you could ring the bell at the top of the pole, but for all the fencing posts and sheep-stakes you had driven into the yird you couldn't manage it, and maybe it served you right for trying to show off in front of the quine, smiling at you there with her sweet mouth and her eyes dancing with mirth. But you was a fair hand at ruggin the swingletree so you would have a pull at the handle on the brass box, where a clock registered your stupid might; but you didn't make much of that either, and you wasn't going to rive at the thing or you ruptured yourself.

You had just got your breath back when who should appear but the old shepherd from Scrapehard, where your father was cottared, the first time you had ever seen the man without a crook in his hand, or his collie dogs at heel, Rip and Fanny, and he was fair taken with your quine and said he would tell your mither he had seen you with a lass at Aikey Fair. Of course your mither didn't know you had a lass and it was a bit embarrassing, and you was a bit bashful with the quine and didn't want to be seen by more folk of your acquaintance than you could help, so you tried to get her away from the shepherd, taking her hand again among the steer of folk, when you ran into your aunt Phyllis, who looked at the kitchie-deem with approving eyes and said she would have to let your folks know about this, because nobody had ever seen you with a quine before. And if you wanted to meet folk you hadn't seen for half-a-century you went to Aikey Fair, and if they were still alive you was sure to meet them on the brae.

So you took your blushing quine further up the brae, out of the steer, away from the noise and the sweat, up among the heather and the smell of fresh peat, where there was peace and quiet, and you could look at the beauty of your quine against the pine trees and the pale summer sky. But you weren't yourselves, for there were a lot of other couples on the brae, kissing and cuddling and having a carry-on, but you didn't want to upset your lass by starting anything like that; well not until you knew her better, for she was really one of the nicest quines you had ever met, and you wasn't going to spoil her feelings by making a fool of yourself, for Aikey was famed for its brazen courting on the hillside, and the quines who lost their knickers among the whins.

So after you'd had a rest a while you takes this bit slip of a quine up to see the Druids' Circle on the summit of Aikey Brae, where it overlooks Stuartfield and Old Deer, the wooded policies of Aden and the observatory tower at Pitfour, with the Hill of Mormond and its white horse in the background, round to Saplinbrae and the rising fields of Bruxie. And you explain to the quine what you knew about the Druids and their weird circles of standing stones that are thousands of years old, and you tell her that under certain circumstances, peculiar to the Druids (though you didn't like to ask if she was a virgin) she might have been slaughtered on the alter stone as a sacrifice to the Sun God, while the Druid priests stood around chanting in their white robes and smearing her innocent blood on the stones. But you said that her hair being black might have saved her, because the Druid priests preferred virgins with corn-coloured hair like sunripe harvest fields.

66

The blood-thirsty creatures must have had a gey chauve to get these monoliths dragged up the hill at Aikey and hoisted on their ends in geometrical formation, and sunk into the ground, for the mathematician lads would have us believe that the placing of the stones had something to do with astronomy, or the measuring of time, like a sun-dial, because the Druids set their stones to catch the noon-day shadows in the same position in most of their circles, and especially the mid-summer and mid-winter suns, what is known as the solstices, and if that be so the Druid circles were the first clocks in existence, long before the sand-glass.

So you are fair engrossed with the Druid creatures and their blood rituals and human orgies and the quine thinks you must be daft or something to be so taken up with a circle of lintel stones that could have been set up on their ends for the nowt beasts to scratch their hides on, for that was maybe what her father had told her. Maybe some day she would learn to share your thoughts, but in the meantime she chides you for tearing her fine net stockings on the whins and briars that grew on the hillside, and striding over the barbed wire around the stone circle.

So you tells the quine about the Monks of Deer and the ancient Book of Deir they had written in Gaelic about religion, written out-bye in yon rickle of stones that used to be the grand Abbey of Deer (though some folks call it Deir) before the Laird of Pitfour carted most of it away to build his farm steadings. She said you should have been a minister or something, and not just a farming chiel when you was so interested in kirks, and you laughed at this and said that you wasn't a bit religious, it was just that you liked to know the history of the place. But you couldn't help telling her that she was standing on one of the most sacred spots in all Scotland, what you might call the cradle of our religion, where the Pagan and the Saint have left their mark.

And you told the quine about the Holy Fair that the Monks of Deir had started for the relief of the poor folks and the upkeep of their abbey; and the Holy Day which had become a hol(i)day and was the real beginning of the fair on Aikey Brae. The monks had started it to commemorate that Saint Drostan chiel, on the third Wednesday of July, the day they removed some of the creature's bones from a cist at Aberdour, and took them to Deir, for the monks liked to build their monastries on the remains of some saint or martyr. And if she didn't believe you she could still see Saint Drostan's Well on the beach at Aberdour, where he had landed from Iona with Columba and Saint Fergus and Saint Colm and Saint Machar, with some others besides, and that was why we had places like St. Combs and St. Fergus and Newmachar, and the Saints converted Brude the Pict, who gave them land for their kirks that replaced the stone circles. But the folk of Buchan were gey dour and ill-schooled and they forgot all about Saint Drostan and named the fair after the tink who fell into the Ugie with his pack or got soaked in the rain and spread his trinkets to dry on the brae. Aikey they called him, so it became Aikey Brae.

And the folks on their way to Old Deer and Maud bought all the trock that Aikey had spread out to dry in the blink of sun between the thunder pelts. So old Aikey came back the next year on the same day with a huge pack on his back, almost all that he could stagger with, and he spread it out on the purple heather and the passers-bye bought every knick-knack that he had. Then the old fool went away and got drunk and blethered to all the other hawkers about the folks at Old Deer that were daft about strings of beads and silk scarfs and brooches and such like, so the next year a great birn of tinks came to Aikey's Brae, and some of them sold their shelts and ponies to the farmin chiels and that was the start of the horse market. There was even nowt on the brae at one time and hundreds of cattle beasts were sold to the butchers from the south and England. Syne the gypsies came with their caravans and their fortune-tellers and their travelling clowns and before long you had a real jamboree on the hillside.

You wasn't sure how it got started on the Sunday, but maybe it was because the tinkers came at the week-end to get their stalls up for the Wednesday, and when there were so many ill-mannered creatures standing about watching they might as well sell them something, so they got yoked on the Sunday, and after all the monks had started it off as a Holy Fair.

Now that there were motor cars and buses folk came from far and wide to Aikey; moreso than the old days of horse traffic. The railway company had even started running trains on a Sunday for the Fair, and maybe that was why the folk referred to the old G.N.S.R. as 'God Never Spares Rascals.' But it was the L.N.E.R. nowadays and they had built a halt anent the Abbey of Deer to let the heathens walk up to the steer that was on the hill. They said it was to accommodate the clergy that wanted to visit the old abbey once in a while, and you wouldn't deny that there were some creatures in long black frock-coats that came off the train on a Sunday, and you supposed that they were monks though they minded you on hoodie-craws that went trooping over the field to the ruin of an abbey, with little more than the dykes of it left, where a bit brig had been erected to let them over the River Ugie, in one of the bonniest howes in Buchan. And you thought the monks would be there for a benediction, until they whips out their fishing-rods from under their frocks and hardly leaves a trout or a salmon in the Ugie for a common body. And they pokes and bores around this cairn of an abbey till you thinks they have taken up residence in the place, reading great screeds of poetry and chanting out loud until you are fair deaved and feart to go near the place after dark. They nearly put you off poaching these unearthly creatures and you could say that there was hardly any need for a water baillie while they were moaning around in the woods.

Och aye but the quine said she knew about the savage Pict creatures being converted by that Saint Drostan chiel that had landed at Aberdour, because she had been there once for a school picnic, and the teacher had shown them the well where Saint Drostan drank, and the ruined kirk above the bents that had been built in his name, besides the chapel in Auld Deer. Abody kent aboot that. There had been a picture about it in her school book; about Saint Columba preaching to the Picts. Did you think she was a dunce or something?

So you changed the subject and brought her up to date a bit, telling her about

Jimmie Sutherland scrubbing the herring scales off his motor lorries and fitting them out with forms for seats and a tarpaulin cover for a hood, tearing out and into Peterheid with passengers for the Fair, though mostly on the Wednesday for fear of offending the fisher folk, who were still as religious as the monks had been; moreso than the country folk, maybe because they were never out of danger on the sea. Aikey Fair was held just at the end of the herring fishing, so there was bound to be herring scales on the lorries, and the smell of herring, which was a fine mixture with the smell of petrol, and next day you'd see the same lorries back at the pier with their herring barrels. You told the quine you'd had a hurl yourself in one of these charabangs going to Aikey, when you was a loon at the school, during the holidays, but you had to sell a firlet of oatmeal to a grocer in Peterheid to pay your fare, a terrible day of thunder and lightning and you was soaked to the skin, and the quine asked if you'd got a lass that day and made you blush in your turn. Then she said her father had told her that Jimmie Sutherland bought his first Clydesdale horse at Aikey Fair, and that the next year he went to Aikey with one horse and came back with seven.

And yon Sandy Burnett from Mintlaw, him that left the ploo at Lunderton fairm, near St. Fergus, and spent all his money on an old bus to drive folks to Aikey; and look at him now with three or four spleet new buses on the road, and likely to get more of them as every Aikey goes by.

Ach but you had blethered long enough about Aikey Fair, so the quine put on her hat and her coat, which made her look like a princess, and you took her warm, friendly hand and the pair of you went linking down the brae to the fair again. Hunger had taken the quine, and as you was a bit jaded yourself the pair of you went into a tent for your tea. There was a lot of noise in the beer tent, but you passed it by, and bought a quarter of Fred's Candy from the Broch at a sweetie stall.

A lot of people were leaving the fairground, so you went and got your bicycles out of Briggie's park, but the road was fair jammed with folk and you had to walk nearly all the way to Old Deer, where the drunks were singing and stytering about in front of the Aden Arms Hotel, and a lad was nearly feart to go bye lest they pulled your quine off her bicycle.

Next day in the hay park you'd get all the banter from the other lads for taking the deem away to Aikey, and they'd tease the quine about it at dinner time; but you didn't care a damn for them, and neither did she, but cheeked them up and said it was none of their business, for something had sprung up between you and the quine that made you sacred to each other, maybe after all that blether about the saints on Aikey Brae, whatever they said, and a wink on the sly was a bond of understanding, until such time as you had the chance to seal it with a kiss, in glad remembrance of a blissfull hol(i)day.

Folks in Black

Life can be a wearisome business for a five-year-old girl, especially when all the bairns next door have gone off to school and there is no one left to play with. I was now age for school but mother said I would have to wait until after the summer holidays. My school-bag and slate had already been bought, and a sliding box to hold slate-pencils, varnished with a flower on the lid, but what good were these if I couldn't have them to show off with.

I had lost all interest in my stocking-dolls and weaving cattie's tails, and what good were hoosies and lames without someone to share them with, or even skipping and beddies without a partner? I was getting big enough to play these games but they just weren't any good on your own.

I had become so frustrated with myself that I started to bite my nails. Then I got a skelp on the lug from my father and he said: 'Ye'll ken what that's for, ma bonnie quinie!' I wasn't sure that I did but it cured me of nail-biting for life, besides making my eyes water and setting the bells ringing in my ears at the time.

So there was little else I could do but run barefoot around the doors of our thatched hovels, which were the cottar houses at Gowanlea, where my father and the foreman lived and worked on the farm. The orra pail stood at our doorstep, where it served as a sink for slop or dishwater, and meantime there was just enough water in it to cover the bottom. I kept dipping my foot in the pail and ran up the close to see how much sand I could collect on my sticky sole.

Megan Handerson, who was my mother, stood watching my antics, while she leaned on the door jamb, her arms folded, waiting for the tatties to boil for the dinner. The folk next door called her Mrs. Stoddart, but Handerson was her own name and she liked it better.

Dave Rafferty, our Irish foreman lived next door, and at this moment he came round the corner for his mid-day meal. He had a large family and he poached for rabbits half the night to keep them alive. When all else was at rest Dave would be out with ferret and nets, while the stars sparkled and the whin dykes glistened with frost.

But when Dave Rafferty saw mother standing in the cottage door he stopped.

'Aye lass,' he said, 'I heard ye comin hame this mornin. Ye made an affa noise hammerin on the door tae wauken Charlie.'

Charlie was my father's name, Charles Stoddart, and he was the stockman on the farm.

'Aye,' Megan replied, 'Charlie had the door barred on the inside and I couldna get in. He doesna like tae bide himsel unless the door is barred. But what time was that, Dave?'

'Oh, aboot one o'clock, mebbee.'

'Weel, ye see, I was at my father's place and I was late or I got hame on ma bike. I had tae rap hard on the door for Charlie tae lat me in.'

'Weel lass, I was richt gled tae hear ye knockin, 'cause it waukened me frae an ugly dream. I dreamed that folks in black were tryin tae get a coffin in at your door and it wadna go. They tried hard tae get it in at your door but it wadna go. They kicked up an affa noise and I fair thocht they had yer door doon. And when they saw they couldna get the coffin in at your door they cam up the close wi it tae me; a black coffin wi toshils on't, I saw it fine. That must hae been when I heard ye bangin on the door. But what pleased I was when I kent it was only a dream.'

'It must hae been the nichtmare ye had,' said Megan.

'Na lass, it's yersel that taks the nichtmare. Charlie tells me he has tae hide the key every nicht tae keep ye fae gaun ootside in yer nicht-goon. He said there was ae nicht ye was tearin the hair oot o the lassie's heid there, and that ye thocht at the time ye was pluckin a hen. I'll bet it had been damned sair, eh quine!' And he patted my head for approval.

Megan laughed at this. 'Oh aye,' says she, 'but there was anither nicht that I was bashin the pram against the room door ben the lobby. I thocht it was a barra, and that I was a quine again and muckin oot ma father's byre, and that I couldna get the barra up the midden plank. It's a wonder that ye didna hear me that nicht Dave.'

'And a blessin that I didna lass. Weel, I'll awa tae ma denner or the tatties will be caul. Charlie's late the day. He's surely been hindered wi the kye. I think the roan coo was like tae calve this mornin.'

'We'll get new cheese than.'

'I dinna like the stuff lass.'

'Nae even wi raisins in't?'

'No lass, I'd raither hae a bowl o yerned melk ony day.'

Dave Rafferty walked up the close to his dinner. I dipped my foot in the pail at the doorstep and followed him gathering sand on my wet sole as I went along. While my back was turned Megan came to the door to 'bree the tatties,' and she strained off the scalding water into the pail, shook the tattie pot and went back into the house. When my foot had dried off I came hopping back to the doorstep and plunged my naked foot into the steaming pail. Then I fairly yelled in agony, and my scream brought Megan back to the door. When my father came round the corner I was dancing on one foot, yelling like mad, while the other was seared nearly to the bone.

About a fortnight later Dave Rafferty was wracked with a hach and a hoast that put him off his work with pneumonia, while I had developed blood-poisoning from my scalded foot. Dave had been poaching for rabbits half the night for a week, sitting out in the cold and the wet till he was fair chilled to the bone. He had no strength left in his legs and came out in a sweat and cold shivers till he was forced to take to his bed. Eight or nine rowdy bairns ran back and forth in the dark lobby or hung around his shabby bed. The man could get no rest for his own bairns and he tossed and turned in his bed till he was ravelled in the head.

The doctor came and had a look at him and sounded his chest and said he should be poulticed, back and front, and gave orders that a bottle of turpentine be mixed with the potion to keep it warm. He also prescribed a mixture, and took one of the older quines back with him to the town to get these things from a chemist, which was a brave thing for the doctor to do because the creature was itching with lice. But before he did this he came in bye and had a look at my swollen foot, which also had to be poulticed, and said he would look in again sometime.

Dave Rafferty's wife was almost witless in her perplexity and the house stank with neglect. Her man got worse in the night and asked for his medicine. She got up from his side in the box-bed and fumbled in the candle-light for the physic. What with worry and want of sleep she was on the brink of distraction, so she just poured out a doze from the nearest bottle on the mantle-shelf. Dave didn't like his medicine, so he swallowed it at a gulp. The hot liquid seared his gullet and made him cough and retch. He twisted his face and shuddered at the taste of it.

'Ye stupid bitch,' he spluttered, 'you've given me turpentine.'

'Turpentine,' said his wife, and looked at the stained label on the bottle. 'Michty mee! What'll I dee?'

So what does the frantic woman do but comes hammering on our door at the dead of night with her bloodless fists, even worse than Megan was doing on the night that Dave dreamed about the folks in black coming up the close with his coffin.

'Oh let me in,' she cried, 'Dave's worse, much worse, oh let me in!' And it seemed she would have the door in staves by the time Megan got out of bed to open it.

She swept in upon us like a ghost from a whirlwind, with a shawl over her night-gown, barefooted, and her black hair was blown about her white, scared face.

'It's murder I tell ye, murder,' she cried, clutching her shawl, 'I've poisoned my man with turpentine and he's stark raving mad. Oh Mrs. Stoddart, I couldna help it. I took the wrang bottle fae the mantlepiece and he jist gulped it doon. He's dyin I tell ye, and it was me that poisoned 'im, his ain wife. Oh, what'll I dee? Mrs. Stoddart. What'll I dee?'

She was sobbing hysterically and fell into Megan's arms like a heart-broken schoolgirl.

'But turpentine's nae rank poison woman,' Megan remonstrated. 'It winna kill yer man. Maybe it's made him drunk, like whisky. He'll be a' richt or mornin. I'll come roon and we'll gie him a dose o castor oil and he'll soon sleep it aff.'

'Oh na na, Mrs. Stoddart, he's waur than ye think. He took a gey big doze o turpentine. Will ye go for the doctor - jist tae ease my mind?'

So Megan dressed herself and cycled six miles to the town to see the doctor. Charles wouldn't go on his bike after dark.

The doctor lived in a posh part of the town, where trees grew out of the pavements, and every house had a front garden. The street lamps were out and Megan could hardly see the brass knocker on his varnished door.

She rattled the heavy knocker and the doctor peeped out from a window on the roof.

'What do you want at this time of night?' he snapped.

'I'm Mrs. Stoddart from the hovels at Gowanlea. Do you mind on Dave Rafferty the foreman there? You've been attending him for pneumonia.'

'Yes, I remember, Mrs. Stoddart. I'm sorry I was so rude with you. But what is the trouble?'

'Well, Mrs. Rafferty has given her man a dose of turpentine in mistake for his medicine and she thinks he's goin tae die. He's ravin mad and she thinks she's poisoned him. She wants ye tae come at once doctor.'

'Delirious eh! And no wonder, after a dose of turpentine. Probably it has raised his temperature a little but it won't do him any real harm. Tell the woman to give her man a good stiff dose of castor oil and I'll be out first thing in the morning. And keep the poultice going. By the way, Mrs. Stoddard, how is your wee girlie's foot?'

'It's terribly swollen and she's affa lame.'

'I can't hear you.'

Megan repeated her statement in a louder voice and it seemed she would wake the whole street.

'Very well, if it's ripe tomorrow - today, I mean, I'll lance it. But don't tell the wee lass; we'll break it to her gently. Good morning! Mrs. Stoddart.'

The doctor's head disappeared and the window went down with a clash. The light went out in his room and Megan was left in the darkness.

Mrs. Rafferty gave her man a dose of castor oil and he quietened down a bit. He fell asleep in a stupor and talked nonsense. Megan sat beside his bed and his wife quietened the bairns. She got them all to sleep ben the hoose and fell asleep herself in the midst of them.

But Dave began to chauve again, tossing the blankets nearly out of the bed, trying to get out of a load of straw he had toppled in the farm close. Syne Gyp and Daisy had bolted at the ploo and he fair tugged at the sheets trying to pull them in. He was hot and steamy and tossed about restlessly on the bed. Megan dipped a cloth in cold water and swabbed his face and temples. Eventually he lapsed into unconsciousness and Megan left the damp cloth on his brow, rinsing it now and then in cold water and replacing it on his forehead.

Megan somehow knew that Dave Rafferty had reached the crisis of his illness. Very soon he would die, or show signs of improvement . . .

Mrs Rafferty got up at daybreak and made tea. But Megan couldn't relish it. The smell of the dirty hovel made her squeamish, and already she thought she felt the itch of lice. Not that Megan really blamed the woman, for she didn't have a chance with all that bairns.

That day at noon, when my father came home for dinner, Megan ran up the close to speir for Dave Rafferty. He seemed somewhat revived but showed only the whites of his eyes under heavy lids.

Megan bent over him. 'Do you know me, Dave?' she asked.

'Aye lass, I ken ye fine. Folks in black were tryin tae get a coffin in at your door but it wadna go. They tried hard tae get it in at your door but it wadna go - so they cam up the close wi it tae me . . .'

His words were mumbled from between cracked swollen lips and the effort exhausted him. Megan ignored what he said and bent over him again.

'Are ye feelin ony better Dave?' she asked.

'Oh aye,' he seched, 'a wee bittie.' But his eyes were glazed with death. He turned his face to the wall and fell into another troubled sleep. Megan felt his pulse. It was weak, almost indiscernible, and his breathing came in short faint gasps that brought pink froth to his lips.

'The doctor's comin back in the efterneen,' his wife said.

Two hours later Dave Rafferty was dead. His wife lay over him and wept sorely. She kissed his pallid face and her hot tears ran down his cheeks. Megan took her away from the bed and set her on a chair. The younger of the bairns cried when they saw their mother greetin. The others gathered round her chair, silent and wide-eyed.

'Yer father's deid,' the mother sobbed, 'and I poisoned him. I poisoned him, bairns, d'ye hear!'

Megan shook her by the shoulders. 'Ye didna poison 'im woman. Get that oot o yer heid afore it takes root. Never mind her, bairns, she's haverin; she didna poison yer dad - he was goin tae die onywye.'

When the doctor had finished with Dave Rafferty he set me on Megan's knee and lanced my foot. He flicked the ugly swelling with a lancet and squeezed out the thick bluish matter with his thumbs.

Megan looked away for a moment. 'Could it be dangerous? doctor,' she asked.

'Not now, Mrs Stoddart, but had we not managed to localise the poison, with the help of poultice, and had the infection got into the girl's bloodstream, I wouldn't care to say what might have happened . . . But you're going to be all right now my wee girl.'

He washed my foot in hot water and swathed it tightly in a bandage. He set me on the rug by the fire and ruffled my brown ringlets. 'You've been a brave little girl,' he said, closed his leather bag with a snap, put on his hat and departed.

'Bye bye!' he said.

Megan went to the door and watched him as he walked down the close to his car, an old 'Tin Lizzie' with a canvas hood. She watched the dust rising from the wheels of the doctor's car until it disappeared on a bend of the road. I was standing beside her on one foot, still reeking of Lysol, and holding on to her long skirts.

Megan turned her head and looked towards the Rafferty's door. She could see the hens pecking around the doorstep but there was no sign of the bairns. Their drab shabby blinds would be down though the sun was shining so beautifully. It would be eerie now to come home late at night and bang on the cottage door. Now that Dave Rafferty was gone Megan felt afraid of the dark.

She bent down and her strong young arm went round my shoulders. In a moment she had gathered me close to her warm skirts and was smothering my cheeks with her hot tears and kisses.

Who Would be a Gaffer?

You had heard about the gaffers in the old days who walked in at one end of the stable at yoking time and out at the other, snapping out orders as they went, never dachlin, and the men trying to catch their words in the by going, but feart to back-speir if they didn't, for woe betide a man gin he back-speired a gaffer in those days. Cairt neeps, ploo and thrash was about the gist of it in winter; hyowe, hay and harvest in the summer months, with maybe a pucklie o peats to cast or yows to clip, so you couldn't go very far wrong with the horse wark, one day was the same as the next and complications were few; maybe the odd beltie broken on thrashin days or a colt to yoke in the spring, the rest was hard work and long hours and you could manage fine without machinery. For ploomen chiels in those days it was mostly 'Jist haud back again lads and blacken a bittie mair!' So there wasn't much to be said at yoking time any way.

But by the mid-fifties all this was changing and it wasn't so easy being a gaffer nowadays: what with they new tractors coming in and the horses disappearing, the changing of implements and methods, working shorter hours with fewer men; and yet you were expected to produce the same results as before, or even better, and at greater speed, because all this new-fangled machinery had to be paid for.

The pickiesae hat and the nickie-tams were gone forever; so were the piked hames, the segs and the harness cleaning, and nowadays you seldom saw a double-cased lever watch or a lad in tackety boots smoking a 'Stonie' pipe and bogie-roll. The old heavies were fast disappearing and a new generation of mechanics were taking their place. The Agricultural Revolution was in full swing and a new image in farming was being created, so different from the old that nowadays you could hardly tell a farm worker from a town billie, except maybe that the country chiel had a bit more colour in his face. Some of them even had motor cars, which didn't give the toon bairns a chance to run after them crying: 'Country Geordie, Brig o Dee, Sup the brose and leave the bree!' as they had done with their fathers.

The old gaffers were on the way out too. Those who were still carrying on were sending men to jobs they couldn't do themselves, and unless they could drive a tractor they were getting in the way. Farmers wanted a 'working' grieve who could handle machinery and take his turn with a tractor. But you had foreseen this and could whip a tractor about with the best of them, although they got a laugh at you for a start, especially when you tried to back it into the shed with a load of sheaves or turnips, but it had been well worth while to persist.

And you could just see yourself stamping into the tractor garage snapping out orders at men dressed in berets and boiler suits, duffle coats and wellington boots; men who had scarcely ever seen a horse yoked, and one of them had asked you what the saddle-trees were for in the old stable. When you told the foreman what to do he immediately kicked up his tractor and the others couldn't hear for the noise, or see you for the diesel fumes, so you had to shout in their ears till you nearly choked, while they consulted their wrist watches to make sure you wasn't a minute too soon. Yoking half-a-dozen horse teams was a pleasure compared with this rumpus, and if you didn't jump out of the way quick they would run you over; what with their haversacks and tea flasks you would think they were off for the day, not just a few short hours and the rest overtime.

You just couldn't imagine what your old man would have thought of this lot; them with their half-days on Saturdays and summer holidays with pay, and never a wet sark sitting in their tractor cabs. Some change from the old days when it was 'stracht theets' for ten hours a day, up at five in the morning and back to supper-up in the evening, and never a bite to eat between meals. This crowd never rose or the postie was by, and their winter day was that short you sometimes wondered how you was going to get everything fitted in. But maybe it was for the better, because some of the men were old before their time in the old days, wracked with work and rheumatism, and never knew what it was to get a holiday beyond the feeing market or a term day.

But the weather was still the real master as it had always been: even with all their contraptions they hadn't managed to alter that, or get the weather to suit the wark. Yesterday you was at the hay-makin but the rain came on and spoiled it, so you had to send the men inside to scrub the 'dry coo' byre. Today the rain had ceased but the hay was conached for the present, rather a pity because it was well matured and almost ready for stacking. Just shows how many irons you must have in the fire at a time like this, and being the gaffer you got to give the men a job: you can't have them digging holes in the ground just to fill them in again to pass the time, the manager would think you was off your nut and maybe give you the sack. So in weather like this you have to have a lot of things going at the same time, and you've got to keep cool when things go wrong. Of course you still got the 'dry coo' byre to paint after the scrubbing, and there's a great heap of coiryarn in the loft to be unravelled and wound into balls. You just threw it aside when you took it off the stacks in the winter time, but you have to get it all ready again for the hairst. A while back you could have the men inside to twine strae-rapes on a rainy day, but that's all past now and the thraw-heuks are thrown aside, now that you've got nets or 'hackles' for covering the rucks.

Being a gaffer you've got a lot more things to think about than the other lads. But you are supposed to be able to crack a joke just the same. You're not supposed to go about with a face that would sour the mannie's milk just because the weather has gone against you. You get bigger paid to carry a lot more in your mind than the other chiels, and if your head is screwed on the right way you should manage it, otherwise you shouldn't be a gaffer. Of course you get the blame for everything but you've got a skin as thick as a nowt beast and you can thole it; and what the men say about you behind your back would make you cock your lugs in your sleep. Not that you lose a blink of sleep over it, 'cause you've learned to trample a lot of the stite under your feet. Damnit man, if you was to listen to all their yammer you would be awake for twenty-four hours a day, and not fit to take a bite of meat for the thought of it. Just because you was a gaffer you knew some folk that would have you on crutches and your wife up the wall, your family all in prison or in hospital, and if looks were anything to go by you should freeze in your boots or go up in a blue flame. But your father was a gaffer before you and you'd learned from him how to settle their hash.

And you had thon manager chiel to contend with, not that he was a bad stock, but he always wanted to know the outs and ins of everything and you had to keep him informed. He had even tried you to keep a diary about what the men were doing every day, but you had drawn the line at this and said that gin you had wanted a job as a clerk you wouldn't be here. Him and his beuks, and all this fash about having everything down on paper. That was college folk for ye, but you had told the creature what he could do with his diary, every flippin page of it, and you thought he was offended. But that was a long time back and the manager had learned since then that you had a crackin good memory and could manage fine without a pencil behind your lug.

The manager had come straight out of college, with nothing but what he stood in by way of clothes, and riding a bicycle; but brim full of fancy ideas, and you had to put him in his place from time to time, or he would have everything growing upside down and all out of season. Not that the man hadn't wit, and he had shown a lot of folk outby that there was more in him than the spoon put in, for it's little they thought of him when he first came to the place. That creature they said will never manage an estate of that size; he's got it all out of books and he'll find it a different thing when he puts his ideas into practice.

But he had opened their eyes the breet, and them that shunned him for a start would now like to pass the time of day over the dyke, but he was a man by himself and wouldn't listen to any of their claik.

And you had to admit that the manager had changed a lot of things and brought the farms really up to date: what with that braw new milking parlour and press-button milking at the Home Farm; the new tattie sheds he had biggit, and big fodder barns that held nearly a' the crap under a roof, so that ye had little bother getting everything inside from the weather. The way he was going he would soon have the whole steading under glass, like a hot house, stacked with manure and implements. You never saw such a creature for manure and you guessed that for every bag of corn or tatties that went away a sack of manure came back. It soon would be that you could manure the grun on an ordinar fairm with the soil of this place. The kye were wading to their bellies in grass but still he stoured it on, and the hay was that rich you could hardly cure it. A 'controlled surplus' he called it but you hardly knew what the creature meant, though it was true that the farms were running more milk, corn and tatties than you had ever seen before.

He wasn't feared of work either the stock, manager though he was, skelpin on in his shirt sleeves from daylight to dark, with nothing on his head, working all day and writing in books half the night, it made you feel half affronted for the little you did in comparison. Talk about a collar-and-tie job; if this man put on a collar he would choke himself, or hang himself with the tie, for he always had his sark neck open nearly to his navel. The man hardly slept either, just a few hours on the pillow after his clerking and he was up in the morning and into the dairy byre as if the place belonged to him. You never saw such a man for work and he fair made a hobby of it: never had time for a smoke or a drink, or a bit hooch of a dance and how he got hold of that slip of a quine for a wife you would never know. Over six feet he was and you had to look up to the man, more ways than one, and behind that ready smile of his was an awful lot of thinking. But maybe it would tell on him some day, for his hair was grey already for a young man, and cropped short as stubble.

You knew fine that the manager was more popular with the men than you was; and no wonder, for since the firm gave him that motor car he was never slack to take their wives to the houdi, day or night, and blin drift made no difference for then he took a tractor; always ready to do a good turn, though sometimes he got little thanks for it, and if he couldn't speak good of a man he held his tongue. But you always remembered that time when you was off work and the manager took your place, and when you came back the men were all on about the manager: it was the manager did this and the manager said that until you were fair deaved with their clipe. But they didn't know him quite as well as you did, or maybe they wouldn't have been so verty, for he said things to you that they didn't hear, and as he had an eye for each man's work individually he wasn't slack to say what he thought of it, for he wasn't above a bit of honest criticism.

But sometimes the lad took things in his head that just had to be dealt with, even though it was only to show that you was still the gaffer; like that time at the start o hairst when he came home from the town in a great fizz because everybody on the way out was cutting their corn and you wasn't started. He had nearly run into a bus from gawking at all the binders tearing round the parks and nothing done at home. You had the men out cleaning ditches at this time of year and maybe he thought they should be clearing roads for the binders. So he comes to you in a great flurry and asks why aren't you started man? Everybody's cutting from here to the toon! You thought of asking him that if all these people jumped into the harbour in the toon, would he jump in after them? But you thinks this would be a bit impudent, so you puts your pipe away and calmly tells the man that the stuff isn't ready for cutting. But he doesn't believe you and wants to know why, thinking maybe that you are a bit thrawn; so you takes him to the gate of a corn field and tells him to go in there and fill his oxter with the stuff, and when he had it all together in his arms it was as green as kale. With that he apologised for his rashness and said he wouldn't have believed it any other way. It would look mighty green in a stook you say, especially if you are going to thrash early as you usually do; man it would hardly weigh in a sack and you would never get them tied. He admits this and then you slyly tells him that he still has a lot to learn though he has been to the college.

And there was that other time in the spring during the war when the neep seed was that scarce you couldn't get it at any price. But you had a few pounds of old turnip seed in the loft, a wee bit musty but you knew fine it would grow in fair weather and the ground in trim. So you shows this little sack to the manager and he shakes his head and says you cannot sow that stuff because it is too old and wizened looking and will never take root. Too big a risk he says and you might lose the crop. You tries to reason with the man but he is as stockit as a newly cogged calf, when round the corner comes his bit quine of a wife and says that he is wanted on the 'phone. When the manager's back is turned you take a dander the way of the tractor garage and pours a droppie paraffin in the bag among the neep seed; a daft like thing to do, but just a little makes the seed trickle better through the seed-barrow, besides brightening its colour. You gives the seed a bit stir with your fingers and shakes the bag, and when the manager appears again you show him what he thinks is a different mixture of seed. He pokes his head into the bag and brightens up immediately. You wonder that he doesn't feel the smell of the paraffin, but no; and he puts his hand in the bag and runs the seed through his fingers. He says that is a much better sample grieve and you were lucky to find it and that you can start planting right away. You wait till he is fully convinced and then you tells him it is the same seed and he nearly falls into the brander at his back. He wants to know how you have managed to make it look so fresh, and how you got up to that trick. But you just laughs and shakes your head and hints that he still has a hantle to learn though he had been at the college for a life-time.

At the moment however there's still the tatties to rogue and it's about the only thing you will get away with for the time being. But you don't like tattie-roguing, and being the gaffer you don't have to go with the men on a job like that. That is one good privilege you've got above the others, in that you can choose your job, at least to some extent, provided you haven't a conscience and that you know the best place to hide. You are blamed for that in any case so you might as well take full advantage of it, so when there's a bit of a hash on or some heavy lifting to be done you just make yourself scarce, because though you stuck your neck out and slaved yourself to the marrow they'd still say the same things about you. So why spoil a reputation that has served you so well for so long?

So once you get the men yoked to the tattie-roguin you could stick your thumbs in your waistcoat and make an errand down to the blacksmith; not that he will have much time to listen to your blab, him being busy like, but it will keep you out of sight for a time, and you could always say that you was down at the smiddy for yon mower blade that needed sortin. What with the second cut of silage comin on you had to have a mower blade. Daggit now that just reminded you it's high time you had the binder canvasses off to the saddler afore the hairst begins, for most likely they'll be needin some repairs. And what with the men's holidays comin on; neeps tae shim, tatties to spray, thistles to cut, hay to stack, one thing or another, so that you began to wonder if ever you would get a holiday yourself, for you didn't get much peace as a gaffer.

The Broken Scythe

Bob leaned over his scythe and felt the edge of the blade with his thumb. He referred to the wooden part of his scythe as the 'sned'. It resembled a deer's antlers with only two spikes left for handles, and the wood was gnarled with age and wear until it looked like polished horn. Resting the scythe on its 'heel' he took a carborundum stone from his belt to sharpen the blade. Upturning the scythe, now with the antlers under his oxter, and the point of the sword-like blade on the ground, Bob began to whet the blunted edge. And now the clash of stone against ringing steel was echoed in the glade like the din of battle just begun.

But Bob's enthusiasm didn't match his action. He had about as much inclination for the work as a fly in a basin of milk.

It was a warm sunny day and the sky was as clear and pure as a maiden's eye. The clouds were no more than vapours, like the breath of angels, drifting across the expanse of heaven in gentle motion. The moisture of the fields was evaporating in the hot sun, shimmering above the cornfields in a rippling haze. The corn was rustling in a breathless swoon, hard and ripe and level with the dykes, ready for harvest.

The skylarks warbled an incessant chorus, mere specks in the blue that rose and fell in their exuberance of song. From the pinewood the cushats were cooing a deeper note in the autumn symphony. Gossamer spangled the grass like fine hairs, dancing in the sun glint, while the spiders hung their webs on whin and broom. The air was somnolent with the hum of insect and the drone of bee; minty with the fragrance of bogmyrtle.

Bob straddled the burn and slashed at the rushes on the banks. But it was a lazy day, drowsy in the ripeness of autumn and above all, it was a Saturday, and Bob had expected a half holiday, the afternoon off from his labours.

But old Weelum the farmer had sent us to cut and bind thatch on the ditch banks, to be ready for the stacks at the end of harvest.

Nowadays the fee-ed loon takes his weekly half-holiday for granted. He does not have to ask it as a favour from his employer: unless he is paid overtime it is there for the taking, a privilege by law, and he doesn't have to trouble himself about excuses for obtaining it.

Sixty years ago such a luxury was unheard of, or left to the farmer's discretion, a most disconcerting state of affairs if one was refused a half-day off at the end of a week's hard work, especially if you had a pre-arranged tryst with your quine in some flowery hedgerow, or had planned to attend a football match.

Half-holidays were most common in summer, when the cattle were on pasture, and didn't have to be fed in byres at week-ends. Some farmers gave their men Saturday afternoons off in summer on condition that they worked extra time in harvest without pay. And half-days off were available in slack periods only, mostly between hay-making and harvest, and even then they were scarce if the farmer worked peat. Some of the cottared men (married men with families) spent their half-days in the peat-moss, driving home their peat for winter fuel.

But of course there were ways and means of obtaining your freedom on a sunny Saturday afternoon, and many were the subterfuges contrived to secure an occasional half-day off. Sometimes your grandmother died suddenly without any mention of it in the papers; but since you had only two lawful grandmothers, and they had to last a whole summer, you had to space them out a bit. And you didn't worry about the next year as you would probably be moving on among strangers. Grandfathers were not so convenient, as they had a habit of turning up at roups or marts or fee-ing markets, and there was always sure to be somebody who knew them, and who didn't believe in ghosts.

I was only a loon at the time but Bob was a man, still single, and his notion of a half-day off was solely for pleasure. He wanted to ply his fishing-rod from the rocks below the sea-cliffs, with a swirl of gulls mewing overhead, and the silvered waters breaking on the shore. Bob fished at the Bullers of Buchan with an earth-worm on the hook, and many a fine trout he landed for the basket. He took me there one Saturday afternoon after the hay-making. I crawled on my hands and knees to look over the edge of the beetling cliffs. I was terrified, but Bob coaxed me on to follow him, and as I had great faith in Bob I managed to get a foot over the edge. We shinned our way backwards down the Grey Mare ridge, astride the rock, (a position which gave it its name) a leg on each side, our faces to the cliff, Bob with his wand and fishing-bag tied to his back, the two of us like flies above the blue swirl of the waters.

But I didn't stay long on the rocks with Bob. I wasn't interested in fishing and my one concern was to reach the top of the cliff again, alive. Bob wouldn't come back with me, so I had to make it alone, shinning my way up the Grey Mare's back hanging on for dear life, fingering every foothold in a dedicated bid for safety and a longer life. I clung to the hard stone with my whole life in my finger-tips, a huddle of fear between sea and sky, schooling myself not to look back, but to think only of the future and the spine grass at the top of the precipice.

So that was Bob's idea of a holiday. For me it was a nightmare and I would rather have stayed at home - even to gather rushes on the ditch banks, just as we were doing now . . .

Bob straightened his back and wiped the sweat from his brow with his sleeve. 'Ah tae blazes,' says he, 'Foo can Auld Weelum nae gie us the half-day aff? Sic a fine efterneen for the rock-fishin at that. And wi the hairst comin on we winna hae anither chance o a holiday.'

I was gathering the rushes into sheaves, binding them with twisted strands, to be carted away later for the stackyard.

'Foo nae ging hame and ask a halfie then?' I suggested. 'It's nae ower late yet!'

Bob kennelt his pipe and spat in the ditch. 'Daggit man,' says he, 'that's nae a bad idea. But first I'll hae tae brak the scythe, or Weelum will jist send me back tae cut mair thack.'

There was no more thatch to gather, so I peeled the green skin from a reed and held up the white cotton-like fibre between thumb and forefinger. 'Ken what folk used that for in the old days?' I asked.

Bob looked quizzically at the white fibre. 'No loon, I dinna ken what they used it for.'

'Well, they dried it and used it for a wick in their oil-lamps tae light their hovels.'

'And what has that got tae do wi us gettin a halfie?'

'Oh naething,' I said, 'I just minded on't.'

Bob hooked his scythe on to a fencing post and tore out the grass-hook, the small strut that held it together, so that the blade fell away from the handle. In other words, the sword came away from the antlers. 'Noo than,' says he, mischievously, 'the snickle is oot o the snackle, as they say, and there's nae anither scythe on the premises; they're a' at the smiddy bein sortit for the hairst.'

'And what are ye goin tae do?' I asked, for I had never seen Bob do anything so reckless.

'You bide here and peel rashes,' says he; 'I'm gaun awa hame tae ask Auld Weelum for a halfie, and if I dinna come back I'll send young Weelum tae fetch ye hame.'

He shouldered the broken scythe and strode away over the pasture, whistling for the dog. Roy was at his heels in a moment, roused from his snooze beneath a golden whin bush. The cattle left their grazing and went after them, curious as they always are at the sight of a dog.

Bob sent the dog at the stirks, snapping at their heels, trying to catch a tail. They disappeared over the hill, Bob and the nowt and the collie, and his bark grew fainter and fainter until they were out of hearing.

It reminded me of a little snatch of a poem we used to recite at school.

> Smock-frock, billy-cock,
> Harvest field and hay,
> A whistle clear for all the year,
> And a heart as fresh as May.

I sat down on the mossy bank, there being no more rushes to bind, and I considered how splendid it would be to have a half-holiday. If I hurried I could still catch most of the afternoon matinee at the pictures. It was so much more exciting than the evening shows when the big folks came. I would have to run

84

three miles to the town, but I would take to the fields for a short-cut. I had done it once before to see *Ben-Hur*, and such a splendid experience that had been.

Today it would be Col. Tim McCoy in *War Paint*, and the Indians would be on the war-path, tearing over the barren prairies on their piebald chargers, their feathered tiaras streaming in the wind, swinging their gleaming tomahawks and whooping their warbling war cries.

Or they would have a pow-wow with McCoy around the camp fires, smoking the peace-pipe, while their squaws plaited their hair in the wig-wams, for Col. Tim McCoy was a ranger to be reckoned with among the Indians.

In last week's serial Tarzan and Jane had fallen into a lion-trap in the jungle. Now I was dying to know what had happened to them when the hungry lion sprang at them from a corner of the pit.

But my reverie was short-lived when I heard Bob come whistling o'er the lea, the collie at his heels, the cattle prancing behind them.

Some of the stots were challenging Roy to a fight, creeping up behind him, as close as they dared, scraping the earth with their front hoofs and tossing the sods over their backs. But Roy turned and made at them, scattering the whole herd to a safe distance.

Surely we hadn't got a halfie then?

Bob had brought me a can of hot tea and two scones laden with ginger-flavoured rhubarb jam. 'Weel loon,' says he, 'Ye winna be hungry onywye!'

I threw a piece of scone to the collie dog. He snapped it in mid-air, then stood wagging his bushy tail, his head to one side, looking for more.

'Nae luck for a halfie then?' I ventured.

'Daggit man,' said Bob, 'Weelum was that concerned aboot the scythe bein broken, and girned sae muckle aboot the cost o repairs nooadays - man, I jist hadna the hert tae seek a halfie.'

'Hadna the neck, ye mean!' For my eyes were smarting with disappointment, and a lump was in my throat, which I managed to wash down with the tea.

'Man,' says Bob, 'It was like kickin a man efter he was doon; sic a lay-off I got aboot the hardness o the times he nearly had me in tears.'

I pointed with my tea-can at the old rusty scythe he held in his hand. 'Where did ye get the Robsorby then?' I asked, that being our Scots name for a scythe, after the maker, Robert Sorby, or some such thing.

'Man,' Bob explained, 'Weelum had it hidden awa in the laft yonder, up in the rafters, lyin amon the cobwebs and the binder canvasses, jist waitin for somebody tae seek a half-day aff at the start o hairst. But fegs, it's that blunt (stroking the edge of the blade with his thumb) it wad hardly cut wan o yer rash wicks, or a print o butter. Come tae think on't I shouldna hae broken the wan I had!'

'There's midgies noo,' I warned, slapping my face with my hand where a midge had bitten me.

'I thocht I felt the buggericks,' and Bob lit his pipe to try and dispel them, for the midge doesn't like pipe reek, black twist especially, better known as Bogie-roll.

He whetted the rusty blade and lashed at the bending reeds. 'Damnit man, she winna cut at a'. That's your wyte loon! Ye wad put ill intae me, and ye've ruined ma gweed scythe!'

'But I didna tell ye tae brak the scythe,' I protested.

'That was a strategem, and it was the diplomacy that failed. Ae thing leads tae anither, but it was you that set the ba rollin.

'Sabotage, I would call it,' I said, disconsolately, 'and if ye was the ba, ye rolled tae nae purpose!'

'Aye, but ye wad get impudent noo! What aboot the drap tea ye got? Ye wadna hae got that if I hadna gaen hame. But ye'd better come awa and gether a puckle mair thack, ye've havert lang eneuch noo!'

And so the Indians would have to wait until nightfall before they started their war-dance, at least as far as I was concerned; and Tarzan and Jane would have to crouch in their lion pit until I saw them rescued.

As for the rock fishing, well, it wasn't much good in the dark. There was always Sunday, as Bob said, but any old man would have told him there was bound to be rain after such a day as this, with all that midges about.

'A' that slammachs on the girse,' they would habber from toothless gums, 'A' they spider wobs on the whuns; and all that bluddy midgicks aboot, it's bound tae rain!' And 'slammachs' by the way was their word for the silver gossamer.

But now a ballet of midges was dancing in the sunhaze, punishing us for our deceit; a thousand hypodermic needles thirsting for our guilty blood.

Every slash of the scythe brought forth a cloud of stinging fury; a curtain of torment that followed us like a shadow, peppering our faces and arms with blistering hot spots.

Bob was raving mad.

'Blast the thing, it winna cut ava. And blast the midgies!' And I echoed his curses.

Sarah and the Angels

Folk said there still were fairies in Lachbeg Woods. Sarah Blossom, who was my grandmother, had good reason to remember it, but she swore it was angels she saw that night when she was in the gig with Gleg. Gleg Handerson was my grandfather, and he said he didn't see any angels. But he said the shilt saw something, because it shied and nickered loudly and fell into the ditch by the roadside. 'The geeg lichts gaed oot,' said Gleg, 'and I couldna see a stime. It was a fine starry nicht and I was fair blint wi a licht as bricht as lichtnin, but ower slow for that, and it rose up intae the sky.' It rose from the hedges, Sarah confirmed, and it went up to heaven, and she swore she saw two angels rise in the midst of it, one from each side of the road, their wings transparent with light.

Megan told me the story a long time ago. Megan was my mother's name, and she told it to me as a bed-time creepie that was supposed to keep me out of mischief for days to come. She had been but a quine at the time and worked on her parents' farm at Kelpieside, just under the Mattock Hill, with the white stone deer on its slopes. Gleg had yoked the shilt early after supper and set off with Sarah in the gig. They were to spend the evening with the Blossoms, Sarah's folks, away up in the Strath where the burnie tumbled doon from the hill; where the troot loupit silver-like in the moonlight and the whaups wheebled over the fens.

'Bick-birr, bick-birr,' the moorhens cried, 'g'wa hame, g'wa hame.'

It was still daylight when Gleg and Sarah left home. Soon they were in Lachbeg Woods, with the laird's dyke on one side and a hedge on the other. The shilt was at a brisk trot and Sarah was well wrapped up in her tartan plaid, a rug on her knees and her hands in a muff. It was almost dark under the trees, but Sarah had sharp eyes, and as the shilt jogged along she spotted an old jacket lying by the roadside; perhaps it had fallen from a cart, or some forester had lost it. 'Look Daw,' she said to Gleg, for she always called him Daw as the bairns did, 'Look Daw, that jacket lyin on the road; if it's still there when we get back we'll stop and pick it up - it micht fit ye Daw!'

Sarah knew fine that Gleg wouldn't have stopped at the first telling anyway. He would have to make up his mind about a thing like that; him deep in his thoughts of kye and parks, ploughin and sowin, and a woman was always nagging about something. But Sarah would have him prepared for it on the way home, and she would remind him to stop for the jacket, a pity to leave it lying there . . .

But by and by they were up in the Strath and nearing the heather. Partridges that were startled from their nests whirred over the darkening moor, clucking their displeasure of the intruders.

'Bick-birr, bick-birr, g'wa hame, g'wa hame,' the moorhens cried.

But Gleg never heeded them. It was a return visit that was lang overdue he said. 'And forbyes, auld Basil's bottle would be fu again, and we'll jist gang owerby and gie 'im a hand tae teem't.'

'Bick-birr, bick-birr, g'wa hame, g'wa hame, g'wa hame, g'wa hame.'

'Noisy brutes,' Gleg mused, and clicked his tongue at the shilt.

Meanwhile at home Megan had her hands full. Being the eldest, she was left in charge, and besides looking after her younger brothers and sisters, she had to milk the kye, sieve the milk and wash the pails; the calfies had to get a suppie in the coggie, and she had to see to the supperin o the horse, Kate and Nell, and fasten in the hens. And the deuks had to be chased hame frae the dam or they wad lay awa in the mornin.

But Megan's biggest worry was Jancey and Teenie, her two baby sisters who had not been well lately. Jancey was nearly two years old and Teenie six months. Before leaving, Sarah had told Megan to give them their mixtures and put them to bed in the kitchen. But Jancey had coughed all evening and Teenie had whimpered and fretted since Sarah had shut the door on them.

It was dark by eight o'clock and Megan lit the paraffin lamp that hung from the roof and pulled down the blind. Jonas her brother was two years younger than Megan. Sometimes they fought, but mostly when they were alone they were friends. Jonas was afraid of being alone in the dark and trusted her completely. So when she had the others in bed she lit a lantern and Jonas carried it to the byre for the milking, while Megan took the pails.

Jonas hung the lantern on a wire from the rafters and waited while Megan milked the kye. It was eerie in the byre without Sarah about the place; spooky too, and Jonas could hardly wait or the cows were milked. He was suspicious of every lurking shadow and paced back and forth on the cobblestones, disturbing the beasts. But he was afraid to go back to the house alone in the dark. Megan said he would see a ghost in the close. She was feart hersel and couldn't let him go, so she threatened to blow out the lantern and leave him in the dark. In this way she could master Jonas and got him to fall to and help her give the calves their milk.

The milkhouse was as cold as a tomb and fitted with blue stone shelves like a mortuary. Their shadows flickered grotesquely on the white-washed walls, enormous silhouettes out of all proportion to their normal size. The air was damp and cold, like the smell of a crypt, a cold dead smell, but in hot weather this place kept the milk from souring. Megan strained the hot milk into the wide brown earthenware basins that stood on the shelves. She went to the kitchen for boiling water to scald the pails, and while she was gone Jonas helped himself from a cheese kebbuck, crawling with mites.

Next to the stable to give the mares a drink and an oxterful of hay. Megan held the warm lantern over her head while Jonas went cannily up to Kate. He was hardly able to lift her pail of water into the manger and she had to get two fills of his small oxter of hay. But Kate and Nell were quiet mares and they knew the touch of Jonas' hand and the sound of his voice. He shook down their bedding with a fork and gave them each a swede turnip, because his father said it was 'gweed for their teeth tae humch a neep!'

Back in the house Teenie still girned. Megan gave her the mixture in her milk and rocked her in the cradle. But she wouldn't take the teat on the bottle and screwed her small face into an orgy of pain. The rocking seemed to sicken the bairn and she vomited. This seemed to help and Teenie was better for a time, and Megan rocked and rocked in an effort to get her to sleep.

Meanwhile Jancey lay in the box-bed and coughed and tossed in a restless stupor.

The other bairns had wearied and gone upstairs to bed. Megan prigged with Jonas to stay with her by the peat fire but he said he couldn't sleep on a chair. She kept vigil alone and even the willow-pattern plates took on a sinister expression as she looked at them on the wall racks. They seemed to stare back at her as if she was a stranger among them. Her eyes wandered round the old kitchen to the passage door, where every moment she expected an apparition to emerge from the gloom. She saw visions in the peat flames in the white-washed hearth. The ivy leaves tapped at the window panes with soft ghostly fingers. She closed her eyes and almost fell asleep, till the scratch of a mouse resurrected her fears. Her ankles ached on the cradle rocker and Teenie began to cry again. Would Sarah never come?

Jancey coughed and coughed till Megan thought she was going to die. The long brass pendulum on the wag-at-the-wa clock swung the hours away. The seconds were measured out into minutes with every beat of its iron heart. The minutes were circled into hours by the fretted fingers on its flower-decked face. Two rocks of the cradle to the long deliberate swing of the pendulum, hour after hour, until it seemed an eternity. And Teenie still puckered her face in agonised spasms of pain.

Megan's eyes rested on the brass knob of the closet door. It reflected the firelight like a beacon. She could almost imagine that it was turning and that the door would open. But the peat flames played a devil's dance on the brass berry-pans under the dresser, they shone like full moons and laughed at her fears.

Would Sarah never come?

But Gleg and Sarah were in nae mood for gaun hame. They stayed with the Blossoms folks into the sma oors o the mornin. After all it wasn't often that they got a night out, and with Megan in charge at home there didn't seem to be much to worry about. The shilt had been stabled with an oxterful of hay and a leepy-ful of bruised corn; the nicht was fine and the peat fire was warm, so there was nae thocht for the lang road hame.

Sarah even forgot for a time aboot Jancey and Teenie that were ailin at Kelpieside, though she had tellt her mither aboot the bairns. But they hadna been sae bad these last few days and the doctor was lookin in bye noo and than. Sarah's mither gave her a tot of brandy to warm her up after her journey in the gig. It helped her to forget things that mattered for a time and she stopped worryin aboot her bairns.

Gleg too had a fair swig o fuskey frae auld Basil. It lightened his mind and loosened his tongue as he shared his troubles with his father-in-law. And there was this body tae rake up and yon cratur tae ring doon, craps and beasts and prices tae be taen thru haun, gweed kens whaur the time gaed till. The tea was good (even withoot melk for Sarah) and Gleg's pipe tasted real grand after the whisky. Old Basil Blossom, Sarah's father smoked a pipe as well, a clay pipe with a fich on't and they could hardly see each ither for reek.

'Weel weel, gweed kens, but we'll hae tae be goin,' Gleg said at last, as he knocked out his pipe in the peat ash. Basil took the lantern and went out with him to yoke the shilt into the gig. Sarah put on her nap coat with the ivory buttons and seated herself on the gig, high above the wheels. Gleg tucked her in with the rugs and she nestled her hands in her muff. He lighted the candle lanterns and you could see the shilt's breath in the flutter of light. 'Gweed nicht than,' said Gleg, and climbed into the seat with Sarah. Next moment they were off, driving into the night.

'I hope Jancey and Teenie are a' richt at hame,' said Sarah; 'and if we see yon jacket on the road hame we'll stop and pick it up.'

The moorhens were silent on the heather and as Gleg approached Lachbeg Woods Sarah watched for the jacket. Sarah had marked the spot well and though it was dark she would get a glimpse of it in the light from the gig lanterns. Gleg slowed the shilt to a trot and the clip-clop of his hoofs rang sharp and clear in the dark silent woods.

But the jacket was gone and in its place a ball of light flooded the roadway, sudden, silent, mysterious. Sarah was frightened. She clutched tightly at Gleg's arm and nearly tore the reins out of his hands. 'Oh Daw,' she cried, 'My bairns!'

Two angels appeared, one on each side of the road, gliding along beside the gig, the light shining on their wings. Sarah was terrified and her scream woke the night. The shilt neighed loudly and rose in the air and toppled Gleg and Sarah out of the gig. Gleg kept hold of the reins but even as they fell Sarah saw the light rise up to heaven with two angels in the midst of it, shining through their wings; up and up until she must have fainted, because the next thing she remembered, Daw was holding her in his arms and shaking her back to consciousness.

'Fireballs come doon usually,' Gleg said to folk years later about this night, 'but this ane gaed up, rose fae the road like a sunrise.'

'And twa angels appeared,' said Sarah, her face all goosepimples when she spoke of it. 'I saw them fine; they ran along beside the gig, one on each side o the road, then they rose up in the air, slowly, the licht shinin in their wings, until they disappeared.'

'She fainted,' Daw said. 'I couldna say I saw ony angels but the shilt saw something, 'cause he reared up and coupit us oot o the gig.'

'And when it was a' bye we were left in darkness,' Sarah chimed in, 'the gig was coupit and the lichts went oot and we were baith in the ditch. But we were neen the waur o't! Daw soon had the shilt in hand again and we managed hame in the dark. But I was that shaken I could hardly stand on my feet, and I kent fine it was my bairns; a warnin fae Heaven that my Jancey and Teenie wad soon be taen awa. I could hardly wait or we got hame.'

'Ah weel,' Sarah continued, 'Teenie died in the mornin, my poor wee Teenie, and never opened her een for me at the last. The doctor said Jancey had consumption; tuberculosis he called it, and she didna last lang efter Teenie. Aye, poor Jancey, she had a hoast like an auld roosty pump, and never stoppit yarkin fae daylicht tae dark. She lived only twa days efter Teenie died. I took her on my knee tae gie her a doze o Ipecacuanha wine and the poor thing never got it doon. She choked in my airms and turned blue in the face. I thumpit 'er back tae get her breath back but it was nae eese. Next meenit she was deid. We had a double funeral. Poor Jancey and Teenie; Janet and Christian was their real names but the ither bairns could never get their tongues roon't.'

'My poor Jancey and Teenie,' Sarah sobbed, 'my twa wee angels. They were too good for this world. Efter yon nicht in Lachbeg Wuds I can believe they are in Heaven. Yon twa angels were waitin tae tak them hame!'

I Wadna be a Loon Again

Every mornin at five sharp Knowie came up the stone stair at the back and rapped with his knuckles on my chaumer door. 'Are ye waukened lad?' he cries, waiting for an answer. I could have seen him in Purgatory but I says 'Aye aye!' and slid out of bed, cold as a seal on an iceberg. I had to light the old paraffin lamp where it hung on the wall, shell-backed and leaking, to let me see to put my clothes on, although the rest of the steading was lit by electricity, generated on the premises.

Down in the byre Knowie fed the kye with draff and bruised corn while I mucked them out with barrow and shovel. He scrubbed their hind-quarters with a long-handled broom, dipping it in a pail of cold water as he went along. The cows swished their lithe bushy tails in my face, sprinkling my neck and bare arms with cold icy drops, which soon shook me out of my sleep.

Twenty-four cows stood in a single row, heads to the wall, tails on the greep, licking their food out of rough-faced cement troughs. Drinking bowls were not then in existence so there was a water cistern at the far end of the byre; fodder barn and turnip shed at the other.

At 5.30 am Knowie's wife and two daughters came in for the milking. They brought their cans and pails from the dairy and took down their stools from a shelf. They sat down, each one to a cow, and very soon they had brimming pails between their knees, spurting the hot milk into the rising froth in rythmic, steady jets, plop-plop, plop-plop . . .

All this time young Knowie had been feeding the horses and mucking out the stable, his own pair and my odd horse, old Bud, a proper bitch with teeth and hoof; dark brown with white rings in her eyes, and her ears mostly flat back on her mane: 'ringle een an her lugs in the howe o her neck,' as they say, and supposed to be a sure sign of equestrian temperament.

Aleck was foreman on the place, but folks behind his back just called him young Knowie, sometimes with a bit of a sneer, 'cause the folk at the Knowehead were a bit stuck-up they said, and young Knowie was the glowerin image o his auld man, but less high-minded.

We went into breakfast, Aleck going first, him bein foreman at the Knowehead, and his auld man liked him to have his thumb on the sneck o the kitchen door at the hour appointed. Knowie came in after us to wash and shave for the milk round. While we slubbered away at our brose and cream he laid off about the work that had to be done in the forenoon, a screed as lang as a kirk sermon, and it made denner time seem an affa distance awa. When his back was turned Aleck gave me a wink. 'We'll jist dee what we've time for!' says he, sort of under his breath, for he was still a bit feared at his old man, him bein only a haflin.

But I was heartened by the label on the syrup tin, which read: 'Out of the strong came forth sweetness!' And there was a swarm of bees bizzin round the carcase of a lion that the mighty Samson had slain with his bare hands.

After breakfast we laced our boots by the kitchen range and stytered out in the darkness to the stable. We were supposed to kaim the horse but we knew that old Knowie was at his porridge so we lay down among the straw in the spare stall. I had a bit blow at my pipe and Aleck lit a fag, never saying a word to spoil it, but each one enjoying his own thoughts. Then we fell asleep. The next thing we hears is the purr of the lorry and the rattle of milk cans, which was Knowie loading up for the town.

We sprang to our feet and grabbed a brush and comb, nipped up beside a mare and banged away at the travis posts. The noise was enough to frighten the rottans off the rafters and Knowie fair thocht he had a pair of gallant grooms. Sometimes he took a bit keek into the stable with a last minute order but never once did he catch us on the straw. Then he got into the lorry cab and slammed the door.The headlights swung round and searched out the trees in the avenue, whining down to the main road.

The women had finished the milking and gone to the farmhouse (while we were asleep) for there was no cooling system to scutter with in those days, and the milk went into the cans warm from the cow's udders.

Aleck harnessed his pair, 'Flo' and 'Tib' for the plough, while I went back to the byre to finish the work of the morning. I fed the cows with neeps and hay, mucked out the byre again and bedded them down with fresh clean straw. I gave each cow a drink in a bucket from the cistern at the end of the byre; honest, I did, every cow, for I've heard of the lad who poked his finger in the cow's eye when she wanted a drink, and a pailful went a long way - the thing is that you put the water in the cow, not in the can. Then I splashed and scrubbed the greep with Knowie's long-handled broom.

When rosy dawn began to tint the east I opened the big sliding door on the dung court and turned the twenty odd heifers out to winter pasture. I then went to the stable to harness old Bud for the cart, driving home turnips till dinner time.

I had to stand on my toes to force the hard leather collar over Bud's stubborn head, upside-down to get it over her bulging eyebrows, then swivel it round on the narrowest part of her neck. You had to have an extra spoonful of meal in your brose for this job, and I've known some lads having to stand on a box, or the 'corn leepy' aye, even grown men, to manage it. Another tussle was getting your saddle off the saddle-tree high up on the wall, when you carried it on your head to your mare's back, then fastened the belt under her belly; and even at this you had to be careful, or Bud would bite or kick your backside, which ever way you bent down. But as I was of fair average height I managed these jobs on my feet, so that nobody could look down their nose at me, or take me to the 'chaff hoose' where you shook hands with the devil, and then you could do almost anything with a horse, or so they said.

But the first morning I tried to collar Bud she backed out of the stall and bolted from the stable. She meant to take me all round the parish at her heels, but I got her on to the sharn-midden, where she floundered to the belly, and I had no more ado than halter her. She meant to sit on the warm muck till dinner time, but I stuck a whin bush under her tail and she soon changed her mind about that.

After that I always closed the stable door before I tackled Bud. I tried another way: I put the saddle on first, which meant I didn't have to loosen her halter chain, but she leaped into the forestall, and the saddle went slithering over her back and fell on the cobble-stones among the dung. One of her fore feet got stuck in the manger and she was standing on three legs. I took advantage of the situation to get the saddle on, but I couldn't manage the collar in this position. I removed the halter and eased Bud's foot out of the forestall, but she sprang backwards out of the stall and ran back and forth in the stable, from one end to the other, while I tried to corner her to get the collar on. This time she nearly had me in tears. She finished up in the wrong stall, and I had to carry the harness piece by piece - collar, haimes, britchen, bridle and reins from the other end of the building. Fortunately the saddle remained on her back, and prance as she would she couldn't get rid of it.

Bud had sharp teeth and quick hoofs that went with her bad temper. She knew that I was only a loon and she wouldn't have tried it on with a grown man, not with those 'strappin chiels' who knew the horseman's word, and all that stite.

Knowehead bein a 'three-horse place', Bud had never worked with another beast as a 'pair' but always as the odd horse, and always handled by a loon, so that I was only another in a long succession of loons whom she had taken the size of, for she was a wily beast was our Bud.

When there was ice on the roads I had to take the mare's fetlocks between my knees from behind, as the blacksmiths did, and hammer spikes into the holes in her iron shoes. At nightfall I had to chisel them out again, or have her stand all night on her stilettoes, which was what she deserved. That frosty mornin I went to the toon without spikes or 'sharps', as they were sometimes called, Bud went slithering down the Broadgate like a new born calf on a wet greep.

Knowie supplied some of the town carters with quantities of hay and straw, and I had to take this through their narrow pends and low arches, terrified that Bud got stuck with a load in a pend, and besides this I had to take the occasional load of corn to the granary, ten sacks to the load.

When mother fee-ed me off as a loon she never knew what she was letting me in for with our Bud at the Knowehead.

And there was that great muckle stone at the cart-shed door. It was so important I should have carried it around on my watch-chain, yet it was all I could do to heave it into the cart. Knowie had told me about the stone at the cartshed door the night he fee-ed me in the parlour, the only time I had ever been ben the hoose; and I was never likely to see the parlour again, unless I married one of Knowie's dothers, and there was small chance of that, because that verra nicht he made me promise that I wouldn't try to sleep with the lassies. He said it in a jocular sort of way, if you could say that Knowie was capable of a joke.

After this, and when he made me swear that I didn't wet the bed, and that I didn't carry lice, he told me what I had to do with the stone at the cart-shed door, as you shall see.

Bud had a habit of bolting out of the cart at lowsing time, before the shafts were clear of her back, so I had to put the stone in the back of the cart before I loosened the chains on the haimes and britchen. I kept hold of the reins and held Bud by the bridle while I tipped up the shafts with my free hand, and then the stone tilted the balance and lifted the shafts clear of the mare's back. She pranced about and chewed on the iron bit impatient to have it over, but no harm was done.

This was something that Bud was really afraid of. She had probably been held in a cart and got a fright as a young mare and never got over it. But I can hardly imagine our Bud on the psychiatric couch and the vet probing her sub-conscious mind.

Then, one evening, I forgot to put the stone in the cart, and when I tilted the shafts they came down again on Bud's back. She lurched forward and sprang in the air, wrenching herself free of the cart and its trappings. I couldn't hold her and everything snapped; a britchen sling caught on a shaft hasp and swivelled the saddle under her belly - one more leap and Bud was free, and the cart shafts clattered on the ground.

Bud made a run for the stable door, where she stood in a tremble, the saddle still upside-down under her belly, and a trail of broken harness behind her. Knowie came running from the byre, where he had heard the mischanter. 'Ye're gettin a bittie over-confident wi that beast!' says he, looking at the bits of harness trailing behind her, and no doubt thinking of the saddler's account for mending it. 'Aye man, a bittie careless. Ye had forgotten on the steen ah doot! Better see and nae lat it happen again!'

I suppose his attitude would have been the same though I had been crippled for life, for he never so much as asked if I had been hurt. That mare could have killed me, a fifteen-year-old loon, for it was a man-sized job to handle her. The insurance lads wouldn't stand for it nowadays. Twice she had nearly split my knee-cap with an iron heel, doubling me up with pain and sickness, and she bit my shoulder when I went up with her corn feed. She bit the hand that fed her, our Bud, and mother saw the marks of her teeth on my bare skin when I changed my sark at the weekend.

Once a week I went to the railway station for a load of draff as cow feed. It wasn't bad really on a fine morning, seated on the fore shelvin of the cart, looking down on Bud's broad mobile back as she swung down the brae, her white fetlocks swinging under the cart, while she shook her head and snorted the hay-seed out of her nostrils.

At the station I had to queue with about thirty other carts until my turn came for loading up with my shovel from a wagon. It was an occasion of great bustle and rivalry, each man trying to get his horse backed to a wagon when another drew away. But first you had to pass over the weigh-bridge to let the station clerk get the tare of your cart. Some of the men had two carts, belonging to the larger farms, and sometimes they had to leave a horse standing bye while they loaded the other. Bein the loon I had to nip in somewhere at the risk of getting my lug clapped, or I wouldn't be home or dinner time.

Some of the lads had high-piked haimes and harness beetle-black, chains and buckles shining, while others had harness as grey as the road and carts that hadn't seen paint or a wash for mony a year and day.

Bud didn't like the trains, and if the engine-drivers were banging the trucks about I had to keep the reins within reach while I was in the wagon. Not that I could have held Bud had she bolted, but it was a pretence that I was doing my best in the circumstances. And if a passenger train came thundering in you certainly had to hang on to the reins; what with the great hiss of white steam, the banging of carriage doors, the waving of flags and the hub-bub of voices Bud's head was in a whirl. The engine on the down train always stopped near the siding and before leaving again the driver blew the whistle for devilment, a piercing shriek that sent the horses neighing and prancing at the wagons. He got a lot of fist-waving from the fairm lads but he didn't care a damn, for he was soon out of their reach in belching steam.

I filled and trampled my cart with steaming draff, hot from the distillery vats, and for one day in the week my feet were warm enough.

I led Bud over the weigh-bridge and propped up the shafts with the resting-pole to get a better reading, just enough to slacken the backchain in the saddle-crup (for I knew Bud's tricks) while the clerk adjusted a sliding marker on a metrical bar, figured in brass and swinging with the load on the platform, and then he checked my gross weight in his notebook.

Once clear of the station (making sure there wasn't a train going under the bridge when I crossed it) I got on top of the cart and sat on a folded sack. Home at the Knowehead I backed Bud into the turnip shed and shovelled the draff into the feed box, where it was mixed with bruised corn, and then it was time to take Bud from the cart and get ready for dinner.

We were well enough fed at the Knowehead, a fork and knife almost every day, eating meat like the gentry, but the long hours of hard work between the meals made me frightfully hungry. By now I could have nibbled at the draff or a slice of swede turnip in the bye-going.

It seems strange to me now, sixty odd years later, that not a railway wagon remains at that once busy station, now overgrown with weeds and grass and the rails torn up from the siding. All the stir and excitement forgotten, and not a horse left in the district. If I was a loon now, and hadn't experienced it, I would never believe that such things had happened. It makes me feel very old to think that I have lived in an age now gone forever and almost forgotten. The pattern of farm life has changed so completely that I can scarcely believe I was once a loon and saw these things which now are only a memory.

There is a sweet sadness in the thought that I shall never be a loon again, and at the same time a gladness that I shall never again be subjected to the slavery of those far-off days. I am glad that times have changed and that life is easier now for a loon on the land. Even with the prospect of my whole life before me, as it was in those days, I wouldn't exchange my later years for renewed youth, not if going through all that drudgery again was the price I had to pay for it.

Lang Breeks!

Well well, it would be my last crack at Aunt Sally, there was no doubt about that. I had smashed a lot of her clay pipes in my time but this would be the last of it. I can see her twisted old mouth yet, her chalky face and apple-red cheeks, her coconut hair, her hat all askew from the whacks she got.

I would be fourteen the day after the school picnic and starting work with Auld Weelum Mackenzie of Fernieden. And besides, I was wearing my father's trousers, and taking a drag at his pipe on the sly. I was getting that big I was beginning to look down my nose at the old man, and I looked ridiculous in knee-length breeks. I had fine sturdy knees and I liked showing them off, but it just wouldn't do any more. I even asked for a kilt but mother said we couldn't afford it. But I think she was afraid of what the neighbours would say if I swanked about in a kilt, or that it would attract the girls prematurely, and then she'd be jealous.

I could still wear my socks with the coloured tops but nobody would see them under the old man's baggy trousers. First day I appeared in them at school the dominie fair sized me up. He had me out in the middle of the floor and walked round about me with his tongue in his cheek. I knew he wanted to take me down to size and making me look a fool in front of the class was one way of doing it.

He never did like me that dominie. I was always late and often absent and always seemed to rub him the wrong way.

'We don't keep cows in here,' he cried, one morning I came in late chewing a Cocksfoot grass; and perhaps next day I would be minus a legging, or I had fallen into a peat bog through looking at the clouds. Sometimes I thought I had a loose screw 'cause something always ticked in my head when I ran, but mother said it was that blow I got on the head from Uncle Simon with the fencing mallet. Not that he meant it, but by the time I got my hand up to feel the bump it was as big as an egg.

But I knew my history and my geography and my Julius Caesar, and I was the most voracious reader in the school, and for these reasons the dominie had to put up with me, though at times he showed his resentment. He was always threatening to 'go up in a blue flame,' and it was a sore disappointment to most of us that it didn't happen.

But he shook his big hairy-knuckled fist in my face and said I wasn't a man yet. He had red hairs on his knuckles, like I've seen on a crab's legs, and eyes like a cat in a rabbit trap. Even the girls resented him. They said his wife had a dog's life and most of us believed it.

But my long trousers fair needled him. 'I'll take you on ten years after this,' he said, his toothbrush moustache bristling red. 'If you would only come to school man, maybe I could make something of you. You have the makings of a scholar but you are a truant lout. You should be thrashed! Maybe your father isn't big enough to do it but by God I am. Get back to your seat and sit very quiet or I'll really get mad.'

If he hadn't been such a tyrant maybe I'd have gone to school more often. But I wasn't afraid of him. Not a bit of it. So I was late as ever and stayed away when it suited me. He pinched my cheeks for it with his vice-grip thumbs and I felt like taking a swipe at his shins. And I couldn't help being the biggest boy in the school; trouble is I haven't grown an inch since then and my poor old father's trousers would still fit me.

But my old man had his faults as well. For years he had complained about my indolence and 'mischief,' with emphasis on the 'chief' in mischief. Well of course I played truant, and the old man had just had his last warning from 'the wheeper-in,' in other words the Officer of Education, that unless he kept me at school he would be run in.

I ran on the old man's bicycle, smoked his pipe, wore his Sunday sark, threw stones, fired arrows, kissed the girls - what was the old man to do?

And damnit he was glad of me too. He was chauved to death in the byres and I ran home from school and sliced his turnips, carried straw, swept up; I even took his place for a fortnight when he was off with 'flu, so he could hardly hit a lad that did that for him - well, not often.

But I had talent that the old man couldn't see; gifts that might have landed him on easy street had he given me some encouragement. I was publishing my own monthly magazine of short stories (hand-written, of course) and sending them round the parish. I had begun a history of Roman Britain with illustrations that might have rivalled Gibbon's *Decline and Fall*. I was coming on as a strip cartoonist and poster artist and even the dominie had allowed me to design and paint the covers for the annual school magazines. He asked for a show of hands in my favour and it was unanimous.

I had the most unique puppet-theatre you ever heard of, all done with silhouettes and a wick lamp on a life-size screen; oncoming trains, stunting aeroplanes, ships at sea, sword fights, bathing beauties - the lot, and the neighbours used to give me threepence a time for a peep-show.

I built model herring drifters that floated on the miller's dam. I made a motor-coach, a binder, and a merry-go-round with swing chairs and painted ladies on the revolving panels. I could make almost anything from cardboard, a handful of pins and water colours. I had to because nobody could afford to give me toys. Anyway, I didn't want a mecanno set or a fretwork outfit because that was someone else's ideas. I wanted to be original and invent my own playthings. But a magic lantern at this stage would have been a real blessing.

I had a standing army of one hundred soldiers, every one a cardboard cut-out equipped and decorated with pencil and paint brush, even Highlanders in kilts. Sometimes I had a war, when I opened up on them with my pea-cannon, and the side left with most troops upright were the victors, and I coloured another part of the map red for a British victory, green, mauve or purple for an imaginary foe.

Compared with this as a geography lesson stamp collecting was a bore and I never touched them. But the old man frowned on my exploits: 'Ye'll get plenty o that when the time comes!' says he.

All this activity made me late for school. I sat up till after midnight preparing my shows; painting my posters, writing my magazine serials, sketching my cartoons. I had a camera-eye for detail on my silhouettes. I could give my patrons a girl's face in close-up even to the eyelashes. A budding Mack Sennett I was when it came to spring-board diving. While my old man snored in the box-bed I was immersed in my late night studies. Sometimes on Fridays I read all night and went to bed when he rose.

What could the dominie teach me anyway? Geometry maybe? Algebra? Mathematics? A dreary lot, subjects probably that I would never have need for, not even as mental exercise 'cause I had plenty of that.

The dominie bored me and I disliked the brute. I had far more important things to learn than he could teach me. I was mad about Haley's Comet for instance and he never even mentioned the Solar System. And anyway when he asked the class a question I had my hand up first. And I could sketch a rough map of the world without a copy. I had read most of the books in the J. & P. Coates' library. The dominie even gave me a prize for general knowledge, second for gardening - gardening, heavens!

But nothing short of an earthquake or a tidal wave could get me up in the morning. I had to run all of three miles to school on a jammy piece, through wet fields and over the moor, my books in a bundle under my arm, sometimes my slate when home to be scrubbed, never a moment to spare.

The only morning I got up early was to watch a total eclipse of the sun. I was up at six with my father to get it on show for my newsreel - a device I used that William Friese-Green would have shook my hand for.

I might have been a Walt Disney, a Beaverbrook, a Sam Goldwyn, a Bernard Shaw - but the old man had never heard of these men. They were only shadows, he said; they had no substance, they existed only on paper - never make a living that way lad!

The only people the old man knew were those that slaved their guts out for the neighbouring farmers. He could see these men, he could talk to them, he didn't have to go boring his head into books to find out what they had to say. He lived in a narrow world the old man and he couldn't read a book anyway, nor even write his name, or count his pay, not without mother looking over his shoulder to see that it was right.

Somebody said to the old man that that loon o his could be on the stage yet. 'Him on the stage!' said the old man, 'none o that for him; I had tae work afore his day and he'll hae tae dee the same. Na, na, he's nae gaun tae loaf aboot idle when he leaves the skweel!'

100

I don't blame the old man really but that was his philosophy. And when I started sending my stories to an editor and they came right back he really had me licked.

'Nivver mak money that wye ma loon, nae wi a pincil ahin yer lug - wark is the only sure wye tae mak a livin; ye'll jist hae tae work like the rest o us.'

Maybe I could make my own way in the world. But what could I do without money, without influence, in my old man's trousers? And for once he had the old woman on his side. She didn't understand me either but I couldn't leave her, not without her blessing anyway.

Nobody understood me, or cared - and why should they? I was such an eccentric oddity, neurotic almost.

But there was still Auntie Sally and the school picnic. And there was this job with Auld Weelum Mackenzie of Fernieden. So I gets up on my toes and looks straight down my blower at the old man, real stern like, to make him look like a twirp, and I tells him flat I'm just not going to work on the farms. It was cheek I know, but a fellow has to put his foot down, even if he tramples his own toes in the process.

The Loon's First Fee!

So it was all settled 'Siven powin,' mither had said before we left the hoose, 'nae a penny less ! The loon's fourteen and he's worth that tae ony fairmer; aye, and mair, come tae that!'

So I went with my father down through the fields to see old Weelum Mackenzie of Fernieden, the three-horse farm among the trees at the foot of the Berryhill. Somebody had told my old man that Weelum was looking for an orra loon tae sort the nowt and work the odd mare, old Bloom.

It was a fine June evening as we strode through the lush pasture, thrashing the white petals from the wet daisies, moistened with dew, so that they stuck to our black tackety boots like confetti at a wedding. We went down through the nowt, newly out from the byres, plucking at the fresh spring grass with their hard tongues, the sunhaze on their backs, too busy and content to bother us. The startled larks sprang up from their nests and sang above our heads, perhaps to distract us from their eggs and young. The peesies wheebled from the newly sprung cornfields, frightened at our approach, while the oyster-catchers were gossipping and running hither and thither on the greening turnip drills.

I was a bit flustered at the prospect of starting work on my own. I wasn't too keen and I had tried various ways to get out of it; away from the grun, the dubs and the sharn and the stink. Yet here I was on my way to get a chain round my neck like a stirk in a stall and earn my penny fee.

Old Weelum was in the farm close, throwing corn to the hens from a pail around the barn door. He saw us at the gate and laid down his pail and came to meet us.

'Aye aye Charlie,' addressing my father, 'that's a fine nicht.'

'Aye, it is man,' replied my old man, 'this'll fairly bring on the neeps tae the hyowe.'

'Aye, jist the thing man.'

Old Weelum then looked me up and down and stroked his stubbly chin, crinkling his blue eyes in a friendly smile. Not that I was a stranger to old Weelum, for I ran through his parks every day to the school, sometimes calling in bye for young Weelum to keep me company, though mostly it was an excuse to save me going round by the road.

'Ye've brocht the laddie wi ye Charlie, I see.'

'Oh aye, we heard ye wis needin a loon tae sort the nowt and work the orra beast and thocht he micht suit ye.'

'Jist that Charlie, jist that man.' And Weelum pushed his cloth cap to the back of his grey head. 'Weel I hinna fee-ed onybody yet. I was jist waitin tae see gin I could get a loon leavin the skweel at the simmer holidays. The last lad we had was gettin owre big and needin mair wages than I could affoord tae pey. That's jist the wye o't ye see: efter ye learn 'em tae work they jist up tail and aff tae somebody else for mair siller. That's jist the wye o't man.'

Now I happened to know that the last loon hadn't been 'socht tae bide' because he had taken old Weelum's pocket-book from his jacket in the turnip shed, where Weelum had left it when he came home from the mart. In fact he was going to hash some neeps for the nowt and help the loon in the byre when his wife called him in for his tea. When his back was turned the loon put his hand in his maister's pooch and took the wallet. It contained £70 that Weelum had gotten for twa-three stirks at the market, paid in cash, and the loon thocht he had stumbled on a gold mine. Weelum got the bobby but it took them three days before they could get the loon to admit he took the money, and when finally cornered he handed it back. But it was a lesson for old Weelum, who had always trusted everybody, and after that he got a cheque book from his banker. I also knew that the last loon had been careless with Bloom when she bolted with a cart and smashed it, and it cost Weelum more than the loon's fee to repair the cart. Maybe the loon couldn't help it but I would bear it in mind if I had to work old Bloom. But Weelum never spoke ill of anybody and we heard nothing of all this from him.

My old man still had his hands in his trouser pockets. 'Fit wages wid ye be offerin?' he asked, looking bashful-like at old Weelum.

'Lat's hear ye Charlie. Fat dae ye think yersel?'

'Fit aboot siven powin Weelum?' And Weelum pursed his lower lip over his moustache, trying to make up his mind.

'Ye're jist stiff eneuch Charlie: ye see there's a month gaen by the term or the laddie leaves the skweel. That means siven powin for the five months till Martinmas, and that's mair than I was coontin on. Mind he winna hae a sair job and he'll be weel treatit in the hoose. We a' feed thegither in the kitchie and he'll get what's agyaun amang the rest o's.'

'Aye aye, I ken that Weelum. I wasna thinkin aboot that. But mind he's nae a greenhorn; he's been a lot wi me in the byre up bye, and he kens aboot the beasts.'

Weelum rolled a pebble with his toe, thinking aboot the loon's experience 'up bye,' as Charlie had put it, amang the nowt beasts.

'Fat wad ye say tae sax powin ten Charlie? Ten shillins less than ye socht - and mind he's comin tae a gweed hame: a cup o tay afore bed-time, sleepin in the hoose; man we dinna even rise in the mornin wi ither folk . . .'

'Weel it's like this Weelum: the gweed-wife said I wasna tae lat the loon awa for less than siven powin, that's the wye I'm sae thrawn!'

'Weel weel, but ye'll jist hae tae explain the thing tae her Charlie, maybe she never thocht on the five month instead o sax the laddie wad hae tae work. There's only ten shillins atween us and I think I'm bein fair eneuch. I have tae gie my foreman thirty powin for the sax month, and he can ploo or dae onything; cut corn, thrash, bigg rucks or fill the barn. Losh man, we only get fifteen bob for a quarter o corn, siven and saxpence the bag, it hardly peys tae ploo nooadays.'

At this moment the collie dog came out of the kitchen and began whacking my legs with his friendly tail. I bent down to fondle his silken head for Roy and I had met before in quite unusual circumstances. Weelum's face was a map of spidery wrinkles, smiling as he watched us, loon and dog. What he didn't know was that until lately I was terrified of dogs, even of Roy here, and that not so long ago, when I tried to saw down a tree for mither's fire in the wood above Fernieden, Weelum's collie came and watched me with his teeth bared. I was half through the small tree and loth to leave it and yet terrified of the dog. I tried to shoo him away but he just stood there and snarled, while I thought of some way of getting rid of him. Then I had a brain wave, so I ran home to mither and asked where was the bone that we had in the broth for Sunday? She said it was in the midden, and what would you be wantin with a dead bone anyway? I said never you mind, trying to hide my cowardice, then ran to the midden for the bone and carried it to the wood on the Berryhill. I had hoped that Roy would be gone by the time I got back. But no, for there he sat, still watching the tree, bewitching it almost, you would have thought, his head to one side, my saw sticking in the rut. Perhaps the dog had more wit than I thought and knew I would be back. Anyway I tossed him the bone and he ran away with it quite contentedly, while I felled my tree and got it into lengths for carrying, for I was more afraid of that dog than I was of the gamekeeper, gun and all.

But now Roy and I were friends and we both watched while the two men bargained for my services.

'A' richt Weelum, we'll jist tak it: sax powin ten as ye said; and as the loon disna need an insurance card till he's sixteen that'll save ye anither powin. And fa kens he could be somewye else or that time. But we winna fecht aboot ten shillin's gin ye treat the laddie weel.'

'Nae fear o that Charlie, nae fear o that. We'll get on jist grand. Won't we loon?' And he crumpled my battered cap on my head with his work-grained hand.

When we returned home mither was darning a sock on the tattie-chapper, though she sometimes used a ladle, the wooden chapper inside the sock to stretch it, the wool in her lap, her fingers busy with the needle.

My old man hung his sweaty cap on a rusty nail at the back of the inner door and sat down beside her at the fireside. 'We couldna get siven powin woman,' he said, 'ye forgot the laddie has still a month at the skweel efter the term, and aul Weelum Mackenzie wadna pay for his schoolin.'

'So I did,' said mither, biting through the woollen thread with her teeth, 'I forgot aboot that. A' the same the hungry brute could of gien the loon the siven powin. It'll hardly keep claes on his back onywye. He needs a decent suit for a start, and that'll tak aboot fower powin; forbyes underclaes, socks and sheen, and he'll need a waterproof for comin hame on a rainy nicht. You men folk dinna ken whaur the money goes and as little ye care. Hagglin aboot ten shillins.

If I'd kent that I wad a fee-ed the loon masel!'

And so it was agreed, and in four weeks' time, when the school picnic was over, and I had bombarded the last Aunt Sally of my schooldays, and broken a few more clay pipes in her mouth, and the dominie had pinched my cheeks for the last time on the day after my fourteenth birthday I would begin work as a fee-ed loon with old Weelum Mackenzie of Fernieden, picking the sprouts from the tatties at an earth-pit round the back of the steading. Looking back I must have been awfully anxious to start, because it was a Saturday (a whole day of course) thinking to have a break on Sunday before tackling a full week.

Rowena Takes a Holiday

There was no kitchiedeem at Whunden. Auld Hosey Rankin said he couldna afford sic luxury. And no wonder when you thought of the bills he had to pay yon Dr. Dalzell who called once a fortnight in his Rolls Royce to examine his wife. Bathia Rankin was a cripple, maybe for life you might say since she fell down the loft stair with a pail of hen feed some years back, stone steps with an iron railing at the gable of the barn. Folk said she could have broken her neck or her back, never mind a broken thigh, which was bad enough for Bathia Rankin, cut down in the flower of life, in the midst of her child-bearing, still with a spark of life in her, and good for a man to look upon. Now she hobbled about on a stick and yon Doctor Dalzell said her hip couldn't be mended; but maybe he just didn't want to lose a good patient, because the guinea a time he charged for his visits helped to pay for those expensive cigars that he smoked. Bathia said that he never looked at the blue patch on her thigh, or even touched it, just stared at her white legs when the blankets were down, as if the sight of them did him a power of good.

And there was old Rowena, Hosey's spinster sister, who had lived most of her life with the family, ever since she had been jilted by yon scoundrel who had married her sister, though maybe Rowena was better off without him from what you had heard from folks out bye. But bein denied bairns o her ain Rowena had lavished affection on the geets at Whunden, young Hosey yonder and his two small sisters, Tess and Lena, spoiling them till they were speaking back to their parents long before their time.

So, as a fee-ed loon at Whunden one of the first jobs you got was scrubbing the flagstone floor in the kitchen, which was hardly what you was fee-ed for, but seein there was no kitchiedeem, and with Chae Cantlay that was foreman milking the kye, and old Hosey feeding the hens and the swine, it seemed that the loon was the only body that could be spared for it, besides picking the sprouts off the tatties, and it was better than that.

You might have said that with Rowena about the place there was no need for a servant quine, and maybe that was so when Rowena was younger; but now she was too old and too fat for floor scrubbing. So, if the sky was overcast, or the fog-horn moaning on the coast like a cow at the calving, neither a day for hay or harvest field, Rowena would rig you out with a sack or harn apron, a bar of Sunlight Soap, a pail of warm water and a scrubber, and you'd get down on your knees at the fireplace and scrub your way out at the back kitchen door.

And if it was a van day you had to hide under the kitchen table until the

106

baker or the grocer or the butcher had gone. 'Jist in case he comes in bye,' Rowena would say, 'we dinna want a' the countryside tae ken we have the loon washin oot the kitchie fleer!' And you'd get a big jammy piece and a bowl of creamy milk for this obligement, and maybe a slab or two of Rowena's home-made toffee.

'And noo laddie, if you'd jist run tae the stack for a basket o peats for the kitchie fire; my auld legs are that wobbly they'll hardly carry me ... and if you'll jist ca the deuks in frae the dam for fear they lay awa in the mornin. Losh aye. God bless ye laddie, ye're a great help in the hoose.'

And so Rowena buttered you up no end, until old Hosey stuck his rosy face into the kitchen and said the sky had cleared: 'God aye,' says he, 'there's a clear bore in the wast, abeen the swines' hoose; I think we'll hae a go at the hey!'

Rowena's room was fitted with a coal burning grate, so that peat was of little use to her, except when she ran out of coal, and then she would waddle over to the stack at the gable of the steading and fill her lap with black stickly peats, picking the best and avoiding all the big foggie divots that would burn better in the big kitchie grate under the swey. Rowena would then come panting back to the kitchen door, one chilblained hand holding the corners of her bulging apron, the other clutching the door jamb, while she heaved her huge bulk up the steps to the passage, ben the lobby to her ain room, warm and cosy, where she slept with the twa quines, Tess and Lena.

Rowena did most of the cooking over the peat fire in the kitchen, where her pots hung from the crooks on the swey, producing juicy clootie-dumplings and sago pudding that was sheer delight for a hungry loon, and rolly-polly made with a clart of rhubarb jam. And she could bake oat breid on her girdle with the best of them, besides scones and bannocks, and if she got you to yark at the long-handled churn for a while she'd make butter, though you couldna thole the buttermilk she offered you to drink in reward for your labour. And sometimes at night she'd pour a suppie rennet in the warm milk when Chae brought it in from the byre and next day you'd get yerned milk for dessert, which was a fair delight with a sprinkling of sugar, and whiles she'd let the milk curdle and make a hangman cheese, hanging it outside on a nail in the wall for nearly a week or it dried and hardened, though in hot weather she had to herd it against the blue-bottle flies that were attracted to the smell of it, and had a fancy to hatching their maggots through the gauze cloth.

The long bare table was scrubbed till the grain stuck out on the wood. It stood in front of the kitchen window and Rowena sat at the end nearest the door. It was furthest from the fire but in daylight it enabled Rowena to keep an eye on the farm road while she ladled out the broth or tattie-soup or handed round the plates of stovies. Spark the collie lay under the table, whacking your toes with his bushy tail, and between his barks and Rowena's quick eye you were soon aware of strangers in the farm close. Between them they could detect Doctor Dalzell's shining Rolls nearly a mile away, and Rowena would warn Bathia of his approach, and Bathia would hirple along the lobby and shed her clothes before he arrived, Rowena holding him up with some tittle-tattle at the door.

'He's a torment of a mannie that,' Rowena would say, when he had gone ben the hoose, 'ye never ken whan he's comin, and for all the good he does he could stay away. But he never forgets tae send in his account though, na faith ye!' And she would spoon out the semolina pudding with great gusto, licking the spoon between each plateful, while the plates were passed from hand to hand along the table, right up to Chae Cantlay at the end nearest the fireplace, the head of the table, him being foreman, where he sat under a coloured painting of Burns at the plough.

Ben the hoose Bathia had hardly got her breath back when the doctor had her by the pulse. 'You've been out of bed again,' he snapped, squinting at his wrist watch; you'll never get better at this rate, you'll have to rest that leg.' He whipped down the blankets and looked at her legs, but never fingered the blue patch on her thigh. 'It's here that it's sore!' Bathia ventured, caressing her swollen hip with her long fingers. 'I know where it's sore woman; but what's the good of that when you won't do what you're told? Maybe we could get a clasp in there if you gave it half a chance to get the swelling down and get rid of the inflamation.' Bathia winced under his withering gaze and pulled up the bed-clothes. 'But I don't want a clasp,' she whimpered, 'and I don't want to go to hospital; maybe it will heal with time.' 'Very well woman, have it your own way, but it will take an eternity and you haven't that time to spare.' 'You mean I could die, doctor?'

'No no, you won't die woman; but unless you allow us to operate on that hip of yours you could be a cripple for the rest of your life!' And with that final warning Doctor Dalzell picked up his bag and snapped out of the room.

Rowena was waiting for him at the kitchen door, beaming like a full moon over the harvest stooks; but before she could say anything Doctor Dalzell cut her short with a curt 'Good day!' put on his hat and departed, sweeping out of the muddy farm close in his great shining car.

'Nasty brute,' said Rowena, seating herself again at the table.

The doctor wasn't more than a mile away when Bathia was back in the kitchen, her long black hair hanging down her back like a school-girl, and leaning on her stick. 'What did he say the day?' Rowena asked. 'Oh jist the usual,' Bathia sighed, 'I've got to stay in bed or it heals.'

'Ach,' Rowena scorned, 'Ye'll be there for a lifetime for all he knows or cares. You should hae been in hospital lang ago!'

'But ye ken I dinna want tae go tae hospital. He was speakin aboot a clasp for my hip the day; but I dinna want that . . . I'll manage fine.' Bathia sounded sure of herself, but the mist of tears in her soft brown eyes betrayed her.

Rowena handed her a plate of soup. 'But if it's for your own good woman, you should be thankful for that. Maybe it's your own fault that the doctor mannie says that your hip won't heal unless you rest it.'

Bathia couldn't sit down to her meals, so she sipped the hot soup standing in the middle of the floor, her staff hung on the back of a chair.

When Bathia had visitors she couldn't be bothered with the palaver of feeding them ben the hoose, mainly to save Rowena from extra work. So everyone was fed in the kitchen, be he factor or packman, and no matter what time of day you went into the old kitchie at Whunden the red enamelled tea-pot was never far from the peat ash, warm and full of welcome.

And when Bathia acted as hostess she leaned with her hand on the back of your chair, craning her neck over your shoulders and pressing her breasts into your back, spreading the trenchers of bread and cheese, scones and pancakes before her guests with her free hand, telling them to help themselves, while all the time her warm breath fanned the back of your neck and her long loose hair tickled your temples.

After dinner you went out with Chae to the stable while Bathia and Rowena had their nap before washing up. Bathia lay down on her leather-covered couch by the wall while Rowena sagged into her heavy armchair by the fireside. The bairns (when they weren't at school) went romping round the steading, playing 'hoosies' or 'beddies,' 'ring-a-ring-a-rosie,' 'hide-and-seek' or 'tackie roon the rucks'. But Chae barred the door to keep them out of the stable, for the quines liked to come and have a tease at you.

On Fridays everybody sat a whilie langer in the kitchie to get a bit squint at the *Broch Herald*. Chae had it first, him being foreman, for there might be a dance somewhere for him and his lass. Then you'd get a keek at it to see what was on at the Picture House, or at French and Shand's 'Empire' on the High Street. Bathia always read the Marriage, Birth and Death columns, and as she couldn't get peace to sit she read them standing in the middle of the floor. Old Hosey being only the farmer got a peep at the bit paperie last of all, maybe to see if anyone had a calf to sell or wanted to buy a few loads of neeps or hay, depending on what he had to spare, and then he would retire to his cubby-hole at the top of the stairs. Here he slept at night with his young son, leaving the big bed downstairs to his wife, because nowadays she said she couldn't be doing with anyone in the bed with her since she injured her thigh. She had to have room to spread her legs she said, because of the pain.

Now there was no chaumer at the Whunden, so you slept in the fairmhoose, in an upstairs bedroom with a storm window that looked on to the garden, just along the passage from Hosey's cubby-hole. At an antrin time in the night you could hear Hosey creaking down the stairs to his wife, pretending to go to the earth-closet at the foot of the garden, and giving the front door a bit kick with his big toe to convince you; but by the time he was away you knew fine he was up to something, and if you could stay awake long enough you could hear him come creaking back up the stairs again.

But all this had stopped and there seemed to be a quietness between Hosey and his ailing wife. She was much younger than Hosey and folk said she had married him for his siller, and the thocht of being a farmer's wife, pretending to be in the family way to get him, stuffing her briest with a pillow-slip, and that it served her right getting a broken hip joint for getting up to such a trick. Her father had been the blacksmith out bye in Haughfield yonder, and Bathia had plenty of lads before she met old Hosey at a 'Meal-and-Ale' down at the

109

Miller's place at Damneuk. And Hosey was glad to have the young limmer, bairn and all, had it materialised, for she was a lithesome change to his fat old sister at the Whunden. Some folk said it would be the death of him, but blind though he was in love old Hosey wasn't long in replacing the pillow-slip with something more substantial, and might have done even better had the randie not fallen down the loft stair. Something he found it harder to forgive than the pillow-slip affair - that had only been the bait, but now he had swallowed the hook as well he began to understand the meaning of misfortune.

And you would have thought for a time that there would be fireworks between the old dame and the young wife at the Whunden, but in this you were disappointed, for they took to each other like a cow with a mare's foal, never a natter between them; the old woman at her wash-tub and Bathia dawdling a bairn on her knee by the peat fire, a young Hosey Rankin to the very toe-nails, and Rowena was glad of it that they wouldn't die childless after all, and that there would be an heir to the Whunden.

After you had groomed a while at your roan mare, and Chae had taken the body brush to Rose and Sally, to put a bit shine on their hair, the pair of you lay down among the straw in the spare stall, listening to the chap of an iron hoof on the cobblestones, or the snort of a mare over her water pail, or maybe you was just dreaming that you had fallen in love and was likely to have a wet dream when you hears old Hosey rattling the sneck of the door at yoking time - 'Come and get a drap tay lads afore we start.'

Not that old Hosey ever started anything, for he dodged around real canny. But he was a good old soul compared with some you'd known, and never fussy about yoking on the dot, and always ready with a bowl of hot tea and a buttered scone when you came out of the neep park to sort the nowt, your feet cold and numb and your hands stinging with frost. There weren't many places where a loon got that sort of treatment, so you were better not to abuse it. 'Ye're nae use tae me wi a teem belly laddie,' Hosey would say, and you'd bite into the scone like you hadn't seen food for a fortnight.

Now like all other human creatures Rowena had her dull days: days when she sat listlessly in her chair, her feet and ankles encased in high-laced boots and crossed in front of her on a padded stool; her lower lip sagging like the stoup of a cream jug, the tired old eyes peering over her spectacles, which had slid down her nose, and her grey hair, uncombed and uncared for, hanging about her face like an old rug thrown upon a dyke.

When in this mood even the foreman had to speak twice to Rowena before she took any notice, and that was saying something because Chae Cantlay was a great favourite with Rowena, like she was his mother almost, and knew all about the quine he went about with, or when he wanted a sark ironed, and as Chae didn't have a mother and had been at the Whunden since he was a loon you began to wonder if old Rowena was a spinster after all.

'I wasna listenin Chae,' or 'I didna hear ye Chae,' Rowena would mumble, startled out of her reverie, moving her thick cracked lips and her dry tongue. But she made no attempt to start a conversation and fell back into her chair while you drank your tea in silence.

A stranger body might have thought that Rowena was in a sulk, or that someone had offended her, but Chae knew the old spinster better than most and he blamed the wag who had jilted her for her sister those long long years ago. Surely she had been a sonsie lass in her day and she earned your secret sympathy. You couldn't say that she was bonnie, jist sic like as your own granny, and yet old grandaw had married her.

But there were other days when Rowena was quite the opposite of despondent - days when she went about her tasks almost nonstop, her round jovial face bright and flushed with a resurgence of richer blood, her beady old eyes gleaming with mirth and her heavy mouth bursting with suppressed laughter. Even the bairns could sense her change of humour, and they would hang about her skirts hopefully, expecting peppermints or pandrops to be handed out forthwith, and this supplied she would 'hish' them off with a flap of her apron and a shake of her fist that sent them running for the door.

When Rowena slumped down in her chair at last a happy sigh escaped her, sometimes a grunt, as if she were an old sow who felt she had done her bit and had sunk down in her sty in restful contentment.

But Rowena was in the doldrums on the day that Bathia said to her: 'You should tak a holiday; I'll manage fine!' And come to think of it you had never seen either of these two women beyond the farm close, not even to the end of the cart road, because the vans brought all that they wanted and they did their shopping at the door. Old Hosey never had a motor car, or even a horse gig, and when he went to the marts to see his nowt sold he took the bus that went past the end of the road on market days.

So it was agreed that Rowena should have a holiday, when she would go and spend a fortnight with a married sister in the Broadsea, though not the one who had stolen her lad. Willie French sent a spanking horse and black cab out from the Broch to take her away, and everybody gathered round to see her off, Bathia and the bairns and old Hosey, while you watched with Chae from the stable door.

Rowena was dressed in her finest black and shining with sequins, a veiled hat to match and smelling strongly of mothballs. The driver assisted her into the cab, handed in her luggage and shut the door, like he was John Brown and she was Queen Victoria leaving Balmoral. John Brown climbed up to the dicky-board in front, took the leather reins in one hand and cracked his long whip with the other, and they were off, Rowena waving her silver-mounted umbrella handle from the carriage window, and Spark the collie barking at the highly polished wheels as they flashed silently out of the farmyard.

During the fortnight that Rowena was away you had to do other things besides floor scrubbing. For one thing you had to get down on your knees to whitewash the fireplace. Rowena usually whitewashed the arch twice a week and the low binks at the sides. The ironwork got rather more attention, especially if visitors were expected, when Rowena would get out her black-leading brushes and polish the lid of the ash-pit, the black swye that swung out on hinges above it, like a gate, and the huge black metal kettle that hung from the crook.

Last thing at night you had to 'rest' the peat fire, gathering all the embers together with the tongs and covering them with a shovel of ash from under the brander; and when you got up in the morning the fire was still a red glow, all you had to do was add more peat and blow the bellows, and you soon had the water boiling for the brose.

It was a slack period in the summer when you wasn't doing much in particular, and you had promised to help with the housekeeping until Rowena's return. Bathia would manage the cooking on her stick they said so you had to do most of the other chores. Up till then you had been scything yellow flowered tanzies and purple-headed thistles in the grass parks and old Hosey said he could spare you for a while. It was a job that wearied your legs and gave you nothing to think about and you almost welcomed the change, though it made you feel an awful Cissy working in the fairm hoose.

Bathia took to her bed occasionally, maybe a bit tired from hobbling about on her stick. Chae and old Hosey were in the fields most of the day, hacking with their hoes at the weeds in the turnip drills, and the bairns were at school, leaving you alone with Bathia in the old farm house, washing dishes and peeling potatoes.

Chae and Hosey had just gone to work and you was drying the dinner plates in the scullery when Bathia called to you from her downstairs bedroom, so you dried your hands on the towel and ran along the passage to see what she wanted.

Bein a loon you was a bit shy at going into the room where your mistress slept, but she told you not to be feart, that she was cold and wanted more fire put on. The room smelled strongly of scent and Bathia was in bed brushing her hair, her eyes strangely bright in her flushed face. Hosey had lit her fire in the morning but it had burned low. So you had a bit poke at the fire and put on a shovel of coal from the brass scuttle in the corner, besides some broken peat that was lying on the kerb. The lushness of the room made you feel a bit uneasy, you being a cottar bairn and little accustomed to anything more than the kitchen range: the thick red curtains on the window that looked into the farm close, the panelled wooden shutters fastened back to the walls, the wallpaper richly embossed and hung with coloured paintings, with expensive looking ornaments on the furniture.

But Bathia was watching you, where she lay on the four-poster bed, the hair-brush still in her hand, the tortoise-shell handle resting on the tasselled quilt. Her hair was down full length and hung about her shoulders in black mercurial strands, long enough to wrap around your neck, and Tess and Lena sometimes plaited it in two long ropes down her back, each standing on a kitchen chair while their mother leaned patiently with both hands on another. Lying there without her stick, her crippled body covered with blankets, you realised for the first excited moment in your young life that you were looking at a really beautiful woman; enough to make you blush and feel shy, especially so when she was your mistress. You was anxious to get back to your dish washing, but just as you meant to go she said she was thirsty and wanted a drink of water, while she reached over and laid the hair-brush on the small dressing-table at her bedside. So you brought the glass of water from the tap in the scullery and placed it in her hand. She took a small sip, hardly touching it, while her soft brown eyes wandered all over your face, pleading, beseeching, you knew not what, until she laid the tumbler on the dressing table. Then she asked if you would like to see her sore leg, but giving you little time to make up your mind about it she whipped down the blankets. You was fair astonished but couldn't help lavishing your eyes on her long white beautiful leg, her broad strong hip with the tiny blue veins running under the creamy softness of her skin, the first time you had ever seen such a sight. She took your nervous hand and placed it on her thigh, hot and soft and smooth and so exciting you didn't know where to look. She drew your hand across the bruise on her hip joint, which was rough and inflamed and slightly swollen. You was mesmerised and wanted to look but you was so afraid and bashful. Now she was pulling up her nightgown and you struggled to get your hand out of her grasp. Both her legs were now visible and she still held on to your wrist. You had no idea she was so strong, drawing your hand nearer her naked midriff, shameless in her strength of desire. Her head was rising from the pillow, pulling herself up with your wrist, until she had your knees against the bed, her free hand about your neck, her hot lips seeking yours, her eyes clear and beautiful. You couldn't have held out much longer, and would have fallen across her half-naked body, but suddenly she let you go and fell back on the pillow, pulling down her nightdress. She was breathing heavily, excitedly, and you saw the pulse beating madly in her neck. Her eyes had changed and were clouding with anxiety, staring at the door, at Doctor Dalzell standing there with hat in one hand and brown leather bag in the other. 'Well well,' he challenged, 'what have we here - another doctor ?' But he wasn't joking. His face was white and stern.

With Rowena on holiday and the collie in the fields the silent Rolls had slipped unnoticed into the farm close. Bathia was blushing all over and pulled up the blankets over her thighs. 'I was only showing the laddie my sore hip,' she whimpered, 'surely there was nae harm in that.' But you didn't listen for more and ran past the doctor out of the room.

You never learned how Bathia got out of her embarrassment, or how much the doctor had seen, and being your mistress you didn't want to affront her further by asking awkward questions. She never mentioned the incident again and you worked on together in the kitchen as though nothing had happened, though sometimes she singed the sago pudding, perhaps at the thought of it.

In the second week of Rowena's absence Lena took sick in the night, ben in Rowena's room, across the passage from their mother at the foot of the stairs. Bathia was up in her nightdress and whacking on the bannister with her staff. Would Hosey send the boy down to help her with Lena that was sick on the bed? So Hosey got up from his cubby-hole and roused you from your sleep in the bed beside Chae and sent you downstairs to Bathia, perhaps the opportunity she had been waiting for.

113

So you got a glass of water for Lena and cleaned up the vomit and sat a while with the girls on the bed, Bathia watching you from the door, her eyes bright as beacons. How could you escape? Caught between two young girls of seven and eight and a sex-crazed mother. Yet you felt that if she touched you you would scream. After all you was only a loon and no match for Bathia. But you wouldn't betray her, a good kindly woman who treated you well in every way, except in showing her weakness, and you were the guardian of that. But temptation and fear had you by the throat and you could hardly wait until the girls fell asleep again.

The Grandfather clock in the hall struck three o'clock; three musical chimes that were so much a part of the night that it scarcely disturbed the silence. Tess never stirred but Lena quivered in the twilight of slumber while you still sat quietly on the bed. Your breathing came faster and your throat dried up while you pondered what to do. Bathia still stood by the door, her face soft and radiant in the warm glow of the paraffin lamp, her hair clustered to the breasts of her pale-blue nightdress, staff in hand, guarding against your escape. It would be so easy to put your hand on her mouth, take the staff away from her and put her back to bed; yet there was a magnetism of excitement which drew you towards her, breaking down your resistance, your will to escape; something mystifying for which you could hardly wait, and even as you sat there on the bed you felt it would be a pity if Bathia ignored you, now that she had teased you up with an inward fire.

A cock crowed outside in the darkness, quite near at hand but it seemed far away, lost on the wind that sighed and moaned among the trees in the garden. Lena turned over on her other side and you screwed the lamp nearly to darkness. You was losing patience with the girl and Bathia had turned to a statue in the shadows. But at last Lena was in dreamland and you slid from the bed in your stockinged feet, blew out the lamp and tip-toed towards the door.

Bathia was waiting for you, barring your escape; afraid of what you would do - perhaps give her away; alarm the household, yet determined to risk it.

In a moment she had you in her arms, her hot blistering kisses raining on your lips; her writhing body warm against yours, her rich beautiful hair all over your face, and the sweet smell of her breath in your nostrils. You could hardly speak or cry out even if you had wanted to, so much was her lips upon your own. Your hands were everywhere, but mostly trying to push her away, though all the time you wanted to embrace her. But now you had no wish to escape and you could feel the warm shape of her in the darkness; a sweet blindness that dug your fingers into her warm flesh, thrusting your body against hers. Now she had you in her power, burning with a passion that was rising within you. In a moment you would be hers, far stronger than she imagined; a man on the instant that would surge upon her in uncontrollable lust . . .

But the fall of Bathia's stick on the floor sobered you in a moment. It fell with a crack and a clatter that was like a tree breaking in the wind; a loud snap that wakened Lena and stirred the household. Bathia let go of you at the sound and old Hosey's door creaked open at the head of the stairs.

114

'Oh aye, Lena's a' richt noo. We'll be back tae bed in a meenit or twa. Nae need for ye tae come doon. We'll manage fine!' Bathia spoke calmly, deliberately, restraining her words in her heavy breathing and a pounding heart.

Lena whimpered a little but soon fell asleep again. You picked up Bathia's stick and placed it in her hand. Once again she kissed you: gently this time, softly; like a kiss of goodbye, touching your lips with a warmth and sweetness that blotted out your boyhood. Then she hirpled towards her door, a crippling vision in the darkness, while you tip-toed up the stairs.

Soon you was back in bed again with Chae, careful not to waken him, though now you was cold and glad of his warmth. But you never slept a wink till morning, dreaming about Bathia. Day by day she was becoming more beautiful for you, more desirable; but she was a woman and you was only a loon.

But at last Rowena was back from the toon and you was almost disappointed at the sight of her. Bathia was much more exciting; younger by far and much more beautiful, and the fact that she was a cripple never bothered you, or that she was your master's wife. In such a world as yours anything could happen; even miracles, and maybe you could learn to be a doctor and cure her . . .

How had you got on in her absence? Rowena had asked, handing you a small present, a pipe or something. Oh jist grand you said, and nothing gave you any trouble at all.

Soon you was back in the parks with Chae, a drab scene compared with Bathia's charms; her sweet soothing kisses and her lithe body that was smooth and warm against your own. But now it was hairst and Chae in the swing of the scythe, slashing the ripe corn into a swath, while you gathered and bound it into sheaves. And Chae cursed you for falling behind, your thoughts far away - obsessed with an impossible dream. Now you was sulky and moody and disliked Rowena. You hated her for coming back and spoiling the most beautiful thing in your life. Nothing would ever be the same any more; discontent and desire wracking your wild thoughts. You had tasted of Eve's apple and wanted another bite. Now you knew what all that stite was about in the bible. Bathia's lips had been the apple, your apple; her arm the serpent, and you wished she had stung you more.

Rowena still dished out the food at mealtimes, licking the spoon between each plateful, perhaps as good as a kiss for any of you, but a poor substitute for Bathia's warm breath. Rowena was a likeable old spinster to say the least of her; a Friar Tuck of a woman who coddled Chae and the bairns. But for you Bathia was Queen of Sheba; Queen of all your little world, where she had launched a thousand sighs. But the best that you could wish for now was that next summer Rowena would take another long holiday . . .

Moonlight Flitting

As a married chiel it was never easy to get a cottar job on the Buchan fairms at the November or 'Martinmas' Term. It was never easy at any time to get decent wark but doubly so if you were looking for it in winter time. Married men always fee'd at the May or 'Whitsun' Term, once a year, but a single chiel could change his job at November if he wished. But as a single billie you had only your kist to move, whereas a married bloke had to shift all his bits of furniture, mostly on to horse carts fitted with harvest frames, wife and bairns and chaff beds, crockery and dishes, pots and pans and the baking girdle, cat or dog and the loons' rabbits, and maybe even a jar of tadpoles that the quines wouldn't leave on the window sill. Sometimes the cats took scare at flitting time and were nowhere to be found on the Term morning, so it was best to fasten them into a box the night before, just as you cooped the hens, for it always broke some bairn's heart to leave a pet cat behind. And you had to be careful to put the wife's pot flowers into the wash tubs on the back of the second cart, for if you placed them on the first cart the horse beast coming behind would maybe eat them down, especially if he had a fancy for geraniums, despite the bit between his teeth. Bicycles, prams and clothes props were another problem and the worst you'd seen was a pair of breeks on the back of the second cart and the man's braces trailing on the road. Of course you had been packing your stuff into boxes for weeks, and all that remained on the eve of the Term were a few cups and teaspoons, a jar of treacle, a half-loaf, milk and sugar and the tea-pot; even the beds had been dismantled and you had a 'shakie doon' on the fleer, lying on a chaff mattress and the curtains down from the windows, waiting for the cock crow and the early sound of horse carts on the Term morning.

Most cottars were on the road at the May Term, moving from place to place, seeking pastures new, maybe a bit more money or just a change of job; from driving a pair of horses to sorting nowt, or the other way round. Maybe you didn't like the neighbours or your growing bairns had too far to walk to school, or you just couldn't get on with the fairmer chiel and he had never asked you to bide on for another year and you just had to leave. But the smallest excuse was good enough reason to be on the road with your flitting, rain or shine, but if it was a fine day folk said the sun always shines on the righteous, or that the deil was kind to his ain, so you could make of it what you liked, depending on your views on religion. But heaven help you if it was a slashing day of rain and your chaff beds sodden and your bairns like drookit rats sitting on the carts among the wet furniture, or walking behind to keep them warm, an old jacket over their heads, and your poor wife with the smallest child in her oxter, the rain drops from her hair falling on its cheeks, chilled and blue with the cold. Folks that weren't moving would be watching you from the comfort of their cottage doors, and the wisest of them would say among themselves that maybe in changing your job you would get a change of a deevil but it would still be the same hell, a hell that got sadder as you grew older and less able to cope, for though you were rid of the bairns you still had a living to make and jobs were scarcer for an older body, now frail and sair from the long years of toil and wet and rheumatism.

But God bless you or Devil curse you, wet or dry, young or old, some folk accepted the May flitting in holiday spirit, even as an adventure; the fond memories of leaving an old home, some sweet some sad, depending how long you had lived there, and the excitement and thrill of entering a new one - all the labour of scrubbing out your old house and the bother of papering a new one. Of course your wife always wanted to leave her old hoose as clean and tidy as possible, brushing down the roofs and walls, even to placing newspapers on the floor for the bairns running out and in, and then you'd go to a new place and the paper all torn off the walls and not a flower or a berry bush left in the gairden, mostly done out of spite by a leaving tenant for some grudge against the farmer. But the worst you'd heard of was the farmer chiel who so disliked his cottar who was leaving that he fired a shotgun over the horses' heads and they bolted with the loaded carts and smashed all the lad's furniture. But for all its set-backs it was still fun to be a cottar; especially for the bairns, the only real holiday they ever knew, a change of scene and school and playmates, despite the slippery stone they say that lies at every doorstep.

But by the time you came of age to be a cottar things were changing a bit for the better, and instead of sending horse carts to flit you, farmers were paying for a motor lorry or a steam-wagon to move your furniture, with cover and ropes for wind and rain, and your wife and the bairns got a seat beside the driver while you could ride on the wagon, waving to the lads in the parks, though there weren't many at work on a Term day, except those that were staying on at their places; maybe the odd grieve with a turnip-seed barrow, or a horseman with a 'bone-davie,' scattering manure on the drills.

Ach but you were tired of the bothies and the chaumer life and thought you would like to set up home yourself. It was almost instinct that you had to become a cottar, just as your father had done, and the food that you got on some of the fairm-toons, or the want of it, was beginning to give you sore bellies, so that the only decent dinner you got was from your mither at the week-end (who could least afford it) when you went home on your bike to change your dirty sark. You were supposed to be working in a land of plenty: a land flowing with milk and honey, beef corn and tatties, producing the nation's essential diet, yet you were sometimes treated like the Prodigal Son at the swine's trough, eating husks and offal. Rather than thole it some lads joined the army at the feeing markets, where the brass buttoned recruiting sergeant was waiting to offer them the King's shilling, which some preferred to the arles, or bargaining money,

117

offered by the farmers, and with a good chance of better conditions, so they rallied round the big drum and the pipe bands that were always at the fairs. Some of the best soldiers in our Highland Regiments were recruited at these slave markets, where the harshness of the fields and the strictness of farm life had bred them well for discipline; men who could endure in all weathers and march on empty stomachs and blistered feet as they had done behind the harrows - men who had seen the blood on nature's claw, and would bury a dead comrade as he would a beast of the field. Yet mony a weeping mither prigged sair with her sons not to join the army on market days: widows who remembered the fathers who had bled to death in the trenches of Flanders.

But you had no hankering for the kilt or the khaki, or the barracks for the chaumer, for at least on the grun your mind had the freedom of the birds of the sky or the wild creatures of the field, and regimentation or conformity was something that you remembered and hated from your schooldays. So maybe a bit wife that could cook a decent diet and having a hoose o yer ain was the better answer to your problem. But you had never been a lad for the quines really; never went to dances or concerts where you could meet them, so you found it a bit difficult in finding a lass that would suit you. Oh you had been tempted once or twice and had met a quine or two at the meal-and-ale or Harvest Home festivities, but it never came to much and they jilted you or you deserted them and that was the end of it. So you took to the pictures, for you were a great admirer of the film stars, especially the quines among them, and you had their photographs plastered all over the walls of your chaumer and inside the lid of your kist, where other lads usually hung their ties or their harness ribbons, rosettes or martingales to decorate their horses. And when the mistress or the kitchiedeem came to make up the chaumer beds they were fair amazed at your gallery of glamour girls, maybe a bit envious that they couldn't compare with your taste for beauty, thinking that you was ill to please, and that you would find it hard to get a wife to compare with those for looks. But those were your dream girls and you were determined to have one just as bonny.

You lived in a world by yourself a bit with your dreams and books and film stars; never taking a dram with the other lads or having a bit hooch of a dance, a bit of a radical you was with a different view of everything from anybody else, though you never got yourself into trouble over it, just thinking deeply, poet like, though you didn't realise it at the time. So the other lads in the chaumer got used to your reading and your picture-going and left you to your own wiles and fair admired your pin-up quines. But sometimes for their amusement you stuck up a quine with not much on, for you were far ahead of your time on the fairms, where a bra or a bikini had never been seen or heard of in those days. But it riled the farmer's wife when she came to make the beds, and she ordered that those 'painted, brazen hussies' should be taken down. But the chaumer billies wouldn't hear of it and she got used to the pin-ups eventually, though not without protest and probably regarding you as a protégé of the devil for introducing them, until she discovered that you sometimes went to the kirk on Sundays, which was more than the other lads did, and then she forgave you completely, perhaps remembering that even Solomon and David had their sins and that you was no worse than them. You even joined as a member of the kirk to please her, drinking the blood of Christ and eating of his flesh at Communion time, cannibal like, until the elder came round collecting for the kirk funds, when you was that hard up you gave him only eightpence, which he said would never get you over the Jordan, though maybe he meant the Red Sea, so you told him to remember the Widow's Mite, and the other billies fair got a laugh at you and your kirk going.

But while you still kept looking for this quine of your dreams, and the other billies came and went at the Term times, and though the food got worse and worse, you stayed on for nearly two years at Slabsteen, maybe because you had an easy kind of job, when lo and behold at the May Term comes the lass you had been waiting for all these years, the new kitchiedeem. She was quiet and bashful for a time and wouldn't speak to any of the lads and you could see at once that she was no ordinary quine. Here at last was your film star in the flesh; your dream become a reality, so that everything you looked upon was radiant with her beauty, arousing the poet that was in you, if only you had the pluck to tell her so, without being snubbed.

Of course you had your rivals at this game, but as none of the other chiels could get the quine to speak to them they gave her up as 'a sulky bitch', bonnie though she was with her head in the air. The Third Horseman was the first to get a word out of the quine, and a bit of a smile as well, which made her even more desirable, and had its funny side to it. It was 'Knotty-Tams' for supper, brose made from oatmeal and mixed with boiling milk instead of water. But they were pretty solid, so that when the Third Horseman turned his bowl upside-down the brose never fell out but stuck to the bowl like cement, whereupon he asked the quine if 'He was good looking'. The quine stared at him in surprise and asked what he meant, or who the 'He' was? So the lad uprighted his bowl on the table and remarked: 'Oh the lad ye was thinkin on when ye made this brose!' The quine blushed and told him she was not to blame; that the mistress herself had made the brose, and that he'd better ask her. But it was all he could get out of the quine and she would hardly speak to him again for his impudence.

Now Francie Gatt, that was Third, was your best pal in the chaumer and you wouldn't have minded a bit though the quine had taken him on. He was the only one who really understood you and your flair for books and sometimes stuck up for you when the others would take the size of you. He was the only one who could swim in the mill dam and could take music out of a stone almost: could play on anything from a saw blade to the bagpipes, with fiddle, dulcimer, jews' harp, melodion and mouth-organ forbye; had even taught you how to vaump on the mouth-organ, and he had spent a whole fortnight mastering David Copperfield, a feat you admired in him more than anything he could do with a pair of horse in the ploo. You had worked with this lad for a whole year on another fairm and had moved together with your kists to Slabsteen; and you knew fine that Francie had a quine o his ain and didna want yer lass, but ye thocht maybe that ye could confide in the chiel, seein that he was yer best freen like, and had taken yer side in ither things, so after a bit tune together on the mouth-organs, sittin on the edge o yer bed, and him on his kist, ye told Gatt how ye felt aboot this quine and what he thocht ye should do about it. So Gatt said she already had a lad, and that the last Sunday he was toon-keeper this lad cam tae see the kitchie quine, and got his denner in the fairm hoose, so that he must be gey far in with her and the fairm mistress and that ye hadna much chance; and besides, did ye no ken that the shepherd was after 'er, sneakin in tae the chaumer here when the lassie was makin the beds, feart that she wad ravel his Sunday breeks that he was pressin under the mattress, but that it was only an excuse tae get a word wi her, or even try something bolder, but that she told 'im off; that she didna want 'im, that she had a lad o her ain withoot tripe like him. Oh maybe ye thocht she was quiet like but she could speak oot when she liked, and she might put ye in your place quick enough. All's fair in love and war Gatt said but that you were a bit slow with the quines and that unless you looked nippy aboot it ye would never manage tae ding oot this ither lad she had, and that Gertie Troup wad be married before ye got started.

Now it just so happened that about this time your old grandfather died and in a week or two your mither asked if ye would put a bit flower on his grave; that maybe the farm wife would give you a bunch from the farm gairden, and that ye could put it on when you went in bye to the kirk. So bein a kirky body like hersel ye had nae bother gettin a bit flower from the farm wife, and what was better, she sent Gertie with you to pluck them. And a fair picture she was with an oxter of flowers, and the sweet smile of her when she handed them over, fond like, as if she was loth to part with them, but didn't mind seeing it was you, the quiet one who never took her on much. And was it true that you wrote poetry? Folk said that you was clever and wrote things to the papers, all about your film stars that were hanging on the chaumer walls. Would you write a poem for her? My but you must be awfully proud of your old grandfather to put flowers on his grave. Not many lads would bother to do that. But how could she be sure that you wasn't giving them away to some quine that went to the pictures with you in the toon? Seein it was Saturday night you didn't deny this was possible, and the farm wife wasn't at the kirk every Sunday to see what you did with them. You were that damned shy you hardly knew what to say, but after a time or two at the flower gathering you plucked up courage to tell the blushing quine that a flower like herself didn't need a flower: that she herself was the loveliest flower you had ever seen in nature's garden; and a lot of other things you told her, and she looked at you so sweetly and said that no lad had ever said things to her like that before, that surely you must be a poet, like the ones she had read about in her school books. So you told her that you wouldn't be wanting any more flowers for your quine in the toon, or whatever she thought you did with them, and that if she waited up for you the next Saturday night in the back kitchen you would bring a flower for her, and maybe the bit poem she had asked for.

So you spent the next week with the muses, mostly in secret, writing a bit

120

poem for the quine in the kitchen, and on the Saturday night you went away on your bike as usual like the other lads, maybe to the pictures they thocht, but you returned in the gloamin, when the farm folks were in bed, and you crept into the back gairden and plucked the loveliest rose you could find, scented fresh from heaven's pharmacy, sun-kissed with colour and tipped with dew, and you tapped on the back kitchen window, where the quine had been knitting in the twilight, waiting for you, just as she had promised, and when she took the snib from its catch, and you pushed the sash half up, ever so quietly, not to waken the farm folk, you handed her this one single beautiful rose and a box of chocolates you had bought at the Bog shop. She placed the dewy rose against her lips and smelt its fragrance, and with the flower against her face she seemed an angel in the mirk, the shadow of your dream come true.

And you had to stand on a backet from the peat stack to reach your quine at the open window. Oh aye you could call her Gertie and you gave her the poem you'd promised her and she said she'd read it in bed by candlelight because she couldn't wait till daybreak to see what you had written. So you whispered to each other till long after midnight, in the smoked-glass light of a midsummer morning, when it is never really dark, while the leaves rustled in the quiet sigh of the wind that was rich with the smell of dewy bud and the tang of earth, soft and sweet and warm as the lips of your quine that you touched with your own ere you parted. Syne you jumped on your bike and dreamed your way home in the colder flush of dawn, while the birds and the cattle beasts were still asleep in the deep green of the fields, and the world quiet about you, and you knew in your heart that something wonderful and mystifying was awakening in your young life. And you wanted to tell your mither about this new quine you had met at the fairm, but when mornin came you thought better of it, because you knew she didn't like you to be goin out with quines, though she didn't object to your film stars on the walls, because they couldn't do you any harm, neither break your heart nor ruin you.

But bye and bye you were spending nearly an hour with Gertie in the back scullery when you was supposed to be shaving and washing your face, taking care you was last for the wash basin, so's you wouldn't be molested, while the other lads were in the chaumer, playing cards or the gramophone; and by the time you went round to supper your horse of a winter evening they were sometimes in bed. But with Francie Gatt on your side they didn't bother you much about the quine, except to say that you were a lucky bugger, and that if ever you married the sulky bitch they'd wash your feet and blacken the pair of you from head to foot. Sometimes you got your tea from the farmwife, you and the servant quine, with home-baked scones and honey, mostly from ben the hoose, for she spoiled the pair of you and the lad that used to come on a Sunday had fair got the go bye. And whiles you'd cycle down to the Bog shop for an ounce of tobacco and Mollie Kane that kept the place would measure out a length of black twist from a roll and cut it on the edge of the counter, and when she put it on the scales she was never far out. So you'd buy a pucklie sweeties for your lass and Mollie would coup the pan from the weighing machine into a paper whirl she had twisted at one end like a cone, and she'd tell you that you had the bonniest quine in the whole of the Bogside, as her mither was afore her day, for fine she minded when she cam tae the shop hersel as a young deem. So you'd make an errand back to the fairmhoose with the sweeties, where you'd find Gertie in the scullery, and you told her what the shoppie wife said about her mither and gave her the poke of sweets. And if the farm-wife appeared you'd ask for a book to read and Gertie would hide her sweeties under the mou of a pot where they lay up-side-down on the skelves. So the farm wife brought you *The Last of the Mohicans*, because you had just finished *Deerslayer*, and she knew you was fair daft on this Fennimore Cooper lad that wrote about the backwoods of America.

So Gertie liked your poem fine, and she wrote you a bit letter back to say she had always wanted a lad like you, and you read it all by yourself in the chaumer and fair thocht yoursel King of the Castle. And so the summer wore on, hyowe, hay, peats and hairst, and sometimes at the shim with your odd beast you would be caught in your sark sleeves in a thunder pelt, but then the sun came out in a blaze of heat and by the time you'd reached the other end of the neep drills you was dry again, thinking all the time about the beauty of your quine and the wonder of the world and not a real care in your young heart. Even on the longest warm sunny days you'd never weary, and you'd jump on your mare's back and drag hay coles from the hill fields down to the stackyard, where the grieve and the farmer chiel would be building and trampling the rucks, with two-three billies on the forks, one on a ladder as the stacks got higher, pitching the scented forkfuls to the builders, while the hayseed went down the back of his neck. But you'd kinch up your rope and hang it on your hames and trot away back for another cole, maybe a bit further afield this time to give the lads time to top their stack, and you'd meet the second billie on the way, with two bairns riding on his cole, and when your quine appeared with the piece-basket they fair made a picnic of it. Then there was the wark in the moss, with a flaggon of loaf saps or sago for your dinner; cutting, barrowing, spreading, rickling and driving home the peat, a job that sometimes lasted the whole summer, depending on the weather and when you could get at it, and you'd have your harness polished and your clear hames and chains glittering in the sun, while back at home the peat stack got bigger and bigger, the grieve building it and a lad throwing up the peats to him, for you just couped your loads and away back for another dracht, and when the stack was finished they topped it with dross to keep it dry, though some folks had a shed to stack their peats in.

Syne the hairst, clearing roads for the binder, swinging the scythe and gathering sheaves and setting them against the dykes, the golden ears of ripe corn rustling in the sun. Then long golden days stooking behind the binders, rows and rows of upright stooks, setting them north and south to catch the sun, tidy as you could make them. And maybe you'd get a glimpse of your quine on her bicycle, when her mistress had sent her with a ball of twine for a binder that had run out of yarn, and the horses standing idle in the hairst park. But soon she would be back with the piece basket, and when she got you by yourself in the lithe of a stook she whispered that you had gone too far with her lately in your 'Garden of Eden,' as you called it, the high-walled gairden ahin the fairmhoose, with its rustic arbour, summer house and lily pond, where you had made your trysts with her in the gloamin, and that maybe you would be a father before you expected it. But she was smiling all the time and bonnier than ever and you knew she was happy about it and trusting in your love. Nor was you unhappy about it either, for you had always wanted a place of your ain and a quine that you liked whatever came of it. But you would have to tell your mither for God knows you had little enough to get married on and you'd need her blessing and whatever else she could give you by way of a little money and some bits of furniture she could spare. But you told Gertie not to worry, that you would stand by her whatever happened, and she said she knew that and gave you the sort of smile that comes from an angel's heart, cheering you on the hairst rigs with a song on your lips. You usually drove a horse cart at the leading-in, 'cause they wouldn't trust you with building a ruck yet, lest you watered and spoiled it, much as you wished to try it, so you had to be content with building your carts and driving them home to the stackyard, where you forked your sheaves to the builder. Then came the thatching and the tattie-lifting and as Martinmas drew nigh you knew you would have to look for a cottar job and a hoose o yer ain for your wife and bairn.

But married jobs were ill to come by at the November Term, and though you bicycled far and near to answer adverts in the papers someone had always been there before you and you were turned away, though some farmers did earnestly thank you for looking in bye. By now the cottar wives at Slabsteen were beginning to claik among themselves about the loon and the quine that were getting married at the Term: 'Still waters run deep,' they said, 'for you would hardly have thought by the pair of them that they would be at it already; and the quine with the mark of the schoolbag hardly off her back, and the lad only a haflin with nothing saved up for a rainy day - and the quine expectin at her age - Gweed sake! What was the warld comin till?'

So you dressed yourself in your best serge suit and took the train to the feein market for single men at Maud, for there was just the chance that some odd farmer billie might be looking for a cottar. But na na, there was nothing for you there but the blether of wark and the swagger of the heavies and the lads that got drunk on their arles, and while you stood there with the bite of the wind in your Sunday clothes not one farmer asked your price for a six months' Term. Dinner was out of the question, you just couldn't afford it so near the Term, for it was nearly six months since you got any wages, and unless you got a fee and some farmer chiel offered you a dram you had to be content with a cup of tea at Morrison's bakery, and then you lit your pipe and made for the station platform to wait for the train. Going back on the Buchan train the face of your quine haunted you; though not unpleasantly, but smiling at you from a mother-of-pearl sky, playing hide-and-seek with you from the pine woods on the hillsides; even as you thought of her the watery sun dried his wintry tears and burnished the autumn gold at the feet of the stricken beeches, filling you with hope that together you had nothing to fear, though you envied the lads at the ploo or pulling turnips, confident and content in their sense of security.

On your way home from the station you got off your bike at the smiddy and told the blacksmith of your plight. But he never stopped tugging at his bellows handle and twirling with a tongs at a red-hot horse shoe in the glowing forge, chewing tobacco and spitting the juice into the tiny flames. 'Ach man,' says he, 'ye'll get a place a' richt, and ye could aye go intae Rascal Friday in Aiberdeen. Ye're hardly startit yet and ye're baith young; a' the warld afore ye and a hist o geets, ye'll be feart tae throw a steen in owre a skweel dyke for fear o hittin ane o yer ain!' This nearly tore the arse out of your breeks so to speak and made you rise from the anvil and make for the smiddy door. And the blacksmith's parting words rang in your lugs like a kirk bell: 'Man, if ye're willin tae work ye'll never want for a job!'

Maybe he was right for you got a cottar place little more than a week before the term, a dairy job, which you had never done in your life before, but you'd have to learn it, now that you was taking a wife. So this new farmer chiel that was called Lowrie took you into his parlour at the Blackstob farm and offered you a £1 a week plus house and perquisites for second dairy stockman on the place. You a dairyman, you that had never milked a cow in your whole life - but before you could make up your mind the 'phone rang and Mr. Lowrie went ben the lobby to answer it. When he came back he said that was another chiel applyin for the job and would you be willin to take it on for something less than a £1 a week, seeing this man was experienced and you would have to be learned to milk with the new machines. But na na, you stuck to the figure he promised and said you wouldn't do it for less: after all maybe it was only a trick because you couldn't hear who was on the other end of the 'phone; maybe it was only so-and-so asking Lowrie for an extra pint of milk on delivery. So you settled for a £1 a week and came away from the Blackstob farm feeling a rich man, because it was more money than you had ever made in your life before, and just wait till you told Gertie.

Gertie was delighted, but the folk at Slabsteen were determined to have your feet washed before you left at the Term, both the pair of you, but what with all you'd been through already you got roused at this and threatened to strike the first one to lay hands on you or your quine. This marriage business was beginning to make a man of you and putting some spunk in your veins. Just let them try it and you'd land the first one in the horse troch if you got the chance. You wasn't worried about yourself but what they'd do to Gertie; maybe not thinking about the condition she was in and the harm it could do. But Gertie tamed you down and humoured you to go through with it for her sake, because she didn't want any fighting, and that they'd never lay a hand on her because the mistress was against it and would protect her. So you bought a bottle of whisky and allowed the devils to wash your feet and blacken you from head to foot, even taking your boots off yourself not to hinder them, though you never missed a chance to give as well as you got, until you hardly knew one from the other, and it took you nearly half the night in the back kitchen to wash yourself clean again. But they never got hold of your quine, for the mistress had been as good as her word and kept her inside, even to milking the kye herself until it had all blown past at the Term. But maybe the cottar wives had some influence on their menfolk in this respect, for they were sure it must be a 'forced marriage,' or how else would you be getting married at the Martinmas Term. But they drank all your whisky and gave Gertie a small present, and when you left at the Term the farm wife threw a horse shoe after you down the avenue, wishing luck to the pair of you in your new venture.

You wasn't getting married for a week after you went to the Blackstob farm, so you'd work as a single man and board next door with the McPhee's, while Gertie stayed with her parents at the Bogside. But you'd never forget the first night that you and your quine approached the Blackstob place. It was in the gloamin of early winter that you went up the avenue on your bicycles, but had to get off when you met the foreman and the second horseman coming out of a dubby field with four tremendous loads of marrow-stem kale; such enormous loads as you had never seen at Slabsteen, and such dubs and stern chiels you thought this must surely be a hard place to work on, and that you had certainly jumped out of the frying-pan into the fire.

But you both liked the little harled three-roomed house down the back road from the farm, with a fine big garden and hen-run and plenty of room for Gertie to hang her clothes line. You had your kist and some bits of furniture gathered together that you had gotten from your parents: an iron bedstead with brass knobs, blankets, sheet and pillows, table and chairs and washstand and an old second-hand dresser that was little better than a hen-coop, besides some pots and pans, kettle, tea-pot, dishes and spoons; some curtain material for the windows, rugs for the floor and a roll of linoleum, and you'd pick up some other things in the sale rooms bye and bye. There were no blinds on the windows but you lit the paraffin lamp and set it on the table to let you see to put some messages you had brought into the wall presses, which were fitted with shelves, scrubbed and clean, though Gertie placed a sheet of newspaper on each shelf before she used it. This done, and Gertie getting the tea ready, the first you'd ever had in your own house, when the door opens without warning and a wash tub is thrown into the little kitchen. Four men stared in at you and your quine from the open door, their faces dimly visible in the light from the paraffin lamp. Two of them you had seen with their loads of kale, now both grinning with mischief in their eyes; the third was McPhee from next door, who would be your boss in the byre, at first glance a proper ruffian, strong and sturdy as a nowt beast. Standing in front of the other three, tallest of the lot and evidently their ringleader was Jock Herd, gaffer at the Blackstob for mony a year, his eyes agleam with mirth and his white teeth shining in his dirty face. All four had flaggons in their hands, brimming with warm milk, which they had no intention of pouring into the tub, so that any visions you had of being treated like Cleopatra were soon dispelled. Na na, water will do the job they said, cold water at that, and Herd ordered you and your bride to get your boots and stockings off so that they could wash your dirty feet. But your birse began to rise at this and you told them that your feet had already been washed at the last place, your quine as well, for you had to tell a lie to protect her, thinking she would fair be in for it this time. But Jock Herd was dubious: 'Expect us tae believe that?' he cried, 'A likely story. Fill 'er up lads and we'll wash the pair o them!' All four left their flaggons outside and went in search of pails and water. Gertie was almost in tears and you was mortally terrified at the uncouth brutes. Surely they would have some sense or pity seeing you was just newly moved into the hoose and everything in an uproar. Jock Herd came back with the first pailful of icy water and poured it into the tub, threatening to wash you stockings an all if you didn't get a move on, and to clart you with axle grease and harness blacking. He hadna time to scutter he said for he was hungry and needin his supper. Then the other three appeared and tipped their pails of water into the tub. That would be enough Jock said and waited to see what you was going to do, solemn like, looking at your scared faces, and then all four burst out laughing. 'Did ye really think that we wad bother tae wash yer feet?' Jock asked. 'Na na, we wis only haverin, and we'll tak yer word for't that ye had them washed afore!' So you told them that you was beginning to wonder if they were in earnest and you gave them each a bottle of stout that you had in your kist and they departed in great glee, taking the tub with them. It was a relief to see them gone but Gertie said she felt sure they wouldn't man-handle us; that Jock Herd looked so like her own caperin father and had quines o his ain and she could see by his face that he was only in fun. So you had your tea in peace after all, and a bit cuddle after the light was out, though it wouldn't do for the two of you to sleep together, not just yet anyway, so you lit your gas lamps and got on your bicycles and you saw Gertie home to the Bogside.

So you wouldn't be seeing Gertie for a whole week, and by then you was fair convinced you had taken the wrong turning with a dairy job at the Blackstob: but as the saying goes 'when you've made your bed you've got to lie in it,' trouble was the damn the very lang did you get to lie - up at half-past three for the milking, and you had bought a new alarm clock to make sure you could manage it. Back at Slabsteen you had lain in your bed till six and didn't know how well off you was till now. McPhee wasn't all that sharp himself but he caught up with you in the avenue, his pockets bulging with empty milk bottles and his fag a red spot in his mouth. But you was still in a daze of sleep, the stars winking down at you, the moon grinning low in the violet blue of the west, while you stole a glance at it with your bleary eyes. But the warm stink of the crowded byre, the cold water you was throwing about, the hard work feeding and mucking out, the struggle with the new-fangled milking machines and kicking cows soon had you out of your day-dreams.

McPhee's wife made porridge for your breakfast, rich with cream that McPhee had skimmed from a can in the dairy, and no sooner was the spoon out of your mouth than you was fast asleep on their couch. McPhee was used to it and after a short nap he sat and smoked and played with the bairns while his wife rigged them out for school. Faith but they were a rough and ready crowd, the worst you'd ever seen but good at heart, though the house was a mess of dirt

126

and stank with casten sarks to be washed and had a bairns' footpath from the door to the fireside, sair needing to be scraped, never mind scrubbing, and empty milk bottles standing everywhere, even in the window sills, where one or two had a bit flower in them. Faith but the woman wasn't all that to be blamed, for she worked hard in the dairy for about a shilling a day, washing cans and bottles, and all that McPhee did to help was to light the boiler fire for her. And what with all that geets and a man like McPhee always on top of her, and always in debt, 'cause he spent so much on fags and booze; and sometimes she was so far behind with the grocer that when she saw his van coming up the back road she went away up the whun-dyke with the bairns that weren't at school, because she hadn't a copper in the house, living on meal, milk and tatties, besides an egg from her hens and what McPhee could steal - and when the vanman had gone (hoping to get his money the next week) she'd come away home again with a birn of sticks on her back, pretending to be in search of kindlers. Syne in the evenin McPhee would be fair cravin for a smoke and he'd send a bairn to the shop for fags on tick, and if the bairn wadna go it got a skelpin. But for all that McPhee and the wife were a lovin pair and you never heard an ill werd between them, and she forgave him everything, even a rough-and-tumble on the straw in the barn with the scullery maid, or a bit cuddle at her in the sly, thinkin maybe it was something to be proud of to have a man that other women wanted, for she fair adored the brute.

On the night of your marriage Jock Herd and McPhee put a sod on your lum, spiced your bed and slackened the screws that held it together, while all the time you had the key of the door in your pocket and never knew how they got into your cottage. You had a piper at your wedding and thought yourself gey braw and came home cock of the walk after midnight in a motor taxi. Oh you fair did it in style and even gave the driver a tip and he carried all your presents into the house from the back of the car. When he had gone you picks Gertie up in your arms and carries her over the threshold into the little dark kitchen, like you'd seen them doing at the movies, right through to the bedroom, where you sets her down and lights the lamp, while she hangs a bit blanket over the window. The pair of you were a bit bashful getting your clothes off together for the first time and Gertie was that shy in her nakedness that she had you screw down the lamp or she got settled at the back of the bed. But the weight of her didn't dislodge it, not until you put your knee on the edge of the bed to get in beside her when the whole damned thing collapsed in a heap, both ends coming together and giving you a nasty crack on the head. Oh it was well contrived and the disturbance set the spice going and the pair of you started sneezing like you would never stop, while all the time through the partition you could hear McPhee and his wife skirling with laughter. So you both gets up again and tries to put the bed together, but when you couldn't find the key for it you lost your patience and threw one of your boots at the wall, thinking to quieten McPhee between your sneezes, for by now you was in a tearing rage, fair bloody mad and threatening to go round and kill the bastard. But Gertie was wiser than you for she knew they just wanted to have you roused and managed to quieten you down before you made a shambles. When the sneezing stopped you managed to get back to speaking in whispers again, setting the ends of the bed aside and lying down together on the mattress on the floor, your arms round each other's necks, your lips together and the blankets over your heads, not caring a damn for anyone. But no bloody honeymoon because you had promised old Lowrie you would be at the milking in the morning, 'cause there was a man off work and nobody to replace you and he would give you a day off later on.

So you only had about two hours in bed the first night of your marriage, lying on the floor at that, but in the morning you never let dab to McPhee about the racket you'd had with the bed; you was quite calmed down by then and wasn't going to give him the satisfaction of making a fool of you, though you knew damned fine it was to make up for being denied the fun of washing your feet, and McPhee would soon be whispering to Jock Herd about the fun they'd got when the sneezin started, and how you had been fair roused and swearing like hell at the lot of them.

But that wasn't all, for there was this bloody sod on your chimney, and when you got home to breakfast for the first time in your own home, sair chauved in the byre, your kitchen was full of smoke and your wife standing at the door hoasting for want of breath and her eyes watering. You couldn't see a stime in the place for the reek, and had to run outside again for breath, thinking that your house was on fire, and you ran round to McPhee to ask for help. So he had another bloody good laugh at you, and his wife fair giggling, while McPhee pointed to the turf sticking on your lum. It was damned provoking, especially on a teem belly, but you was that relieved the house wasn't on fire you was beginning to see the funny side of it yourself, though it was all at your expense. McPhee gave you a ladder he had taken from the farm to let you up on the slates, and when you stood up on the coping to get hold of the chimney pot the confounded thing came away in your oxter and you nearly lost your balance. Can and sod went crashing to the ground while you held on to the stonework. But it stopped the laughter and while you came slithering down the slates McPhee held the ladder for you, a bit white-faced and scared lest you should fall. Back at the farm you told Lowrie that you would need a new chimney, but he looked stern like and said 'Damn the fit, ye'll replace it yersel, or I'll keep it aff yer wages!' But you saw him winking to McPhee and you knew that he was only joking, for he was as bad as the rest of them with his pranks on newly married folk.

But it wasn't long before a slater lad was clambering on your roof fixing your new chimney pot and you got a ton of coal as your first perquisite. A wagon load of coal was shunted off at Binkie Station for the Blackstob and Jock Herd sent the horsemen with their carts to drive it home to the cottars. It was Scotch coal because English was considered too expensive; but it was a whole ton of coal to yourselves, more than you had ever possessed in the world before, and even though you were come of cottar folk, both the pair of you, it was a bit of a thrill having it couped at your own shed door. Gertie was that excited about it that she gave you a hand to shovel it into the shed, happy you were the pair of you at it, by the light of a cycle lamp in the evening, and all your other set-backs were soon forgotten. Next day you got three bolls and a firlet of oat-meal, which is about 4 cwt., and the foreman carried the bags into the kitchen and set them on chairs, where you left them until the grocer came to buy the meal off your hands or take it in exchange for provisions over a period. Of course you had ordered a girnal to hold your meal, a fairly big one with a desk lid and lined with zinc to keep out the mice, but the joiner hadn't finished making it yet, so you kept a bag to store in it for your own use. Then you got ten sacks of tatties, which you buried in an earth-pit, to protect them from the frost, but again the grocer relieved you of half of them. It wasn't until you had a big family that you needed all that stuff, and you got another supply in six months time, so in the meantime you sold as much as you could to buy the bits of furniture you needed to set up house in earnest. Besides all this you got three pints of milk a day and £4 a month in money, with the balance at the Terms, less £1 in six months for Insurance, so you considered you was much better off now than you had been in a chaumer, and with a quine all to yourself for company and to keep you warm at nights.

About six weeks after your wedding old Lowrie decided to give you a day off for your honeymoon, the first whole day you'd had to yourself since you came to the place, so you fair looked forward to your holiday. You were that excited you didn't even take a long lie and got up about an hour after you heard McPhee leave for the milking. He had been sleeping-in lately and you usually gave him a bang on the wall to make sure he was up, but today being your honeymoon you didn't bother, and you couldn't have cared less though he had slept till dinner time.

It was a fine mild morning for mid-January, with a dark dreamy sky outside the window and a star winking here and there and the cottars' cocks crowing to each other with all the promise of a beautiful day. So you dressed yourselves in great excitement and had your brose and cocoa and set sail in the dark on your bicycles for Binkie Station to catch the first train for Aberdeen. At the station you blew out your gas lamps and left your bicycles in the waiting room and bought your return tickets and waited on the platform for the train. The signal was at green so you didn't have long to wait, and when you got on the train it was all lit up and not many folks in it so you got a whole compartment to yourselves with fine red plush cushions and pictures under the luggage racks. Gertie had never been in a train before so you knew you was giving her a real treat, so you just sat and smiled across at each other as if you were the richest and happiest pair of creatures in the world. Outside in the dark you could see the lights on the passing farms and you knew that folks would be at work in their byres and stables; but this was your day of adventure, your day of days, your's and Gertie's, and you were going to make the best of it.

It took the train nearly two hours to reach the black tunnels in Aberdeen and by then it was daylight and the lights all out in the carriages and a great bustle of folk when you got off at the station. By now you was hungry, so the first thing you did was to get your tea in a restaurant, not too posh because you couldn't afford it, and then the two of you went linking down Union Street, hand in hand, on a shopping spree. Gertie had you inside 'Raggie Morrison's,' at the corner of St. Nicholas Street, and the Guinea Shop, where she told you she had bought her wedding frock for twenty-one shillings, when she was in the city with her mither and one of her sisters at the Term. Now she wanted some hanks of wool to knit something for the coming bairn. Then to 'Cockie Hunter's' place at the head of the Castlegate, which used to be the old Sick Children's Hospital, but now so crammed with everything that you could hardly get up the stairs. Cockie used to boast that he could sell you anything 'from a needle to an anchor,' or could get it for you if you wanted one, but you settled for a second-hand dressing table for your bedroom, which cost you a fiver, and an overmantle for your kitchen fireplace, with a mirror in the centre and a picture by Constable on either side, which you had for about three shillings, besides a roll of linoleum and a huge hand-painted flower pot at 10/- that Gertie fancied for her front window nearest the road. And when you paid Mr. Hunter for these things he promised to send them out with the carrier that passed your way once a week.

In the New Market you was a bit shy to go upstairs because of the quines, but maybe with Gertie with you they mightn't be so bad. When you was a single chiel they used to torment you at the Term time to buy a broach or a pair of stockings for your lass, when they knew you had the money, and unless you snubbed them proper or just clean ignored them they had you into their shabby booths by the arm or the tail of your jacket and you was glad to buy something to get rid of the bitches. They just sat at their stalls like a spider at a web, waiting for the unwary fly that might come in bye, mostly farmers and country chiels that were a bit canned and careless with their money; but some of them offered to buy the stockings if the quines would bare a leg to let them try them on, which usually quietened the limmers, and if some of the chiels took hold of them they were glad to leave the lads alone. But you wanted to get to Low's bookstall, which was at the other end of the building, and though the quines pestered you a bit it wasn't nearly so bad with Gertie by the hand, and you being such a lad to read you got plenty to choose from at Low's, where the books were piled to the roof and cheap enough for your purse.

Then you'd go along to WOOLWORTH'S 3d. & 6d. STORES, where nothing was dearer than a sixpence, including gramophone records labelled 'Victory' and 'Eclipse,' and the hit of the moment was 'Little Grey Home In The West,' sung by Wilfred Eaton, a boy with the sweetest voice you ever heard this side of heaven, and having a special appeal for you at this time you just had to buy one. There were plenty of places where you could have your dinner, even in the New Market, but you remembered a place in King Street that was plain and cheap, where you had gone as a loon with your parents, Stephen's Restaurant, so you went there with Gertie and had a grand dinner of mince and tatties, plum-duff or trifle, tea and cakes, and a blow at a fag to finish it off, though Gertie never smoked. But she waited while you looked through the books you had bought, and then you daundered up Union Street again, dodging the trams and the horse dung, and the lorries that clattered over the causey

130

stones, up to Stead & Simpsons, where Gertie bought a pair of shoes and you stood her a black leather handbag. Back on the streets the tram-cars were whining and grinding to and fro on the rails, double-deckers powered along by a steel finger on their roofs attached to an overhead cable slung between the houses across Union Street, while here and there a Rover or Bydand bus, even folks on bicycles, threading their way among the motor traffic and the cars of the gentry, though they were few in those days. So you went back to St. Nicholas Street, just behind Queen Victoria's statue, to have a look at the suits in the windows of 'The Fifty-Shilling Tailors,' which was the price of their suits; comparing them with those at Claude Alexander's, Hepworth's and Montague Burton's, an area which you had always regarded as Jews' Corner, and many a day in the dreich of the neep park or the trauchle of the byres you were cheered by their enterprises, for you had read in the *Picture Post* that the Jews had made the desert blossom, growing fruit and oranges where once was sand and scrub, and you being a young lad still full of dreams and ambitions you wondered if some day you could match their enthusiasm, or perhaps become an H. Samuel and fill your lighted windows with golden rings and watches.

Having but one short winter day in the city you couldn't venture far from Union Street in case you lost yourself, or couldn't find your way back to the railway station, where the last train left at seven, but you went along George Street as far as Jerome's to have your pictures taken, especially as you didn't have a wedding photo. Gertie said that when her brothers came to the town at the Term they always went to the scenic railway or to see Harry Gordon at the Beach Pavilion, but you hadn't time for this after all that shopping, so you took her to the pictures, which she had never seen before, up at the old La Scala in Union Street, where they were showing the new 'Talking Pictures,' and your quine was fair mystified, especially when they sang and danced 'Way Down Upon the Swanee River,' and it was a fine rest after walking so long on the hard pavements, you being accustomed to the soft grun or the sharn midden. When you came out of the darkened picture house the streets were all lit up cheerfully and as you walked to the station down Bridge Street with your parcels you had a cup of coffee as a final treat and then made for the train. Back at Binkie Station you lit your gas lamps and cycled home with your parcels in one hand and steering with the other, tired but happy, the pair of you, after your honeymoon, and you'd have to be up for the byre again in a few hours' time.

In about a week's time your dressing-table, overmantle, flower-pot and bit of linoleum arrived with the carrier, so Gertie paid the chiel and he gave her a hand to carry them into the house. What with the curtains that your wife had made and the rugs she had clicked on a frame from old coloured rags in a pattern of her own, the papering she had done on the walls, the pictures she had framed, your varnishing of chairs and table and the old dresser, and your lino laid down, your house was almost furnished, even with a chiming clock for your mantleshelf, which Gertie had bought at a sale in the toon. She was getting big with her bairn but bonnier than ever, and sometimes in the dead of night she would take your hand and place it on her naked midriff, where you could feel the child turning inside her and bulging the skin, like a little Jonah in the whale's belly, so you kissed her fondly and turned on the other side and fell asleep, for morning and another anxious day was soon upon you.

Sometimes a cow calved during the night and being head cattleman McPhee had to get up in the small hours to deliver her calf, and although he never got anything extra for this he never came home empty-handed, and you'd be wakened from your sleep with a big thump on the floor that you heard next door through the wall and it was a huge lump of shining English coal that McPhee had pinched out of the farm coalshed, and when you tackled him about it next day he told you bloody plainly that he wasn't going to rise to their cow calvings for nothing, and before long he had you so much in his confidence that in the dark mornings you'd take one end of a railway sleeper on your strong young shoulder and McPhee would take the other, down the road to your coalshed, 'cause it was nearest, and in the evening you'd get a cross-cut saw and share it between you. You'd been a born cottar but never in all your days had you seen such thieving as went on at the Blackstob. Had you been soft enough McPhee would have had you into the hen arks for a dozen pullets coming on to the lay, but here you put your foot down and refused to join him. And he told you how he and the man before you had been locked into a field henhouse by the kitchiedeem, she not knowing they were there, and how they had to burst the door open after dark or stay and be caught in the morning.

But nowadays you had to waken McPhee every morning, banging on your bedroom wall with your fist until he answered you that he was up, depending on you entirely as a sort of alarm clock. Jock Herd said you should let the bugger lie and sort your own side of the byre, but you had been so much obliged to McPhee for showing you how to work the milking machines that you didn't want to offend him; and he shirked enough as it was, capering with the kitchie quines and newsing to folk out-bye, expecting you to do more than your share of the wark, quite enough without having to help him out after a sleep-in, which would have happened in the end, being the sort of lad you was, so you shielded the brute from getting the sack and thought it better to get him out of bed for a start to save trouble. And after all McPhee was your neighbour and Jock Herd would have liked fine to see trouble between you, so you had to be tolerant and use some diplomacy to keep the peace, though you felt all the time that you was being taken advantage of by force of circumstances.

But McPhee had a better idea and got both of you an extra while in bed in spite of everybody. The diesel engine was supposed to be going about a quarter-to-five for the milking, driving the pulso-pump, after you'd fed the kye with draff and bruised corn and mucked out their stalls, but McPhee didn't get up till half-past four and started up the engine as soon as he reached the steading, so that old Lowrie would think that everything was going normal when he heard the engine purring. So McPhee hid his empty milk bottles by the dairy door and started milking immediately, while you went before him with your draff hurlie feeding the beasts, and when finished with this you started mucking out behind him, while he worked all the machines himself and carried the milk to the dairy and watched that the cans under the cooler didn't overflow. He certainly had a full-time job and you wasn't sure but that he had the worst of it: in fact you thought it was an excellent idea because you were doing two jobs at the same time, and you had finished mucking the byre or he was half-through milking, thus giving him a hand to finish and feed the calves. But Lowrie of the Blackstob had just gone in for tuberculine-tested milk, first in the district, him being an enterprising kind of farmer, and it gave him a half-penny a pint more than his neighbours on the retail side of the business, though a lot of his cows failed in the test and he had to spend a lot of money replacing them with accredited stock. Cows that failed went to the outfarm and their milk went to the pool at the usual price. But when Lowrie was short of tuberculine free milk he dispatched a lorry to the outfarm for a couple of cans of diseased milk and bottled it up with T.T. milk at the higher price for his customers. Now you were supposed to be much more particular with the production of this new germ free milk; wearing white coats and caps and wellington boots, washing the udders more thoroughly and stripping off each cow for dermatitis, making sure there were no curds in the strainer before you put the milking cups on the teats. But Lowrie got up earlier one morning to see what was happening (or maybe Jock Herd had told him) and he was waiting in the darkness of the byre when McPhee switched on the lights, fortunately hiding his empty milk bottles before doing so, but a good half-hour late as usual. So Lowrie had fair caught you this time and he ranted and raved at McPhee about how things were being done to deceive him, starting up that damned engine to make him think you was on the job as usual, while all the time you were cheating him and mixing muck with milk in a certified T.T. herd. And what would happen if the Inspector called and you without your white coats and caps? Surely you had to think of that and you fair thought that McPhee was going to get the sack on the spot. And Lowrie took you aside and asked how long this had been going on, but you wouldn't tell on McPhee, and when Lowrie saw that he couldn't get anything out of you he said he knew you could rise in the morning and that you should come up at the proper time and let the tink lie, and then he'd know how to deal with him. But McPhee was too smart for Lowrie and comes up to him and says he could produce clean milk though the beasts were on a sharn midden, which was no worse than mixing rotten milk with good, and Mr. James Lowrie being a councillor he knew fine what McPhee was hinting at and left the byre in a sulk, so that everything went on much as before, except that it stopped the sale of infected milk to innocent customers.

But you never forgave McPhee after you saw him killing a premature calf with a hammer, smashing in its forehead until it died, for he had little patience with them if they wouldn't take a bottle teat or sup their milk from a bucket. Two or three days he hungered them and if this failed he splashed the milk in their faces and killed them. You had never seen such cruelty and was fair shocked though it did save you a lot of time scuttering with the ill-nourished creatures, lacking the instinct to suck the teat, which nature would have given them had they remained the normal time in their mother's bellies, nine months with the umbilical cord instead of the seven or eight caused by abortion. And Lowrie wouldn't have thanked you for 'phoning the knackery cart for a wee calf that had died, and as you didn't have much time to dig a hole you toppled it into the dung court from your barrow and covered it with sharn, thus spreading the disease where in-calf heifers were wintered in the building, besides angering Jock Herd and his horsemen when they came upon the stinking carcase with their graips while loading their carts in the springtime. And much as Lowrie wanted you to keep the mother in milk McPhee did his best to put her dry; turning off her water supply and cutting down her share of turnips, even rubbing her udder with vinegar, and in his ignorance was preventing the spread of brucellosis, which was little understood in those days and known in humans as undulent fever. But as the beast wasn't isolated it wasn't long before you had another abortion, unless you used plenty of Jeyes Fluid, which did something to prevent it. Indeed it was a long time before the agricultural colleges got on to the scourge in dairy herds, though you suspected all the time what was causing it but didn't know the cure, except that your old grandfather kept a billygoat in the byre to save his cows from 'casting their calves!' Eventually, when the veterinary lads came round in their white coats and wellington boots with needles to inject your heifers against abortion before serving you discovered they were trying out a vaccine from the goat, so maybe your old grandad had been right after all, but merely using the breath and discharge of the goat in his old-fashioned way among the few cows that he kept, until the disease went rampant as the dairy herds got bigger and more commercialised. But just think what might have happened if you had taken this disease home to your poor Gertie that was expecting her bairn shortly.

But for all his faults McPhee never teased you about your wife expecting a bairn, whereas Jock Herd in his crude way never missed a chance of comparing beast with body, and how the first calving was always the worst, until he had you nearly out of your sleep with worry, especially after that case when he'd had to help you with the ropes and fencing tackle to relieve a young heifer of her calf, four or five of you pulling with all your might, and another holding the arse of the beast that was chained by the neck to her forestall, lest you should haul her on to the greep, while she lay on her side panting and foaming at the mouth and bellowing in agony. And you pulled so hard that the forelegs of the calf came away in your hands, and you had to tie the rope around its neck and strangle it in delivery to save the life of its mither. What with these experiences and Jock Herd's taunting you became feared for your wife and wished you had never caused her such trouble, and next day McPhee would halter a cow that was in season and take her round to the bull, trying to make fun of it, while you began to understand the blind instinct and cruelty in the life force and survival of nature. And some of the cottars would tell you that most of their bairns were mistakes, or that they could hardly shake their breeks in front of their wives and they were nicked. But for all his taunting Jock Herd would give a bit hach of a spit in the wind and say it wasn't so bad as all that for some. Ach these were really bad cases and his wife would look after Gertie for you, seeing there was no district nurse; that she was damned good at that sort of thing, being a midwife like, having had a few herself, though she was past it now poor bitch. And there wouldn't be much to worry about with yon Dr. Craw, 'cause he left most things to nature and used chloryform at the end to make things easier for the creature that was having the bairn.

Of course you never mentioned any of these things to poor Gertie, who got bigger and bigger as the weeks dragged on, and the bigger she got the more you pittied her sitting there knitting by the fire while you tried to settle your mind to a book. But books didn't seem all that important nowadays since you had been in contact with another human being and caused her a great hurt which you was going to have to answer for. The thought of it nearly made you sick, and you wondered how poor Gertie could smile in your callous face so patiently, so sweetly, while she held up the garments she was weaving for the bairn, which you now regarded as a sort of demon you had created within her. But after all she was herself one of ten bairns that her mither had suffered with, all born at home in the box-bed, and all brocht into the world by the same doctor, yon fat cloart of a chiel they called 'Whistling Rufus,' because he sat on a chair and whistled all the time the woman was in her pains; but right clever he was too, for he had cured one of the bairns that had St. Vitus' Dance, by making it sit on the sunny doorstep for days on end twirling its little thumbs between its knees until the rest of its body stopped twitching. And when another of the bairns swallowed a safety-pin he wouldn't let them give it a drop of liquid, but had them feed it on nothing but dry meal for three days, until the pin came right through the creature harmlessly. But surely Gertie must have seen or heard her own mither in the throes of this hideous thing - yet she never mentioned it and you were afraid to ask. Maybe she could laugh your fears to scorn, you silly chiel that had only one sister and had lived in a dream world with your books and film stars all your innocent life. But after all the things you had seen in the dairy byres you just couldn't forget the savagery of nature. You had always worked on the beef producing farms, where they kept only two or three old pet cows that calved easily, and you'd sometimes helped with the ewe lambing; but with heifers it was different, heifers were young cows with their first calves, and Gertie was a heifer, a virgin before you'd touched her.

There had been a fluffert of snow in March and you had to sweep and shovel the snow from the drills to get at the turnips, your feet freezing and your hands numb with the cold. And when the storm cleared McPhee went away to a wedding all by himself and was that drunk he spent a week's wages and left the wedding present on the train. You had to lend the poor devil some money to buy fags because they couldn't get any more credit at the shop. His wife had taken to the whin-dykes again when the butcher or the baker called, sitting out there in the snow, and the poor woman was that much in debt that Gertie shared with her what she could spare, for she had confided in Gertie of their poverty. Yet she wouldn't hear an ill word of her man though he spent every penny, and from what you could hear of them in their beds through the wall they were a loving pair, though sometimes she protested loudly that he was going too far with his

135

foolery, and that she didn't want any more bairns when they were so much in debt. And sometimes old Lowrie took McPhee's bairns home from the school in his car and his wife gave them tea in the fairmhoose, almost made a party of it. But McPhee didn't like this sort of charity and it sobered him up for a while, trying to make ends meet.

But somehow you dreaded that a day of reckoning was coming for McPhee, when he would have to settle these debts that were hanging about his neck like a mill-stone, tightening the noose with a creditors' list that would drive them to plundering his household in a bill of sale, by warrant of sheriff, for the little it was worth, as you can't take the breeks off a Highlander, as they say, when he wears a kilt.

But now the knife-edge winds of a late spring were blowing on the budding trees, but with little heat in the sun to nourish their growth; a dry, cold withering blast that swept across the frost-bitten fields with a pittiless hand, where the sprouting grain struggled to keep alive in such a heartless world. A haze of dust rose behind the dancing harrow and the hungry gulls sailed aimlessly in the wind, placquered against a chill blue sky of broken, fleeting cloud. Sometimes a lark went darting into the cold sunlight, chirping out his hearty song that was carried away in the wind. Out-bye you could hear the eerie wheeble of the teuchats, 'peezie-weep, peezie-weep' over their broken nests, angry with the horsemen that were disturbing their peace, darting down in defiance of the ceaseless furrow, skimming low over the heads of the horses straining at the yoke, and the chiel hirpling between the stilts, steering by the coulter buckled to the beam of his plough, and the reins from the horse bridles twisted round his wrists. Aye it was cold out there where Gertie hung your sark and your drawers to dry in the wind, but inside it was warm with the sun at the windows, where you might put your finger in a flower pot to feel the warmth of the earth and the green smell of the plant.

You knew in the cold grey of morning that you were likely to be a father before nightfall. You could feel the sword thrust in Gertie's back and you could see the anguish in her whitened face, so at breakfast time you went down to Jock Herd's wife and told her what you thought, so she ran up to your Gertie and you 'phoned the doctor from the parlour at the Blackstob, not caring a damn for your muddy boots on the carpet. The doctor's car was at your gable by nine o'clock, where you saw it from the turnip shed, and it was still there at noon when you had your dinner in McPhee's kitchen, not to disturb your wife. You wanted to go inside at yoking time, but the doctor being there you were shy, so you denied her the little comfort that even the sight of you might have given her.

Even at milking time the big black car was still at your gable. My God! What were they doing to Gertie all that time? You could hardly settle to the milking and fell behind McPhee, for you kept running to the door of the turnip shed, where you were sure you heard the screams of your wife on the wind. But you could stand it no longer so you took your jacket from a nail on the wall and left McPhee to the milking and ran down the road to the little white house where all your world existed. Shame or guilt or fear had no power over you now, for

136

you must see at once what was happening to your Gertie.

But when you reached the door there was silence, not a scream, nor even a whisper, while you stood there listening, the whip of the wind in your ears. But you opened the door and walked inside just the same, cap in hand, not knowing what to expect, though you had every right to know. Your wife was almost naked on the bed, a lifeless crucifix of mortal agony, her nightdress rolled above her navel and her knees apart, the doctor between them with his bare arms, one foot on the floor and a knee on the bed, a gentle but powerful man, pulling at the bairn with brute strength, while Herd's wife had both arms under Gertie's oxters, her knees against the bed, holding with all her weight against the strength of the man lest he pull your wife to the floor, a tug of war between life and death, and your loving Gertie the awful sacrifice. She lay athwart the bed, her sleeping body writhing in the grapple of pain that seized her, her bosom heaving quickly with her breathing, her rich black hair ravelled over her sweating face, her mouth convulsed in speechless motion, her white feeble hands still clinging to the iron bed-rails as she had sunk into the chloroform. Dr. Craw glanced at you over his shoulder; merely glanced and ignored you, while Herd's wife shook her head and glowered at you with big frightened eyes full of concern.

Then you heard the first faint cry of the infant, its crimson head cupped in bloody irons in the doctor's hands, pulling it forth in a flush of blood and water. The doctor cut and tied the ends of the umbilical cord, while Herd's wife relaxed her hold on your still unconscious Gertie. She poured a bath tub of lukewarm water by the fireside, then took the bleeding bairn from the doctor and held it in the water, all the time skelping life into the creature until it began to move and breathe and cry. 'You've got a loon!' she cried gladly, looking at your scared face. But you was watching the doctor, while he hid your wife's blood-stained hips with the blankets. He untwisted her death grasp from the bedrails and slapped her cheeks through her ravelled hair, flexing her arms and speaking to her until she opened her eyes, half smiling at you standing there like an overgrown schoolboy. Then Dr. Craw got a needle and cat gut out of his bag and said bluntly that he would have to stitch your Gertie. But you had seen enough to scare you for a lifetime and you dashed out of the house, never even looking at your skirling infant - back to the Blackstob and the milking, but with a strange new gladness in your heart, the first young pride of being a father.

You had your supper at McPhee's again and then went round to see your wife, the house smelling strongly of lysol and baby powder. The doctor had gone and Herd's wife left when you entered, promising to be back after she had suppered her man. Gertie was peaceful now, lying with your bairn beside her and her black hair laced over the white pillow. It was a loon she told you and you said you knew and looked at his puckered crimson face in your wife's oxter; and then you kissed her sweetly and fondly, holding her gently in your young strong arms. But your quine was possessed with a great gnawing hunger she said, and had a great craving for corn flakes, so you got on your bike and went to the shop for corn flakes, the first time you had ever seen the stuff, and you shook out a plateful from the carton, with sugar and cream, and fed your wife with a spoon, lovingly, until she was satisfied, and not allowing her to make any effort on her own behalf.

So you thought everything was fine, and the sun at your windows again, bringing forth the flower from the buds in the lovely carved bowl that Gertie loved so well on the sill, where she could see it from the bed, as the petals stretched forth their colours to the light. But on the second day of the doctor's absence a fever took your young wife that quickened her pulse and redened her cheeks and sent her into delirium. Dr. Craw came in the evening and injected Gertie with a serum which was supposed to arrest her fever, but it merely opened her closing eyes to the misery of your face, for even as you placed your rough loving hand on her burning forehead your tears landed on her cheeks - now hot now cold, but growing slowly colourless and feeling not the touch of your fingers in the creeping hush of death. Dr. Craw cursed himself and said he should have been sent for sooner. But it came upon your Gertie so quickly and Herd's wife said she had never seen it before, this child-bed fever that had sneaked up like a thief in the night, when the doctor's back was turned, and stole away your Gertie. Milk-fever, child-bed fever, call it what they liked, but of all the terrors you had seen in the byres that this should kill your loving wife, her that should have been in a hospital ward, where they might have saved her. For had you not seen the vets inflate a cow's udder and tie her teats with tape, injecting her with glucose and calcium to save her life and managed it. Your Gertie had been a human being but was now a stiff corpse in your little bedroom. Up in the Bogside they had a district nurse for looking after the women, but not in this parish at the Blackstob.

So your mither took your wee son off your hands and you buried Gertie back in the Bogside, among her ain folk, where the kirk bell could be heard at Slabsteen, your Garden of Eden, the shrine of your betrothal, the Paradise you had lost. Your mither had also taken away the coloured things Gertie had knitted so fondly for her bairn, looking forward to its birth with such cheerfulness and patience, such bravery of soul, such confidence; and she had been right in her choice of blue, for she always said it would be a loon, but you couldn't stand the sight of them lying there on a chair; it brought a lump in your throat and a tear to your eye, though you'd have to get used to your son wearing them.

So you were back where you started at the Blackstob, but without your Gertie, living alone and sad in the little home you had built up between you; your 'Little Grey Home in the West' you had sung about so cheerfully in your courting, and Gertie smiling so sweetly at your boyishness as you pedalled along on your bicycles, thinking maybe that you would never grow up, this loon that she had married so hastily, so unavoidably. But now you'd grown up all right and your laughter had turned to tears.

But you still got a bite of meat from Mrs. McPhee, and the poor woman mothered you almost and sometimes turned her face away to hide the tear on her cheek. Life must go on but you had little interest in it and your care for your work seemed without purpose. And you were feart to look folk in the face lest you lose control and weep, folk like Jock Herd and his poor obliging wife who in her ignorance did all she could to help - except call the doctor in urgency, which might have saved your Gertie.

Then one morning in your sleeplessness you banged on the wall to waken McPhee and there was no reply. Maybe they had all died of food poisoning or something, and in your grief and bitterness of heart you didn't really care. But even in the midst of your returning sorrow you struggled into your working dungarees and grabbed your torch and went round and rapped on the door. But all was silent as you stood there in the cold loneliness of the morning, the full moon grinning down at you from an almost starless sky, when the full glow of his face dims their glory. His expression was mocking and mysterious and he only had to wink an eye to look the mischievous image of McPhee himself, lurking home with his lump of shining coal in the midnight hours. It was an expression that could tell it all: of what he had heard and seen in the silent midnight hours of your sleep, before your returning grief awoke you to tossing restlessness. So you shone your torch in at the black curtainless windows, shining on blank bare walls and a house devoid of its occupants. They had taken a 'Moonlight Flitting,' as folks called it, mostly flying from debt to God knows where, and local traders found it hard ever to trace them again. Folk like that got another job in secret, mostly by 'phone from the papers, even without references, maybe a hundred miles away, among strangers, where they could make a fresh start, and the contractors who flitted them were either bribed or sworn to secrecy.

But for a moment your sadness left you, lost in the thought of the plight of others, then suddenly it struck you that you were all alone at the little cottages, that no loving Gertie would come after you with a coat about her shoulders, her sweet kind face asking what ailed you; her soft tender fingers wiping away the tears that sprang in your bewildered eyes. Oh Gertrude! Even the thought of her ghost was a comfort that thrust all fear from your heart. No you wouldn't run like an excited bairn to tell Lowrie what had happened; you'd just walk quietly up the brae and knock loud and clear on the front door till Lowrie's light went on in his upstairs bedroom. For though you were numbed with grief, your manhood purged in youth, you must stumble on in your darkness of soul, and the memory of your Gertrude would be as a new star in the heaven of your heart.

Snowfire!

The river was frozen over to a depth of seven inches. You could see the ice encroaching from the banks as the days passed, closing in upon the flowing current, until only a trickle ran in the middle, and finally this disappeared and the water ran under the ice. And if you stuck a fork handle in the river at the Latch Farm you could barely touch the bottom. Snow blizzards came sweeping over the barren hills and whitened the fields and haughs in mounting drifts. Trees were exploding in the frost and turnips were bursting in the drills. And if you took hold of a wire to stride over a fence it stuck to your fingers and nearly tore the skin away. The old folks in Buchan couldn't remember the likes of it in their time; only once before could they mind on the river being frozen, away back in the 'eighties, when a fee-ed loon took a short cut over the ice, going home to his folks with his fule claes at the week-end, carried in a small bag over his back, what they called his 'chackie', and on his way back to his place the loon fell through the ice at the Latch and was never seen again.

It was the winter of 1941-42 and the Russians were fighting for their lives in the siege of Leningrad. The folks in Buchan said they were getting the tail-end of the Russian winter, though others said it was blowing straight from the Arctic; but in either case it gave everybody a good idea of what the Russians were putting up with. Hitler was at the gates of Moscow, and you were damned glad he had turned on Stalin and saved your skin, so you thought about the Russian folk starving and dying in their fight for Leningrad and you tore at the neeps with a heartened will.

So you dug the snow from the turnip drills and tore at the frozen bulbs with a pick or an adze, and all you'd get for an afternoon's wark was enough to fill a horse cart, scarcely a starvation diet for all the beasts that were chained in the Latch byres, besides those loose in the courts. There was an ample store of bean and green corn silage in the concrete tower, hay and straw in the barns, but as everything was frozen up and no water supply available these had to be balanced with the moisture giving turnip. The storm had caught Gerald Sansom of the Latch Farm with his breeks down, so to speak, without a store of fresh turnips in a clamp, and he had neglected this because for so many years he had stored neeps and never required them, relying on silage in normal snowstorms to see him through. But already the beasts were getting hard in the dung and dry in the hair as the storm lengthened. You couldn't carry water in pails to all your beasts, about a hundred and twenty, including calves and the three milk cows for the cottars' milk, especially when everything was frozen up but the kitchen tap and the horse trough, the latter supplying one of the courts. And those twenty-odd Irish heifers in the other court, which normally was supplied with rain water, in a trough from the roof - these were the biggest problem, and already howling in their thirst. Sansom had bought them just before the storm broke, and since they came off the boat he had been compelled by law to keep them in quarantine for three weeks as a precaution against transit fever or foot-and-mouth disease. He bought a batch every year and wintered them with the bull. Each one yielded a calf, and when the calf had been suckled and weaned he sold the mother fat at a profit. The calf in its turn added to his stock, which saved him buying so many store cattle at the marts as replacement when he sold his fat beasts. This year the ink was scarcely dry in his Record of Movement of Stock Book when the white inferno engulfed the turnip fields.

It was the hardest winter Gerald Sansom had known since he came to farm the Latch twenty years ago. The Sansoms were the landed gentry hereabouts, Gerald and his brothers, though he was the one that farmed the Latch, like his father before him, and you could walk from one end of the parish to the other and scarcely be off their land, except when you crossed the road, when likely as not you'd meet a Sansom with a flock of sheep or a drove of nowt, and you'd have to stand aside to let them pass, for they usually filled the road; and they would be off to eat up some lad's grass who needed money badly or he wouldn't let a Sansom on to soil his parks, for they would eat it to the bone, till you could see the dung of the beasts like molehills, and the field as bare that you'd never lose sight of a mouse from one end of it to the other.

And maybe he'd have to wait a while for his cash the lad, for they were slack payers the Sansoms and liked to have you come begging for your money, like you was a tink or something, or a dog eating crusts from their table. The crofters said you was always better to go to the Latch when Sansom was off in his big car, for then you'd get his wife at the back kitchen door, when she would rant and rave at her man for his neglect and you'd get your money right quick after that, for she was a right decent body Mrs. Sansom they said, and it was a pity she had married that Sansom brute.

But the main grudge that the crofters had against the Sansoms was that their father had bought some of their holdings over their heads, land that was clay and the steadings were done, and no local laird to repair them, only a syndicate that had no interest in their affairs, so long as they paid their rents and asked nothing in return. When the Syndicate wound up and the places went up for sale the tenants got the first option. But some of the sitting tenants couldn't afford to buy their places, nor could anybody else for that matter, but the Sansoms had the money and they bought the crofters out. Some of them were glad to go, because they couldn't afford the horse or the oxen they'd lost in the dreich darg of the clay, blue and dour in the turn of the plough, setting hard in their tracks, till the harrows barely scratched it, and they couldn't make a loam to take seed; iron hard or a squelch of myre, depending on the weather, and the crops were hanged in the baking clay or drowned in a spleiter of rain that spread out on the parks for weeks, because it couldn't get through the clay. By summer it had all

141

dried away, leaving the land cracked and bare, so that the crofters had to cart water for their thirsting beasts, and the grass parks were seared and brown in the scorching sun.

And if a crofter ever looked back he'd see that the Sansoms had his place all in grass and crawling with sheep, after they'd waited a while and tilled in a season that would take seed, coming away fine on the clay that takes grass and clover better than free land, once it takes a hold, and will last longer. And the Sansoms had a shepherd in the old farmhouse and the steading in ruins, for the Sansoms had no use for a steading, all they needed was a few lambing pens and a dipping trough, and a fence round the place that even reindeers could hardly jump.

So if you was a Sansom you got yourself a bad name among folk, but God knows, being a Sansom you knew you didn't deserve it. You couldn't let the places go to rashes and nettles just because nobody else wanted them, or hadn't the money to buy them, and sometimes you left a tenant in his farmhouse and gave him a job fencing the land or working at the Latch in a busy season - damnit, what more could they want?

But since the war started the Government had compelled Sansom to plough up some of the crofts again, and sent him big motor-ploughs that mastered the clay, growing flax on land that wouldn't take corn the first year, because of a weevil in the soil, and Sansom remembered how it had taken on the blue flower on the sweep of the hill, and the Government lads came back to harvest the stuff with plucking machines that bound it into sheaves like a binder. And Sansom only had to stook the flax till it matured like rank heather, then build it into stacks until they were ready for it at the factory, but he got plenty of prisoner-of-war labour for that at a cheap rate, and the motor lorries drove it away. Sansom was on to a gold mine growing flax for the Government on land he had bought for a song, and the evicted crofters resented it and called him ill names for his better fortune. It never struck them that Sansom was doing a good job for the country, growing flax that was made into hose-piping to fight the great fires in the big cities, like London and Coventry, devastated by the German bombers in the night, while the crofters lay snugly with their wives in their warm beds.

But as much as they condemned Sansom and approved his wife, the crofters didn't know all the outs and ins of the Sansom household. True enough Sansom was a bit tight-fisted among poorer folks, and maybe you wouldn't trust him with your teenage daughter, but for a long time there wasn't a man or a cottar woman about his place who would breathe a word against him, for they knew he wasn't so bad as he was painted, and that Mrs. Sansom had become a crack-pot who gave him a dog's life, and they wondered that the man had patience with the creature and didn't wring her dainty neck. She had grace Mrs. Sansom, Clara as he called her, a cultured, emotional, sensitive, delicate woman, and she moved about the farm mansion like a ballerina, sometimes singing and throwing flowers about, or splashing water on the floor, just for the sight of the maid on her knees drying it up, because one day she had seen her man give the quine a playful skelp on the hip in the bye-going, a daughter of one of the crofters who now poisoned his name in the district.

Nowadays Sansom took to his bed by himself and his wife hardly spoke civil to him, and she'd hold up his dirty sark with a dainty thumb and forefinger, as if it belonged to a tinker and crawling with lice, and she'd drop it out from his upstairs bedroom window, where it landed on the green, and the dog wiped his paws on it, then carried it away in his big mouth and buried it among the bushes, the earth flying on to the gravel path where Sansom was dutch-hoeing in his shirt-sleeves, hat on the back of his head, pipe in mouth, watching his wife at the window. And Clara would skirl with laughter and then shut the window with a clash, like a guillotine on a criminal's neck.

And Mrs. Sansom would ask one of the men if he had seen a tramp wandering about the steading, pretending to be the farmer at the Latch, and the man smiled to humour her and said that he hadn't, though he knew fine who she meant, then went home and told his wife so that the clipe of the Latch got about the Buchan howes and everybody knew what the mistress had said.

Sometimes in desperation Sansom took it out on his men, just to prove his authority to somebody, and even among his own cottars his name was beginning to stink, so that past kindnesses were forgotten and they said among themselves that Sansom should have his doup kicked, or that he should be tarred and feathered and set fire to, or thrown in the river with a stone about his neck. Fancy that, and you the farmer about the place, strutting about like a bantam cock and everybody waiting a chance to thraw your neck. It was a sad state of affairs and you a big farmer among the gentry and expecting to be looked up to in the parish.

It had been fine in the old days when the bairns were young, before young Irvine died, and while Errol and his two sisters, Gail and Muriel were still at school. These were happy days and Gerald Sansom remembered them fondly, when they were all around the log fire in the big bay sitting room on a winter's evening, the light shining bright from the electric candleabra, glinting on Clara's golden hair and her blue eyes laughing at the bairns, while they tumbled on the big divan or rolled on the carpet, its lush depths littered with their toys, while the Red Setter lay by the fire, his snout on his paws, with one eye watching the bairns, lest they sneak a ride on his back. Sometimes Clara would play the piano and they would all have a sing song, or she would read to the bairns till they all fell asleep in Wonderland, when she and the maid would carry them upstairs to bed, each hugging a big doll or Teddy Bear, and a deep silence fell upon the house. Then Clara would get out her easel, palette and brushes, daubing on the paint to form some sylvestral scene from her own lively imagination, while her finished works graced the walls in frames of figured gilt and ivoried wood.

On a summer evening Sansom would take them all for a run in the Chrysler and treat them to ice-cream, and he'd drive them round the crofts and his shepherds, and Clara would get out of the car and visit them, like a queen among her subjects and the shepherd's wives thought her a right genteel woman, whom they all loved and respected (whatever they thought of Sansom) though the sight of her jewellery dazzled their poorer eyes, and her perfume was not of their gardens. And Clara seemed so happy; a radiant, kindly, loving wife and mother, and Gerald Sansom thought himself blessed and fortunate in the arms of providence.

But then the Gods withdrew their smiles from the Sansom household, and they smote their youger son with a long and withering illness that took the roses out of Clara's cheeks, yet left the trembling dewdrop, a transparent tear upon the pallid skin. Clara had never been quite the same since Irvine died, though it had given her Joy to see their daughters married, Gail first and then Muriel, and now living abroad, while only Errol, their elder son remained, working on the Latch with his father.

And then Clara's smiling lips had gradually turned to snarl at Sansom, and the eyes that once caressed his soul changed to beams of hate, her lilting voice more like the hiss of a snake. And Gerald Sansom searched his heart for any reason why he should deserve this, and he could find none to merit it, unless it were the slapping of a lassie's thigh, which was nothing to speak of, but you'd think to hear Clara that he had raped the poor quine in the barn. Seeing the way the wind was blowing Sansom told Clara she could sack the maid, thinking maybe it would give her peace of mind and no cause for suspicion. But Clara insisted it would hurt his feelings and then used the quine as a weapon against him, and Sansom was sore perplexed about the fickleness of womankind.

Things had reached a pitch just before the war, and Sansom remembered the day they were going off in the car, Errol driving and his mother in the back seat, laughing and giggling at nothing, and just before leaving she nipped off Sansom's hat and threw it out at the window, and when he jumped out to pick it up, chasing his rolling hat across the windy lawn, Clara had Errol put the car in gear and drove off without him, leaving Sansom standing on the drive like an idiot, hat in hand and a strange curse on his lips. But he was puzzled about his wife's behaviour; she was so much changed from the Clara he once knew and loved. She seemed to get fun out of provoking him, a malicious sense of humour that cut him deeply, though he never spoke back or sought revenge, thinking maybe that if she was ill and anything should happen to Clara he would have no regrets about hurting her wilfully. That the loss of their son had disturbed her was understandable; but it should have brought them closer together, not driven them apart. There was something sinister in her obsession about his familiarity with the housemaid, even to the extent of poisoning Errol against him, judging by the latest event in their relationship. Clara had the whole thing out of proportion.

When the war came Errol was called up for the militia. Gerald had tried to exempt his only surviving son from military service but it was refused him, and Errol had told his father he wouldn't accept it anyway. Errol had been captured at Dunkirk and was now a prisoner-of-war in Germany, while Sansom was left with an estranged wife in a surly Arctic winter.

But while the snowdrop faded and the lily bloomed, as the crocus withered

144

and the sunflower glowed, while the petal fell and gave way to fruit, while season followed seedtime into harvest and autumn into winter - in the passing of time Clara's illness crept upon her, revealing itself in a cough and a slight breathlessness; in her transparent, wilting beauty, in the lunar depths of her distant eyes, like dying stars where once the diamond sparkled. But when Sansom suggested a doctor Clara threw a vase at him, smashing it against the papered wall, scattering the fragments about his feet, and then she was seized by a fit of coughing and a lapse of consciousness. While she lay in a swoon the first big snowflakes came ogling across the lawn and melted on the panes of the great bay windows. During her revival they came thicker and faster, sticking to the glass and darkening the room. In her saner, more compassionate days, what Clara had always feared was beginning to materialise, for she had always dreaded someone taking ill in a snowstorm and all the roads blocked and no way of getting a doctor or an ambulance to take them to hospital, just in the same way as she always imagined a steading fire during a snow blizzard and no way of getting a fire-engine, quite normal fears and anxieties that Sansom always dimissed with a shrug and a smile, telling Clara that her imagination was running away with her better reason. But even as Clara opened her eyes the world was now engulfing her, closing in upon her with a soft white suffocation, and while Sansom pleaded for her permission to 'phone a doctor she cried out against the rising blast. But Sansom rose from her trembling side and picked up the 'phone, Clara staggering behind him but unable to deter his stronger arm.

'It's a conspiracy,' she cried, tearing at his shirt sleeve, 'you just want me out of the way so that you can marry that girl!' She struggled to get at the 'phone but Sansom fought her off and she sat down on the divan, breathless and weak, worn out with emotion and illness.

But now the doctor was at the front door, like a snowman from the wastes of nowhere. The maid took his snowy coat and hat and hung them on a peg in the hall, then conducted him to the bay room, while she herself retired to the kitchen. Doctor Crammond didn't know how he had reached the Latch in such a blizzard and he was deeply concerned about getting back to town. He set down his bag and shook hands with Sansom, and before he could speak to Clara she had risen from the seitle to rebuke him. 'I don't need a doctor,' she protested. 'Gerald 'phoned you on his own. There's nothing wrong with me but a chest cold, and if you think you are going to get me into one of those horrid sanatorium sheds in the garden, like the one Irvine died in you are sorely mistaken Doctor Crammond!'

Crammond was taken aback but he grasped the situation immediately - 'Glad to hear it Mrs. Sansom, even if I am on a wild goose chase to treat you for a chest cold!' And he wiped the moistened snow from his spectacles. 'All the same Mrs. Sansom, seeing that I'm here on such a day I should like to have a look at you. Surely you wouldn't have me come all this way for nothing; after all a chest cold should be attended to before it gets worse and a tonic mixture might build you up a bit. As for putting you in a sanatorium Mrs. Sansom - I have no intention of doing any such thing, least of all in this weather, and with a chest cold - good heavens woman . . . you'd catch your death of cold! No no, we can't have that!'

'But I assure you doctor . . .' But Clara was wracked with a fit of coughing and sat down again on the divan.

'Now now Mrs. Sansom, I really think you should let me have a look at that chest cold. Would you be such a good woman as to go upstairs to your bedroom and let me examine you?'

'Oh, very well doctor, seeing that you're here.' So Clara was persuaded and went upstairs to her bedroom, weak and short of breath, the doctor going up a few minutes later, glancing at Sansom almost with a wink in his eye as he climbed the stair.

He examined Clara thoroughly, talked to her, gave her a sedative and left her lying quietly on the bed, then came down to Sansom in the living room.

Sansom took the doctor into a side room for a wee dram to cheer him on his way, where they could talk freely out of Clara's hearing.

'Good God man,' Crammond said, tippling his glass, 'I should have been here long ago. The last time I saw your wife her general health gave me no cause for anxiety, but now this . . . And why the hell didn't you send for me sooner? You must have noticed that your wife's health was failing. Surely you don't want that on your conscience.'

Sansom stared at the doctor in great alarm. 'Surely you know me better than that,' he said, 'and what's the matter anyhow?'

'Tuberculosis!'

Sansom sat down flabbergasted. 'Oh no, surely not doctor. I never dreamed . . . after all she isn't all that different. She's a bit thinner I'll admit, but she still eats and sleeps, as far as I know (we don't sleep together any more you know) and she's never had much of a cough. Anyway she wouldn't hear of a doctor. Even now I 'phoned you against her will.'

'You want to know the truth Sansom?' Crammond asked, sipping his whisky.

'Of course doctor, let me know the worst.'

'Your wife has tuberculosis of the lungs, well advanced, and I dare say an x-ray would reveal them like a sponge. I think you should get her to hospital as soon as possible, now; before the storm closes in completely. Persuade her, tell her it's for an x-ray, anything, but get her there somehow, and the sedatives will help. I'll send an ambulance as soon as possible.'

'Why is it so urgent?' Sansom interposed.

'Because I'm afraid for a lung collapse, or even a haemorrhage, and furthermore I think her mind is affected. She has tuberculosis of the brain!'

Crammond rose from his chair and walked to the window, hands behind his back, where he stood for a moment watching the snowflakes whirling at the glass, coming ever faster in the rising wind, now howling in the chimney and moaning at the doors. Sansom sat with his elbows on his knees, rolling the whisky glass between his palms, a dry fear in his mouth, his eyes glazed with tears.

146

'You mean she will die?' he asked.

Crammond came back from the window, his face wrapped in thought.

'Well there's been some spitting of blood or bowel discharge and I'd need a second opinion on the brain infection. But most likely the whole thing will escalate eventually; what is sometimes known as Galloping Consumption, and believe me it isn't called that for fun, but for its speedy end to the patient.'

A glimmer of understanding came into Sansom's mind. Crammond's words explained a lot of things: Clara's strange behaviour, her obsession about the housemaid, her little fits of spitefulness, now he forgave everything; oh my God, that it had come to this .

'Doctor,' he asked, 'do you think she will last till Errol gets back? I know she would like that. Maybe it's impossible to get the girls home just now but after the war it would be easier.'

Crammond sat down and faced Sansom across the table. 'Depends how long the war lasts,' he said, 'but I hardly think so; a month or two perhaps, maybe less. Look Sansom, I'm sorry about all this but when the end comes we could handle Clara better; you've got to get her to hospital before the storm breaks, this thing can't wait, it's urgent!'

'Does she know?' Sansom asked.

'Of course not,' Crammond admitted.

'Then you'll never get her to hospital.'

Crammond was uneasy, fretful, and worried about the storm. 'Can't you tell her something Sansom, even a lie?'

'I haven't the heart to tell her the truth, after what happened to Irvine.'

'Heavens no, Sansom, anything but that,' and Crammond rose from the table. 'I'll have to push off now while the roads are still passable. The wind is getting up and they could be blocked in a couple of hours. Get your wife ready for hospital and I'll 'phone an ambulance.'

But the ambulance never reached Clara. Even while she was being prepared for hospital a howling blizzard enclosed the Latch, a white and furious holocaust that raged for three days and nights and had barely spent itself at the end of a week; then terrific frost and blowing snow that cut off the farm completely from the outside world. Sheep were buried everywhere and the shepherds on the crofts were digging them out at the risk of their own lives. For lack of turnips the cattle in the byres were bellowing for water, and those Irish heifers in the dry court were howling their heads off. The Latch farm was two miles from the main road; two miles of wind-packed snow, level with the hedges and still blowing. Sansom got two of the cottar wives to look after Clara, because she resented the maid, and they took it in turns, day and night, looking after her, but intruding as little as possible, because she wouldn't hear of being an invalid. Sometimes in her sedation she cried out for Errol, thinking he was an angel, and could fly to her on wings of silver, shining bright. She was being gently doped into submission and didn't seem to realise the full significance of her plight.

Sansom 'phoned Doctor Crammond and told him the roads were blocked.

Crammond said that if Sansom could dig his way to the main road and take Clara on a horsesledge he would send an ambulance to meet her.

'Can't it wait or the storm blows over?' Sansom asked, his voice crackling in the frost over the wire.

'No Sansom, it can't wait. The storm could last long enough at this time of year. Get digging in the first lull and let me know when you're ready. The snowploughs are stuck on the main road but I expect they'll get through in time. Keep in touch Sansom. Bye for the present.'

But it was into the second week of the storm before the folk at the Latch could get about with their shovels, clearing paths from the cottar houses to the steading, to their wells and hen-runs, and all were short of food because there were no vans to supply them. There was no postman either, and no newspapers, though John Snagge and Alvar Lidell told them on the radio how the war was going; how the gallant Russians were still holding out at Leningrad, and how our convoys were still reaching them with supplies at Murmansk, despite attacks in the Arctic by German submarines, and the risk of pocket battleships.

Though there was no meat for their dinner the cottars at the Latch boiled a frozen turnip and made neep brose, supped with fresh cream. Only on a Sunday would they kill a laying hen to make broth, for though it lasted a family for two or three days it was something of a sacrilege when you thought about the folks at Leningrad.

For the cottar bairns it was something of a holiday because they couldn't go to school. Nobody died in their little world and everybody lived to be terribly old. Sledges and toboggans were out in strength on the slopes and the quarry brae and the snowballs were flying from every nook and cranny. When the snow freshened a little they rolled it into balls and made a snowman in the front yard, with little bits of coal for eyes and one of father's old pipes stuck into his mouth, a carrot for a nose, and an old hat on his head, sometimes with a bit coloured scarf about his cold neck, flapping in the wind.

Sansom had the three horsemen and the grieve working on the road, heaving snow to a height of nearly eight feet, while it stuck to their shovels in the frost, giant sugar lumps piled above their heads. But the powdered drifts still whipped across the fields and covered in their tracks again. Even the main roads were still blocked, with no chance at present of an ambulance reaching Clara. But Sansom would have his men dig the two miles and take Clara by horse-sledge to the main road, where he hoped there would be motor-ploughs and a chance of reaching the town. Even the fields were over a foot deep in wind-polished, crusted snow, swept by choking powder drifts that filled the burns and piled against the dykes and hedges, impassable barriers for man and beast. The trees were crystalized in the sun-frost and razor-edged wreaths curved around every corner and gate-post, spiralled into whirls of white phantasmagoria. Winter's ruthless artistry was perfected on every stalk of withered grass and glistening pine-needle, her most worthless trifles jewelled in a moment of her careless snow-broom.

Meanwhile Sansom had to think of his stock, parched for want of water and without turnips, for they couldn't endure long on silage and dry fodder. The turnips in the sheds were for the byres, and even these were frozen. Kevin Porter, head stockman at the Latch was smashing the stone-hard swedes on the floor with a fencing mell, because they wouldn't go through the slicer, and when thrown in the feed troughs the animals thawed the pieces with their breath. Sansom told Kevin and his assistant, Geordie Thom to carry the old house bath into the dung court and water the crazed heifers with pails from the kitchen tap, the only one that was running, for he couldn't stand the noise of the brutes, and they were disturbing Clara. He hadn't lied to her but had told her plainly they were taking her away by horse-sledge for an x-ray, and that it was for her own good. She protested at first and then cried about it and said she hated snow-storms. But the sedatives Doctor Crammond left were beginning to take effect, and Clara dried her eyes and seemed to be looking forward to her sleigh-ride; it would be so jolly she said just like Christmas, with holly berries and tinkling bells, and Errol would be waiting for her at the end of her journey. Poor boy, he must be weary of waiting.

The horsemen still toiled on the road, never even taking time off to run their horses out on the snow, so that their legs were swelling for want of exercise, standing idle in the stable, such a long time away from the plough. So the men cut down their hay and corn feed and the horses stood in the quiet stable all day long with their lower lip sagging and one hind foot behind the other, fair in a sulk it seemed for want of a trot round the steading in the snow. The grieve said the men would have to thresh a stack of grain shortly, but while the straw still lasted in the barn the mistress came first. Neighbours came to help on the road and the small army of shovels managed about half-a-mile a day. The snow was freshening slightly, leaving their shovels cleaner. In three or four days they should break through. Sansom kept in touch with Doctor Crammond on the 'phone.

But there was no satisfying the thirst-crazed heifers in the court. They drank water faster than the feeble tap would run, fighting to get at the trough, ripping each other open with their cruel horns. Even the horse trough for the store bullocks was licked dry and Kevin suggested letting all the animals out to eat snow, in spite of the quarantine. But Sansom thought he had a better idea, for he remembered Kevin smashing turnips with the fencing mallet, so he told him to take it and smash a hole in the ice at the river's edge, big enough for an animal to drink - to hell with restrictions, and he and Geordie would bring the heifers down to the haugh. It was the day the men reached the main road and at last an ambulance would be waiting there for Clara. The path cut by the men wasn't wide enough for motor traffic, but would take a single horse and sledge, so the men would be ready about an hour after dinner, once they got the sledge rigged out and a horse harnessed. Sansom would take the beasts to water and be back to see Clara off; he wouldn't like her to leave the Latch and all that nowt howling, and he would like to kiss her goodbye, for if the storm came again it might be the last time . . .

Even the frost had gone at mid-day and a dazzling sun shone upon the snow.

Icicles were forming on the byre roofs, like glittering rows of sharpened spears, where the heat of the cattle had melted the snow. Above the howling of the nowt came a sound like distant thunder, while a great mass of snow avalanched from the slates, silencing the beasts in their fear for a time. At night it would be brittle frost again, especially with a growing moon, but during the day it was a warm, blinding desert.

Kevin Porter shouldered the 14lb. mell and struggled through the sun-flashed snow. Red-breasted robins twee-twee-ed at him from the naked hedges and a lone hare loped across the fields. The ice on the river was iron hard and he could only chip the surface with the rebounding hammer. It seemed that nothing short of a charge of dynamite or a German bomb could smash a hole in the steel-grey roof that covered the running water. Kevin swung the hammer until he was out of breath, but for all his labour he failed to crack the ice, merely smashing it into sugar in a slightly deepening bowl. But eventually he broke through and the hammer splashed in the water, now running under eight inches of ice, strong enough to carry a horse, Kevin thought, or even a herd of nowt, if anyone cared to risk it. Now it was easier and he hammered the ice to break the edges, to make a hole wide enough for a beast to drink.

He had barely finished when he heard the heifers come bellowing from the farm. Sansom hadn't wasted any time but had opened the doors of the court and let the cattle out, a snow-blinded, thirst-crazed, stampeding horde that floundered in the deep drifts and plunged towards the river haugh, Sansom and Geordie panting behind them, and the black Labrador that Sansom kept as a game dog sniffing at their heels, though he was little use among cattle beasts.

On they came, plunging through the snow wreaths, their red mobile backs arched in a stifled gallop, their hot breath rising like steam, heading straight for the water hole, drawn by the scent of the water. Kevin did his best to head them off, swinging the hammer in their faces and over their heads, stopping them in their tracks, allowing only one animal at a time to the water hole. But the press was too great for Kevin to hold them and he cried for Geordie. Kevin yelled and laid about them with the hammer, but it was a useless struggle, and for his own safety he had to step aside. Geordie couldn't get near him, and while one animal drank the others pushed her forward on to the ice, two and three for a start, now half-a-dozen, the dry sugary surface holding their hoofs, and several leaped on from the snowbank, skidding to a halt on their hurdies, landing on the ice with a sickening thud. Sansom kept shouting to hold what they had on the bank and tried to send the dog on the ice to turn the others back. But the dog merely broke their ranks and more and still more heifers sprang on to the ice. One got stuck in the water hole, tearing her legs on the sharp edges, while she struggled in vain to get out. Of the twenty-five heifers only two now remained on the snow, Kevin and Geordie holding them back, and no one would dare go on the ice for the others.

Sansom stood on the sunlit bank and cursed himself aloud as a fool; dreading every moment that the ice would break. If it did the Insurance company wouldn't cover his loss and he would be heavily fined for breaking the quarantine rules. Better that he had continued watering the beasts from the kitchen tap, slow as it was, but it was no use now crying over spilled milk. And then he remembered Clara, even now they would be wrapping her up on the horse-sledge and he would have to hurry back to say goodbye! Oh the folly of it! But how could he drag himself away from the dreaded spectacle before him? A score of Irish heifers sniffing about for water on a death-trap while every moment he expected to hear the first deafening crack on the ice. Now he was in a fit of anguished indecision: whether to watch his heifers drown or hurry home to kiss his dying wife. By now she would be under way. Silly that he thought he heard the noise of sleigh-bells, mingled with the mooing of the cattle.

Kevin was first to see the 'plane, a great black bird that came shining out of the westering sun, the sign of the swastika under its wings, flying low over the snowy landscape, spattering the steading with rapid gunfire. Next moment it was roaring over the river, spurting hot bullets into the ice, stampeding the cattle, the rear-gunner's dome-shaped turret glistening in the sun, its twin stings swivelling downwards and spitting bullets at the running heifers, strafing them with deadly fire, a staccato that ricocheted far up the quiet valley, while the great stinging wasp sped on, a black shadow on the snow, an angel of death spattering gunfire on the distant farmsteads.

'Great God!' Sansom cried, but even as he spoke the first crack in the ice was like a gunshot. Several cattle lay dying in their own blood and the others burst into panic, scared by the noise of the plane and the gunfire they charged at each other in frantic bellowing fear, horns goring deep in hide. There was another succession of cracks, clear and sharp in the winter sunlight, and visible splinters appeared on the ice. The next moment the river split open and half-a-dozen heifers disappeared. Great sheets of ice slid apart and toppled the roaring animals into the blood-stained water. They pawed and scraped at the toppling edges as huge chunks of ice gave way. Animals were swimming desperately in circles while others vanished helplessly under the ice. Up and down the river where the cattle ran the ice gave way, and the crackling of ice and the lowing of nowt went far up the silent haugh, the swift black current sweeping the animals under the ice-roof, while some few sprang to the banks and safety. Only the dead now floated, blood seeping from their bullet wounds, and Sansom could look no longer. The little red and blue veins were blotched on his face, his teeth a chatter with cold and anxiety, his eyes stark and dazed. He turned wearily towards the Latch, his stick going deep in the snow, the black Labrador behind him, while Kevin and Geordie brought back the five surviving heifers, tamed with fear, shaking the beads from their wet hides and trembling in the cold.

Sansom had just missed Clara, the horse and sledge a mere pencil point between the distant snowbanks, where the white arch of the world met the china blue of the skyline. He met one of the cottar wives in the close. 'The mistress has gone, Mr. Sansom,' she said. 'We had her on the sledge, all wrapped up in blankets and two hot-water bottles for her hands and feet; then that terrible 'plane came over, a German it was, shooting at the steading, and it frightened the horse till it bolted with the sledge, but my man held on to the reins and it didn't get very far in the deep snow, yet owre far to call them back to see you. Your wife got a terrible fright Mr Sansom and she cried out for you from the sledge, I could hear her; but she came to no harm poor soul, and now she will be gone on the ambulance on the main road. It's the second time the Germans have gunned up everything hereabouts. Mind the last time when they nearly got one of my bairns going to school?'

'I remember, Mrs Burr,' Sansom said calmly. 'I remember, and thank you so much for attending to the mistress.'

'It's been no trouble Mr. Sansom, and it's just a pity that we couldn't do more for your poor wife.'

Clara had just gone in time, for by evening there was a fresh on-ding of snow. Cottar folks could see it in the darkening sky when they fixed their black-outs on the windows. This time it was driving sleet that stuck to the tree boles, then electrifying frost that killed the birds or sent them twittering to the steadings for food and shelter.

Next morning, when Sansom picked up the 'phone to enquire for Clara the line was dead. The sleet and frost had thickened the wires with a weight of ice that brought them down on the snow, snapping between the poles. Sansom came out of the farmhouse and saw what had happened, and as he looked beyond the steading he saw hundreds of crows in the stackyard, ravaging the corn rucks, scraping at the snowy summits and tearing out the corn stalks with their hungry beaks. It wasn't what they devoured that a body grudged but what they wasted, strewing the snow with good corn still on the stalk. Some folk took a gun to them, if only to frighten them off to a neighbour, but somehow in the midst of his troubles Sansom hadn't the heart to shoot them; after all they helped you get rid of the tory-worms in the Spring so you couldn't grudge them a bite of keep in the winter.

By nightfall all the lights had failed at the Latch and Sansom said the turbine wheel must be frozen to the wall of the water-shed. Next day the men set to with hammers and chisels, chipping at the ice on the water-wheel, frozen at the spokes to the stone wall. But their efforts were in vain, because the buckets were solid in ice, a mere trickle of water coming from the chute, freezing like candle-grease as it dripped over the wheel. The paddle-wheel drove a generator that supplied the farm with light, though not the cottar houses, and up till now it had never failed, day or night, except perhaps when there was a spate, which floundered the wheel in water, when the light would rise and fall with the speed of the wheel, because it was direct current and no storage batteries. It was a cheap and reliable source of power, diverted from the river, where once had been a meal-mill, even driving the turnip slicer on a three-phase system, and Sansom had never bothered to instal accumulators or an engine in case of break-downs.

Before the war the Latch farm was all lit up at night and folk passing on their bicycles in the dark thought it was a great sight. They could see the road for half-a-mile on either side of the farm without their gas-lamps, and for miles around you could see the Latch lights twinkling on the river, a little Venice in the night. Sansom was proud of his illuminations, and maybe that was why some folk called him the Bantam Cock, seeing he wasn't a big man, rather short and stocky, so perhaps it was because the folk outbye had to be content with stable lanterns that they called him names.

Of course the war and the black-out had ended the illuminations at the Latch, but the wheel had never stopped until the present freeze-up. Now it had failed Sansom in his hour of greatest need, and he didn't have a single lantern to light his farmhouse, nor even a hurricane lamp for his steading, nothing but a bundle of candles, which he handed out at nightfall to his workers; for stable, barn, courts and byres, and told them to be careful in case of fire, and he would see to it that such a thing would never happen again.

So Kevin and Geordie stuck a lighted candle on some of the travis posts along the double byres, two or three on pillars in the courts, and one in the barn, though not above the straw. At supper time they collected all their candles and put them safely away until morning, then they were lit again for the usual routine of feeding and mucking out the fattening steers. During the day they still carried water to some of the beasts or struggled in the neep park with a pick and shovel, for the frost still persisted, especially at night, when the moon blizzards swept the fields, while by day great mountains of snow cloud towered around the blue horizon. Sometimes a trio of Spitfires would zoom overhead with a gladdening roar, veterans from the Battle of Britain, training young pilots from Tortorston Fighter Station. In the far meridian a white thread of vapour might reveal a Flying Fortress, a mere spec in the blue, or you would hear the friendly purr of an Avro-Anson from Coastal Command watching the sea.

In 1940 Government sappers had planted wooden poles all over the Buchan fields, about a dozen to a park, depending on its size, and these were meant to break the wings of German 'planes trying to land invasion troops, and now these derelict poles stuck out of the snow like the remains of a petrified forest, as far as the eye could see between the hail squals on this white wilderness.

Folks were having to wade knee-deep in snow to the nearest shop for provisions, some waist-deep across the howes to Jake's Emporium, because the roads were still choked, and where the cottagers had cleared a path the snow was as high as the eaves. Some even took their shovels inside at night, because mostly they had to dig their way out in the morning, their windows battered with snow and their rooms in darkness.

Jack Frost sketched flower patterns on the window panes, and intricately laced caricatures that were a sneering reminder of summer, thick on the glass so that the cottars couldn't see out, not unless they took a cloth or sponge and a pail of warm water outside to wash them off, otherwise they were still there the following evening, because the sun was never strong enough to melt them.

Kevin and Geordie went to the shop in the evenings because they hadn't time during the day, and Jake would give them their ration of fags and tobacco for the week, and maybe a box of matches if they didn't have flint and fleerish and saltpetre for a light. It was a sair trauchle in the snow after a day in the byres, but they didn't mind so much since all Home Guard duties had been suspended in the Bourie Hall during the storm.

Sansom yoked the foreman with his horse and sledge, to try and get provisions from the town, and maybe see Doctor Crammond, but the track the men had dug was blown full again and he had to turn back. So Sansom sent two men to Jake's during the day, each with a pillow-slip, and they brought something for everybody, besides a tin of tobacco for Sansom, for the man had to have his smoke, especially at a time like this when everything was going wrong with him.

Sansom was not a religious man, but in these first lonely Sabbaths of the storm since Clara left he yearned for a little spiritual comfort. It was such a long time since he had been at the chapel, him and Clara, that he had almost forgotten what she looked like then, before the children were born, and a soft tear flooded his eyes. In those days Clara had been the light of his world, his better self, the joy of his heart, and now it was ended. Was this the cross then that had been hewn for him in the tribulation of life? A time of trial so that he might be judged accordingly? But he was the stoic always and would bear with patience, even as Job in his affliction, something he remembered from the bible readings at his mother's knee.

A fortnight had passed with the candles at the Latch, Kevin lighting one from the other to save matches, when one evening he saw a fat stot swipe a burning candle from a travis post with his tail. Kevin searched carefully for the missing candle, turning over the straw among the feet of the animals and even their dung, but he never found it. It must have been thrown to the ceiling, concealed but still burning, perhaps against a cobweb or an electric cable, or dripping fiery tallow on to the straw in the cattle hakes on the walls, for by nine o'clock the Latch was ablaze, a perfect target for the German bombers that came over from Stavanger in Norway, only three-hundred miles across the North Sea. Sansom had always wondered why the Germans had invaded Norway, but now he was beginning to understand, and the merchant seamen didn't call the Buchan coastline 'Hell's Corner' for nothing.

Kevin Porter and Geordie Thom were coming home from Jake's Emporium when they saw the Latch on fire, the skylights red in the darkness, and a tongue of flame on the roof, rising ever higher, licking the night sky. They started to run, but it was difficult with Wellington boots in the deep snow, and pillow-slips stuffed with groceries. As they approached the Latch they heard the moaning of cattle, deep in the byres and muffled in the snow. Kevin and Geordie ran breathless to tell their wives, dropping their pillow-slips at the doors, then to rouse the grieve and the horsemen, and finally Sansom, who had fallen asleep by candle-light in the big bay sitting room, the labrador at his feet, while the maid was visiting the cottar wives.

Sansom's first thought was the telephone. Then he remembered the wires were down, and the snow-ploughs hadn't yet come near the Latch. In war time it was all they could do to keep the main roads clear. There was an ample supply of water where Sansom had drowned his heifers, but no fire-engine to pump it; about six hundred yards to the river, too far to form a human chain, he would need half the parish with their own buckets to do it, and by the time they got to the Latch in the deep snow it would be burned down. These were futile, impossible thoughts, like clutching at burning straws, but they flashed through Sansom's mind with the red fire at his windows, the nowt now screaming in his ears from the blazing byres. And there was alway the risk of German bombers. A recent pub fire in the Broch had been a night target that had cost the town forty lives. All the things Clara had dreaded were now becoming a reality, almost the fulfilment of a prophesy. Now Sansom cursed the bombers. 'Hell and damnation' he cried, as he ran into the close. 'Damn the war! Damn the snow!' He was usually a quiet forbearing man who took life in his stride, but the fire had brought him to breaking point. What with his son a prisoner of war; his wife dying in hospital; his cattle drowned; his steading on fire and no fire-engine! Great God! Just how much could the man take?

But even as the Latch burned the frost was losing its grip. The stars disappeared and the sky grew darker, and a freshening wind sprang up from the south-west, fanning the roaring flames and lifting the smoke cloud that hung above the steading. The red orange glare of the fire lit up the white countryside, turning the snow to crimson, a throbbing glow in the darkness that brought neighbours in from miles around, struggling in the snow to reach the Latch.

Men folk were already in the hot byres unchaining the frantic nowt beasts, clambering over their backs as they pranced about in terror, fighting their neck chains that the men were trying to slacken. Once free the beasts charged to the far end of the byre and came back with their hides on fire, tiny flames licking along their spines as they rushed outside to the wind. Men struggled desperately in the heat to set them free, choking in the dense smoke and tugging at the chains with hot sticky fingers. They ran outside for breath and couldn't get in again for charging bullocks. What with the roaring of cattle, the neighing of horses, the squealing of pigs the cackle of poultry, the yelling of humans, the crackle of flames and the sough of the wind it was hell let loose at the Latch. Fiery rafters caved in and trapped the chained beasts still in their stalls, roasting them alive till the boiling fat was running down the urine channels, yellow flames licking at the trickle. Falling slates came in a shower and bursting glass flew from the skylights. Heat and smoke overcame human effort. Men stood back aghast, their faces blistering hot, their eyes smarting from timber smoke, their mouths parched with fear and excitement. The inside byre walls glowed like an oven and there was a sickening smell of roasting flesh and burning hair. A cry went up that the roof was falling and the last daring men ran out from the turnip shed, chased by fire maddened, careering stirks, froth at their nostrils and tails in the air. A great arc of fire crashed down and smothered the dying animals in an avalanche of flame, while the wind took showers of sparks over the steading, floating like tiny stars till they died in the snow.

Freeing the horses had been easier because the flames hadn't yet reached the stable; only smoke, which was bad enough, but each man haltered his pair and led them out to a park, rearing and neighing at the sight and din of the fire. Once free they galloped about in the drifts, their nostrils wide and their eyes bright with fear, kicking at the squealing pigs that ran at their heels in the beaten snow. Men threw open the doors of the dung courts and chased out the cattle, herding them into nearbye fields for the night. Hens were cackling from the tree-tops and ducks were quacking in the snow. Cockerels still safely on the roost behind the steading thought it must be morning and were crowing in the din. Out bye on the brae you could hear the bleating of sheep, safe from the fire but huddled in the snow wreathes. Cats ran about with kittens in their mouths and rats and mice were leaping everywhere, running along the blackened rafters and falling into the fire.

Somebody cried out to Sansom to halver the steading, to cut the roof apart at the corner where the barn joined the stables, and save the remaining wing. So the men ran round the back to get the ladders out of the implement shed, and a cross-cut saw, while Sansom gave them a bushman and a long-handled axe out of the logging hut. Volunteer neighbours scrambled up the ladders and began smashing the slates with hammers to get at the sarking boards and rafters, but by the time they got the first cross-tree to sag the heat and smoke was upon them, funnelled along by the wind from the gutted byre; so the men stood back on their ladders, exhausted in the heat and the suffocating smoke, and were finally forced to the ground. It was all too late to do anything but stand back and watch the wind-whisked tongues of fire whipping into the dry seasoned timber with devouring relish.

The straw in the barn was now a raging inferno, wrapping the threshing-mill in sheets of flame, feeding on the greasy oil-bearings and licking out at the paraffin tank in the engine room. Slates came clattering down and rone pipes came away from the heated walls. The barn roof blazed like a herring-bone bent in the middle, where the embered cross-trees gave way and crashed in an upsurge of flying sparks, the heat exploding the paraffin tank in a muffled bang, spewing liquid fire into the stackyard, but the rucks were wet with melted snow and the flames died on the thatch. The dung in the cattle courts was blazing like a peat moss, fanned by the wind from the open doors, the iron roofs sizzling hot, the latticed wooden tresses a scissors work of spreading fire. The granary floor collapsed with tons of smouldering seed corn, smothering the raging furnace in the stables below. Fire raced along the canvas conveyor belt and ravaged the hay-loft, reddening the skylights and splintering the glass, while a spiral of smoke rose mockingly from the old bothy chimney. The men had pulled out the horse carts from the arched pends under the hay-loft, and all the hand tools they could rescue. Most of the heavier implements: binders, mowers, drill-sower, manure distributors, ploughs, harrows and rollers, besides a yellow Fordson tractor were all safe in a large shed behind the steading, near the tower silo, seventy feet of reinforced concrete that wasn't even warm from the fire. The mansion house was never in any danger, secure in its scarf of trees, and while the garage burned fiercely Sansom's car was pushed safely to the front drive.

156

It was long past midnight and the heat so unbearable that folk stood back in a ring round the steading, standing in slush from the melted snow, their faces aglow in the firelight, while the wind still carried sparks and smoke far across the snowlit fields, dotted with cattle and wandering pigs. 'It's been a quick thaw!' somebody joked, and a ripple of quiet laughter went round the spectators. 'Aye,' said another, 'but it's a good job that Jerry didna come ower.' But the conflagration was dying and Gerald Sansom looked around at the many faces who had come through the snow to his aid. Some of them were evicted crofters of his father's day, now old men with bent backs and sharp piercing eyes: had they honestly come to help or to gloat over his misfortune? Others were neighbours of long acquaintance and some were folk he had never seen before, so that he couldn't tell farmers from cottars, master from man. But to Sansom that sad night all were friends; more than he had ever hoped to share in the days of his triumph, and the thought of it warmed his breaking heart and moistened his eyes with tears.

He invited everybody into the farmhouse for a dram or a cup of tea, something even he could ill afford in these days of rationing. But Clara's cupboards were amply stocked and everyone got a share, while the maid and the cottar wives served them at table or on chairs in the candle-light.

Then somebody cried out 'Fire-engine!' and sure enough, when everyone ran outside a fire-engine stood in the close, white with snow and clustered with helmeted men. Folk in the toon had seen the red glow in the sky and told the police. A snow-plough had been despatched to open the road and they had struggled through, alas too late to save the steading. But the firemaster had a message for Mr Sansom: a last minute telegram from the hospital in Aberdeen, sent to the police, and they had asked the firemen to deliver it. Sansom took the small pink envelope from the fireman with a trembling hard, and as he slit it open and read its contents his great heart broke at last. So Clara had not lived to see her dear Errol home from the war. It had been his earnest wish but even this had been denied him. Gerald Sansom turned his broad back upon his friends and walked slowly through the slush to the farmhouse, the black Labrador at his heels, all eyes watching him as he went through the garden gate to the front door. He didn't want them to see him cry, to see his body shaking in the great sobbing that soon would overpower him, the final humiliation to his shattered manhood; these were for the Labrador and the quiet of his ain fireside.

'Water!' cried the fire-crew, 'where can we get water?' 'To the river,' someone shouted, 'this way to the river!' Aye, it had been the tail-end of a harsh Russian winter. The Buchan folk were sure of it, and while the storm lasted eight people had been suffocated in her barren fields. But for Gerald Sansom, this little Napoleon of the Buchan farmlands it had been something of a retreat in the snow from the flaming gates of Moscow. Even as he sobbed quietly in the great bay sitting room at the Latch, the busy firemen were snaking their hoses towards the broken ice on the river, pouring loss upon loss to quench the last embers of a dying snowfire.

The Secret of Tormundie!

The Old Laird Wouldn't Allow Anyone to Alter the Steading, and People Wondered Why?

There was a new laird in Tormundie House, you could tell by the alterations they made to the steading, especially in the barn wing, 'cause that was a part of the buildings the old laird wouldn't allow them to touch, him or his mistress, while they were alive. Of course it didn't matter at all in the old days, but what with all this mechanisation, tractors and machinery, combine-harvesters and such like, steadings had to be altered to suit the new conditions. Some folks were even knocking their steadings down flat and rebuilding from scratch, and what with drying kilns, tower silos, Dutch Barns, milking parlours, self-feed cattle courts and sludge-pits, the new steel and concrete structures look more like rural factories than fairm toons.

While the old laird and his lady were alive the manager and the factor had worked round the barn wing, not daring to touch it, but changing this and that in a haphazard sort of way, for even then there was a crying need for labour-saving development. Heaven knows what would have happened nowadays had they still been as thrawn to change anything: what with the urgent need for a corn-drier and storage bins the barn wing would have been a must for conversion, and when the new laird took over it was one of the first things he started on . . .

So from what you had heard of Tormundie you had never expected to see the old mill thrown out of the barn, but there she was in the close, her great wooden hulk lying where the tractors had left it, for it had taken two of them all their might to wrest her from her trestles and drag her up the steep slope to the road. The scrap merchant had robbed her of her fine brass bushes, roller-bearings and steel stripper-drum, while all her leather belting, elevators and riddles had yet to be disposed of, and maybe a bonfire was the quickest way for that. The great length of chain elevator for the straw had been taken down from the rafters and fitted up on wheels, which would be a great help in lifting bales of hay and straw in the new Dutch Barns, saving labour in years to come. The only thing they'd forgotten was the 'shackin spoot' for taking the corn along the loft, where it was still suspended on its lath sticks from the rafters, perhaps a memorial to puzzle future students of an agricultural heritage.

There had been a threshing mill at Tormundie since the days of the flail, driven first by a team of horses on the revolving spars, what is known as the 'mill course' or tread-mill, which rotated a steel shaft connected to the workings of the mill. You could still see the hole in the wall where the shaft went through, though the spars and pinion-wheels have long since disappeared. Tormundie was a hill farm, where it was impossible to irrigate water in sufficient volume to drive a threshing mill, so there was never a mill-dam or a water-wheel on the place, and wind-mills were never popular in Scotland for this purpose. But you could still see the covered opening in the blackened roof of the engine-hoose where the brick lum stood in the days of steam, and the old rusted cinder brander still lay in the stackyard. 'Oh aye,' they would brag in the old days, 'Tormundie was a gey toon, she had a stem staak and a styag aboot 'er!' meaning of course a smoke stack and a stallion, a prestige that could only apply to a farm of considerable size, and with the resources to support it.

Then came the internal-combustion oil-fired engine and you can still see the concrete base where this monster stood, chugging away with his great fly-wheels and tireless piston. In our own time this was replaced with electricity and press-button threshing, which was a long way from the flail and proved to be the ultimate in barn threshing when the combine-harvesters appeared. But the old mill had been through it all, and though she had given you mony a 'het sark' a body never thought to see the day she would lie stripped naked in the farm close. But there she lay in her cobwebs, a relic of the bye-gone days of farming, and many a time in your sweat you could have wished to see her in smithereens, though you never expected it to become a reality.

And they've just had the close concreted at Tormundie and the farm road tarred, not a dub about the place or a weed to be seen, nae mair scrapin dubs or howkin weeds roon the steadin, they canna pay you for that nowadays, and what with that glass roof over the place you would think you was working in a railway station, were it not for the stink of the silage. All this self-feed and slatted floors, sludge-pits and tanker sprays they're just hauling the craps home from the parks and putting it through the nowts' bellies and spraying it back on the grun again, with hardly a teeth mark on it, and the stink of the stuff is enough to drive you to the drink. This is modern farming and you've just got to accept it, though you rather fancied the smell of the old dung cart and the sharn midden, which was a healthy smell compared with this sludge stuff.

But never a load of muck to drive out nowadays or a load of neeps to bring home in the gloamin; never the knack of a wooden cartwheel in this age of machines, nor the neigh of a horse or the whistle of a ploughman, now drowned in the jangle of transistor radios in their tractor cabs, and they've even got them in the dairy byres, where the kye are chewing the cud to the tempo of the Top Ten and letting down their milk to the Beatles and the twang of electric guitars.

But the new laird hadn't demolished the barn, for he had left the walls standing and repaired the roof before he installed a corn-drier and storage bins for the corn and barley that would come off the combines next harvest. The barn wing also contained the corn loft with the cartshed pends underneath, key-stoned arches of dressed stone that rested on enormous square pillars of stone and lime, a lasting credit to their builders. These he had blocked up with bricks and cement between the pillars, which still preserved the original appearance, so that you could point out to a stranger where the horse carts were penned in the old days. But the loft floor had been removed, and with it the hatch over a pend where the horsemen used to back their carts to load corn, dropping the sacks through the opened hatch into their carts. This was the part of the steading that really mattered to the old Laird and Lady Margaret; the arched pend that went under the hatch in the loft floor to the old dung court, a very old octagonal building with a pagoda like thing on the roof, as if its builder or designer had spent his life in the Orient. Nobody had dared to touch this part of the steading while the old laird was alive, or his lady after him; they wanted it left just as it was, and they had bought the whole estate to keep it that way.

Now you may ask what the old laird and his lady could be wanting with a draughty hole of a cartshed pend when they lived in a mansion fit for a prince, not at Tormundie of course, but up at Kingowrie yonder where they had built a palace so grand that common folk were feared to go near it, unless you were employed on the estate. Great dykes had been built round it with stone lions at the gates, and when you shone a light on them at night their eyes glittered like diamonds. Folk said the laird had spent all his money on this 'White Elephant' and that he couldn't afford to repair Tormundie, which they said he had bought for sentimental reasons, to please the Lady Margaret, who had once worked there as a kitchiedeem, as he himself had done, as a stonemason.

But when you hear folk say that so-and-so was 'born in a cartshed' they usually mean that so-and-so always left all the doors open and nearly starved you to death, because there are no doors on a cartshed pend and so-and-so had never got into the proper habit of closing them. But the laird wasn't born in the cartshed pend, nor his lady either, for folk would tell you he was a barfit loon out of Pitarrow yonder, where he had served his time as a stonemason, and when he was sent to bigg up the dykes at Tormundie, where the Lady Margaret had worked as kitchiedeem, her father, who was grieve on the place, fell through the hatch in the cartshed pend and broke his neck. He was looking over the place at night, without a lantern, up in the loft where he fell through the hatch, where the horsemen had been loading corn during the day and left the lid off.

When the old grieve died and his widow left Tormundie the kitchiedeem got a job as nursemaid with the local dominie, looking after the bairns for his wife. But then the dominie goes and does a most extraordinary thing, for he gives up his job as school-master, sells off all his furniture, packs up the rest of his belongings and sets sail for that Bolivia place in South America yonder, where all the tin was being mined, and people were getting rich quick, and the dominie takes his wife with him, and the bairns, and what was more important - the serving quine to look after them.

Och but there was a great hue-and-cry about the tin that was being dug up in that Bolivia place, and also about the gold and diamonds that were being mined in South Africa, so that people went mad with a sudden lust for money, and a lot of them clamouring to go abroad. Quite ordinary folk, who had always been content with a bite and sup, and somewhere to sleep, now had a frantic desire to get rich quick, and they just up and off from their daily darg like a dry leaf in the wind of fortune, which they hoped would fill their laps with gold. Even our stonemason got caught up in it, for ach, he was fed-up with Tormundie and his dykes for all he got for it, so he gets a few of his cronies together, and they decide to have a go at the diamonds, which they thought would be richer than tin, working their passage as deck hands on a boat to South Africa. But just about the time they landed at the Cape, the Boers started a war with the British, more likely as not about the gold and diamond mines which they said was theirs in the first place, since they were Dutch settlers and had been there before the British, and the lads were likely to be involved, which was not their intention at all, because there was no money to be made fighting the Boers, and maybe get killed in the process, so they gets on a cattle boat and works their way across the wide Atlantic ocean to this Bolivia place, where the dominie and his wife had gone and the little kitchiedeem from Tormundie.

So they all gets dug in at the tin, each man to his claim, employing cheap local labour and making a lot of money in a short space of time. And folk said they didn't treat the natives any too well, paying them little more than pocket money for a hantle of work in bringing up the tin from the mines, lashing about them with whips and cursing at the creatures till they gave themselves a bad name and some of the natives threatened to shoot them in revenge. So they just got out in time with bulging pockets before the tin boom went bang and they had to sail for home, but not before the stonemason had met up with the dominie's nursemaid again and got married because they knew each other at Tormundie. But now they were a wealthy pair, and a son was born to them out there in Bolivia, who was nearly ready for school when they returned to Scotland. But they had to have somewhere to live, somewhere splendid, now that they could afford it, and they made up their minds it would be awfully nice to buy Tormundie, that grand mansion where they had first met, for the quine had loved bidin there and she had been loth to leave it when her father died; surely it would be the thrill of their lives to own a place like that, where they could be lord and lady where they had once been servants, a dream to be realised now they had the money. The only snag was that Tormundie was not in the market, nor could the resident laird be tempted out of it with money, so they would just have to wait, and maybe some day . . .

In the meantime they bought the estate of Kingowrie, which was miles from their beloved Tormundie, but they had no choice, and here the stonemason built a huge mansion, one of the most beautiful homes you ever saw, and planted the grounds with trees and shrubs and flowers and made an artificial lake where the white swans floated gracefully in delightful settings. But even in the midst of all this grandeur and luxury the laird and lady of Kingowrie still sighed for Tormundie and its fond associations with the past.

But before the new laird of Kingowrie built his mansion house he and the Lady Margaret travelled extensively in Europe, where the laird studied the classical ruins of Greece and Rome; he became a great scholar and studied the works of John Ruskin on 'The Seven Lamps of Architecture' and together the laird and lady of Kingowrie visited a great many of 'The Stately Homes of England', the great country mansions built by the Smiths and the Adams brothers, and other famous architects. Kingowrie was modelled on what the laird had learned in study and travel, a classical structure of mixed design, something in the nature of a Grecian Temple, supported on a double colonnade of Corinthian, Doric and Roman pillars, with a flight of marble steps leading up to the front entrance, and a glass observatory on the roof where you could look at the stars through a giant telescope. The stonemason cared nothing for tin, but for what he could do with the money it brought him, and while his interests abroad still flourished he threw it about him with a lavish hand. His only regret was that it had not been spent on Tormundie.

But after a year or two even this aversion was overcome and Kingowrie began to gain some affection in the hearts of its creators, and but for a terrible tragedy might have earned their love and Tormundie would have died in the past, forgotten in the joys of raising their young son to inherit the fruits of their labours on the new estate. But their short-lived joy became a lasting sorrow which turned them against Kingowrie for ever, for their only son was killed in a riding accident, thrown from his pony against a tree in Kingowrie woods, which broke his back and killed him instantly, so they took him down to Tormundie and buried him in the local cemetery, as near their old home as possible, and folk thought it was a queer thing to do with their only bairn.

But now they were without an heir, so there wasn't much point in adding to their estates, and to minimise death duties the laird declared his assets as a private liability company, under his own chairmanship, with a factor in direct contact with his tenants and the farms he worked himself.

And so the years passed, and by the time Tormundie came on the market the laird of Kingowrie was an old and disenchanted man, crusty with the rigours of life, and his lady but a withering leaf of her former self. But they had their chauffeur drive them down in the Rolls to Tormundie, the old man with a staff, a rug on their knees, and they drove round the estate and looked at their old home from the road. They swung in at the lodge gates, smooth and silent, and up the drive, now ablaze with rhododendron flowers, mauve, white and purple, and the sun flashed down on the shining black Rolls through the tall beech trees that lined the avenue. Finally they stopped at the big house where the chauffeur got out and opened the car doors to assist his master and mistress on to the gravel path. But so eager were they in sight of a great fulfilment that hardly any assistance was necessary, and they met the estate agent at the front door with broad smiles, and with footsteps that were lightened with the memories of youth. The agent took them into the great drawing rooms, still richly furnished, where they hadn't dared to set foot as youngsters, the laird not at all, and his lady only on a special errand for her lord or mistress.

But it was a disappointing dream: a dream realised too late in life and the laird almost wished he had never seen the place again. What he had lavished on Kingowrie he should have spent here. In his watery eye was reflected the palace he would have made of this fading mansion, for he still had a notion for masonry; for the classical moulding and the chiselled stone, and his eye for landscape gardening had not dimmed with the years.

When the old couple left the mansion house the laird told the chauffeur to drive slowly round the steading, and to stop at the arches over the cartshed pends, where the Lady Margaret's father had been killed, and they peered forward to look at the old cottage in the woods where she had played as a girl. But for these circumstances they would never have been laird and lady of Kingowrie, perhaps never even lovers, or at best only a pair of ordinary cottar folks you'd never have heard a cheep of again. It was indeed a day of nostalgia for the ageing couple as they drove back to Kingowrie, half happy and half sad with the memories and prospects their journey had aroused.

So they bought Tormundie, which, besides its several farms, also included a smithy, a joinery shop, a meal mill and property in the village; a self-contained estate, and the purchase price ruled out any intention of restoring the mansion house to the glory they had already made of Kingowrie, whereupon the Laird and Lady Margaret decided that Tormundie should remain in their day exactly as it had been in their youth, stone upon stone, which in time was to prove a great stumbling block when the age of machines burst upon the land, and but for the farsightedness and dogged persistence of the resident manager would have left Tormundie as much out of touch with the present as a Highland croft of last century.

The factor now ran the two estates, comprising perhaps a dozen farms between them, large and small, and a resident manager was appointed to each Home Farm, one for Kingowrie and one for Tormundie, run as independent units and both responsible to the factor. The factor stayed at Kingowrie, but you could easily tell when he was visiting at Tormundie, about once a fortnight, when you could see his big posh car parked in the drive in front of the mansion house, where the manager lived with his young wife and family. Most likely they would go over the books together, the factor and the manager, and then, after tea on the lawn, if it was a fine day, you'd see the pair of them taking a stroll across the fields, or motoring round to one of the farms on the estate, where some alterations might be taking shape. And what you might ask could the factor creature know about farming? Him that used to be a barfit loon selling newspapers at the street corners down in Glasgow yonder, for the lad had fair gotten up in the world, starting as a clerk for old Kingowrie and now running the show himself, or so you would have thought, but as far as farming was concerned the managers kept him right, though they couldn't match him at counting up figures.

And so the years wore on and the laird became a dottard and endured stroke upon stroke like hammer blows which slurred his speech and crippled his limbs until he was eventually confined to a wheel-chair. He was now in his seventies and taking little interest in what they did at Tormundie, which perhaps was a good thing, because agriculture was in the throes of the new mechanical age and alterations to the steading were an absolute necessity if the place was to survive economically. The manager made his suggestions to the factor, who conveyed

163

them to his mistress at Kingowrie, who, in her common sense, consented to everything except any interference with the barn wing; this she insisted must be left intact, as she and her husband had agreed upon before his senility, for she wouldn't break her trust with the dying laird.

The old stonemason was now confined to one of his grandest rooms in Kingowrie mansion, where the purple walls were hung from ceiling to floor with silk and wool embroidery, damask tapestries in richly coloured scenes from myth and legend: battles, flowers, saints and landscapes, peopled with incidents from history seemingly still alive in their transparency and brilliance, fine art treasures bought in the salons of Europe and Asia Minor at incredible prices. Heavy velvet curtains, likewise emblazoned, shrouded the mullioned windows, while marble statues graced every corner of the room, with busts of great men in the alcoves. The ceiling was carved in polished wood without a nail that would rust, and painted with oil periodically to make it everlasting, while suspended from the centre on a golden chain was a chandelier of purest shining crystal. The floor was also inlaid in wood and scattered with the skins of lions and tigers, still with their heads on and showing their teeth and eyes that glittered in ambient life. The furniture was carved as from ebony, inlaid with brass, stolid and elaborate, and adorned with ornaments of priceless value, amethyst, ivory, pewter and bronze.

Here the old laird of Kingowrie and Tormundie spent the whole day in his chair tearing up old newspapers, tearing them into strips until the heap was as high as his knees, when he would fall asleep by the marble fireplace and the blazing logs. A watchful maid would then tip-toe into the silent room and remove the heap of torn newspapers and replace it with the latest editions from the city, for the laird in his own way was still following the share markets and dabbling in high finance. The maid would then tidy the room, moving in elf-like silence on the animal skins, add a few more logs to the fire, replace the safety-guard and then retire into obscurity. When the laird woke up he began tearing the pile of newsprint into strips again, and if you had given him pound notes he wouldn't have known the difference.

Day after day this went on, week after week, month upon weary month, year upon year, while the ageing Lady Margaret watched over her husband with pitying gaze, reflecting on the tragedy that a man so gifted and resourceful should come to this: the prospector, empire-builder, business magnate, classical mason, landscape gardener; the architect of great mansions like Kingowrie, now like a child in a nursery, depending on her and her servants for his every bite, for his every want.

Then one day suddenly the rustle of paper ceased. The listening maid thought the laird had fallen asleep again, or maybe he was dead, for he sat so still in his wicker wheel-chair. She tip-toed into the quiet room as usual to remove the customary heap of torn newsprint, and while she knelt to pick it up the laird spoke to her. The quine got such a fright she nearly screamed, almost ran from his presence, for she had never heard him say a word before. But she composed herself and stared at the old man, waiting and listening. He wasn't

164

looking at her but staring at the fire. Then he habbered something and she bent closer to hear him. In a jumble of hesitant words she thought she managed to make out 'Take me to Tormundie!' She was sure that was what he had said, and she repeated it herself to see if it made sense 'Take me to Tormundie!' The old man was silent now, not even nodding his head, but the maid dropped the paper rags and ran to tell her mistress.

The Lady Margaret came into the room in great haste, bent and crippled though she was, eager to catch the laird in one of his lucid moments, which were few and far between. He was still awake with his palsied hands on the arm rests of the chair, peering vacantly at the glowing fire. She knelt down in front of him, listening hopefully, but all she heard was his hoarse breath coming and going gently and moving his frail body with each little spasm. She looked at his wan face in the firelight. His eyes were strangely blue and clear but vacant and far away, seeing not what was presented to him but that which his contorted mind reflected, as in a broken mirror, far in the past. She knelt there till she was nearly cramped, waiting and listening, watching his shrivelled frame rise and fall gently with his steady, mechanical breathing. Surely the maid couldn't be mistaken. Perhaps it would be too late to make sure. She touched his cold quivering hand on the arm rest and eventually it crept over hers. He never looked at her but his parched lips were moving again, mumbling something that brought froth to his chin, a mutter of broken syllables that sounded like '...back to Tormundie!' But the Lady Margaret understood, and she knew what she must do, and she fell upon his breast and wept.

The 'phone rang at Tormundie House and the manager's wife was told to prepare one of the best rooms for the laird, to have beds in it and to air them, to light a fire and fill a box with newspapers, and next day at noon, when it was warmest they wrapped the laird in a plaid, with a hot-water bottle at his feet and drove him in his smoothest Rolls to where he wished to die . . .

The Lady Margaret did not long survive the laird, and the great mansion of Kingowrie has been stripped of its finery and its empty rooms are used as a store for fertiliser and animal feeding stuff, its beautiful oak ceilings still resplendent but its peeling walls a stark reminder of its former glory. The farms on the estate were sold to their tenants and the only semblance left of the old laird are to be found in the neglected but beautiful policies which still surround the mansion house. But you will search these grounds in vain for a gravestone or memorial to its former owners, nor will you find them in the local churchyard, and you may ask - 'where then did they bury the Laird and Lady of Kingowrie?'

Perhaps you could ask the new laird of Tormundie, where the cartshed pillars have been blocked up but not obliterated, where above the old pends you can still perceive the strength and perfection of the great key-stone arches, and there, as sure as you may find a Pharoah in the heart of a Pyramid, or a living martyr built into the walls of a monastery, there in these bricked-up cartshed pends you will find the Secret of Tormundie, you will find it in the shape of a silver casket, containing the ashes, and maybe the spirits of its former owners.

Harvest Home

Jonathan McGillivray had been the blacksmith at Bourie for as long as most folk could mind, and he had shod their horses and metalled their ploughs and rung their cart wheels since some of the fairmer chiels were in hippens, comin on for forty year maybe and nae much change in the man: a bit crook in his back from leaning over horses' hoofs with a burning shoe, held with a spike in his hand, his fingers gnarled into the curve of the hammer handle, his old bald head polished like a yellow turnip for the spring show, but as swack as ever at the picnic races and still as fond o a dram. An gin there was a concert in the Bourie Hall he could give you a tune on the fiddle, skreichin awa up there on the stage, his red face like a full moon newly risen at the end o hairst, and again you would find the blacksmith at the Meal and Ale celebrations.

But Jonathan McGillivray was a name far too long for the fairming chiels in the Bogside, especially in the hairst time when they were hurried, so they just called him Jotty, and Jotty it had been for some of them since they were toddlers. So the hairst comin on folk began to look out their binder canvasses that were mostly kept on the rafters of the corn loft, away from the vermin, and they would take them to the saddler for repair, maybe a bit stick to tack on here and there and some patching to do and buckles to be sewn on; and besides his harness duties the saddler was fair stacked up with wark, so that he had to send some of the binder canvasses to the sail-maker down at the harbour in the toon. The farmer billies had forgotten all about their canvasses in the height of summer, when the saddler was slack, and now they all came jing-bang, in the mou o hairst, and there was a great clamour for repairs at the last minute. Others had forgotten to order binder-twine and the agents' lugs were ringing with the dirl of the telephone, which was something new in the Bogside.

Some folk had to take their binders to the smiddy for mechanical repair and there was another hue-and-cry for spare bits. There were the few who were methodical and had things done on time, but most of the farming chiels were easy going and left everything until the last minute; and maybe you couldn't blame them when you thought of the patience they had to have with the weather, waiting an opportunity to handle their crops, long over-ripe and rotting in the process. Nature was their schoolmistress and she had taught them patience from the day of their birth, snatching at her skirts but wary of her moods, awaiting her smiles and the shake of her apron, when they could gather in plenty from the sunny fields. It was an environment that would have sent the factory-bred boardroom mind to the wall; and maybe it accounted for the tolerant attitude of the farming chiels, 'glad of small mercies' as they say, the children of a mistress whose tears are slow in drying. Some of them will tell you that the weather clerk is boss and the banker is the farmer; that they themselves are only caretakers looking after the place and the most they can hope for is to die in debt.

The factory chiefs have only strikes to contend with but the farmers have Mother Nature, and when she weeps over the harvest fields her tears are a desolation. In 1927 she had a fit of weeping, the likes of which their fathers had never seen before, nor their children since. In fact the farmers thought she had pished herself and when the sun appeared they said he was only out for a wee-wee. Sometimes he came out on stilts to keep his feet dry, staring down those shafts of light piercing the storm clouds the sunscape artists love to paint but are hated by the farmers. Almost every day there was a 'tooth' in the sky, mostly on the sea, the broken pillar of a rainbow, the other end of it shining in somebody's park of wet stooks, with a bit missing overhead, and this phenomenon appeared so very often that folk began to talk of the Rainbow Hairst, and whether it was at even or morning it was always a warning to the farming billies that the umbrella sky was leaking.

'Sic seed sic lead' they used to say, meaning that the harvest would be as the seed time had been, yet the spring of that year had been a moderate one, so the farmers never trusted Dame Nature after that. Most of them had barometers on their lobby walls and when they tapped them in the mornings they nearly fell off the hooks, always at rain and still falling, while outside in the close the hens refused to take shelter and the cats in the steading washed over their lugs, sure signs of rain, while old men complained of rheumatism and stinging corns. Over the parks the oyster-catcher birds were skirling for more and still more of Mother Nature's tears. There were even jokes about it; like the loon who said to himself 'The mair rain the mair rest,' hoping to get a sleep in the straw, but when the farmer overheard him he changed it to 'The mair rain the mair girse (grass)' and the farmer forgave him.

Our farmer chiels are the unspoilt sons of Mother Nature and in 1927 she threw the book at them: rain hail sleet snow and thunder; frost that turned their turnips to stone, and when they burned their useless crops she sent gales to fan the roaring flames across the corn fields, the night skies red with the conflagration. That which was too sodden to burn went under the plough and the spring of the following year was a paradise. It seemed that Mother Nature relented for her sons and she gave them a harvest that lasted only a month, but with a slightly lower yield than most.

But when the farmers brought their binders to Jotty the blacksmith he dirled his hammer on the ringing anvil and said: 'Damnit tae hell, couldn't ye have come sooner!' thinking that experience would have taught them better over the years, though it never did, and they never listened to his advice or admonishment. Now as always in late summer Jotty was surrounded with binders, so that folk with their motor cars could hardly get by on the road: what with Deering, Albion, McCormick, Massey-Harris, Hornsby, Sunshine, Milwaukie, Wallace

(Frost & Wood), Osborne, Bisset etc., all the popular makes, and all waiting for spare parts from the makers, delivered by bus or carrier from the agents in Aberdeen, like Barclay Ross & Tough (later Barclay Ross & Hutchison), or Reid & Leys, or even from as far afield as George Sellar & Son Ltd. in Huntly, more famous for their ploughs than binder spare parts. Jotty's wife poor soul was up to the eyes in invoices and accounts, with hardly time to tidy up her house or cook a decent diet for her man and his assistant. What with the usual wark of shoeing horses and his ain crop to harvest, though it was only a few acres, Jotty had his sleeves rolled up to his arse-'ole almost, all day and half the night, with hardly time to fill his pipe, smoking more spunks than tobacco, and for want of nicotine he was short tempered and ready to snap your nose off as soon as you put it round the top half of the door that was always open in daytime.

On Monday mornings Jotty would tell you he had worked all day on Sunday while you was sitting sleeping in the kirk, and that the minister worked only one day a week while he worked seven; unless there was a wedding or a funeral, or even a christening, which wasn't all that often in the Bogside, and you said it wasn't all that wonder then that some blacksmiths had gone in for the clergy and turned their collars back to front. But this only angered Jotty worse and he refused to shoe the shelt you had brought with you, riding on its back to the smiddy. 'Damnit tae hell,' says he, his fusker sticking out like a byre broom - 'it's jist sae muckle a body can do!' So you had to threaten to take the shelt away again before he would shoe it, and he was a bit feared to let you do that, lest he offend the farmer chiel you worked for; so you just had to be prepared to duck quick if a hammer shaft came flying through the hoof reek if Jotty's birse was up, for he spent his busy life solving everybody's problems but his ain. Some blacksmiths had a reputation for their ill nature and Jotty was no exception.

Jotty had just gotten the telephone and the linesmen had cut down the old chestnut tree where the wires came down from the pole to his parlour window. Jotty's wife was fair dumfoonert with the dirl of the thing in her lugs: farmers asking for Jotty or his man to come and look at their binder that wouldna bind a sheaf, or anither that wadna cut a stalk o corn, and no wonder when you remembered that some of them stood outside all winter, rusting and rotting in the sleet and rain, with never a drop of oil or a clart of grease on the knotter mechanism or the cutting bar. What did they expect when they didn't look after their machinery!

Shoddy Davidson yonder biggit a ruck on top of his binder at the finish o hairst, which at least kept it dry when he hadn't a shed to hold it in, and Jotty said a lot more of them could take a leaf out of Shoddy's beuk; lads like Spootiehowe and Snibbie Tam yonder, for you might still see last year's clyack sheaf sticking out of their binders in the middle of a stibble park, never even troubling themselves to take it to the gate, let alone transport it on the road - at least it was still there at the back of the New Year, the last time you was in that airt.

Snibbie Tam went over the parks to the Mains to ask for a bang on his telephone ('cause it was only the big farmers that had them) and he dialled Jotty's wife at breakfast time and said he liked the smell of her bacon frying that was coming over the line, just to humour her like, and said that a bicker of brose did fine with him, and when he heard a bit 'Ki-hee' of a laugh in his hairy lug he speired gin Jotty or his man would take a jump on his bike and come up to Kirniehole and take a gander at his binder, 'cause it wadna bind a sheaf, and when it did it was no thicker than a dog's leg, dammit tae hell.

But Jotty hadn't the time to go near Snibbie Tam, so the daft gowk yoked his three-horse binder in a yaval park and cut a whole day throwing loose sheaves. He was that anxious on sic a fine day (and there were few of them that year) and Jotty never putting in an appearance that the chiel went fair starkers. Hardly gave the horse beasts time for a munch of hay at dinner time, or a blibber of water, but had them trailed out of the stable and away to the hairst rigs as soon as he had a tattie over his ain thrapple, hardly taking time to chew it he was in such a fash. Next day he had everybody out gathering and binding up the sheaves, even the kitchie quine and his auld mither, and a tinker that was passing on the road. The tink happened to look over the dyke to see what the daft creatures were at, thinking maybe that Snibbie was scarce of binder-twine, or that he had been using an old back-delivery reaper. So Snibbie cried 'Hie' to the tink and the creature came over the stubble with his pack on his back and Snibbie said 'Can ye mak a ban?' And the tink said 'Aye, fine 'at,' and Snibbie said 'Weel, gie us a hand tae gether up this stuff.' So the tinker left his pack at the fairm hoose, where he got a bowl of hot soup from Snibbie's wife, and a fill to his pipe, and syne he got yoked to making bands and tying sheaves and stooking them, and right good he was at it too, and tidy in his work, and though it was a long sair trauchle of a hairst Snibbie kept him on for the leading, for he was a good hand with the fork as well, and he slept in the barn and got his food in the kitchen. Atween times, when the weather was bad, Snibbie had the tink yoked to the Smiler, like a horse beast, with a rope over his shoulder, raking between the stooks, but when Snibbie was out of sight the tink turned the rake on its back, upside-down with its teeth in the air, so that he had an easier go and nearly ran off with the thing. Snibbie paid him three pounds a week for this, besides gathering strabs and opening out sheaves that were sprouting in the bands, so that as a hairst hand he made as much or more in three weeks than a loon got for a six months' fee.

So that was Snibbie, and he went right off his food that year of the bad hairst in 1927, the worst in living memory and there has never been the likes of it since, folk chauvin on till the New Year in the hairst parks and burning whole fields of corn when it was dry, not worth the cutting for all the corn that was left on the withered stalks. And Snibbie didn't sleep at nights for the batter of the rain at his windows and the thought of his corn sprouting in the stooks, and his wife was at her wits' end with the breet and right glad to see the end of that ill hairst and the stirks all chained up in the byres.

But never mind Snibbie though he be throu, for as far as Jotty was concerned the hairst was only startin, and a lot of binders still to be sorted.

But bad hairst or good, horses still died of grass sickness and beasts took ill and the vet was another lad that was sore tormented when the farmers got the telephone. There was old Johnnie Rettie from the Myres that was seldom sober and cleverest when he was drunk. Johnnie had the 'phone before the farmers, but now he regretted it, for they had him out of bed in his sark tail any hour of the night. But Johnnie's wife took over the 'phone, and as she had a sharpish tongue she soon sorted out the farmers and they thought twice about ringing her up at any hour of the day, and when this didn't work she stiffened the accounts a bit. She kept the books as well because Johnnie couldn't be bothered, and left to his own wyles the farmers would have had his services for nothing. In the old days of the shilt and gig Johnnie's sheltie knew all the places and took him there and back drunk or sober, but since he got a motor car he had to have a chauffeur to drive him about. And Johnnie would pull an aching tooth or lance a human boil or even deliver a bairn if he had to, and sometimes save the doctor a lang journey to some ailing body who needed no more than a dose of salts and treacle.

But Johnnie was getting old and a bit dottled folk thocht and near the end of his tether, so they sometimes tried him out to see how clever he was or to see if he was losing any of his skill. Now there was a chiel they called the Wiley Rottan who warsled on a place on the Hill o Jock that had a mare with the colic, and when he 'phoned the vet Johnnie told him to put a sack on her nares, which meant over her back and rump to keep her warm or he came to see her. So the Wiley Rottan told his foreman to put the sack on a healthy mare to play a prank on Johnnie Rettie. Now the vet had a squeaky kind of voice, like he always had a greet in his throat, a fraiky kind of wye of speaking to animals, in a language they seemed to understand, and he had got into a habit of speaking to humans in the same tone, maybe because he thought them no better than animals sometimes, and whiles a bit worse. Anyway, when he got warsled out of his car and stytered over to the stable Wiley's lads were waiting at the door to get a laugh at Johnnie, but he just smiled in the passing and went swaggering along the stable in his checked tweed suit looking at the mares, right to the far end of the stable, where five mares and a horse stood in a row. The sack was on the first mare in the third pair, fifth from the door, but Johnnie Rettie passed her by and came back to the second mare in the foreman's pair, went up beside her in the stall and took off his pickiesae hat and listened at her bellie with his best lug, poking at her ribs and flanks with his soft skilled fingers, syne he told the foreman to get hold of her head and put a stick in her mouth or he got a look at her teeth, for Johnnie was a dentist as well as a vet. 'That's the wrang ane,' says the Rottan, coming to the door and thinking to catch the vet off guard. 'But na na,' says Johnnie, like a bairn choked on his medicine, 'ye thocht ye wad play a trick on Johnnie Rettie, eh! But I'll tell ye this Wiley, that yer mearie's gaun tae hae a foalie!'

'I ken that,' says the Rottan, still crowing like a cock on the midden plank.

'Aye,' says the vet, with a bit sparkle in his cunning eye, 'but ye didna ken that she was gaun tae hae twa.'

170

'Twins vet?' Wiley asked, fair stamygastered.

'Aye twins Wiley; twa foalies, so I'll gie her a ballie and file doon her back teeth a bittie, so that she can chew better, and gin ye mend yer manners Wiley I'll maybe come back and foal the cratur for ye.'

'God's sake vet, afore ye leave come owre tae the hoose for a dram.'

Now when Dargie Thomason saw the vet's car standing in the close at Wiley's place he sent his loon on his bicycle to tell the vet to come up to Sandyknowe 'cause he had a cow with the staggers.

'The staggers, loon,' said the vet.

'Aye,' says the loon, fair in earnest.

'And have ye been layin on 'er wi a stick, loon?'

'No, I hinna touched 'er!'

'Ah weel, tell yer father I'll be up jist noo,' said the vet, and went in with Wiley for his dram.

Up at Sandyknowe the vet met Dargie in the close and he took Johnnie to the byre to see the ailing cow.

'The wife canna melk 'er,' Dargie explained, 'she's aye tryin tae mak her watter and staggers aboot a' owre the place.'

Johnnie Rettie stood on the causey greep and glowered at the little black cow with mounting interest. 'But gin she had the staggers Dargie she couldna stand ava, lat alane fit aboot. G'wa and get a basin o warm watter and a bittie soap and we'll hae a look at her in-timmers.' And Johnnie Rettie took off his pickiesae hat and his jacket and gave them to his driver, then rolled up his sark sleeves and waited for Dargie with the hot water. When he returned the vet soaked his hands in the soapy water, and while Dargie held the cow's tail aside he thrust his bare arm full-length into the uterus of the ailing cow. After about five minutes he withdrew his hand and washed in the basin, then put on his coat and hat again.

'She'll nae trouble ye again Dargie,' he said, 'and she'll stand at peace to be milked.'

'What ailed her than, vet?' Dargie asked.

'Ye kent that yer cooie was in calf, Dargie?'

'Oh aye, I kent that vet.'

'Ah weel, the calfie had a wee foot in the water passage and she couldna mak 'er watter properly, that's the wye she was staggerin aboot. I've jist put the foot back in the womb and yer cooie will be a' richt noo Dargie.'

A skeelie mannie was Johnnie Rettie the folk said, and they knew they owed him a lot.

But all this time we've been with the vet Jotty the blacksmith has got the binders sorted and they're back in the hairst parks, transported from their bogey-wheels and ready for cutting. The canvasses have been buckled on to the elevator rollers, the blade sharpened and fixed to the driving-rod on the cutting-bar, the needle threaded and the driving wheel screwed doon, the divider in position and the platform adjusted.

The three-horse team are yoked to the drag-pole, the driver in his seat, the whip in a socket at his elbow, as long as a fishing-rod, though you never saw him using it. Maybe you could stand on the platform going round the first time, seeing there wasn't a job stooking, slicing round the stubble roads made by the scythemen, the corn reels striding into the standing grain, swathing it on to the cutting bar, the blade in lightning motion, slashing the feet from the ripened corn as it falls on the platform canvas, to be hustled into the guts of the machine, the packer arms grabbing furtively at the corn stalks, getting them into bundles with the ears to the tail of the binder, the wooden butter tidying the shear of the sheaf, the long steel needle curving up through to put a string round it from the canister under the driver's seat, the knotter tying it, the knife cutting the string, the delivery arms tossing the bound sheaves on to the shorn stubble at regular intervals, all as quick as the eye can follow, faster than a human being could ever perform it. And as the long rows of sheaves increased so the stookers picked them up and set them on end, stubble to stubble, eight or ten sheaves to the stook, set north to south to catch the varying winds, the corn clustered to the sun and weather, row after row, park after park until the weather broke . . .

Then the noise and clatter of the binders ceased and you were yoked with scythes to cut the lying holes, corn that the rain had flattened and would choke the binders, so you bound the sheaves by hand and trailed them to the open stubble, where you stooked them clear of the standing crop. And the rain of 1927 was no ordinary rain for it fair lashed doon, not for days, but for weeks on end, almost non-stop, so that the grun wouldn't carry a binder, and some folks scythed whole parks and bound it by hand, the women sore trauchled at the binding. Others yoked their horse-mowers and cut it like hay, in long swaths that had to be gathered up and bound by hand; but it stood so long in the stook that the corn sprouted at the bands of the sheaves. Far away on the Buchan coast you could hear the growl and boom of the sea, like you had a buckie at your lug, and thousands of white gulls landed on your sheaves and stooks, filling their craps with your corn and vomiting the husk on your stubble, glued into little balls with their stomach spit, and your sheaves and stooks all whitened with their guano. 'Damned fishers' hens,' Hilly called them: 'I wish they'd bide at hame and ate their ain stinkin herrin!' But maybe Hilly forgot that the herring boats had all gone south to Yarmouth at this time o the year and that the gulls had no other option but to turn on the farmers for a bite to eat. Yet it was the cushie-doos and the craws that Hilly and the Mains gunned doon and you'd never see them fire a cartridge at a herring gull, maybe because they minded the good things they did when the ploughing started, devouring all the grub and sic like beasties that damaged their crops in the spring-time.

So it was stook parade for the farming chiels, days and weeks of it, the most hated job in agriculture, re-setting stooks that had been set up many times before, blown down by the equinox winds or had simply collapsed from bad stooking; but whatever the cause a wearisome, disheartening, leg-weary ordeal, especially if you was sweating in oilskin suits, and the only consolation was to look over the hedge and see your neighbours at the same trauchle.

But as the sky loured and the days of rain lengthened you were driven inside to twine straw rapes between the empty stalls in the long double byre, or up in the corn loft if it were empty. The long cement greep gave you the full length of the byre to twine a rape without going outside to the wet, enough to wind a ball or cloo for the ruck thatchin after hairst (if it was ever going to finish this year you wondered) and you twined and twined walking backwards all the time while the grieve or the foreman sat on a trochie at the far end of the byre and thrummed the straw through their fingers, further and further from your thraw-heuk, while the rape lashed the bare greep like a quine's skipping rope. The greep wasn't all that wide, so that if there were four of you on the job, with two rapes going at the same time you had to watch not to entangle them. The straw had been 'drawn' beforehand, plucked from the ribs of a ruck with your bare hands, a process that straightened the stalks and made better rapes for the thatching.

'Nae sae fast loon,' the grieve would cry when his rape had spun into a rottan's tail and snapped in the middle, so that he had to get up and splice it. So you kept your mind on the job for a while, away from the quines and moonlight trysts among the stooks. But there was a great art in letting out a straw rape, even and smooth through your fingers to form a trig and tidy rope, not a loose and hairy one that broke on the top of a ruck and made you nearly lose your balance. Making edrins was another ploy some lads excelled at, pear-shaped cloos that could be laced under the main rapes, forming a sort of net to keep the thatch in place in the howling winds of a winter's night.

When you had a great bing of cloos and edrins, enough you thought to rape the whole cornyard you could make a pair of ploo reins, using a thripple or three-pronged thraw-heuk and binder twine; thin ropes that were pliable in the horseman's hands, tight and hard till the oil oozed out of them in the twining, and a thicker pair of cart reins would come in handy, or great thick girdins that would rope a cart load of hay or straw, for you never bought ropes at a fairm toon.

And then the kitchie quine came in with the piece basket and a kettle of steaming tea, for at the Knock fairm you got a piece as long as the hairst lasted, fair or foul, though it were three months, including the ruck thackin and the tattie liftin, be ye single or cottared, and maybe in return you'd do a bit of unpaid overtime when the weather cleared, an hour or two at the cutting or stooking in a fine evening, or an extra load of sheaves at the leading time, when the great big harvest moon would be rising cheerfully over the dew that was settling on the stubble fields. But there were some places where you didn't get a bite between diets unless you were actually harvesting, which made you hellish hungry when you weren't, and even for this you was expected to do a bit extra on a fine night, so the Knock was a good place to be at as far as this was concerned.

But sometimes if the price was promising Knockie would have the feeding byre half filled with thriving stots taken in from the grass parks to fatten on tares and green corn for the Christmas sales. So you would have to scythe the tares and cart them home to the turnip shed, about a cart load a day, mostly in the wet or dewy mornings or the stooks dried, while the horsemen would be oiling their binders or sharpening the blades and spreading the damp canvasses to dry on a stook, or maybe making ruck foons with the whin and broom you had cut around the quarry brae, or carting home the reeds and sprotts you had scythed and sheafed in the peat-bog. Oh aye, you never wanted for a job on a fairmtoon, fair or foul, and there was always the byre to lime-wash while it was empty, or sweep down the cobwebs from the rafters, and if the worst came you could always turn the sharn midden or wash the horse carts or clean out the dam. But if you had to twine rapes in the little bailie's byre they might be a bit shorter, because he sometimes had a shorter byre, with smaller stalls for young store cattle, and you was minded of the stranger who went to the fairmtoon and the farmer chiel was showing him round the steading when out of a door and over the close goes a great strapping chiel, near twice the size of an ordinary body, and the stranger being impressed said: 'By Jove, but that's a fine figure of a man, and who might he be?' So the farmer listened to the iron heels of the lad on the causey stones and he says: 'Man, that's oor little bailie!' 'Good heavens,' says the stranger, polite like, him being of the gentry, 'if that's your small cattleman I should certainly like to see the big one!'

But the weather began to kittle up a bittie, blasts of wind that blew down your stooks again and a bit spunk of sun to dry the ground. But on clean land where grass had been sown in the wind couldn't move your stooks, because the grass had grown nearly up to the bands of your sheaves, and unless you threw them over on a fine day, to let the sun and wind get at the butts of the sheaves you were likely to get het rucks, for the damp grass would boil and steam in your stacks and ruin your grain samples. Then one fine dewy morning you'd see the rucks steaming and the farmer chiel sticking his arm into the ribs of a ruck up to his elbow and pulling out a few stalks of corn or barley to feel if it was hot, and if it was on the lowe he'd be off to the telephone to the contractor lads to come and thresh it before it got worse. Or maybe he'd yoke his men to turning the rucks and making them smaller, sheaf by sheaf, to let them get the air, with a tripod in the middle to ease the pressure as the stack got bigger and heavier, which he should have done in the first place to prevent fermentation. Syne the chiel would go and blether to folk that he'd lost his gold watch in one of the rucks at the leadin, but he couldna mind which ane it was so the men were turning all the rucks you'd biggit to see if they could find it. But the story of the lost watch was getting a bit thin as an excuse for bad management and folk just took a bit snigger of a laugh behind your back and said it served you right for not shifting your stooks sooner and giving them a new stance on the grass before they got so sloppy.

And sometimes you'd see Hilly's lads throwing down a whole park of stooks on new grass stubble, old Hilly in his hat leading the foray, away out in front of his foreman billy, and him fair gnashing his teeth at Hilly for slaving him, every lad throwing down as many stooks as he could batter, rag-tag and bob-tail, mostly in the forenoon, just before the sun was at its highest, smiling down on Hilly's lads with their jackets off and sweating like tinks in a brawl.

174

But you knew fine what Hilly was up to, for by the time the lads had gotten their dinner the sun and the wind would get at the butts of the sheaves and dry out the grass before Hilly stacked it in the afternoon.

And if Hilly thought he hadn't enough stooks flattened by dinner time for an afternoon's leading he'd yoke a cottar wife to ding doon the stooks, as he sometimes had a woman on the fork anyway, pitching up the sheaves to the carts. But woe betide if the rain came on again about piece time and Hilly had knocked down too many stooks, for the men would have to put on their oilskin suits and set them all up again, and yon foreman chiel would be cursing like hell and speiring where was thon lad with the hat that was in sic a hurry tearing down the stooks, for you'd never see Hilly setting them up again, and most likely he'd have a cooie to calve or a sooie to pig, or some such lame excuse to keep him out of sight or things simmered down a bittie. But the lads at the stookie knew fine that Hilly would be in the kitchen, with his hat on a peg and his feet on the mantelshelf, reading the daily paper - the 'Buchan Leear' or the 'Ellon Squeak', and not even a cat kittlin, let alone a coo.

But there was no meal and ale for 1927, or very few, and some single billies finished the rakings at one place and left at the November Term, only to find at their next place that the hairst was still unfinished.

There are no Meal and Ales nowadays, when you got your bowl of sowens that you supped with a horn-spoon, with maybe a sixpence in the bottom of the empty bowl if you were lucky. The real Meal and Ales disappeared with the horse wark, and when the tractors started folk called them Harvest Home Festivities; a sort of dinner and dance among the bigger farmers, known as the annual Farmers' Ball. The Kirk has upheld tradition with its yearly Harvest Thanksgiving, when the walls are decorated with corn dollies and the congregation brings gifts for the poor, like sacks of potatoes, flowers and vegetables, and the poor nowadays are known as the Old Age Pensioners. The whole thing is a bit of a sham anyway, for it is sometimes held when there are still acres of bales on the stubble fields, and parks of wasted corn and barley yet to be harvested. 1927 was a bit like that; when you didn't know where to draw the line, some folk finished and some folk not, and some others so disgusted they never bothered with Meal and Ale.

But whatever Meal and Ales were going that year old Jotty the blacksmith would be there, his fiddle under his chin, scraping away with the bow, a dram at his elbow, and nothing further from his mind than binders.

'Damnit tae hell,' he would hiccough, 'a body maun hae some fun!'

And the farmer billies of the Bogside would put their heads together and hire a contractor and thresh his three stacks of grain, for they knew they would be clean lost without Jotty the blacksmith, though he signed himself in their accounts as Jonathan McGillivray.

Johnnie Rettie got an invitation to the Meal and Ale on the Wiley Rottan's place on the Hill o Jock; maybe because he had promised the Rottan twa foalies when he was only lookin for one. After the feastin on roast turkey and the suppin of sowens and a good dram Wylie asked the vet to say a few words by way of a speech, most likely because he knew that Johnnie Rettie would say something to make them all laugh and raise the spirits of the company.

So the vet dabbed his moustache with his white hankie, for there was no such thing as a table napkin at Wiley's place, and then rose up from his chair, a bit unsteadily at first, until he got stanced, while his wife held on to the tail of his jacket, ready to give it a sharp tug if he said anything out of place, which wasn't uncommon with Johnnie Rettie when he had a good dram in.

He began with a few serious words on the ill hairst they had just experienced, the worst that he could mind on he said since he came to the Bogside, near forty years back, and it was the first time he had ever seen snow on the stooks, or the ploughing so late in starting, and he hoped for the sake of everybody concerned that he would never live to see it again, whereupon some of the billies cried 'Hear, hear!' and Johnnie glowered at them from under his glasses and took another sip of his whisky.

But not all harvests were bad, the vet continued, sticking his thumbs in the waistcoat pockets of his natty grey suit; not all harvests were bad, and he could mind on the farmer chiel who had such a grand hairst that he held a ball at the end of it, not just a Meal and Ale like Wiley here, but a grand affair in the barn and folk were invited from miles around to come and have a fling. Now this farmer chiel had an affa ugly dother near thirty years old who had never been kissed or cuddled in her life, nor even winked at by the working chiels on her father's farm. So the farmer told his quine to dress up well for the occasion and maybe she would get a lad in the leith of it.

A lot of folk turned out for the ball, farmers and their wives and their sons and daughters, besides some of the working chiels and kitchiedeems for miles aroon, and some of them came without invitation, just for the fun of the thing and all were made welcome.

But not a lad speired for the farmer's daughter, nor asked her up for a dance, so the quine was a bit crestfallen in all her finery, and when all the folk had gone she broke down and wept. 'But never mind quine,' her father said, offering her his hankie to dry her tears, 'next year we'll hold another ball for ye, and maybe ye'll have better luck next time.'

The next hairst wasn't all that to blow about, but the farmer chiel held a ball just the same and a hantle of folk attended it. The lassie dressed herself brawly and practised her steps for the dance but she fared no better than the year before. She sat the whole evening on the weighing machine in her fine clothes and watched the others enjoying themselves, while never a lad gave her a second glance in the passing nor asked her for a dance. The farmer cried out several times for a Ladies' Choice, and though the quine got a birl or two from the lads she picked up they just ignored her afterwards and went back to their more amorous partners.

It was a disappointing experience for farmer and daughter but as the next year's harvest came on the quine thought she would have another go, another last try to get a lad, even though it was only a farm servant - maybe she would be third time lucky. But as the winter drew on and her father never making a

176

move she asked him if he was going to have another ball for her.

'Na na,' says he, fed up to the teeth looking for a lad for his ill-faured dother: 'Na na, if ye canna get a man wi twa balls ye're nae likely tae get ane wi three!'

Johnnie Rettie's wife gave his jacket a tremendous tug that pulled him down in his chair. Her face was as long as a decanter, with never a smile to pattern it. She knew most of his stories but this was a new one she had never heard before; harmless enough when he started but the ending caught her by surprise. But whatever his wife thought the folk fair skirled with laughter, especially the women, and thanks to their vet it hadn't been such a bad harvest after all, for all its trauchle.

Man in a Loud Checked Suit

Now Forbie Tait of Kingask never knew it but although he had fee-ed you to work for him body and soul (shades of *Uncle Tom's Cabin*) in that he had every ounce of your physical effort and some of your mental activity - taking a fervent interest in his cattle beasts and in pulling his turnips (or so he probably imagined) but actually, and mentally at least, Forbie had only engaged part of your energies, because most of the time only part of your mind worked for Forbie and the best of your thoughts were far away on higher things. Had this not been so, or in other words if you had conformed to the frigidity of rustic life, contenting yourself with its dullness and monotony, harnessing your mind to its soulless illiteracy, its almost sterile simplicity - then people like Forbie Tate and Badgie Summers would never have existed beyond their mortal deaths, whereas your enlightenment has enabled you to breathe new life into their dry bones, to give them flesh and muscle and blood in the brain cells of readers yet unborn; to bring them alive that were dead, and surely this is the greatest glory that man can achieve, in the image of God, his maker, in resurrection.

When you was spreading muck or pulling turnips on the brae above the farm you was there only half the time, and only part of you at that, and not the better part, for your heart and soul was with the arts in whatever form you could find them: whether in books or magazines or even newspapers; films, posters or gramophone records, and as radio was just beginning to catch on in the cottar houses it didn't have much of your attention. You might be flinging muck about you with nothing further from your mind than sharn, your thoughts away with Jack Hulbert and Renate Muller in that wonderful British musical of the early 'thirties *Sunshine Susie,* with its delightful songs and dances, its carefree youthfulness and its music bringing an exuberant glow into your drab life; putting a lilt in your voice as you sang to yourself on the brae, the shit flying about you, your thoughts enlarging on the subject the more you dwelt on it, for days at a time, like being in love with someone beautiful beyond dreams, until the vision faded and lost its colour and left you with a pleasant memory, which is the accolade and surely the ultimate of which the human soul is capable. On the wings of song you might call it, when your thoughts are extrovert, going out to meet the world on the wings of angels; but woe betide when your thoughts become introvert, turning in upon yourself in a deep depression, when your angels come home to roost, drooping their feathers, in the simple Freudian thesis of melancholia. Being eccentric is like being on a tightrope, performing to an applauding audience, a delightful experience so long as you don't fall off, with only a frail net to catch you.

When Forbie Tait thought you was being punctual in the byres you was mentally in the projection box of some imaginary cinema screening the *Pathe Gazette* or the *Movietone News* on the stroke of eight; indeed your regularity at work was inspired by the consistency of the newsreel people in keeping up to date with world affairs. The bread and butter efforts of the film producers made everything worth while, and if the Hollywood moguls produced a masterpiece you was elated. Without the cinema backdrop in your daily drudgery you was without a guiding star, and if ever there was a round peg in a square hole you was the kingpin. But of course Forbie Tait knew nothing of the workings of your mind but he said he liked a lad who was punctual in the byres feeding his nowt. He even mentioned it to Badgie the foreman that you was punctual and conscientious and that he was pleased enough with your work. So long as you did your work Forbie didn't much concern himself with your own private pursuits. But it was the movies that turned you on so to speak, and made you tick, and you couldn't have cared less for the running of Kingask. That you had given a good performance was automatic; a means to an end, without enthusiasm for the daily darg.

During your second harvest on the place Badgie Summers taught you how to build a corn stack. Maybe he was just tired of crawling on the corn rucks and wanted a change. Anyway he took the cart you was driving and put you on the stack and showed you where to lay your sheaves, round by round from the inner circle, with plenty of hearting in the middle and a gentle slope to the outer edge, Badgie forking all the time and directing you right to the topmost pinnacle of the stack, then gave you a hand to rope and secure it against wind and weather, and you came down the ladder gratified, proud of your achievement.

It was quite a feat Badgie had taught you, the beginning of your stack-building career that was to last for thirty odd years, in which time you was to build an average of forty or fifty a year, depending on the size of the various farms you worked on, or the sum total of something like two-thousand corn, wheat and barley stacks, besides an experiment in flax building during the war, until the combines came in during the 'sixties and killed this skilful art. It was one job that gave you a pride in your work over many difficult years; a prestige and reputation with the farmers and sometimes though not often an extra pound or two to your meagre wages, besides a better chance of finding a job.

That was something you had to thank Badgie Summers for, him that was foreman at Kingask; otherwise you can't think how you would have managed it, or even made a start, and because of the art involved (or architecture if you like) it turned out to be a job you became really fond of, in spite of your aversion to farming in general. But when Forbie saw the stack you had built he told Badgie he'd better thrash it first in the season in case it watered. Badgie said there was no fear of that but knowing the old man he had to comply with his wishes.

Kingask kept a lot of hens; thousands of them, in sheds of weather-boarding scattered over the grass parks. Forbie believed in a policy of mixed farming, so that if one project failed the other might support it: just as some beef-cattle farmers went in for sheep or pigs as a sideline so old Forbie went in for hens. Young Tom was chief poultryman, with a fee-ed loon from the village to help him out, the two of them with a pony and cart filling the feed hoppers and the water fountains, mucking out the sheds and collecting the eggs. Tom's two sisters, Deborah and Edith, cleaned and packed the eggs into crates for the shops, and a van called twice a week to collect them. Badgie was on regular call to move a henhouse from one park to another, sometimes in the snow, or to take it home for repairs, for Tom was something of a joiner as well as many other things and good with his hands and a kit of tools. And Badgie would hitch the yokes and swingletrees to the hooks on the shed runners, like a sledge, and Jug and Kate would haul it out at the gate and over the road to where Tom wanted it in another park, mostly not far from the steading, so that he could take a rifle shot at the crows and the cushie-doos that hovered round the feed troughs. Tom and the loon had a steady job cleaning out these hen-arks, and the only time you was involved was on wet days, when Forbie whistled you home from the parks, and you went up to the corn loft, mixing feed, with a heap on the floor all the colours of the rainbow as you emptied it from the sacks; then turned it over and over until the colours dissolved into a whole of slatey grey, when you shovelled it back into the sacks again for feeding in the parks.

Though there was no electricity on the farms Tom was experimenting with the new inc ̇ators to raise their own chickens, maintaining the heat with oil lamps, as he did with the brooders after hatching, thus making a lot of the broody hens redundant and easing the work load in replacing the stock. Good laying breeds were selected and crossed with suitable cockerels. Tom also had a go at the battery-hen system, with the birds all in cages, food and water in front of them and laying their eggs where they stood; imprisoned for life and never out in the fields for a healthy scratch with other birds, and mostly their life-span ended with their moulting, when they were culled from their cages and taken to the butcher's shop, which was a good thing when it happened at Christmas time, because the cottars got a hen for dinner in the leith of it. Old Forbie didn't like this new-fangled idea of caging the birds for life and thought it was proper cruelty. He complained also of the lack of colouring in the egg yolks and thought there was something lacking in their diet. 'By gum,' he said, rocking his false teeth, 'it's nae natural keepin hens in there Tom; and besides, foo wad ye like tae be keepit in they cages a' yer born days and never seein a member o the opposite sex?' But being a bachelor himself Tom had a ready answer for his old man. 'What ye never had ye never miss,' he said, glimmering through his glasses, with a wink to the loon who was standing beside him. But even without the hen Christmas and New Year were grand times at Kingask. The cottars got a cherry cake from Mrs Tait, and a big fancy tin packed with cream biscuits, with sweeties for all the bairns. Even the tin was a luxury and Kathleen kept it for years to hold her oatcakes, because she liked the crinolined lady on the lid, and the sights of London round the sides, Buckingham Palace and all that. Even in those so-called Hungry 'thirties it is a fact that fruit cake was so cheap from the grocers' vans you were still eating it half through January; every time you had tea you had currant or sultana cake, till you was scunnered at the sight of it and glad to get back to loaf and treacle, oatcakes and stovies, peasemeal brose and porridge. Bread and fancy cakes of all kinds were also cheap and plentiful, in fact the pound sterling was so elastic it could be stretched to such an extent that when people were sensible there was no real hardship in the cottar household, except perhaps in the bigger families, though these were tending to get smaller. Whisky and beer were unheard of except in the pubs (which you never visited) but wine and soft drinks were easily got, provided you returned the bottles. Tobacco and cigarettes were at throwaway prices and smoking was fashionable. Very few women smoked or drank and most of the men smoked pipes filled with thick black twist.

Your first Christmas at Kingask was the best one, maybe because there was snow on the ground and all the countryside like one big Christmas card standing wide open; even without the trees, for there were no trees in the wind-torn parish of Pittentumb, except for a few survivors at the manse of Peatriggs and the old ruined castle of Spitullie. But the blue of the sea and the white of the land was a dream in bone china, the sky feathered with wind-blown cloud and ramparts of snow on the far horizon. The sea itself was surly, grumbling all day against the land, with a deeper tone in the boom of the surf; angry at night when the tide rose in a snarl of sleet, stabbed by the lighthouse beam from Brochan, swinging over the sea and the parks. It swept the braes at Kingask on the darkest nights, without a star in the sky, showing you up like a thief in a searchlight, lurching home with an old fencing post to light your fire, so everybody was honest at Kingask, or what you took was in daylight (which wasn't very much) but then nobody suspected you.

It was cold on the feet while you plucked turnips on the brae, jerking them out of the steel hard earth with a twin-pronged adze (for want of a better description) your mittened hands stinging with frost, though the sun shone warmly at noon, slanting across the snow in an autumn glow, crystallizing the crusted fields like champagne in amber glasses. Folks were driving out fresh dung on the snow, warm and steaming from the sharn middens, the smell of it like perfume on the brittle air. The hairs of your nostrils froze like spikes and your breath rose like steam in front of your face; your ears anaesthetized, while your shadow dodged behind you like a man on the run. There was nothing for it but action to keep the blood going, work or starve, and as there was only one day off at Hogmanay there was no excuse for feeling the cold. With plenty of food in your belly you never really felt the cold, which was easy at New Year time with all the titbits, but at other times with the long drag between meals your stomach ached for food, for there were no tea breaks. Even though you had your own house you daren't be seen with a snack and a thermos flask; such a liberty had not yet come into fashion, though it did later. Meantime you would sometimes sneak in by your cottage and gulp down a cup of tea and a bun Kathleen had ready for you when you left the turnip field, going home to the byre. You just hoped that Forbie or the women folk hadn't seen you from the

181

farmhouse windows when you left the cottage, for though it was only five minutes of truancy it was frowned upon and you didn't want to be caught in the act. The farmhouse of Kingask stood like a sentinel over the parks and you was never out of sight of its peering windows. Whether they saw you or not nothing was said, but you didn't push your luck too far just in case, and sometimes you missed your fly-cup if you saw anyone in the farm close, or if Forbie whistled you home earlier for a shower of rain.

But in spite of the cold and hunger, hard work and frustration, you had one other consolation - you was a film fan and Garbo and Harlow were at their loveliest, filling your skies with their radiance, larger than life itself in those days of your youth, though now in your old age you can see you was only chasing shadows, for the cine film is only shadows reflected on a bedsheet. But in those days they were real enough and the Empire Theatre in London was offering three-thousand seats daily at one-and-sixpence each to watch them: Garbo as *Camille* (Lady of the Camellias) and Harlow in *Red Dust* - and you had never heard of such riches from such beauty and wished you'd been a film producer, far from the neep parks, the snow and the sharn. Film going was becoming a religion in the realms of angels, and the women had gods in the shape of Clark Gable, Robert Taylor and Spencer Tracy. Shirley Temple was everybody's child and now they were adopting Little Lord Fauntleroy; Deanna Durbin sang at the gates of Paradise while Bing Crosby was catching *Pennies from Heaven*. Frank Capra had found his *Lost Horizon* and Cecil B. de Mille had made *The Sign of the Cross*. Claudette Colbert had bathed in asses milk and we had seen *The Last Days of Pompeii*. Sonja Henie had just cut the figure 8 on silver skates and Paul Muni was digging in *The Good Earth*. But the crowning glory was the coronation of King George VI and Queen Elizabeth in colour, shown all over the country on the day it took place, May 12th 1937, almost as quick as television, and old Forbie was obliged to give you the day off to watch it in Brochan, seeing it was a national holiday. There had been three Kings on the British throne within a year: George V, Edward VIII and George VI, whereupon Forbie remarked: 'By gum, ye get a new king ony day o the week nooadays!'

It was during your second summer at Kingask that old Forbie ran short of hens corn, having sold too much for seed in the spring. This wouldn't have mattered to you at all but for the fact that you couldn't get corn for your own hens. Badgie Summers had been wiser than you or better informed and had bought a bag in advance, before the shortage became acute. He didn't have to worry about hen feed but he told you where you could buy a bushelful to tide you over till harvest time, up at Stovie Roger's place, beyond the smiddy; so off you set one sunny evening with an empty sack on your bicycle and five bob in your pocket to visit Stovie Roger. What Badgie didn't tell you was that Stovie would speir you inside out before he would give you the corn: your name and where you came from and why you couldn't get corn from the farmer you worked for? - and why come to him for corn when there were so many other places where you could have got it? He also wanted to know where you had worked before you came to Kingask? - How long you had been there and why you had left it? He even wanted to know where your parents lived and your wife's folk; where they lived and what they all did for a living? You told him they were all cottar folk, but you felt like telling him he could keep his bludy corn and maybe you would get it from somebody with better manners and who was less inquisitive; though you could by no means be sure of this in a scarcity round about Kingask, where you was still a comparative stranger and everybody had to know about your dirty washing and the size of your shoes and whether or not you slept with your wife before they would trust you out of their sight, or part with the dirt under their finger-nails on your behalf. Badgie Summers had qualified for such trust and respect after twelve years as foreman at Kingask, while you was only banging the door knocker.

But at last, after about an hour of interrogation, Stovie was satisfied that you wasn't a born thief: that you wasn't just spying out the place and where the dog slept, and that you wouldn't come sneaking back some dark night and steal his hens or a sackful of peats or set fire to his stack-yard or let the water out of his dam - or even sleep with his kitchiedeem - for such a thing was not unheard of, even among married men. Stovie also seemed to be convinced that you hadn't just escaped from the convict prison or the lunatic asylum and that you was really fee-ed at Kingask, though it was a wonder he didn't ask the colour of old Forbie's eyes, just to make sure; or what was his swear word, and you felt sure that if he'd had a telephone, and if Kingask had one, he would have rung up Forbie to ask for your credentials.

So you went up to the loft with Stovie and he filled you a bushel of corn, strake full, that means he took a broken fork shaft (though some folk used a scythe - broad or scythe-straik hence the 'strake') and scraped it over the rim of the wooden bushel, scraping off the surplus corn, to make sure you didn't get a grain of it more than you was entitled to, but just for bonus he licked his thumb and picked up two ears of corn from the loft floor, sticking to his moistened thumb print, and flicked them into the bushel, then tipped the lot into the empty sack you held out for him. He took the two half-crowns you offered him and put them in his waistcoat pocket, while you clambered down the loft stair and set the half sack of corn across your handlebars then jumped on your bike, Stovie watching you with the dog beside him till you was clear of his premises and on to the main road, bound for Kingask.

Next day you told Badgie your experience and he said that was what you would expect from Stovie Roger, but that he was one of the best farming chiels in the parish of Pittentumb, and that he never missed a Sunday at the kirk; which gave you a mighty poor opinion of the farmers round about Kingask, and even less regard for the folk that filled the kirk at Peatriggs. But when you told Badgie this he said: 'Tyoo fie man; it was Stovie that put the clock in the spire o the kirk, paid for it himsel, so that folk would mind on him, and of course he's an elder!'

The story went around about Stovie, that before the Rev. Thow came to Peatriggs he complained to the former minister about a kitchiedeem from one of the farms who came to the kirk on Sundays with a plunging neckline. So the minister had a word with the quine in the vestry after the service and explained to her that one of the elders had lodged a complaint about her low-necked dress and wondered perhaps if she could possibly wear something less revealing. Personally he had to admit to himself that she certainly had something to display and he had no objection. Trust Stovie Roger to go and spoil things, because from where the lassie sat in the congregation the minister had an unclouded view of the valley of sunshine and could have tossed a pandrop nearly down to her navel. But the lassie insisted that she wore a low neckline because her lad liked to see her dressed like that and she wasn't going to change it to please a narrow-minded kirk elder, whoever he may be, or though it had been the Laird o Pittentumb himsel. She said that when she lay down in that dress and her lad put his head on her bare breast and listened he said he could hear the angels singin. But the minister wasn't convinced of this and said he would have to try it himself before he would believe it. So the lass lay down on the vestry couch and the minister knelt beside her and laid his lug on her naked bosom. After a while he looked up and said: 'I canna hear ony angels singin, lassie - but maybe I'm on the wrang wavelength?'

'Och no Reverend,' said the quine, now flushing to the lips: 'It's nae that; ye couldna hear them that wye - ye're nae plugged in!'

This was the minister who got on a bus from Brochan and unavoidably sat down beside a drunk. After a while the drunk became abusive and the minister upbraided him and said he should think shame of himself going home to his wife and bairns in a state like that. But the drunk argued that he wasn't all that bad and at least he didn't have his collar on back to front like the minister. 'But look at me as an example,' said the man in black, 'I am never drunk!'

'Never drunk,' said the man; 'nae even on Communion Sundays on a' that wine that's left efter the service?'

'Least of all on Communion Sabbath,' said the minister, 'for on that day I am the father of thousands!'

'The father of thoosands! Gweedsake Reverend, it's yer breeks ye shid hae on back tae front, nae jist yer collar!'

Now you was a member of the Peatriggs kirk yourself by now, having changed your membership from your last place when you came into the parish, though you hadn't gone very often, only twice the year before to the communions. But now Kathleen wanted little Brian baptized. She wanted it done before she had another one, because she was with child again, and it would be born sometime in the spring. But you would have to get a new suit. You couldn't go to the kirk in your marriage suit nowadays; you had worn it so often to go everywhere on your bicycle that the arse of your breeks was polished smooth as a bus driver's seat, the lapels of the jacket sticking out like a donkey's ears, the pocket lids dog-eared, the trouser legs creased like a melodeon, the knees paper thin; in fact Stovie Roger had a better suit on his scarecrow, but since he took it inside every night there was little chance of stealing it. So you would have to get a new suit, which meant you would have to ask a half-day off from

Forbie (which was like asking for the Pole-star) because the tailors in the toon closed their shops about the same time as you shut your byre doors at Kingask, so you'd have to go and get measured on a Saturday afternoon.

But Forbie was in a thraw that summer about half-days off and rather than let you go he'd have you sheiling the sods from the verge of the farm road, or creosoting henhouses with a tar brush, seeing he was short of work, rather than see you off on your bike or away with the wife and the pram to the toon, no matter what your errand was. Maybe he thought you'd just be spending your money anyway and better to keep you at home where you might be saving it, the little you had. It was Badgie's week-end with the cows that you asked off to buy your suit, thinking that this would be most convenient, and you had expected that Badgie would be about the place on the Saturday afternoon. But as things would have it Badgie and his wife had a wedding that day and couldn't oblige you. You could have waited another fortnight but you was anxious to have the suit before the christening. You told Forbie all this but even though he was an elder of the kirk himself he wouldn't let you off. It was like trying to brasso the moon while it was still full, before the waning started, wondering how you would get up there in the first place. Forbie made the excuse that Badgie being off as well there wouldn't be an able-bodied man about the place for a whole afternoon; and what if the beasts 'ran a heat' (tormented with gadflies) and broke out of the parks, or the place caught fire - what was he going to do? There was some sense in what Forbie said and you could see his point of view; but you said you would be gone for only a couple of hours or so and you would be back by cow time at the latest. All the same it wasn't the done thing Forbie said and he wouldn't budge. Now it was said of Forbie Tait that he prepared for the day he would never see, and that he feared the death he would never die, and you was beginning to see the truth of it. And besides there were enough of them left about the place to run for help or cope with these unlikely disasters: what with young Tom and his sisters, the hen loon, the kitchie quine and the mistress, and old Forbie himself, enough of them to herd a whole park of nowt or pish out a fire before it got started. So you just ignored Forbie on the Saturday and never turned up in the stable for orders after dinner, but dressed yourself and went sailing down the brae on your bike for the toon.

Now you hadn't had a decent suit for a long time and you was determined to have a good one while you was about it; not a really expensive one but the best you could afford. But the tailors in Brochan had nothing on the hooks to fit you: neither Hepworths nor Claude Alexander nor Burtons; not enough padding to bolster your sloping shoulders, too wide in the waist or too narrow across the chest; too short in the arms or too long in the legs, and anything that sort of fitted you wasn't the right colour. Nothing for it but have one made to measurement, and you settled with Claude Alexander to have it done, seeing he was 'Scotland's National Tailor', and they measured you up and gave you a book of patterns from which to choose your colour, something you was about as good at as picking out the separate colours of the rainbow, and you should have had Kathleen there to help you. Now you'd had nothing but dark brown

185

and deep blue suits ever since you'd come out of short breeks: 'cottar broon or fisher blue', as they were called, something you could always put on for a wedding or a funeral, seeing it was the only decent suit you could afford, and your old one would be good enough for 'Go-ashore' purposes as they said, like feeing markets or roups or Saturday nights at the pubs, or in your case for going to the pictures. But you was tired of all the dismal Johnnies and thought that for once you'd have something brighter; something that would set the fashion in Pittentumb, and to hell with convention and poverty.

So you choose a loud check for your suit that would dispel all this gloom of mortal living and set a new image for the farm workers: away from the Hodden Grey and Kersey Tweed, Blue Serge and moleskin that had dominated the attire of the Scottish farm worker from the days of Burns and James Hogg, and you supposed that English farm workers were much the same. But you later discovered you had chosen something that no self respecting horseman or stockman, married or single, drunk or sober, would have the effrontery to be seen in, either at fair or market, kirk or ploughing match. What you had chosen was something for the Chep-Johns at Aikey Fair they said, or the swanks down in London yonder; or what the Laird or the factor might wear on the twelfth of August for the grouse shooting, but certainly not on a Sunday for the kirk at Peatriggs. Maybe you had gone too far because you had never thought of this when you chose the colour of your suit; so eager was you to be unorthodox it was nearly a week before it struck you that you would be an oddity in a suit like that to be seen anywhere, never mind the kirk. You was about thirty years ahead of your time with the suit but you would have to stick to your guns now and nail your colours to the mast. It was too late to mend matters because the tailors would be busy on the cloth by now with their long shears. Nor could you afford to buy another suit length and you had already deposited £2 on the one you'd chosen. Kathleen laughed outright when you told her of your discomfiture. She said you could dye it but that seemed silly, and she added that you should have had more sense. Who did you think you was anyway? Clark Gable or the Laird of Cock-pen? Maybe you should have bought a kilt when you was about it. So you got little sympathy from Kathleen.

The tailors had promised to have the suit ready in a fortnight, and that you could pay by instalments if you wanted to. It cost you £8.10. but Kathleen said she could afford to pay it cash from money saved from your monthly wage of £4. Forbie hadn't said anything about not turning up for work that Saturday, and as you had returned about four o'clock in the afternoon and had changed into your working clothes and was driving in your cows at the usual time for milking he let it slip. When you told him you wanted another couple of hours off to collect the suit a fortnight later he was less thrawn and said you could go. On the Sunday morning after breakfast you was in high spirits about your suit and wanted to try it on. Kathleen said it was just grand: a smashing suit with a waistcoat, and she had a shirt and tie to go with it, and she said you never looked better in your life, and she put her arms round your neck and kissed you, which made you feel like a million dollars, in movie language. She had just bought you a new armchair, because the stuffing was sticking out of your old one, and she had paid for it in Brochan from a surrendered insurance policy you couldn't afford. Seated in your new armchair with the *Picturegoer* was like the first sweet smell of success; if only you had been a film producer instead of a clodhopper, and Kathleen had been your leading lady. Of course you never told Kathleen about your ambition to be a film director; nor did you discuss any of your thoughts with her about the movies, though she was bound to think it strange that you had all these film magazines lying about, and did a bit of writing on the sly, reading Shakespeare and all that sort of thing, which most other lads forgot about as soon as they left school. Not at all like her brothers you was and most likely a bit 'picter daft' as folk said, though she stuck up for you if anyone tried to make fun of it in her hearing. But your suit was fine she said and first class material, if only you had chosen a less gaudy colour. What would all the kirk folk think when they saw you in a braw thing like that? But this annoyed you, and you said to hell with the kirk folk and got up from the chair and put on the checked cap you had bought to go with the suit and strode out of the house, up the road for a stroll. And who should you meet but Forbie, on his Sunday morning round of the parks, and when he saw you in the brash new suit he nearly fell over the dyke he was straddling, but saved himself with his staff. 'By gum,' he said, nearly dropping his pipe from his mouth, 'but that's a braw mornin!' If he had said: 'That's a braw suit!' you might have felt heartened, but as it was you had scarcely noticed what sort of morning it was, until Forbie drew your attention to it, when you was aware of the sun blazing down and that the dirt flies were everywhere and the sea blue and calm and motionless, with scarcely a murmur from its tumble on the beach. But you knew by the way that Forbie went hytering down the road that he couldn't get home fast enough to tell the women folk about the daft like suit the bailie lad had bocht.

You was that abashed that you put off your visit to the kirk as long as you could, leaving it till the sacrament Sunday, when you had no other option or excuse, especially when you wanted the Rev. Thow to baptize little Brian later on, so you would have to face the music. As it was you had left it a bit late because he had started swearing and you was worried about what he might say when the minister poured the cold water on to his head. You couldn't say where he had learned the swear words because you seldom swore yourself, something you was real particular about, and so was Kathleen, but as soon as the bairn could speak 'Bugger' and 'Damn' were among the first words he used; and even worse from time to time, and when you tried to check him he swore the worse, until you had him in tears. Nor could you any longer discuss something private in his hearing, or speak about the folk next door, or he up and told them about it and you didn't know where to look to avoid their reaction, your faces crimson with guilt. Spelling out the words puzzled him however and you got away with that.

On the Sunday morning of the Sacrament, when the pair of you were rigged for the kirk, Kathleen took the poker and rapped on the back of the grate with the point of it, to let the Summers folk know you was ready, when young Esma came round for the bairn, fair delighted like a quine would be, and the four of you walked up the road for the kirk, Kathleen in her blue and white hairy coat, like the hide of a New-Foundland dog, and a trim little hat like a brose caup with a rim on it, and Mrs Summers rigged out as black as the Ace of Spades, with an enormous hat spiked with feathers and draped with sequins, both with bibles in their black gloved hands, while you and Badgie walked behind, pipes in mouth past the smiddy, where the blacksmith was rigging a granny on his lum, and he cried to Badgie to put in a good word for him at the kirk, seeing he would be needing it, working on the Lord's day. Within sight of the kirk you put your pipes away, and although you was a bit self-conscious in your new suit you was now determined to go through with it bold as brass. You was a bit early and stood about the door a minute, newsing to the farm folk, getting out of their cars and gigs and some on foot. A lot of them you had never seen before, or if you had you had forgotten them, and one of them in particular came over and shook hands with you, nice as ninepence and asking how you liked to farm Pitburn, thinking you was the new tenant of the place, until Stovie Roger comes over and tells him you was cottared at Kingask, when the man dropped your hand like it was a blighted potato and turned his back as quickly and spoke to somebody else, being taken aback with your new suit.

The bell began to ring and Stovie took his gold watch out of his waistcoat pocket and checked it with the clock he had biggit into the kirk tower and said we should be moving inside, reminding you to hand in your sacrament token in the porch beside the collection plate, Stovie being the elder for your corner of the parish. The inside of the kirk was like a cathedral (though you had never seen the inside of a cathedral) with bare stone walls and candlesticks on the altar and brass lamps hanging on long chains from the roof. While the kirk was filling up some folk sat with bowed heads while others glowered at everybody coming up the aisles, so you had time to look around at all the plaques on the walls in memory of the former ministers of the parish, and some of the bigger farmers, now deceased, though none of the Laird's folk were to be seen in this corner of Pittentumb, and maybe they had a private chapel and burial ground at Bogenchero. Outside you could still hear the bell ringing, high on the belfry, crying out to the heathens of the parish to 'Come awa, Come awa,' until the bellman changed his hand on the rope, when it said, very distinctly 'Ye're ahin, ye're ahin; Collection, Collection!' until he got the swing of the rope and the rhythm again. Now you could feel the throb of the organ, playing ever so sweetly, like you sometimes heard it in some of the bigger cinemas, until the Rev. Thow appeared in his surplice, ready to partake of the Lord's Supper. He took his sermon from the fifty-third chapter of Isaiah, in a language that the patient folk of Pittentumb could understand, and in the declamation of it you would have heard the proverbial dropping of a pin, or better still, the gritting of a ewe's teeth chewing the cud. The Rev. Thow was an excellent reader of scripture, you could see that from the start, lifting his text from the Old Testament in a voice so clear and distinct that every word was like a falling dew drop; like the clisp of shears in snow white wool, the rasp of scythe in ripened corn, the clop of hoof on causey stones, the fall of a chain on byre cement, or the chop of axe on wood-block; and then he called them to repentance: 'For though your sins be as scarlet,' he cried, 'yet they shall be as white as wool,' and the folk of Pittentumb remembered the shearing, and could identify themselves with what the Rev. Thow was driving at. He led them in the green pastures by the quiet waters and in the shadow of death he gave a comforting hand; filled their cups to overflowing with the wine of everlasting life.

'Who hath heard our report?' the Rev. Thow was asking, gazing out over his congregation, pausing in his quote from Isaiah, as if waiting for an answer; but as none was forthcoming, beyond a clearing of throats, he continued: 'And to whom is the arm of the Lord revealed?'

Another quiet hush filled the kirk, while those in the gallery could see the gravestones around the building; the budding trees trembling in the cold wind that beat against the window panes, the green fields awakening to the throes and joys of springtime.

'For he shall grow up before him as a tender plant, as a root out of dry ground,' and some of the farmer chiels remembered their turnip seedlings in a dry season.

Once he had their attention the Rev. Thow brought Christ into the picture: 'He hath no form nor comeliness; and when we shall see him, there is no beauty that we should desire him.

'He is despised and rejected of men; a man of sorrows, and acquainted with grief: and we hid as it were our faces from him; he was despised, and we esteemed him not.

'Surely he hath borne our griefs, and carried our sorrows . . . He was wounded for our transgressions . . . and with his stripes we are healed.

'All we like sheep have gone astray . . .' and just as one old farmer was nodding asleep he suddenly remembered the lambing at home and sat bolt upright.

The Rev. Thow continued: 'We have turned everyone to his own way; and the Lord hath laid on him the iniquity of us all.

'He was oppressed, and he was afflicted, yet he opened not his mouth: he is brought as a lamb to the slaughter, and as a sheep before her shearers is dumb, so he openeth not his mouth.'

Then some old crofter woman remembered her pet lamb on market day and the Rev. Thow had all her sympathy and deepest respect. He didn't believe in flights of fancy but stuck close to the earth, and the good folks of Pittentumb revered him.

The blood of the Saviour was passed round the pews in a big goblet, old men dipping their beards in the wine, the women taking a dainty sip and passing it on from hand to hand, likewise the trenchards of diced bread. 'Can you drink of the cup of which I drink?' the Rev. Thow cried out to his congregation, and when nobody spoke in the moment of silence he replied for the disciples to their Master: 'And they said: we can drink!' This was something you had seen on the war memorial to the soldiers of the parish who had died in the war, and you knew that in their case it meant blood. But like Badgie sitting there by you they had not flinched and had drunk their fill. Badgie had survived to tell the tale, and he said he had seen a lot of Christs killed in the war; even crucified in the snows of the Alps on the Italian front, and not much said about it, because you couldn't make a religion out of all their individual sufferings, so we had to have one Christ to atone for all.

After the hymn singing the minister gave his blessing and the benediction, then went to the door to shake hands with everybody as they left. But like the women folk comparing their hats you looked in vain for another suit like your own among all the congregation of Peatriggs. It made you feel terribly conspicuous and you couldn't bear the thought of it a second time; everybody looking you up and down and whispering among themselves like you was a criminal in their midst. Nor could you afford to buy another suit, so you had the Rev. Thow come to the house on some pretence or other, rewarding him with a high tea and home bakes that he enjoyed immensely, and little Brian never swore a word when he was christened and you was thankful for that.

Winifred was born in the spring, a fine healthy eight-pound girl and you left Kingask at the end of May, back to a place in the Bogside. But nowhere could you find comparison for that suit, not even in Brochan, and though everybody said you looked just grand in it you could never quite forget yourself when wearing it; not even in the pictures, and that was saying something. It was well on in the summer, the very first time you had been to Turra Show, where you went in the bus with Kathleen and Brian and little Winifred (Winnie you called her for short) still looking for somebody with a suit like your own. You was beginning to feel something of a martyr and the damned thing had become an obsession; not in any serious sense but as a sort of game, like looking for the last bit of a jig-saw puzzle that had got lost, an awfully important bit, and Kathleen had even joined you in the search, scanning the crowd where you sat on the grass in the Haughs o Turra, watching the sports. It was the year that Harry Gordon opened the show, the wee Laird of Inversnecky in his kilt and sporran, and steam trains were still arriving at Turriff station, bringing folk from as far afield as Banff and Inveramsay, though Alexanders' buses brought a lot more besides from all over the place, so that the Haughs were thronged with people, and you thought that surely from all that crowd you was bound to find somebody with a suit like yours.

But not among all the thousands of men at Turriff Show did you see one suit like your own, not one. Kathleen pointed out two or three that were quite near it but 'not bright enough', she would say disappointedly, or 'it's a different texture; duller, nae nearly sae noticeable,' and 'na na, that one's nae the same at all!' Out of all the hundreds who came and went on the haughs there was no corresponding suit. So engrossed was you in the search that you missed the parade of farm animals, sparing only a glance at the parade ring while you scanned the crowd. Even the sports were only a sideline though you nearly forgot yourself in the tug-o-war teams, especially the Bells from Tyrie, pulling everything in sight, from Alness to Strathdon, Wartle and Tarland; and all the Heavies were there, George Clark from Grange, Jim Anderson, Norman Murray, A. J. Stuart, tossing the caber, weight-lifting, wrestling, throwing the heavy hammer (though Harry Gordon said it was the heavy bag-pipes) and such was the cheering at these events, and great surge of enthusiasm among the spectators that you got completely carried away, forgetting all about your daft suit till Kathleen gave you a nudge with her elbow and directed your gaze in the other direction. And there she was, not more than two feet from your right-hand side, a fine young girl in a costume suit exactly like your own. She must have come down the terrace from the back, for even Kathleen never saw her approach, not until she sat down beside you where someone had left a vacant seat. Well, well, that was it; the end of your search for the missing piece of jig-saw, the culmination of your obsession, though you had never expected a woman to solve your problem. Had she done it on purpose? Both of you looked at her but she pretended not to notice. Kathleen looked at you in a half-smile and you winked back at her, message understood. But somehow the suit looked fine on the girl; maybe a woman wouldn't look so bad with a suit like that in church - or anywhere, she was so nice. If you looked half as well in the same outfit you had nothing to worry about.

But could you let her go without saying a word? Never in this world were you ever likely to see her again and it was so funny. You knew nothing about her: where she came from, nothing. And being a married man it was none of your business. The kids were getting restless and soon you would have to go. You whispered your thoughts to Kathleen and she agreed you should speak to the quine: ask if she had spied you out in the crowd and had sat beside you on purpose? But you was so shy. It was such a silly thing to ask anybody; especially with your wife and kids sitting beside you . . . maybe a bit different if you had been a single body. It was on the tip of your tongue several times but you just couldn't say it. It was so embarrassing. It was just as awkward for Kathleen and she wouldn't say anything either. Maybe the quine would think she was being accused of trying to flirt with you. And anyway Kathleen was preoccupied changing Winnie's wet nappie. You tried to catch the lassie's attention by just looking at her, without any positive approach, watching her face, but she averted her eyes and looked at the sports, smiling rather shyly when something pleased her. You felt sure she stole a glance at you when you was whispering to Kathleen. You could almost feel her soft pleading eyes on your back, on the colour of your suit - but when you turned round quickly she looked away again. Perhaps she was feeling as you had felt; shunned and neglected, wanting to say something, she knew not what nor how. Strange that she didn't have a lad with her, a pretty girl like that. How long had she searched for you and how far? Maybe she had detested her costume and couldn't afford another one? Perhaps she had used it to attract your attention, by sitting down beside you - until she discovered that you was not alone, that Kathleen was your wife. How was she to know really among all the crowd? Maybe the whole damned thing was just plain coincidence - though not likely, not among all the

191

thousands of folk at Turra Show and only two of you dressed alike; birds of a feather and you had sought each other.

But now you were going. You had to get your supper before bus time, up in one of the restaurants in the town. You were on your feet but the girl still sat there, merely giving you a glance when you stood up, a little forlorn like you thought but maybe it was just your imagination. You took Brian in your arms and followed Kathleen down the hill, Winnie in her oxter, now fast asleep. When you glanced back the lassie was still sitting there, her hat tilted slightly on the back of her head, now staring after you, watching you all the way down the brae, and you could still pick her out from the sports ring when you reached the bottom. You would remember that colour anywhere, wherever you saw it again - but you never did. Once was enough and you was satisfied. Yes she was still sitting there, still watching you - such a pity you hadn't spoken to her after all.

But you wore that suit for years after that; even for Sunday until you could afford another one, cottar brown next time so that you could go to the kirk somewhere for the christening of Winnie. But whenever you felt abashed in your loud checked suit you just remembered that lonely quine sitting there in the Haughs o Turra; for at least there was one other person in the whole wide world who had a costume suit exactly the same as your own.

And if you had been a film director you might have signed her up on contract, even without a screen test, because of her loud checked suit and the satisfaction it had given you.

Hardwood!

The fog being down on the countraside when you couldna see a stirk in your ain parks in broad daylight was the time that Hardwood Harry chose to disappear. Harry Hernie was an old widower who had lived with his twin son and dother on the fairm of Clayfoons since his wife died, which was as many years back that younger folks couldna mind on't. Harry had been a joiner and undertaker in his younger day, before he took over the fairm from his father, and when his own turn came for growing old he handed over the lease to his unmarried twins, Wattie and Bannie Hernie, who had been born at Clayfoons and lived and worked there all their days, and were well on in middle-age when their father handed over the place to them.

But when the old man retired he had a hankering to go back to his joinery, or maybe it was just that he couldna rest and content himself in idleness, and there wasn't all that wark for him on a pair place of sixty acres, for Wattie and Bannie did most of it, so he started making barrows for the farming folk round about Clayfoons, lightsome kind of wark making box-barrows for mucking out their byres and stables, and lighter, flat-leaf barrows for wheeling out their peat in summer, peat barrows with a broader wheel for the soft lairs. Hardwood became a dab hand at the barrows, and they were that well made with good seasoned wood and lasted such a long time that they carried his name all over the district, and if you didn't have a Hardwood barrow sitting on your midden plank you just wasn't worth speaking to.

Hardwood had built a fairly big shed at the gable of the steading, near the peat stack, and set up a bench in it with a vice, and a rack along the wall for all the hand tools he needed for making and repairing barrows, besides a round concrete base outside where he heated the iron rings when he fitted them on the wheels, kindling a fire with peat like the blacksmith did with the heavier cart wheels. The box-barrows he painted blue, with the inside and the wheel red; the peat barrows a dull brown, so they had a fine smell of fresh paint about them when you went in by with a horse cart for one of Hardwood's barrows.

Trade was brisk, because there was a lot of knacky work in making a farm barrow, and there weren't many joiners who took the trouble, so Hardwood got steady work to meet the demand for barrows. By and by he was earning more bawbees from his barrow making than his son was doing on the farm, so that a bit of jealousy sprang up between Wattie and his father, and even Bannie took sides with her brother against the old man, which wasn't surprising maybe them being twins. And sometimes Bannie kept the money when honest folk came to pay their accounts and there was a fair din about the place when the old man found her out. Hardwood would charge the customer a second time and when the body told him he had already paid his dother at the back kitchie door the old man was dumfoonert that his ain flesh and bleed could treat him like this. So he kept the books himself and told his customers to pay him in the shed, 'to keep things right', as he said, though folk kent fine what Bannie was up to, and they thought it a right shame to swick the old man.

But he ups and gives Bannie and Wattie a right tinking with his sharp tongue and says they wouldna have done that gin their mother had been alive, poor soul, for it was enough to make her topple the stone that held her down in the kirkyard at the Bogside, and them huggin and kissin at one another, what would she think of that? Oh aye, he'd seen them at it he said, he wasn't blind or very deaf, and it wasn't a way for a brother and sister to be carrying on, even though they were twins. And what did they want with his money anyway? Wouldn't they get it all when he was dead and away, and they already had the lease of the place; but if they didn't mend their ways he would wipe them out of his will and leave every penny to others more deserving that he could think of.

But this outburst had little effect on the twins, in fact it made them worse when they knew that their relationship had been discovered; so they plotted and planned between them to make the old man's life a misery. So Bannie scrimps her old father at the table and treats him like a tike at the door, so that he could hardly light his pipe in the kitchen, living on kale brose like a caterpillar on a cabbage runt. So the old man took to sleeping on a couch in his joinery shed, covered up with rugs and old jackets, and kept himself warm with a bit peek of a stove that he burned with wood shavings and sawdust and broken peat, till he was nearly smoared with the reek, and his old brown eyes like to run out of his head, and when customers found him like this the twins at Clayfoons became the claik of the Buchan howes.

Folk that were ill-mannered and spied in at the window after dark said that Wattie Hernie and his sister both slept in the same bed, and that they kissed and cuddled at each other like they were man and wife, and were likely to be doing most other things besides, though nothing had come of it and maybe they were just lucky. And they said that this annoyed the old man more than his ill-usage or taking his money, for he knew fine what was going on and that was why he had taken to sleeping on his couch in the joinery shed, maybe to spite them and set the neighbours talking, which might arouse a little sympathy for himself or bring the twins to their senses. But there were others who said plainly that the twins had shut their old father out of the farmhouse so that he couldn't spy on their courting, and that it was what the old fool deserved for giving them the farm in the first place.

Och but they said everything but their prayers in the Bogside, and Bannie Hernie didn't seem to care that much what they said, or maybe she just got used to their wagging tongues; so the old man lay on his couch till his hurdies were sore and the rheumatism stiffened him, and what with the want of proper food

194

for his belly he became as thin and unwashed as a starved tink and fit to scare the craws from your tattie dreels. Fell crabbit he was too in his old age and like to bite off your lug of a morning when you went in by with a barrow wheel that needed to be fitted with a new iron ring on it for a tyre. And if you hadn't given it a dabble in the mill-dam to wash off all the sharn you heard about it from old Hardwood, which was odd you thought when he was sorer in need of a scrub himself, and folk thought he was getting a bit dottled in his old age, though he still had a waspish tongue.

But he wasn't as dottled as they thought the stock, for after his day at the barrow-making old Hardwood began working at something in the evening, so that if you went past Clayfoons in the dark on your bicycle you'd see a light in the far end of Hardwood's shed and the old man plaining and chiseling or spokeshaving at something in the lamplight, so that though you got off your bike and went to the window for a peep you still couldn't make out what he was working at; maybe just another barrow you thought, and that he couldn't cope with the demand, and though you made an errand in bye in daylight he always had the thing covered up, longish in shape it was, like a boat, though you didn't like to ask lest he told you to mind your own business, for he could be snappish at times.

Then Hardwood locked his shed and disappeared into the fog that had been hanging about for days on the hairst parks, so that you couldn't see the lads at stook parade, and the fog-horn at the Battery Head moaning all day and night like a cow foonert at the calving. When her father didn't go in for breakfast Bannie went over to the shed to waken him. She tried the lock and hammered on the door but when there was no response to her knocking she looked in the window. He wasn't in his couch either so she went to the far end and looked in the other window. The light was coming in slowly but she saw the naked coffin on its trestles, uncovered now for anyone who cared to look at it, and Bannie got a sore fright, for there it stood in polished oak, with brass handles on the ends and black cords and toshels draped along its sides, with a lid on top. Bannie couldn't think of anyone who had ordered a coffin from her father, nor could she mind of a new death in the Bogside, or anybody like to die that would be needing one, and it was the first coffin she had seen the old man make in his retirement, though she knew he had been an undertaker in his younger day.

Bannie tried the door again but it wouldn't budge, so she walked round the shed and came back to the window where the coffin was, staring in at it until she had a daft idea that her father must have made it for himself, that he would be lying in there now, and she rapped on the window with her knuckles, hoping to waken him up, half expecting the lid to be raised and the old man look out at her in his working clothes, reminding her of her ill-treatment and making her promise to mend her ways with her twin brother. Guilt began to rankle in Bannie's mind and she promised herself that though the old man was only playing a joke on her she would mend her ways, and the hot tears came into her eyes and she hammered on the window till it shook and cried out 'Father, oh father, speak to me. I promise father, I promise . . .' and the greet grew loud in

195

her throat, until you could hear it across the road, and the tears ran down her face and the dog came barking round and then Wattie to see what ailed his sister, thinking maybe that somebody had ravished her at the back of the shed.

Wattie took Bannie in his oxter but she thrust him aside, pointing at the coffin through the window. 'Father's missing,' she cried, 'and I'll swear he's in there now, waiting for us to promise something. All the time we've been wicked he's been watching and this is our last chance. We must promise never to do it again Wattie!' She was sobbing hard and Wattie said 'promise nothing' and pressed his nose against the glass, shading the growing light with his open hands against his cheeks, and when he saw the gleaming coffin on its trestles he was sore taken aback. 'So that was what he was hammerin at in the evenin's. It's a pity Bannie that we didna take a look over to see what he was at. I jist thocht it was anither barra.'

'I'll go to the hoose and see if I can find anither key,' Bannie said, a bit calmed down since Wattie came round, but she could find no other key to the shed. Wattie shook the door by the knob but it wouldn't move, so he threw his weight against it and burst it open, near going head first after it into the shed. Bannie followed him past the couch and the bench, the floor deep in wood shavings and a fine smell of wood and rozin and paint, with half-finished barrows propped against the walls and wheels on the floor, bits of sawn wood, sawdust and nails, and the coffin at the far end. The twins stood beside it, afraid to open the lid, like bairns with a Jack-in-the-Box, afraid that when they opened the lid their father would leap up in their faces and cry 'Bah!' A sudden frightening shout that would scare them to fits; or he would be lying in there asleep or dead, white and cold as snow and would never speak to them again in this world.

'You open it Bannie. I did my bit bursting the door.'

'No I couldna, and what if he is in there listening to us arguing aboot wha will open his coffin lid.' And Bannie was near to tears again.

Wattie plucked up courage and prised his thick thumbs under the heavy lid, until he got his hand under it and lifted it up on its edge, holding it there, wide open, while the two of them stared into the empty coffin, lined with white cotton, and Bannie couldn't think where her father had gotten all this stuff, unless he had ordered it through the post.

But the old man was not in the coffin, nor hiding in the shed, or anywhere about the steading or the farmhouse, for they had searched high and low for him, though Bannie was sure the coffin was a sign or a warning that they would find him dead somewhere. So they searched all the burns and hedges on Clayfoons and crawled under all the stooks on the hairst rigs looking for him, or simply threw them down in despair, hoping that they would find their father asleep somewhere and nobody would know about his disappearance, and they would be kinder to him after this scare, for he had certainly given them a lesson and they wouldn't forget it.

But no old man leapt out at them from any stook, and he had disappeared at a time that would give them plenty to think about, this misty season in the middle o hairst when he would be ill to find, and when most other folks would have other things on their minds, what with their uncut corn drooping and weeping in the seep of the rain and the stubble as wet you could hardly set a stook on it, the burns all in spate and the snipes wheebling in the segs, though you couldna see them for the fog.

Before the day was out Bannie had to run up to Whistlebrae and tell them what had happened, and would they telephone the bobbies to come and help them look for her father. A sore disgrace it would be to the pair of them, but things had reached a stage when they felt they would be worse guilty if they didn't report it.

For two whole days half the countraside searched for the missing joiner, in the burns and hedges, in the segs and on the braes, among the whin and broom around the quarries, and up among the fir trees on the Spionkop, the highest hill in the Bogside. Folk even drained their mill-dams, thinking old Hardwood would stick in the sluice or go down the lade, but there was never a sign of him, not even in the miller's dam. The polis looked everywhere they could think of, and even the school bairns were told to look out for the old man when they went over the moors and through the woods.

The stone quarry at Spionkop was a deep hole of water on the face of the brae, and the polis got a fire-engine out of the toon with long hoses that went over the grass from the road and sucked the quarry dry, but the firemen shook their helmeted heads when they came upon all the rubbish at the bottom of the quarry but no sign of Hardwood. Folk wondered about the moss pots filled with brown peaty water that had no bottom to them, where a body might sink far enough and never be seen again, and they shuddered at the thought. Lads on stook parade in the hairst parks expected to find old Hardwood in every stook they shifted, and when you thought of all the multitude of corn and barley stooks in the Laich o Buchan where an old body could hide you knew fine the old man wasn't a dottard; that he had chosen the right time to keep folk on the move, especially the twins at Clayfoons, for they hadna steekit an eye since he went missing.

Now you couldn't see the hill of the Spionkop from Clayfoons, though it was but two miles as the crow flies. You couldn't see it for the strip of wood on the Berry-hill, even though the cottars had thinned it with their axes over the years; beyond was the moss and the segs and the grass parks that lay on the shin of the Spionkop. It was an unco name to give a bit hill and you thought maybe it was that if you went up there on a fine day you could spy on the folk in the howe; but it took its name from the fairmtoon high on its slopes, where a Dutch chiel from South Africa had bought the place, and being home-sick he changed the name from Fellrigs to Spionkop, and some said he was a Boer, seeing his name was Vanderskelp or something. But since he came to live there on the face of the brae they called it the Spionkop, which well-read folk told you was somewhere in Natal, and had something to do with a battle that the British had out there with the Boers, those ill-mannered chiels that were but farming folk and shot at the British like they were hares in the parks. But maybe the

Vanderskelp chiel meant no harm, because the Boers got a thrashing at the Spionkop, and yon General Buller had to run with his breeks down, so maybe the lad was giving you credit naming your Buchan hill after a Boer defeat. Anyway the fuskered postie said that was the new address, and when you thought of other places in Buchan with foreign names like Waterloo, Pisgah and Jericho you wasn't surprised. And the postie said the Boer was a right civil chiel to speak to and that he didn't have a barking dog that would tear the arse out of your breeks like some he knew in the Bogside.

You had gone up on the Spionkop yourself in your time, looking for a Druids' Circle in such a likely place, but not a lintel stone did you find there from the olden days, nor any sign of a fort, for the Buchan Howes had small protection from the Vikings when the horned chiels came over in their long-boats from the Norse Lands, though King Malcolm had licked the Danes at Cruden Bay, and you could still see the cairns that marked their graves at Cairncatto, and such a song of the curlew there it was like an eternal requiem for the dead in their long forgotten burrows.

But down at the foot of the Spionkop lived Maggie Lawrence in her thackit biggin, where the fuschias hung their ruby bells over the stone dyke the long summer through, and the dog-rose clung to the walls, while the smell of dewy honeysuckle on an evening clear would nearly sicken you with pleasure, like you had drunk too much wine for your stomach's sake. Maggie was an old toothless body that could neither read nor write, and she lived there alone but for the rats that fed with her at table, and if you looked through her peep-hole windows with the little lace curtains you'd see old Maggie with her pets, and if any one of the creatures was impatient enough to snatch a morsel from Maggie she would give it a right quick smack with her hazel stick and cry out: 'Get doon ye Ted!' And the long-tailed rat would slink away to the other end of the table, with great respect for Maggie when her ire was up. When Maggie died your grandfather had to sit up with her corpse at night to keep the rats away from her coffin, and right glad he was when the funeral was over because he was afraid of the brutes.

But meanwhile Maggie was still very much alive, smoking her clay pipe and gathering whin sticks on the brae for her fire, and any of the divots that she could rive from the heather. She carried her water from a wee well on the edge of a grass park just beyond her door, and Maggie would put on her bit plaid of red tartan with the tassled edges and a yoke on her shoulders, with two galvanized pails hanging from it, her clay pipe in her mooth, the blue reek taking over her canty shoulder, away to the well for her drop water.

It was but two or three feet deep Maggie's well, a tender spring out of the sand with a trout in it to keep the water clean, and sometimes a frog that leapt in to keep him company, and whiles a shrew-mouse that fell in by mistake, swam itself to exhaustion and drowned, and was thrown out by Maggie when she caught it in her pail. Maggie spoke to her trout like he was a human body, and they said he cocked an eye at her when her reflection hit the water. So it was a great surprise to her that day when she found this great big trout in her well, soon as she opened the gate that was for keeping out the cattle beasts, for here was this man standing in her well up to his thighs, his back bent level with the ground, his white head jammed into the water so that he couldn't fall over, his body supported by the rim of the wall. Old Hardwood at last, where nobody thought to look for him, drowned in Maggie's well. She dropped her pails and took the wooden yoke from her neck, stuck her bit pipe in the pocket of her apron and wondered where she would go for help. But first she went a bit closer to the human statue, crouched with its feet and hands in the well, bent in supplication the creature seemed, praying for death with its mouth in the water. Maggie went down the step and put her hand on the cold stiff shoulder, like a stuffed thing, swelling inside the damp clothing. She knew he was dead but she wasn't afraid of the poor old man, just wondered how he came to be there, and how she would ever have the heart again to drink the crystal clear water from her wallie. A pity she couldna see his face to see who he might be, for she knew nothing of Hardwood's disappearance, though she kenned that sic a body lived in the Bogside. His jacket pockets were bulging in the water and Maggie lifted the sodden flap to see what might be in there, thinking maybe it was bawbees, though it didn't seem likely when he had done away with himself, or so she supposed, for nobody could put an old man into a well like that without a struggle, and he was as composed and peaceful as a sleeping lamb; not a speck of blood on him, nor a tare in his jacket, not a hair of his head ravelled and nothing in the well, nothing but the trootie, straight as an eel in the bottom. His jacket pockets were stuffed with coiryarn, coconut-hair rope that the farmer chiels were using nowadays to hold down their rucks and strae-soos, instead of straw rape, and Maggie thought the poor creature had been fell determined to put an end to himself, and that if the drowning failed he would hang himself from a fir tree on the Spionkop.

The fog had cleared and Maggie warsled away up the hill to Mr Vanderskelp, who was kind of a landlord to her, 'cause her clay biggin was on his grun, though he never charged her any rent for the sagging roofed venel that she lived in, little more than a cairn of stones and clay with one lum and an earthen floor, a hallan that some crofter chiel had biggit for his family a hunder years ago, with stones gathered on the hillside.

Mr Vanderskelp heard Maggie's story and said he had been through the park counting his cattle that very morning but never thought of looking in the well. It seemed impossible that anyone could drown himself in such a shallow trough. Maggie would have called it a wee skite of water, but never mind, she knew fine what he meant and she agreed with her laird. Mr Vanderskelp then telephoned the bobby and told him to get the doctor, and they came and lifted the dripping Hardwood out of Maggie's well and laid him on the yird, all but his false teeth that they found later and Maggie hadn't seen, and maybe just as well, for it might have scunnered her completely from taking water there.

Two of Mr Vanderskelp's men lifted the corpse on to a springcart and took him to Clayfoons, the water still dripping out of the cart, and followed by the school bairns that were on their way home at the time. So the undertaker came in his black coat and stretched out Hardwood on a board and shaved him and laid him in his home-made coffin in the ben room. And Bannie bibbled and grat over him like a long lost bairn and would hardly bide in the hoose without a neighbour woman for company or the funeral was by. And such a trail of a funeral that the likes of it had never been seen in the Bogside, the road fair jammed with phaetons and gigs and Governess carts with their shelts and ponies and a motor car or twa, and the kirkyard black with folk, like the craws after a thrashin mull, and Wattie Hernie by the gate when they left, shakin as mony hands ye would have thought he was ca'in a pump, with saut tears hingin at his mouser.

So that was Hardwood and his barrows, and they survived him for mony a year and day, keeping his memory green in the Bogside, green as the sod where he lay with his wife at the gable o the kirk yonder. But the twins didn't stay long in the fairm after this, maybe because they had a guilty conscience, though the neighbours gave them no cause to feel it. They had a roup the two of them the next May and sold nearly everything but the furniture and the grandfather clock. Everything else went: horse, nowt, pigs and poultry; pleuchs, harrows, grubber and rollers; binder, mower, scythes and horse-rake, all the hand tools and two or three of Hardwood's barrows and wheels that gave a stunning price. Sic a steer there was and a day or two after this the twins got a stem-waggon and lifted all their gear and set sail out of the Bogside and that was the last you ever heard of them.

The Souter

All through the first summer at Kingask, the place you was cottared at, and through the long winter evenings of your spare time, and now into spring, you had laboured at the Queen Mary - nine precious months you had expended on this labour of love to create a model ship that was the cardboard image (or very near it) of the famous Queen of Clydebank, a queer hobby for a fairm body and folk jist thought you was a bit daft.

You got your cardboard in the village, down in Candlebay there by the sea, and most of it from Jimmie Duthie the souter, who gave you spare shoeboxes when a customer didn't want them. He also gave you two sheets of tough hardened leather three feet by fifteen inches to make the hull, which cost you nearly a fortnight's wages, and thread waxed with rozin to stitch it together. Jimmie had been a pal of yours almost from the first month you came to Kingask, when you had gone down to have your Sunday shoes soled, and a pair of Kathleen's that needed the heels built up, and Jimmie Duthie had made such a good job of it and had charged so little that you always went back. There was another shoemaker in the village called Tackie Broon, because he tacked his trousers to his wooden leg to scare the bairns when they annoyed his budgerigars. Tackie had lost his leg in the war but he said he still had cold feet from standing so long in the wet trenches. He kept budgerigars in cages all round the shop, the chorus of birds all chirping away while he hammered in the tackets on a last between his knees, sitting on a wooden chair as natural like that until he stood up you would never have noticed that he had a wooden leg. Tackie Broon had done well for a time and was awfully popular with the bairns, who came in bye after school to see his birds, and to listen to their chirping in the cages. But Tackie Broon wasn't all that fond of bairns, nor did he have any of his own, though he was married, and his wife came through from ben the hoose occasionally to feed the budgies and clean out their cages and tidy the shop. But the bairns were a bit of a nuisance to Tackie Broon and he felt they were upsetting his aviary, the birds dashing themselves against the wire meshes, until he devised a way to get rid of the bairns; so he started driving the tackets through his breeks into his wooden leg and this fair frightened them, especially the younger offenders, who couldn't understand about the wooden leg. It kept the bairns away for months but he lost trade over it, because the bairns took their parents' shoes for repair to Jimmie Duthie, who was a bachelor and genuinely fond of the bairns, but was now swamped under the load of work they brought him, hammering away in his back shop while his sister brought him jugs of hot strong tea to keep him going at his last.

So like the bairns you didn't bother Tackie Broon very much, because he was a bit surly at the best of times, so you became great friends with souter Duthie, and after a whilie newsing together he learned of your daftness about boats and the sea, and when he learned you was also a reader he gave you books like Southey's *Life of Nelson; Buccaneers of the Pacific* and *The Riddle of Jutland,* all of which you devoured with relish, and when you told him about your hobby, and your cherished ambition to build a model of the Queen Mary, which had just been launched on the Clyde, he gave you all the strongest cardboard you required and shoe-wax to seal your stitching and to make it water-tight along the three-foot length of keel. Jimmie added that his father had been a great reader, and so was his sister, and that the house was stacked with books, so if ever you wanted a book just come in by.

The first thing you did was to make a wooden platform with notches to hold the keel, so that the giant ship wouldn't topple over, because you wouldn't have room to work with side supports. Then you shaped the hull, first with a yacht bow, both sides exactly the same; cut out the port holes with a sharp knife, then stitched the two sides together with Jimmie Duthie's thread, using an awl to punch the rivet holes, the glossy surface of the leather outmost for painting, and to make the ship water-tight, pouring hot wax into the seams. The walls of the giant hull were now prised apart and straddled with double deck supports fixed with sprigs or small nails, forcing out the bilges to the shape required and pulling in the yacht bow to a shorter angle, then filling with cement to keep the shape and reinforce the hull, judging the correct amount to serve as ballast, though more weight could be added with pebbles through the holds when launching the ship. You had cut the hull walls with a slightly upward curve in the middle, arching from bow to stern, so that when pulled apart they were now level for laying the deck, fitting masts and funnels, building the bridge and cabins, tasks that are usually completed in the fitting-out basin after launching, but in this case would have to be done beforehand, because you couldn't really guess the weight of your superstructure, which would have to be corrected with the final ballast.

During the launching of the real Queen you had cut out all the photographs from the papers and weekly magazines and these you studied in great detail, even closer now that actual building had begun, though you wasn't going to do it to scale, rather using your own judgement in the size of things, which you thought would be good experience when you turned to scale building with some future models.

The Queen Mary now occupied the whole of the kitchen table, when Kathleen had cleared everything away to let you work, meanwhile gazing at this monstrosity you was making; something she had never seen her brothers at, them being country loons and more interested in ploughing and horses. Maybe it was the time in your boyhood you had lived in the town that had drawn your attention to ships, when you was always at the harbour after school hours; the harbour or the railway station, which were linked by a single set of rails for coaling the herring drifters. Now at Kingask by the sea you were trying to recapture this early influence; to express it in art form, though other folk might say you hadn't grown up properly and was still a loon at heart, which wasn't a bad thing really when you came to think about it.

At table-leaf level your Queen was a magnificent ship, her graceful, forward sweeping bow towering above the teacups at bedtime, her long sleek sides and decks stretching to her stern at the other end of the table, awaiting a rudder and propellers in the normal method of ship construction. When work was in progress Kathleen had to guard the Queen with her life almost; guard it against little Brian, your small son, whose fingers were just now reaching the table, and at bed-time every night the liner was carried upstairs out of his reach next day.

It took a whole evening to make one cardboard funnel, about the size of a modern beer tin (which would have served the purpose then - had it been invented) papered over to hold it together (before the days of sellotape) a flat disc inside to keep the shape, then slipped into the hole shaped for it in the upperstructure behind the bridge. It took about the same time to make an air vent; two evenings to construct a lifeboat complete with ratlines and tarpaulin covers, rudder and propeller, and even oars in case of engine failure; and as there were three funnels, six engineroom vents and a dozen lifeboats (though the real Queen had twenty-four) a body gets some idea of the time and patience spent on the upperstructure, prior to launching in this case; including the bridgework, sweeping out over the side of the hull, and the actual wheelhouse and control room, tennis courts, swimming pool and railings (using gramophone needles) linked with white thread, masts and companion ways, and as the new polythene paper had just made its appearance you used this for glass in the portholes and cabin windows. It was the most wonderful thing to date you had ever made in your life and strangers in the house gazed at it in wonder. Its great size captured everybody's imagination from the start, though a closer study by experts would have revealed your lack of scaling, but quite proportionate in every detail, down to the anchors and capstans on the foredeck, which was scored with pencil to simulate boarding - rope ladders, shrouds, wireless aerial, stairways and crow's nest.

The final painting was done with Japlac, black enamel gloss for the upper part of the hull, red keel to the bilges, with a white stripe for the waterline and plimsoll markings; varnished decks and masts, white cabins and lifeboats, black funnels with red tops and a white stripe between, and red propellers and rudder, with tufts of white cottonwool in the funnels.

During construction of the 'Queen' your kitchen was a miniature John Brown's shipyard, except for the towering derricks and the hammering of rivet guns; everything in a muddle for the final achievement, and there were even strikes and suspension of work when you was too tired or just not in the mood to go on, but after an evening or two in your armchair you was back on the job again. Cunard halted work on the real Queen Mary for lack of capital in the hungry 'thirties. The great ship was abandoned for nearly two years and unemployment soared on the Clyde. Eventually the Government provided funds and work was resumed on the skeleton hull. The gesture was more to ease distress than to finish the luxury liner, though the final result is unparalleled in maritime achievement.

But before the launching in the miller's dam you thought that Badgie Summers the foreman next door should see your masterpiece. His daughter Esma had looked at it several times during construction when she had come round for little Brian. Mrs Summers had stared at it with folded arms over the kitchen table and said you was at the wrong job feeding nowt and pulling turnips when you was so good with your hands. Most likely they had told Badgie of your accomplishment but so far he had never seen it. So one fine Sunday morning after byre time, after you'd had your tea and a smoke, you went upstairs for your 'Queen' and set her on the kitchen table. She really was a magnificent sight, the fresh smelling enamel gloss gleaming in the morning sunshine, perfect almost in every detail, even to the guy-ropes of black thread holding the masts, all ready for launching.

You told Kathleen that you wanted to show the foreman your boat, because you felt so proud of it, but she said you shouldn't bother because most likely he would only laugh at you; that you knew fine he hadn't much time for such capers, nothing in his mind but his work, and that he never even troubled himself to put soles on his family's shoes (as her own father had done with their large family) but sat in his corner chair all evening and left it to Tackie Broon the shoemaker. No, Kathleen said, Badgie had no time for hobbies other than his work and wouldn't likely be interested. All the same you took the great ship in your arms and went down the close to Badgie, rested the 'Queen' on your knee and knocked on the door with your free hand, and when Esma opened it you walked in and set Queen Mary on the table by the window. Badgie and the blacksmith were seated in armchairs on each side of the fire, Badgie nearest the window, where he leaned round to gaze at your handiwork. The blacksmith glowered with mild interest across the kitchen, but neither of them rose to give your ship a closer inspection, while you stood in the middle of the floor like an overgrown schoolboy showing off a fabulous new toy, the only difference being that you had made the thing yourself.

'Aye faith,' says Badgie, trying his best to be complimentary, 'some wark gaen intae that thing. It's a wonder ye have the patience. lt's mair than I could dae onywye.'

Badgie's wife sat apart, admiring the model from afar, as if it were in Candlebay harbour and she was feared to go near the water. 'A bonnie piece o work,' she said, 'I dinna ken fut wye ye can be bothered; but I suppose it's fine for takin up yer attention in the winter evenin's.'

Finally the blacksmith offered his criterion: 'But that thing wunna put onything in yer pooch man; there's nae bawbees tae be made at that kind o wark!'

Your answer to that remark would have been that if you was going to spend most of it in the pub like he did it didn't matter, but of course you didn't want to be cheeky; and after all none of them had asked you round to show off your boat. But you was showing them a piece of intricate art contrived by serious study and concentration and all they could think about was money - how much you could get out of it materially - without a thought for the satisfaction of your achievement and the many happy hours it had given you. So you just lifted your boat from the table and politely left the house, wondering what the blacksmith had said after you left. 'A queer lad' (most likely) 'makin boats: naething tae be made at that!' But most likely Badgie would stick up for you: 'Aye but he's a' there though, mair than the spoon puts in; a sober stock maybe but he can cairry a bag o corn up the laft stair wi the neist ane - and he's nae a feel either!'

Kathleen asked what they thought about your boat, and you said 'Oh, not very much; a waste of time showing it to them, they're nae interested in boats, naething in their heids but money.'

'No,' she replied, 'they wouldna understand ye as I do, though it taks me a' my time whiles the things ye get up tae.'

The launching in the miller's dam was perfect, with just the right amount of ballast to keep the ship afloat, swinging slightly in the breeze, so that you didn't have to open the hatches to add more pebbles. She was strung with flags between the masts, with a Union Jack on the stern, and a string from the bows to your hand on the dam bank, where you guided her over the ripples, her stately bow dipping slightly over the waterline. Some of the village loons came up to watch your one-ship regatta; seeing there wasn't a yachting pond in the village, nothing but the harbour, with its patches of oil and barrel staves floating at the pier. So you asked one of the loons if he would go and get hold of Jimmie Duthie the shoemaker, seeing that he had provided the material, and when he saw the Queen Mary afloat on the miller's dam he hailed you with 'Hey there! Anchors ahoy! All hands on deck!' But we didn't break a bottle over her bows, which would have been like hitting the *Titanic* with the iceberg.

Jimmie Duthie was the most amazing shoemaker you had ever seen, hammering away in his wee back shop with a mountain of boots and shoes of all descriptions piled on the floor, some of them without name or number, and when Jimmie threw your pair on the heap you felt you could never be sure you would get your own boots back again. But James Duthie Shoemaker (as on the board above the door, his father's name) knew everybody's footwear in the village of Candlebay and half the parish of Pittentumb (except for those who went to Tackie Broon) from the costly shoes of the mistress of Kingask to the cheaper mail order variety on the feet of the kitchiedeem at Fleamiddens, including the bairns of the parish; though some of his customers put a label on their boots and tied the pairs together in case they got lost in Jimmie's back shop, and some of the most mindful of them tucked a pound or a ten-shilling note in the toe of a shoe, hoping that Jimmie would find it when he put the shoe on the last, because he hadn't charged for the previous repair, or sent an account for it.

Over the years the dusty heap of boots and shoes in Jimmie's back shop seemed to get bigger and bigger; never smaller, and now nearly counter high, and you sometimes wondered if he had ever been at the bottom of it; sharny boots and muddy boots, boots that Jimmie would have to scrape and clean before he ever got a start to repair them, just as the cattlemen had left the byre with them, or the ploughman the furrow. The wooden floor was also shovel deep in leather cuttings, shoe nails, iron heel and toepieces, discarded protectors, studs, tackets, sprigs, broken bootlaces, and the cigarette packets, match boxes, fag ends and matches thrown down by his various customers. Why Jimmie Duthie's shop wasn't burned down during the night you couldn't imagine (or even during the day) because there was only one ashtray, the lid of a boot black tin, over by Jimmy's bench, always heaped up and running over, and when the place was crowded and the lads couldn't get near it, they just heeled their tabbies into the years of leather cuttings on the floor, and some of them landed inside a shoe and were left to smoulder. Folk said that Jimmie needed a wife to tidy up his shop, that his sister wasn't able for it, but both were in celibacy and likely to remain so. Lizzie Duthie was such a frail sickly lass that the lads never bothered her, white faced and frizzy headed and slightly bent in the back, with a small lump between her shoulder blades. Jimmie never had a lass they said, though he teased at the quines who came into his shop, servant lassies and the like, though he was far too shy to go the length of kissing them, and if they had taken the initiative most likely he would have sprinted through to his sister in the kitchen. His only relaxation was his weekly game of indoor bowling and shuttlecock in the Masonic Hall in Brochan on Wednesdays, when his shop was closed all day, and if he was a member of the Masonic fraternity he never mentioned the fact.

Down at Tackie Broon's, at the other end of the village, things were much more orderly, even though Tackie had bother getting out of his chair, because his wife looked after the place. You laid your boots on the counter and pulled a string that rang a bell in the kitchen, when Tackie's wife came through and labelled your boots and set them on a rack beside her husband's chair; entered your boots in a ledger with your name and address and told you when to come back for them.

But Tackie Broon had his frailties too. The want of his leg was an affliction that troubled him sorely and sometimes drove him to drink. On occasions he wanted to forget the static, hum-drum world into which his affliction had thrust him. But for months on end he wouldn't touch liquor; *the drink;* his hammer flying from the last with the rhythm of a conductor's baton, while he cupped a handful of sprigs and threw them into his mouth, humming a tune like 'Tipperary', or 'Pack up your troubles in your old kitbag', broken at intervals while he took a sprig from between his teeth and hammered it into a shoe.

At other times Tackie Broon's eyes had the appearance of a gathering thunderstorm, when he would rise up from his chair, cast aside his chamois leather apron, get into his jacket and hirple down the road to the Spittoon Bar, where he really made a night of it, and some of his old cronies had to carry him home from the pub. Next day his wife would put a notice in the window: NO REPAIRS MEANTIME, and never unlocked the shop door. But after a day or

206

two to recuperate, Tackie was back at his last again; happy and contented, fumbling in his tins for hobnails, his right thumb smooth and scored from long years as a buffer for the keen-edged knife slicing through the leather.

When the war came Tackie was scared of the bombing. He had nightmares about lying on his back in a deep trench, the Germans in their steel helmets and fixed bayonets leaping down on him, landing on his chest, stamping his heart into his throat until he gasped with palpitation, and he couldn't get up because of his wounded leg, the blood seeping through his kilt. He gasped himself into consciousness and his wife would be comforting him, smoothing what grey hairs remained on his throbbing temples. He wanted to shout, to scream, to run away from it all; then buried his head in his wife's bosom, while she swabbed away his tears.

But Lizzie Duthie wasn't able to help her brother to this extent, and since their mother died things had gone from bad to worse with them. But she managed to cook his meals for him and do his washing, go for messages and send out his accounts when Jimmie remembered to tell her who had been in the shop. Jimmie never wrote anything down, relying entirely upon memory for all his customers, and those he remembered filtered through to his sister's ledger, and those he forgot were those who left money in their shoes, while others conveniently forgot and Jimmie cobbled their boots for nothing, at least for a time, until his sister saw them from her front window and sent in an account. But Jimmy mended many a shoe he knew he would never be paid for, and yet he hadn't the brazen heart to refuse, and there were those he repaired for a few coppers, knowing their owners were poor or had big families, and for the poorest of the poor, those who were on parish relief or the old-age pension (which was only ten shillings a week) Jimmy sometimes forgot to tell his sister intentionally. And if she happened to see them in the shop he would only allow her to charge for the materials used; nothing for his work, sometimes charging only a few pence for long hours of work on the footwear of large starving families, rather than see the bairns go to school barefooted. Jimmie Duthie was the Good Samaritan who was never inside the kirk door; the anti-hypocrite who was more of a Christian than the elders whose boots he was obliged to lick. Jimmie hammered far into the night, when most of the village was asleep and the moon peering in at his window. In day time he could have been working in the country, his back to the village and its clutter of houses, before him the open parks and birdsong, looking over the wide farmlands stretching up from the sea.

James Duthie's only real complaint with the world was that though his customers brought him plenty of work they seldom bought their footwear in his shop. Most of them went to Brochan, or even to Aberdeen, where they could buy them cheaper in the big stores, and have a holiday at the same time. Others dealt with mail order firms, especially the women folk and young quines, buying cheap trash that wore out in weeks; cardboard and wax they brought to Jimmie, and when he tried to sole them with real leather they fell to pieces, all for a few pence that wasn't worth the hours of sleep he lost over it.

Jimmie was a late riser and worked mostly at night, getting up at dinner time and hammering away till two or even three o'clock in the morning, his sister in bed, a light in his back window in the early hush of a summer morning, the first cocks crowing at Kingask, the seagulls winging inland from the sea, when Jimmie would retire at last, the mountain of work on the floor slightly reduced and grown into another heap, awaiting customers who didn't know their own boots, until the souter picked them out of the new miscellany, and even though you was a stranger he was seldom wrong in his identification.

But honest, hard working souter Duthie had a reason for spreading his work load; for turning night into day. He liked working in the evenings when the back shop was full of farm workers and lads from the village, a gathering place for idle youth after the Spittoon bar and the bus garage had closed, when all would flock to Jimmie Duthie's back shop for a news and a blether. Sometimes it was standing room only and the place so thick with fag reek you could hardly see Jimmie at his last by the darkened window, his tilley lamp hanging from a beam in the roof, sizzling away until somebody stood on a chair and pumped more air into it with the brass plunger and it brightened into life again. But Jimmie never stopped hammering, a string over the boot he was working at to hold it down on the last, looped over the instep of his left foot; his mouth full of sprigs, studs or tackets, taking them in his fingers one by one and plopping them into the new leather he had hammered on to somebody's worn out shoes. Then he would take a seat by the coke stove, waxing thread with rozin and threading his needle, stitching a patch on the leatherwork of some bauchled old shoe, for he didn't have a machine and did all his sewing by hand.

Jimmie worked through all the banter between the farm chiels and the village lads, some of them fishermen, while others worked in Brochan; but he didn't like fighting and serious argument, and when this happened it was the only time he spoke up. But the teenagers respected Jimmie's quiet remonstrances and the quarrels never reached physical reaction; or if they did they went outside to settle their differences, but as the Candlebay constabulary was never far away they would shake hands peaceably in the cold darkness and sneak inside again to the warmth and comfort of the souter's coke stove in the back shop.

Constable Sim turned a blind eye and a deaf ear to the revelry in the souter's shop. There was no drink consumed on the premises, for Lizzie Duthie wouldn't allow it, and faith the bobby thought it kept the rascals off the street, where they might get up to worse mischief. So he thought he could go home after the pub closed to his wireless set by the fire, his big splay feet on a padded stool and his pipe alight, his tunic on the back of a chair, his peaked cap on a peg in the hall, with nothing to bother him unless the phone rang; which, thank heaven, wasn't often, and mostly his wife answered it, saying that the constable was still out on duty, unless it was a real urgent case, like somebody had set fire to the harbour or putten a sod on the minister's lum down at the Free Kirk manse, in which case he would have to get the firemen on the job, and they wouldn't thank him for that.

The story goes that when Constable Sim was a young bobby in the toon, and had charged a drunken youth for spitting on the pavement in Constitution Street, he fixed the lad by the lug and took him round the corner to spit in King Street, which was easier written down, because Sim couldn't spell Constitution Street, nor transcribe it from print to longhand though he had been looking at the nameplate on the wall. It was also rumoured of Sim about this time that he was summoned to the Police Inspector's office on a reprimand for being too lenient with young offenders. The Superintendent pointed out that this wasn't the way to get promotion; and at the same time insisting that every apprehension must be recorded, however trivial, even though it was only a drunk making his water up a close in the dark. So the next time that Constable Sim was out at night on his rounds, trying the locks on all the shop doors, he also flashed his torch up every lane, and when he came upon a young couple having intercourse against a back wall he flashed his torch right in the lad's face, blinding him for a moment and demanding: 'What's this ye're at min?' When the lad replied that surely the constable must know what he was at with a quine in his oxter Sim replied: 'Weel it's a damned good job ye wasna jist makin yer watter or I'd a run ye in!' Folk said this was how he got his nickname - 'Pee-See Sim'.

Another version of the story was that when Sim asked the youth what he was up to the lad said: 'Och nae naething constable!' Whereupon Sim handed him the torch and said: 'Stand aside than and maybe I'll mak mair o't masel!' But knowing Sim as a respectable policeman a body is inclined to believe the earlier edition: the big clumsy brute that he was with his feet at ten-to-two on the clock, or one-fifty as a body would say nowadays; him that could hardly be bothered to throw his leg over a bicycle, never mind a woman.

The most ridiculous story about Pee-See Sim was the time that a sex-starved sailor came off the train at dusk, determined to have the first prostitute he could find and take her up a dark pend for urgent intercourse. But there wasn't anything in skirts available for his purpose, nothing but a respectable middle-aged lady on crutches, so he grabbed hold of her with one hand and held the other on her mouth, then hustled her up the nearest pend, trailing her crutches behind her. He was doing his bit when Sim came into the close and tripped over the crutches in the gloamin: 'Shift yer barra oot o that min,' he cries, searching for his torch 'Ye're blockin the traffic!' 'Aye, aye,' cries the lad, still gagging the woman, 'but hold on man till I ile the wheel!'

But Pee-See Sim had his good points too, and he didn't charge every lad he met in the mirk without a gas light on his bicycle. Like the chiel he met one dark night with two bicycles and only one light and that on the one he was riding, while he steered the other bike with his right hand, nearest the traffic, though there wasn't much of it in those days, only the odd car. Sim stepped out from the hedge and stopped the lad with his torch, grabbing the spare bike in passing, asking why there wasn't a light on this one. The lad replied that he only had one light and that he had only just bought the lady's cycle and he was taking it home to his sister, giving an address that the bobby knew. Sim asked the lad if he could take the spare bike on his left-hand side, away from the traffic, because he might cause an accident, but the chiel said that he couldn't hold it in his left hand and the bike would land in the ditch. 'Ah weel,' says Sim, 'tak the licht aff yer land horse and put it on yer aff-side beast and we'll lat ye go wi that!' Which shows that Constable Sim (for all his faults) had once been a farm-worker himself and knew about ploughing with horses and what he was talking about.

On another occasion Sim stopped a young farm servant on his motor-bike for speeding through the village. In the summer evenings he tore along the High Street like ricocheting thunder, endangering the lives of the bairns crossing the street, until the folk complained to Sim and he had to caution the lad. So the chiel stopped his machine in front of the bobby and left it ticking over until Sim had his particulars. Sim got out his notebook and licked his lead pencil and put his foot on the pillion, with his knee as a pad to write on. But the lad had heard about Sim and his spelling blunders and gave him an incredibly long and ridiculous name for the place he worked at, and while he spelled it out for the bobby and watched the puzzled look on his face he slipped his bike quietly into gear and sped off, leaving Sim standing in the High Street on one leg like a hen with cold feet in a farm close.

The last time Constable Sim was in Souter Duthie's shop at night - well he was hardly inside for the crowd of folk, but just had his head inside the door to show his authority, or that he was still around if anybody was looking for trouble; his long horse face white in the light of the tilley lamp, his hard topped cap at a bit of an angle on his balding head, and just touching the door lintel, for Sim was well over the six feet required to be a bobby. 'Inquisitive Sim' they called him because they said his curiosity would lead him up a gas pipe; or that he would speir the bloomers off a tinker's wife and then speir where she tint them. Anyway, Constable Sim was showing his silver buttons in the souter's shop when some ill-mannered devil let off a tremendous fart; a beer fart as you might call it, then looked at the bobby and called out: 'I bet ye couldna dae that Constable Sim withoot leavin fern-tickles (freckles) on yer drawers!'

'Naw,' said the bobby, taking it in good humour: 'That's nae bad aff the dole!' Then he shut the door and disappeared, the souter's shop ringing with laughter.

Sometimes when a quine went into the shop the lads had their hands up her skirt, pulling the elastic of her knickers away from her bare hips and letting it back with a sharp snap. Some of the quines took it well enough but the next one would slap their faces. But of course the lads knew the ones to try it on with and they never molested strangers. Half-a-dozen quines of the village were regular visitors and sat on the counter of the back shop most of the evening, near Jimmie Duthie at his last, and being a bachelor he enjoyed the female comaraderie; telling them jokes that made them skirl with laughter, kicking the counter with their wooden-heeled shoes, their flimsy skirts well above their knees and the lads crowding round to hear the latest porn-kister.

Souter Duthie's was a great place for porn-kisters: the bars or dirty jokes the ploughmen told in their stables and chaumers or at the hoe, and if you

210

wanted to hear the latest crack you just listened in the back shop at the souter's place.

There was the one about the two housemaids in the big house who were both invited to the same wedding; but their mistress wouldn't let them go, only one she said, as she didn't want to be left alone. So the two lassies tossed a coin for the privilege of going to the wedding, their presents having been delivered beforehand, and they agreed that the one who won the toss should relate to the other all that went on at the wedding on her return, no matter how late it was. So one lass went to the wedding and the other stayed at home, sitting up in bed waiting for the news of the wedding. When the other quine returned and was taking off her clothes she was telling her friend the events of the evening: 'And you know,' she said, 'there was a man with a beard sitting at one side of the fireplace playing a big fiddle with its bottom on the floor and the stalk of it as high as his head, plucking the strings with one hand and scraping away with the bow in the other, and the big fiddle was saying 'She's been bored afore! She's been bored afore!' Now on the other side of the fireplace there was a thin man with a bald head playing a little wee fiddle tucked up under his chin, sawing away at great speed with his bow, much quicker than the big fiddle, and it seemed to be saying 'A-doot-it-A-doot-it, A-doot-it-A-doot-it!'

After hearing that story, when the lads of the village saw a pregnant woman one would say 'The big fiddle's been there, nae the little ane!' and his companion would add 'A doot it, A doot it!'

Then there was the one about the country schoolmaster who became sexually involved with one of his girl pupils, and when he found himself in prison over it he asked his cell mate what he was in here for? 'Oh, for robbin a waggon,' said the prisoner. 'Ah well,' said the dominie, 'I'm in here for waggin ma robbin!'

And there was the dominie who couldn't sound his rs. Tipperary was a typical example and also his biggest stumbling block, so he told his scholars: 'Don't you say Tippawayway as I say Tippawayway - just you say Tippawayway wight away!'

Jimmie Duthie liked the stories, conundrums, riddles and tongue-twisters, no matter how often he heard them, and new versions of the same story were always welcome. Sometimes he repeated one himself; one he had heard from a customer or a traveller during the day, and one of his favourites was about the woman who had left the village a long time back and had returned to look up her old friend and neighbour Mrs Bile. But in her absence Mrs Bile had left the village and nowhere could she find her. The woman tried everywhere but nobody could tell her where Mrs Bile had moved to. She tried the Post Office, the Police, the Fire Station, even the doctor and the banker and most of the shops, but she was none the wiser. On leaving the village the woman met the postman on his bicycle and she thought now this was the man who should know the whereabouts of Mrs Bile. So she hailed the postie and when he got off his bike she cried out: 'I say postie, excuse me, but have ye got a Bile on yer route?' 'Oh fie na woman,' says the postie, somewhat taken aback, 'but I've got a blin lump on my backside ridin this bicycle!'

The next time you was down at Jimmie Duthie's with your tackety boots for repair; heels, toes and tackets as they said, he told you about the loon who had been in the other day with his father's boots for cobbling, and he told the souter to keep the right toe well back, and when Jimmie asked why he should do that the loon replied 'because that's the one he kicks my arse with!'

Then Jimmie asked you how the Queen Mary was doing and where you kept it, and when you said upstairs he said nobody would see it there; such a pity to keep a thing like that out of sight, like keeping your candle under a bushel, why not bring it down and he would display it in his front window? Oh, he would watch the bairns that they didn't tamper with it, though it wasn't likely they would go behind the counter. He would get his sister to tidy up the window and remove the odd pair of shoes; such a grand place for your boat, where everybody in the village could see it, and anybody passing through, maybe even someone who would buy it, and then you could have a sideline making boats.

So you brought the Queen Mary down from Kingask on your bicycle, the giant model stanced on the saddle and handlebars, while you pushed the bike along very carefully, the village loons chasing after you to see the boat and to watch where you was going with it. Lizzie Duthie had cleared the unsold shoes from the front window for the ship and you placed it there while the bairns gathered outside for a grandstand view.

The Queen Mary aroused considerable interest in the village, especially among the fisher folk, and a great many people admired your handiwork, going inside to ask Jimmie about the ship and who had made it; even some of the farmers of the parish, who, unlike the blacksmith, thought it was a fine piece of craftsmanship. But nobody seemed keen on buying it or even asking about the price. Maybe the size was against it, because it nearly filled the souter's window and it would be expensive making a glass case for that size of a ship. The only real reaction was that when Trail the grocer's son saw the ship he wanted you to make a model for him, though much smaller, a steam drifter, which you did; entirely from cardboard this time, without the leather hull, as he didn't want it for sailing, only for show, and he had the joiner make a glass case for it and kept it in his bedroom. Constable Sim had a look at the liner, and bent down to examine it more closely, his peaked cap under his arm and putting on his glasses, but he made no offer of purchase.

Lizzie Duthie cleaned up the front shop for the occasion, dusted the shelves and tidied up the boxes of unsold shoes, polished the window, shook out the mats and swept the floor. But Lizzie couldn't tackle the back shop, so all the youths who gathered in the evenings put their heads together and cleared out the souter's back shop, and Lizzie covered your boat with brown paper before they started because of the dust. Five barrow loads of solid rubbish they carted out and buried it deep down in the kailyard at the back; swept the place clean with byre brooms and Lizzie's rug brush for the corners; arranged the mountains of shoes on separate shelves and Lizzie gave them all their tea for their trouble. Now you could stand in the middle of the floor and there was room for chairs, and Jimmie's only complaint was that he couldn't find his tools; his awl and his beetle, turcas and chisel, after the spring-clean. Things were where they should be but the souter was happier in a muddle; or what seemed a muddle to ither folk, though Jimmie knew instinctively where everything was in his own eccentric way. He was even finding it difficult to trace the shoes of his customers on the shelves, something that had never bothered him while they were in a heap on the floor.

But Jimmie Duthie never recovered from that dust up, and though the lads meant well they were merely tidying up the place for his funeral. He had coughed through it all and had hoasted for days after it, until he had a lung haemorrhage and was taken away to hospital, where the doctors discovered from x-rays that Jimmie Duthie had lung cancer. He had been a dying man for years though nobody ever knew it, and if he suspected it himself he never complained. His sister was the delicate one and never far from death's door; frail and sallow-faced, like the leather her brother worked with, her body wracked with only forty years of living, yet she survived Jimmie for many lonely years and lived in the same house till the end of her days.

Jimmie had a fag hoast for years but the spring-clean brought his illness to a crisis. In the months that followed his condition degenerated. Mostly in those days it was called decline or tuberculosis, the patient just wasting away and nothing anybody could do to revive him; a condition which, unfortunately, has not improved in modern times, though a little more can be done to ease the suffering, like pain-killers and taking fluid from the lungs.

Though Jimmie was sent home from hospital his shop was never the same again. His customers dwindled and took their work to Tackie Broon, while folk stared at your boat in Jimmie's window in the clean empty shop and the wasted figure bending over the last. When Jimmie wasn't to be seen they sometimes rapped on the house door to ask for the souter, but Lizzie shook her tousled head and said he was still in bed and wouldn't be able to work that day. He had given up his beloved indoor bowling and shuttlecock and now his shop was closed almost every day.

The last time you saw Jimmie was in the back shop, a pale unshaven creature with the look of death in his sunken eyes; the shrivelled skin stretched over the bones of his face, while he leaned painfully on the counter for support, though strangely enough the cough no longer bothered him, maybe because he had given up smoking. You asked permission to take away your boat and Jimmie said he was sorry he hadn't been able to sell it for you; always thinking of other people before himself as usual. A few weeks after this Jimmie had a lung collapse and died in hospital, and his funeral was one of the largest ever seen in the village. After his death his sister put a notice in the paper claiming all debts owing to her late brother; but all you owed Jimmie Duthie was gratitude and respect for one of the most generous-hearted of men you had ever known in your life, a martyr almost of his own selflessness.

But now you had to go to Tackie Broon with the others for your shoe repairs, and on your very first visit he asked about that boat of yours that was in Jimmie Duthie's window before he died. Did he want to buy it you asked. No, he said, he wouldn't offer you money for it; such things were beyond monetary value 'but take a look round the shop: see all these fine birds in their cages? ... Well, you can pick any bird you fancy, cage and all, and you can have it for your boat!'

So you swopped the Queen Mary for a budgerigar in a hanging cage, something that would be easier flitted at the Term than a giant boat. And Tackie Broon would have a glass case made for your ship he said where it wouldn't gather dust, for already you had been trying to clean it with a bellows and sweeping the decks with a feather.

Jockie the green and yellow budgie lived for two years in his gilded cage and became the darling pet of little Brian; though by this time he had grown out of the adjective and stood as high as your waist. But Jockie developed the same symptoms as Jimmie Duthie and pined away in his cage, drooping his green feathers and blinking his eyes for want of proper bird seed during the war. Brian cried his eyes out when Jockie died and wouldn't give him up for burial, hiding him under the cushion of an armchair, believing he would revive with the heat of the fire. He even had his mother fill a hot-water bottle, blaming her for starving Jockie to death, which of course was a false statement. Eventually he buried Jockie at the foot of the garden, and with a tearful face he set a small cross of fir on the tiny grave and a saucer filled with water.

But in the years that followed you sometimes wondered just how much longer Jimmie Duthie would have lived if the Queen Mary had never been built.

Mutch of the Puddockstyle!

Faith but he was a strushle brute Bert Mutch, never even dressed himsel for the marts or a roup, jist oot o the byre in his sharny boots and away on his bike wi a piece in his pooch, an unlit fag between his thick sulky lips (and most likely it would still be hangin there when he came back in the afternoon) for he was loth to light a fag when it lasted longer chewing it, and saved bawbees forbye, jist as a piece in his pooch saved him buying his dinner, and the bicycle saved his bus fare, for in Jehova's life nothing was so important as money.

The folks round about called him Jehova because he never swore, always respected the Lord's name and used 'By Jove!' instead, his biggest swear word though the roan mare had stood on his foot with an iron heel, or he had chapped his thoom with a claw-hammer; though it sounded more like 'By Chove!' to the farming folk, so they didn't know what to make of it and just called him 'Jehova!' It wasn't out of any ill-will they called him names, but just for the fun of the thing, never thinking they were sinners taking the Lord's name in vain. Not that he was a kirk-going body, for the chiel could never be bothered to rig himself for a pulpit meeting, though he never drank or chased the quines either.

But the folk had never quite forgiven the chiel since he kicked his fee-ed loon doon the chaumer stair for sleepin-in; tore him out of bed in his sark tail and kicked him on the bare doup with his tackety boot, nearly breaking the lad's neck in the fall. 'By Chove!' he cried, from the top of the stair, 'that'll learn ye tae rise in the mornin, and ye'll get no breakfast for yer pains. Get yer breeks on and yoke yer horse or ye'll get mair!' He went hammerin down the timmer steps and loupit over the crumpled heap at the bottom, off to the byre in his ill-temper, thinking maybe that would be the end of it, the halflin being an orphan and nobody to speak up for him.

The lad got warsled up the stair, bruised and swelling, and sat on the bed a while, greetin, nearly a grown man but feared to lift his hand to Jehova. He put on his claes and hirpled over the grass parks to the cottar wife at Shinbrae that did his washing, the only hame he knew since he came out of the orphanage in Glasgow yonder. The woman had loons of her ain on the fairms, and when she saw the chiel come hytering over the close and had looked at his sores and heard his story she was fair roused and sent him straight to the bobby, and she said that the loon could bide with her or he got anither place. The Sheriff's Officer and a bobby came out from Brochan and had a look at the chaumer at the Puddockstyle, a bit loft over the stable with nothing in it but a box-bed and a chair, not a spark of fire and a bit skylight on the slated roof. The seams were stuffed with old newspapers to keep out the draught and there was a rat hole in the wall skirting and mice dirt on the floor. They had a look at the steep stair where the loon had bruised his hurdies, and no wonder they thought when they saw the depth of it. They cornered Mutch in the byre and he was fair taken aback and they told him that anything he might say would be taken down in evidence against him, and all that palaver, and then they said he was to be charged with malicious behaviour and assault with injury and for taking the law into his own hands. The Procurator Fiscal gave him a further reprimand in the court-house for his ill-treatment of his servant and said that the accused was fortunate that the youth hadn't suffered worse injury, and that orphans had to be protected from tyrants like himself in industry. A lawyer chiel stuck up for Mutch and said that the youth was loose-living and stayed up late at night and spent all his money on smoking and drink and girls, pestering the accused for 'subs' or advance payments of his wages almost every week from a six-months' contract, besides over-sleeping in the mornings. But the loon had a solicitor as well and he conceded that the accused had paid the youth weekly from his six months' wages contract, due at the Term, but he said there was no evidence that the young man was a profligate, and even if he had been he should have been given a warning on his behaviour, and a chance to mend his ways, instead of which he had been brutally assaulted by the accused. The Fiscal fined Mutch £10 and warned him on his future conduct, ordering that he pay the defendant the balance of his wages yet owing to him, and to stamp his Insurance card to date as the lad wouldn't be returning to his employment; and furthermore the accused must put a fireplace in his bothy or build a new one for the accommodation of future employees. It was all a bit of a stamagaster for Mutch of the Puddockstyle and it made him think twice before he lifted his hand again (or his foot) to a working body about his place.

Mutch had been a long time single, near forty when his mither died and never a woman in his life. As an old creature, frail and sair from the chauve of the Puddockstyle, the widow sometimes wondered what would become of the chiel when she was under the green sod, for she had trauchled on her lane without a serving quine to tempt him from his bachelor ways. But at the end of her tether the old woman wasna able and she was forced to fee a kitchie quine, an ill-faured creature with a hare-lip, a stammer and a squint eye that couldn't get a place easily and wasn't likely to arouse any strange feelings in her son. Now that his mither had gone the quine washed his fule sark and sewed a button on his breeks and cooked a bit meat; she was cheap and strong and could melk the kye and ca the churn and mak butter and cheese and siller and pleased the man fine though he didna share her bed.

Back in the old days you would have seen Mrs Mutch weeding carrots in the windswept parks, down on her knees with an old waterproof on her shoulders and a scarf about her head; a sturdy big-boned woman that could handle a fork like a man and was never afraid of the glaur or the chauve of the farm wife. In her young day she had hoed in her bare feet, with her pram on the end-rig, all these years ago till her bairn got bigger and began to take an interest in the place. Her man had died young of a bowel complaint, struggling to the end the breet, pulling turnips on his knees when he should have been under the blankets, even on a Sunday, and kirk-going folk thought he was beyond redemption, but never gave the man any help to feed his nowt beasts; not that he cared, for he had an independent turn of mind and a game wife that could take her turn at the wark with the best of them. But that was a long time back, and when her man died the mistress of the Puddockstyle put most of her place to grass and leased the parks for grazing, working the rest of it with her loon when he came of age; maybe spoiling him a bit in his youth, for want of a man, so that he soon began to show her that he was the boss.

While Bert Mutch was still at the school some of the neighbours ploughed the widow's fields and gave her some help with the hairst, until one of them tried to take advantage of her in the barn, when young Mutch came over his back with a horse yoke and sent the scoundrel hirpling home to his wife with a different story to tell. From then on the widow and her son managed on their own and the loon was between the plough stilts while he was still at the school. In his teens he ploughed in all the parks for cropping again and fee-ed a single man for the chaumer, giving him the pair of horses to work while he sorted the nowt himsel, with a bit of dealing at the marts and roups on the side.

But over the years young Mutch had never changed, and in his middle-age he still went about like a tink and chewed his fags to make them last; still cycled to mart or roup to save his bus fare, and still carried a piece in his pooch to save the expense of buying his dinner. Some of his neighbours had got the length of a motor car and had sold their gigs and shelts and went tearing past Mutch on his bicycle on his way to the mart, sometimes nearly running him down by the way he swaggered about on the road, his thoughts deep in nowt and corn and siller, his sharny boots on the pedals and his long coat getting in the spokes of his back wheel, nearly throwing him off balance on a windy day; a rain squall slashing at his red face, his wet fag drooping from his stubbly mouth, his bonnet tilted to one side on his grey, balding head.

Some of the neighbours had offered Mutch a lift once or twice, trying to show off their new cars, sneering in his face when he refused, and saying among themselves that he would be safer on the bus, but that most likely he grudged the fare. They were inclined to look down their noses at Mutch, though they knew he was better off than they were: Them with their thriftless wives and big families and new cars, and him still a single man running a bicycle and his pound notes stuffed into moggans and stockings and a big band-box under his bed, under lock and key, 'cause he wouldn't trust a banker with it or pay tax if he could help it. Hadn't the hare-lip quine seen him at the band-box when she was polishing the stairs, surrounded by stacks of coin and paper wads, like a miser over his gold? And the ill-gotten creature had lisped out her excited story to the grocer's vanman at the gable of the kitchie; the one who always lifted her frock or took a pinch at her bare hip when he closed the van door, the quine laughing and slivering down her chin, not to mention what he might have tried with her behind a whin bush, or anywhere else that was handy, had he not been feart that Mutch or his man would be watching from some glory hole about the Puddockstyle.

But in spite of his greed for wark and siller Mutch had a still greater hankering for a wife and bairns to share it. For all his rough ways he was at heart deeply human. His meanness he couldn't help and going about like a tramp never harmed anyone. He got great satisfaction in scrimping himself, in saving bawbees where others were spending. But as the years grew upon him, and especially since his mither died, Mutch felt a great need for a family to share it; for an heir to take over what he had gathered and scraped to save, for without this the man felt a great emptiness in his drizzen life; a hollow knocking from within, for he was not the true miser and his grasping seemed without purpose. But getting the right wife was chancey, aye faith! He would have to ca canny aboot that.

Now you would have thought that if the chiel was looking for a wife he would have spruced himself up a bit; but na na, he still went about ill-clad and hungry looking, like he didn't have a copper to spare; but maybe he thought that if it was dress and gear that the woman was after she wasn't for him, aye faith it was chancey. But he would bide his time or he found the right woman to share his bed and look after his bawbees. He knew fine there were randies in the Bogside who envied his money hoard and a chance to share in it, but he never gave them a chance to untie his bootlaces or to put him to bed in a drunken stupor, for he never attended any of their jamborees, concerts or dances; nothing where the limmers could get their grasping fingers into his pockets, neither at the pictures or the fairs, so that by the time he was forty the spinsters in the Bogside had given up trying to invite Mutch to any of their goings on and left him to his bachelor wiles with the hare-lip and his treasure kist.

But at mart or roup he could out-bid his neighbours for anything that he wanted, like a good thriving steer or a gelding that took his fancy; especially if he thought that by selling again he could make a pound or two, which he usually did, for he could see that if anyone wanted something badly enough to bid with him to the last shilling they wouldn't grudge a little more to have it at the second chance. He was a sharp dealer at the ringsides and sometimes made a damned sight more than he ever did on the fairm, with all its pleiter. Some folk hinted that he should make a full time job of it, and put the fairm back in grass; a collar and tie job, which was maybe a jibe at his greasy sark, but Mutch said it was risky and that he'd keep it as a side line. But with a wink or a nod to the auctioneer he could sometimes take money out of thin air, chewing on his fag and eyeing up the beasts and gear with a wizard's instinct for a bargain.

But the more money he made the shabbier he grew, and a wife seemed as far away as ever. Mony a neighbour's wife said she would enjoy giving him a good scrub and a new rig-out of clothes, for he was a man well built and with fairly good looks, though as things were folk began to steer clear of him for the smell of his unwashed body. It was a wonder, they thought, that the hare-lip didn't look after him better, even though she didn't share his bed, for she might share his will, seeing that the chiel had nobody else to leave it to directly, unless it were some distant cousins who never looked near him, though they might attend his funeral, should anything happen to the stock, to see if there was anything left for them at the bone-picking.

But for all their claik the chiel bided his time, and bye and bye, at the roup on Whirliebrae he met a woman body that took his fancy. Above all the steer of the folk and the scrachin of hens and the howling of nowt he noticed the woman as soon as he came off his bike and took the clips out of his breeks. The fine head of her, upstanding as a high priced ornament, the brown gold of her hair, plaited and spun into a bun on the nape of her neck, the wide-brimmed hat shading her pleasant features, soft appealing eyes with a sparkle in her glances, her small nose slightly tilted at the tip, and her rather wide mouth always on the brink of a smile; the gold pendant on her bare, open breast, the frilled pink blouse, velvet tunic and a half-pleat tartan skirt, narrow at the waist and flared out wide just under her knees, silk stockings on her shapely calfs and buckles on her little black shoes; and the jaunty spring of her walk as she picked her way over the grass and the dubs of the farm close, swinging her soft skirt in a grace of movement that fair caught a body's eye.

Mutch had no eye for the nowt that sunny day of early May, or for the sturdy geldings that were trotted out for the farmers around the close. He was bewitched by the woman and couldn't take his gaze away from her. The auctioneer looked in vain for his customary wink while he whacked the wooden pailing with his stick. Mutch shunned his searching eyes that were darting over the crowd, stick raised in the air, poised, waiting, lingering, then down with a smack to the last bidder. But Mutch wasn't interested; his thoughts that day were all of the woman. Where had she gone? He must watch and follow her.

For the first time in his life he realized that this was something money couldn't buy; something he eagerly wanted but the last bid would count for nothing. She wasn't for sale. For the first time also he suddenly became aware of himself; of the tramp he was among all the folk that were dressed, and he took the fag from his mouth and threw it in the myre. He had a mind to fly home and rig himself like for a funeral, the only decent suit he had; but there was no time, the woman might be off or he got back. She would have to be put to the test, rags and all, and By Jove she was worth it! His only chance was to watch what the woman bought, or tried to buy, and he must out-bid her for it, price was no obstacle; then maybe he could tempt her with a second chance. The idea came to him in a flash; one of his old tricks with a new and definite purpose, the only way he could buy the unsaleable.

The cattle sale was over and the auctioneer was striding over the park to the rows of implements, all painted and numbered, the clerk at his heels with pencil and notebook and a troop of folk crowding round. But there was no sign of the woman in the flared tartan skirt. Ah well it must be the furniture sale she was after and Mutch strode round to the close, to the farmhouse, where some few were gathered, mostly women, coming and going from the kitchen, where they were permitted to look at the articles for sale. He was about to go inside when the woman came to the door, her violet eyes looking him in the face, but with no disdain in them, no resentment of his ragged appearance; kind they were and smiling as she stepped aside to let him pass. Now he must wait and watch; he mustn't let her out of his sight again while the sale lasted.

It was a long time to Mutch but at last the auctioneer came round with the folk and the sale began around the kitchen door. Mutch kept his head down, his gaze away from the auctioneer; watching the woman, her every move, every gesture, every look, but so far she made no bid. The auctioneer stuck with a sale and cried out his name in a joke, for Mutch usually saw him out, but today he took no notice; he didn't want to become involved. He was watching the woman.

Several things had gone: tables, chairs, pictures, carpets, rugs, and now a suite, and still no bid from the woman. Then someone brought ben a wag-at-the-wa clock, polished wood with bold figures and coloured pictures on its face, brass chains and weights slung underneath; a solid thing, so that the bearer could hardly hold it up for the ring of folk round the door to see it. The auctioneer began with his usual patter, pointing at the clock with his stick. 'How much am I bid then? Who'll say fifty pounds, forty, thirty, twenty, ten, a fiver? . . . who will give me a start then? . . . One pound, ten bob, five bob? . . . Thanks lady, five bob I'm bid; five, ten, fifteen, a pound,' his stick flicking over the crowd and always coming back to the lady at the door. So that was what she was on! But he would bide his time; no need to make it dearer than was necessary, and the bidding was brisk yet. He would catch her on the last hop, when the others had been weeded out - when she thought the prize was hers. His eyes and ears were needle sharp. 'Fourteen pounds,' the auctioneer was saying, resorting to one-pound bids. 'Come on, the brass chains are worth more than that - fifteen pounds, sixteen, seventeen, eighteen . . .' But the bids were slowing down, slower yet. Mutch stood on his toes to watch the crowd. Four or five hands still going up, now four, now three. 'Twenty-seven pounds, twenty-eight . . .' It was risky. What if the woman should fall out? Ah well, he would buy the clock in any case. What, another bidder? Somebody must be nodding; or maybe just a wink. Surely he wouldn't be taking bids out of the air for a clock at that price? 'Thirty-one pounds . . . thirty-two . . .' The lady was still there and the stick came back to her, level with her daintily-tilted nostril. She hesitated, shook her head slowly . . . 'I'll take ten bob,' the auctioneer was saying, and she went on, on. 'Thirty-five, thirty-five-and-a-half . . .' Mutch could wait no longer and he whistled the auctioneer, the lady far too concerned even to notice it. The stick was pointed straight in his face. 'Thirty-five-pounds ten sir,' the auctioneer treating him like a stranger but fully in his confidence; aware of his move to boost the bidding, whatever the purpose. 'Thirty-six . . . thirty-six-and-a-half . . .' Now it was Mutch and the woman, ding dong, ding dong, but he won, and he took the clock in his great oxter and went away over by the stable door to set the thing down safely somewhere.

He went over to the open window at the farmhouse and handed in his payment to the cashier, who gave him a receipt, and when he went back to the clock the woman was looking at it, just what he expected her to do. 'I did so want it,' she said quietly, disappointment clearly in her face. 'But you out-bid me for it. I couldn't afford all that money anyway. I don't know what came over me!'

'Folks lose their heads at roups,' Mutch remarked, 'and they throw money aboot like cauld watter.'

Her soft velvet eyes creamed over his face and he thought that little more would bring them to tears.

'Would ye still be wanting the clock then, Miss . . .'

'Oh yes . . . Joyce Allardyce is the name. I'm from the manse at Bourie,' and she held out her white-gloved hand.

'Mutch is my name, Miss Allardyce; Bert Mutch frae the fairm o Puddockstyle yonder, in the Bogside.'

They shook hands, her gloved fingers warm and tender in his big rough fist.

'Oh yes, Mr Mutch, I still want the clock. In fact I came here on a special errand to get it. But it's out of the question now. I just couldn't afford all that money.'

'What would ye be willin to pay for it than?'

'So you would sell it again, Mr Mutch?'

'That was the general idea. Name yer price! The most you could afford to pay for it.'

'Oh but I couldn't. It's beyond my reach; you paid thirty-nine pounds for it, an awful lot of money for a clock. My brother would be so upset.'

'Your brither, Miss Allardyce?'

'Yes, you see, he's the minister at Bourie and I've been his housekeeper since his wife died two years ago.'

'Oh I see,' and Mutch was overwhelmed with a sudden burst of generosity.

'Well I'll let you have the clock for twenty-five pounds,' he said. 'Could you manage that?'

'Oh but you couldn't Mr Mutch; it's a shame, and you'd be selling at a loss.'

'I dinna usually deal in clocks, Miss Allardyce, so let's say that I was a bit rash in buying it.'

'And you are determined to let me have it for twenty-five pounds?'

'Aye, and it's a grand clock, I think!'

'It is, lovely. But you must have a reason for this, Mr Mutch.'

'Well I would be glad to get it off my hands, and I was a bit sorry to see you disappointed; the sad look on yer face when ye looked at the clock after the sale. You was nearly greetin lass, and ye look sae much bonnier smilin.'

A faint blush heightened the colour on her cheeks. 'Thank you Mr Mutch. But it's so sweet of you; and if I take the clock how can I repay you?'

'Never mind that. Where will we put the clock? Have we time for a wee cup of tea to seal the bargain?'

'Oh that would be nice! I have my car Mr Mutch. Oh yes I'll take the clock, though it makes me feel ashamed Mr Mutch, and I don't know what my brother will say. He has his scruples you see, being a minister. Perhaps if you would carry the clock over to the car for me.' And she fumbled in her small handbag for the money.

Mutch carried the clock over to the car and she gave him the twenty-five pounds, mostly in fivers, though he never counted it but thrust it into his hip pocket. 'You could always say the devil tempted you Miss Allardyce,' he said, with a sulky laugh, 'or just never let on. Say you paid twenty-five pounds for the clock and keep it a secret between us.'

'Oh but I couldn't deceive him, Mr Mutch; not for the world, and some of the congregation might tell him what the clock was sold at. I even spotted one or two of our Elders in the crowd. You'll just have to come up to the manse sometime Mr Mutch and explain it.'

'Ah well Miss Allardyce, I'll be quite willin tae do that, though I'm a bit bashful meetin gentry folk.'

Miss Allardyce smiled at his awkwardness and the way he put it. 'Oh but we will make you feel quite at home Mr Mutch; have no fear about that.'

It was getting chilly and she took her coat out of the car and put it on, Mutch holding it out for her. They went to the marquee in the grass park, where there was a smell of cigarette smoke and brewing tea, the clatter of dishes, voices and laughter. They found a small table for two near a tent pole and Mutch ordered tea and cakes for two, holding up his hand when Miss Allardyce tried to forestall him.

They waited shyly, facing each other, and both looked around the tent.

'I hope you won't mind, Miss Allardyce, me being such a track, like; but I jist came oot of the coo byre,' falling through his English.

'Of course not, Mr Mutch. I know how it is with farming people. And you can call me Joyce if you like.'

'Thank ye, Miss Allardyce; I mean Miss Joyce. Folk usually call me Bert, but I'd prefer Bertie, if you don't mind.' He thought better not to tell her his nickname. It wasn't funny.

He felt an awful gowk in her genteel presence, among all the toffs that were dressed and respectable, and him like a tink in his shabby waterproof, the tails of it on the grass, his piece still in his pocket; his baggy trousers glazed with dirt, his boots as grey as the road.

A waitress came and spread out the tea things in front of them from a tray.

So they had a fair crack over the tea leaves, the two of them, the lady and the tramp as you might say, each trying to find out as much as possible about the other, in a round about sort of way; two shy people who had never seen much of the other's side of life.

'I'm an aul tea-wife masel,' Mutch assured her, pouring a second cup for both of them, and Miss Allardyce smiled to hear it.

But she fair opened up the heart of the chiel, and the honeyed smile softened his hard exterior; winning him over in a way he would never have believed possible with the women folk. It was a new experience to the clumsy chiel and he blethered the gist of his life story with his big mouth full of apple-tart. Miss Allardyce sipped her tea, listened and smiled under her wide-brimmed hat, her brown gold hair against her lillied cheeks, two small pearls at her ear-lobes that

222

the chiel hadn't noticed before. But the violet depths of those wondrous eyes changed the colour of his skies; swept away all clouds, and the sun was shining on autumn woods and golden harvest fields, green parks where kine were fed on milk and honey, and the sweet fragrance of her perfume filled the land with her presence.

The chiel was so much taken out of himself that before he realized what he was saying he blurted out that he would pay for both teas. He could hardly believe his ain lugs when he heard himself speaking, and surely he would have to take himself to task about it when it was all over. Him that had never given a penny to a bairn or a crust of bread to a tinker wife, and here he was treating this genteel stranger to a High Tea which, in normal circumstances, he would have grudged even for himself, gloating over the cost that his self-denial had spared him.

But he wasn't himself that day the chiel and he paid gladly for both teas, softly rebuking the woman when she offered him money, and he considered it a bargain for the riches that their meeting had brought him.

He walked her back to the car park, past the beer tent, where the drunks were leering at the door flap, throwing taunts at his back, one calling out: 'Aye Jehova!' But he took no notice, and neither apparently did Miss Allardyce. The sale was almost over and folk would soon be taking the road, though the sun was still well up in the sky.

Miss Allardyce was seated at the wheel of her little Morris car, the precious clock in the back seat. She pulled the starter and the car purred smoothly. Mutch was standing by the door, the handle in his grip, loth to let the woman go; watching those diamonds that sparkled in her eyes while her parting smile caressed his weary heart. He would take the old cart road from Whirliebrae, a grass-grown short-cut to the Puddockstyle, in the other direction from Miss Allardyce.

'Maybe at some other sale I'll see you again Miss Joyce, and next time I'll be better dressed.'

'Oh never mind that Mr Mutch - or should I call you Bertie? You have been so good to me; and if you are not too bashful we shall be delighted to welcome you sometime at the manse of Bourie.'

'Oh that would be grand Miss Joyce. I shall certainly look forrard to seeing you again. I'll close your door than and be off. Ta-ta Miss Joyce. I hope we'll meet again!'

The car moved off down the grass brae and the chiel lifted his hand in a wave of farewell, rather sadly, with a nip in his eyes that made them moist. He sighed at her going, the lovely Miss Allardyce, while he went to get his bicycle.

Bert Mutch could safely say it had been one of the happiest days of his bachelor life when he met Miss Allardyce, for he certainly believed he had fallen in love with the creature; and maybe she with him he hoped, by the way she spoke, so friendly like. From what he had gathered she would be in her thirties: a spinster body who kept house for her brother, who was the minister at Bourie, not that he knew the place very well, only in passing, but in his present mood it wouldn't be long or he was visiting in that direction.

It was a wonder he thought that a good looking woman like that was still single, but maybe that was something he should be thankful for and nae ask questions that were none o his business. And efter a', her brither had tae hae somebody for a hoosekeeper, seein his poor wife had died. And maybe Miss Allardyce would have a pucklie siller behind her, bein come o the clergy like, so she wouldn't come empty-handed to the Puddockstyle, and she looked like a body that could be trusted with what he had already. Maybe it was a pity that she wasna of the farming stock, and could melk a coo or churn butter, though her hands were too lady-like for that, white as lilies and the scent of her as sweet. There wasn't the likes of her in the Bogside or he'd have been married long ago. Ah weel but he could mak her a lady and the hare-lip would do the wark; aye, that was a better idea, and that would gie the neighbour folk something tae craw aboot - a lady at the Puddockstyle. What's mair, maybe he could buy a motor car and start a new life athegither, aye faith!

It was at this point he suddenly realized he was on his bicycle, spinning down the brae from the roup. He had no recollection of leaving the sale, so engrossed was he in his future plans to be almost in a trance, carried away with his thoughts of Miss Allardyce and the manse of Bourie.

He had never been a kirk body but By Chove he never swore and it wasn't likely he'd say an ill werd in front of Miss Allardyce. Oh aye, he'd had to pay for his sanctimony, for there were ill-mannered folk who took the size of him, and made a joke of his swear words, and had given him a nickname, the blasphemous heathens, for he had overheard them from time to time calling him Jehova! But they'd pay for it yet, those sons of Satan, for the good Lord would protect his ain, and once he had Miss Allardyce under his care he would surely be doubly blessed.

And surely he would have a family too. Oh aye, a loon for a start to take over the Puddockstyle, and maybe a dother or twa later on, Miss Allardyce wasn't too old for that yet. All things in their time; everything comes to him who waits he had heard it said, and he had waited well and lang for this great day.

He was speeding down the long brae but hardly aware of it, his thoughts on wings of romance, never heeding the dead-end crossroads at the foot of the hill, where the track from Whirliebrae joined the main road, and the odd motor car that was passing there. He never dachled but sped on deep in thought, gnawing on his drooping fag, his waterproof flapping behind him, the whin and broom obscuring his view of the main road, where everybody had the right of way, and at the last moment he applied the brakes on his bicycle.

But alas too late, for he was on the main road before he noticed, smack in front of a car at slashing speed. There was a screech of brakes and a scream of tyre skids and Mutch was tossed into the air over the bonnet of the car and catapulted head first against the stone dyke, his body hitting the wall with such force he rebounded back on to the road.

The car climbed the bank avoiding him but bounced back on to the road when it stopped, some twenty yards from the crossing. Two farming like chiels

224

came out of it, staggering a bit, as they hurried back to the bleeding man on the road. They stood over him, wondering if he was dead. One of them bent down unsteadily and turned him over so that he could see his face. 'God almighty,' he cried, 'it's Bert Mutch!' The other man hiccoughed. 'Who the hell's Bert Mutch?' he asked. His companion swayed a little as he stood up, spreading out his hands, his fingers tipped with blood. 'Why,' he cried, 'the bastard that threw me doon the chaumer stair at Puddockstyle!'

Blood was seeping from Mutch's ears and mouth and a small pool was gathering on the road. His cap had gone and there was an ugly gash on his head.

'Is he dead then?' the other asked.

The younger man kneeled down again, feeling awkwardly for Mutch's pulse and listening for his breathing. 'I'm nae sure,' he replied, 'but I think he's still breathin.'

'Ripe his pooches,' the older man ordered, lighting a fag.

The youth on the road went through Mutch's pockets, starting with his coat. 'Just a piece,' he shouted, throwing out the jam sandwiches. Then he tried the jacket. 'Ah, a pocket-book or wallet or something; now I'll try the hip pooch. Ah, something here, a bundle of notes, aye, OK.'

The other man was getting impatient, watching the road. 'Come on,' he cried, tugging at his companion, 'let's get tae hell oot o here; we dinna want onybody tae catch us here, smellin like a distillery, especially the cops. Come on Mike, for Christ's sake!'

He ran forward to the car and tore the mangled bicycle from under the front axle and threw it against the dyke.

'But I didna mean tae kill him,' the other protested, now stricken with sudden remorse, the blood speckled notes in his hands. 'God knows, he didna give me a chance tae spare him!' He stood half-way between the car and his old employer lying on the road. Tears now glistened his eyes and he threw the money in the air. 'I dinna want it,' he cried, 'I didna mean tae kill him!'

His companion came running back and gathered up the wallet and the scattered bank notes, bundled the weeping youth into the passenger seat and slammed the car door. 'I'll drive,' he yelled and threw away his cigarette, then ran round the car to the driver's side. Even as he drove off another car was in his mirror, but he soon lost it when it stopped beside the body. After all it wasn't really their fault that Mutch's thoughts were so far away that late afternoon, and not on the road he travelled, but with Miss Joyce Allardyce at the manse of Bourie.

Cap in the Wind

It was towards the end of your first summer at Kingask that you had a visit from your old school pal Bryce Holt, who had been Best Man at your wedding; him that had been so taken with your pretty Kathleen before you married her, though he never had a chance to go courting with her, but made it plain enough in his looks and with an occasional remark on how much he admired your choice of a bride. You had been milk boys together in your schooldays, selling milk in the toon from his father's milk cart, and though he was a farmer's son and you was only a cottar loon he had always treated you as an equal; sharing his tips and his chocolate on Saturday mornings when the housewives paid their milk. But in the two years since your marriage you had forgotten all about Bryce and his infatuation with Kathleen, and as you hadn't seen him since your wedding day you thought he had forgotten about it too. But apparently he hadn't, nor had he gotten a lass of his own, or if he had she had jilted him, though God knows why, for Bryce was a handsome chiel and a farmer's son and you would have thought he would have had no bother getting a quine. But he had been moping about your Kathleen all this time she had been married and borne you a son, little Brian, with his mother's eyes and face, but his hair still in baby curls the colour of straw, so that you couldn't tell if it would be black like his mother's hair.

So things had come to a crisis with Bryce in his celibacy and he takes a funny notion in his head that he might have your Kathleen after all, which you thought was strange in a bloke who had never envied anything you had before, and was always readier to give than to take away. Queer how things take shape in folk's minds and it is sometimes years before you realize what they have been up to behind your back.

Bryce arrived on his motor bike one fine Sunday afternoon, just about the time you was down at the farm, feeding a calf or something, and for nearly an hour Bryce had Kathleen all to himself, whispering sweet nothings in her dainty ears, while little Brian played on the mat or ran outside to the neighbours. So here was you with a brimming pail of water, coming up the brae to the cottar houses, 'cause you never liked to come home empty-handed when you was passing the water tap down at the farm, for all of it had to be carried up the hill. Your little son comes running down the brae to meet you, his baby-fat legs wobbling under his growing weight, though he doesn't have the sense to tell you there was a stranger with mummy, which might have put you on your guard or aroused your suspicion of Bryce. So you takes your little boy by the hand, on the other side from the water pail, walking up the hill, and you pass the time of day with the foreman, Badgie Summers, who is sitting on the grass by the side of the farm road, reading the Sunday paper, his teenage dother beside him, Oslena, her that always gave you the glad eye at the week-ends, when she came home from the place she was fee-ed at, and would have had you away from Kathleen in no time if you had given her any encouragement. And there she was, staring at you with her green-grey eyes as round as marbles, smiling cheekily, her brown hair in curlers under a headsquare, with dabs of rouge on her cheeks, her lips like ripe strawberries, her thin skirt well above her dimpled knees, stockingless and wearing her mother's carpets, home for the day with her parents. She gets up and grabs your bairn in the passing and soon has him on the grass, tickling the life out of him while he squeals with laughter. Then you spies this big motor-bike standing in the close, with a helmet and leather gloves lying on the saddle-tank, and you couldn't guess who it might belong to. You leave your pail of water in the porch and walks through to the kitchen, and here is Bryce at tea with your wife and she pours you a cup when you sat down at the table.

Of course you was pleased to see your old school pal, almost shook hands with him, though it isn't much done among working folks: you just say 'Aye aye, fit like?' and he says 'Nae bad; fit like yersel?' and you say 'Fine!' and you are off to a flying start. You said you couldn't think who the motor-bike belonged to, and Bryce said he had just bought it second-hand from a dealer in Brochan, though it was only a year old and in fine fettle, and that he'd like to take you for a run on the pillion. You thought maybe he wanted to take Kathleen out; but no, that wasn't his plan apparently and it was you he wanted. You was only being evil minded and suspicious, because you minded how he used to look at her before you was married. It was a shame to think such things of Bryce and it was good of him to come and see you, which was more than some of your other pals had done and you felt pleased about it. So you newses away about not much in particular, mostly the weather and how you liked to work at Kingask, seeing you had been there a couple of months now. For all his good points Bryce was a deep thinker and you felt you could never get to the bottom of him, what with his half sniggering smile and sly poking humour you was never sure if he was taking the raise of you or no, though he was always friendly and good-hearted and had never done you an ill turn since you had played together as bairns on your father's place in the Bogside.

For nearly an hour you blethered and Bryce said he had sometimes looked for Kathleen and you up at his father's place. But you reminds him that you don't have a motor-bike and side-car for the wife and bairn; that you couldn't afford such a thing, only push bikes, and that Tilliehash (his father's farm) wasn't all that handy for a bus, so he said he would come and meet you with the gig if you thought about it. He said he had just come down for a run on his new bike to see how you was getting on, and that Kathleen looked bonnier than ever and that the bairn was fair growing he thought for all the short time it seemed since you was married, and he gave Brian a half-crown for his piggy bank. But you wasn't all that keen to go for a ride on his pillion, because you wasn't dressed and it was your Sunday on duty at the farm. But Bryce wouldn't take no for an answer and he said it wouldn't take long for you to change your breeks and you would be back again before cow time.

You couldn't think why Bryce was so anxious to have you on his motor-bike, unless it was to show you how fast it could go, a big 500cc Norton with the new saddle-tank, twin-port exhausts as clear as a sixpence and twist-grip throttle control; silver streak you might have called it shining there in the sun. Bryce put on his helmet and gloves and adjusted his goggles and pushed the big bike off the stand, wheeling it to the gable at the roadside. Kathleen came to the gable-end to see you off, with little Brian by the hand, and Badgie Summers had gone inside with his daughter for their afternoon cup of tea. You got on the pillion behind Bryce and he stood on the kick-start until the huge bike snorted into motion, then slipped in the clutch and moved off slowly down the brae, while you lifted your feet to the foot-rests and held on to Bryce round the waist, your face sheltered from the wind by his helmet, and under you the throb of the bike like a powerful horse that you rode smoothly without a gallop. 'What do ye think of her than?' Bryce shouted back at you over his shoulder, once you was on the main road and he had opened her up, the wind whipping at his words. You had put on your cap back to front in case you might lose it in the wind. 'Oh grand,' you cried out; 'just grand!' trying to please him, and to make him feel you was impressed, and yet not wanting to start a conversation at such speed, for you felt sure Bryce was trying to scare you to death or give you the thrill of your life on his big new motor cycle. The sea was a speeding strip of blue on your right, and on your left the farms and crofts and cottages like punctuation marks that measured the speed you were going; flying like a bird, except in the villages, where Bryce snorted her down with the twist-grip on the handlebars - then off again, up hill and down dale like a switch-back, through Badengour and along the narrow road to the cliff-tops, where Bryce stopped and both of you got off and he stanced his bike on a patch of sand and pebble.

You was just beginning to enjoy it and wondered why Bryce had stopped so soon; for if he had wanted to give you a real joyride he should have gone further, taken you for a long detour inland, a round-about way for getting home, giving you a chance to see the country. But that was not his intention apparently and though you was a little displeased you didn't say anything; after all the bike was his and he could go where he pleased, you was only his passenger. Bryce removed his gloves and goggles and put them in the pockets of his leather coat, but kept on the small helmet that was fastened by a strap under his chin, then the two of you sauntered off in the direction of the towering cliffs, the cry of the gulls getting louder as you approached. It was past the gull egg season and you wondered what Bryce had brought you here for, unless it were to enjoy the grandeur of the scene, where a lot of young gulls were on the wing, like white sparrows at such dizzy heights, diving down from the cliff face and levelling out smoothly above the greenish waters, then rising again with a scream of triumph that echoed against the cliff walls. Although you had never actually been here before you knew something of the history of the place: the saga of Dundarg castle for instance, and the early settlements of the flint-knappers, long before the Picts - but Hell's Lum you had never heard of and that was what Bryce wanted to show you. It was a massive cavern with only a small crack on the cliff top where you could just squeeze inside and listen to the waves in ceaseless turmoil in some mysterious subterranean passage far underfoot. It was like the noise of distant thunder, frightening in its mystery, while you tried to imagine the convulsion of water that made that dreadful noise, struggling far inland under the cliffs, thudding against a prison of rock, black and fathomless, where the sea had entered from a small cave at high tide. You both stood inside the fizzure of Hell's Lum, the cold draught from the flue hitting your faces while you peered over the edge, tilting the cap on your head, while you stared down the black chute to hell's cauldron, though you couldn't see anything in the darkness beyond the ledge of rock. Nor was it really dangerous, as further passage was blocked by a huge rock at the entrance, with only a tiny crack where a man might squeeze through with difficulty, or someone could push you through in a struggle to almost certain death beyond. Bryce said it had been used by the smugglers in the old days, when they entered the cave at low tide and unloaded their boats on the rock shelves, then hauled their booty up the lum or rock chimney with ropes to the ledge where you was standing, most likely tobacco, rum and brandy, then carried it off in the night when all good excisemen were supposed to be in bed. It was all very interesting and of course you knew something of the caves yourself on this cliff girt coastline, though you had never seen them, especially the Hermit's Cave and that of Lord Slypigo, where he had concealed himself after Culloden, hiding from the Redcoats, while the peasantry on his estate brought him food and drink in secret, in peril of their lives, though none would betray him. He was afraid to go near his castle (now a ruin near Spitullie) which had been seized and guarded by the Government, and you had been told he had hid himself in the house where you was born; a thackit biggin with stone-clay walls, under the box bed, which was timbered up and wallpapered, while the searching Redcoats jabbed the chaff mattress with their bayonets though they never found him. All this you told Bryce, while the pair of you cowered back from the black abyss and the awful thunder that trembled the cliff under your feet. And maybe your telling of it took your pal's mind from more serious intent, like pushing you into Hell's Lum - but maybe his courage had failed him.

Outside the sun was shining, and far out in the thin haze you could just make out the hills or Paps of Caithness, shimmering on the misty blue horizon across the Moray Firth. You wandered along the cliff top and then the two of you sat down on the spine grass, smoking your pipes and gazing out to sea, where here and there a fishing boat laboured on the waves, bound for Brochan or Candlebay. Was Bryce still thinking of Kathleen? He had become so suddenly quiet watching the sea, his thoughts far away while he puffed at his pipe; not a word between you, both staring into space. But the devil was working overtime in his mind, scheming how to be rid of you without trace so that Bryce could have your wife. Of course you never suspected this. It was long afterwards when you looked in the mirror of life and you saw an action replay; when you fitted all the pieces together that the jig-saw became clear.

Right now you never realized the danger you was in and you was taken by surprise. You just couldn't make out what had come over Bryce to take off your cap and throw it in the air, whirling in the wind towards the cliff tops. Now he stood over you without a smile on his face, stern as rock; pipe in hand, a challenge in his eyes. You stood up beside him, while he put his pipe in his breast pocket, and you realized you couldn't do the same to him, the leather helmet strapped tightly under his chin. If it was meant as a joke you couldn't return it. 'What was that for ?' you asked, surprised by the stern, half mocking look on his face. 'I bet ye wunna climb down for it,' he said, while you put your pipe away and stared towards your checked cap tilting in the wind on the cliff edge. It had just failed to go over and lay on a green slope overhanging the water. Maybe he was just bluffing but you would try to get your cap back; if he thought you was scared you would make a damned good try to prove him wrong. Maybe you should have been less hot-headed and asked him to retrieve your cap; after all it was him who threw it away and he should have to bring it back. That was only fair. But it was a challenge and you had accepted it. Bryce was testing your courage, like he sometimes did at school; daring you to reach for the cap, and as you slithered down the slope he came after you, but stayed at a safe distance. Your cap lay on a grassy slope just beyond reasonable hand-grasp, where the cliff edge overhung the sea, the white green waves swirling underneath and the young gulls screaming in beautiful ballet on the eddying wind, dipping and rising gracefully above the swell of the sea. Bryce came a bit nearer, sidling down the slope, his leather jerkin open in the breeze, while you tip-toed nearer the cliff edge; now on the slope that was like standing on a barrel, rolling towards the sea. The sky was a hotch-potch of white and smoky cloud patch, the sea a surge of white green water, the wind from the cliff-top ruffling your hair over your eyes, while you straddled the barrel of stone, nearer and nearer the giddy edge.

You couldn't stand any longer and got down on your knees, then lay flat on your belly, crawling towards the cap, your arm outstretched to reach it - now at your fingertips, ever so close; one more shove forward on your belly, with the shout of Bryce in your ears: 'Come back,' he cried, 'never mind the bonnet, let it go - I'll buy ye a new ane!' He had lost his nerve and couldn't do it. At the last moment his courage had failed him and he couldn't push you over. He couldn't come near enough to give you the final shove. You had crawled beyond his reach. If he had got you on a sheer edge he might have tried it, but not on this sloping barrel. Still he shouted but you wasn't turning back now; not with the cap at your fingernails, lying on a patch of daisies and crow-foot anemone, scrabbling at the stone and sea-grass with your free hand, an anchor for your body on the overhang. You had disturbed the gulls and they screamed over your head in confusion; Bryce still shouting, your arm at full length, the diced cap tilting to your touch, your body writhing on the crumbling edge of earth and pebble. But now you had it, your cap firmly in your eager grasp, and you edged your way back up the grassy slope to sanity.

Bryce grabbed your arm and pulled you up the slope, thankful it seemed that you hadn't gone over the edge. 'I couldna have done that tae save my life,' he said calmly. 'Ye've mair guts than I thocht!' Of course you never suspected him at the time and thought it was all a silly joke that had nearly misfired; a challenge maybe to test your courage and you had won. Bryce had done that sort of thing at school and sometimes you had lost, taunting you to tears almost over it, and then he would treat you to a bar of chocolate and all was well again. But this time the prank seemed more sinister; more contrived, with some evil purpose behind it you couldn't yet understand. But you told him it was a damned silly thing to do all the same; risking your life like that for nothing. He said he didn't mean to throw your cap so far, but that the wind caught it and took it nearer the edge than he intended. You could have come back when he shouted he said: there was no need for you risking your neck like that for a bludy bonnet and you shouldn't have taken it so seriously, even though it was a challenge. But Bryce had a curious sense of fun you thought and mostly at your expense. But now he was in better spirits than he had been all afternoon: thankful perhaps that his ill-hatched crime had not been committed; that he had thrust the devil behind him, or at least thwarted his evil purpose, and that he could face the world again with a free conscience.

You brushed the sand and grit from your clothes and Bryce adjusted his goggles and put on his leather gloves again. The pair of you got on the big motor bike and Bryce stood with all his weight on the kick-start, wurting the twist-grip while he paddled it on to the road, slipped in the gear and you were off, purring back along the coast road to Kingask. The wind was in your back but colder now; the sun a white disc in the western sky, but still time to spare before cow time. Bryce dropped you off at the cottage but wouldn't come inside. Perhaps he couldn't face Kathleen again but said he had promised to be back home before tea time.

Not until Bryce was away on his bike, and Kathleen and you were alone in the house after tea, and she told you how Bryce had tempted her while you was away at the farm - not until then did you begin to suspect him, and then only partially because it seemed so ridiculous. Bryce had asked Kathleen how she would like to be a farmer's wife instead of a cottar, turning out his pocket-book and showing her wads of paper money, comparing his well-to-do position with your comparative poverty. But Kathleen had merely smiled at him and said that money could never come between her and her marriage. She was embarrassed beyond measure she said and glad to see you pass the window on your return from the farm. She said you had come back at the right time or he might have gone a bit further.

Maybe some day you would tell Kathleen of your experience on the cliff-top; once you had figured it all out. But not now; you wasn't ready for it yet, and you didn't want to give Kathleen an ill opinion of Bryce. Oh that was just like him you said, always wanting to impress folk; he had always been like that, even at school, but only joking really. Maybe it was all mere chance and coincidence; yet so neatly contrived that time put a seal of truth on it, or at least a measure of probability, and you was sure the devil had a hand in it.

And it was just possible you could have fallen off the cliff by accident, reaching for your cap, while Bryce flew for assistance on his motor-bike, telling everybody (including Kathleen) that you had gone too near the edge. There was nobody to contradict him. The perfect crime, and maybe he could have had your Kathleen after all.

But it is a fact that Bryce Holt never came to visit you and Kathleen again, not in all his life; nor have you seen him since and he died a bachelor.

Dockenbrae

Old Sally Birse of Dockenbrae had never been the same body since the place was burned down a couple of years back. She aye thought she heard the howling of the nowt in the burning byres and sometimes she had the nightmare over it and wakened her man with her screaming. Folk said that old Magnus Birse had set fire to the place himself to get the insurance money to build a new steading and re-stock his byres, and that it served him right if his old woman took the nightmare over it and kept him from his sleep. But outsiders always said something of that sort if a fairmtoon was burned down and maybe they were just lucky that it didn't happen to themselves. But old Magnus had got his new steading in spite of them and was back on his feet again with a fine new herd of fat nowt and a puckle swine forbye.

But if you looked in by at Dockenbrae at a dinner time you might see the old wife making her water in a brander by the kitchen door, holding up her skirts a bit and letting it run down her legs into her high-laced boots. And if the kitchie quine didn't get a clatcht on old Sally she would hyter down to the stable door to give the men their orders for the afternoon. Otherwise Tom Buyers that was the new grieve would put two fingers in his mouth and whistle for old Magnus, who would emerge from some hole or bore about the steading and take his wife to the farmhouse, out of sight of the men folk.

But in her young day Sally Birse had been a different woman and wore the breeks folk said and kept Magnus in a tight corner. It was nothing new for her to give the men their orders at yoking time, and if Magnus said something she didn't like she soon spoke up. The men didn't like it either, taking orders from a woman, and they sometimes wondered if she had grown a stroop, seeing there were no bairns about the place, for maybe she had changed her sex. Nowadays Sally never got the length of the stable but pished herself or she was clear of the kitchen door, something to do with her nerves since the fire folk said, that she wasn't like that before. All the lads were new at the Term anyway, 'cause Magnus had a clean toon when the old grieve left; but they had heard about Sally in her young day though there was no doubt about her sex when they saw her over the brander.

Since all the cottars were new it took a while to size each other up and for their bairns to get acquainted; some of them wondering if they had come from the hay to the heather, from the clover to stubble, or if old Magnus was as black a devil as he was painted, or if his wife was as dottled as they said she was. And Magnus had notions too, thinking that maybe he had fee-ed the wrong lad for

233

second-horseman, because he wouldn't take in his pair from the grass park to be ready at yoking time, neither in the morning nor at noon (not that he slept-in mind you, for he was always there on time) but just sat on the cornkist smoking his pipe and kicking the wooden box with his heels or yoking time, while the other lads harnessed their beasts for grubber, harrows, or rollers, drill-plough or dung cart.

Then, if it were noon, and just about the time that old Sally came out to the brander, Runcie Smart would loup from his cornkist, take a few cubes of oil-cake from under the lid, his halter ropes from the forestalls, and away he'd go, whistling for his mares, a pair of dapple greys that had survived the fire and were the pride of the countryside; better than Buyers' pair (him being foreman as well as grieve) and it caused a bit of jealousy between the two of them - that the second lad should have a better pair of horses than the foreman.

So Runcie got hold of his pair, just inside the gate, where they were waiting for him and the handful of cattle cake that Runcie had stolen for them, never troubling to run off while he slipped the thin rope through the iron ring on their halters and led them through the white clover to the gate. But this was after yoking time, when the foreman and the loon were pulling out of the stable with their horses fully harnessed, ready for a yoking's wark, while Runcie still had to harness his beasts and give them the chance of a drink at the horse trough.

In her young day Sally Birse would have spoken to Runcie Smart right quick about this breach of contract; which was what you might have called it, though it was never in writing, but a customary habit among the horsemen of the Bogside, and the farmers believed from long tradition that they had a right to expect such service. But Sally never got half-way to the stable or somebody grabbed her, or even yet she might have told Runcie what she thought of him and his foreign ways, for Runcie was a man from the Mearns and not accustomed to Buchan ways; though some said he was just being downright thrawn because he didn't like Buyers and wanted to pick a quarrel with him. Old Magnus didn't say anything to Runcie but he put Buyers up to it; loading the gun as you might say while Buyers was expected to fire it, and thus stand the consequences if it back-fired, though Magnus never expected that it would.

So Buyers spoke to Runcie and told him right sharply to have his horse in the stable by yoking time. But Runcie up and tells him he will do nothing of the sort; that down in the South a man never haltered his pair or yoking time and he wasn't going to start it here, just because the Buchan farmers were such greedy lads for wark. They nearly came to blows about it; Runcie like a wee bantam cock and Buyers a big bubbliejock with his tail fanned out and his wings trailing on the ground, sparring round each other in the close and the feathers like to fly from tooth and claw. Runcie took his pipe from his mouth in case it got broke and dared Buyers with his stickit nieve. So Buyers went away in a sulk, muttering something about letting old Magnus do his ain dirty work. But he must have told Magnus the upshot of the thing because at the end of the month when the cottars got their pay Magnus gave Runcie the sack and told him to get out of his cottage.

So that was that and Buyers the grieve was fair cock-a-hoop about getting rid of Runcie Smart, and having a laugh with the other billies and saying how hard it would be for Runcie to get another cottar job six weeks after the May term.

The hyowe was just started, when everybody that wasn't there got their character, or 'their kale through the reek,' as they said, from the Laird himsel to Joe Meeks, the tramp that went with the threshing mills and sleepit in the barns 'cause he had lice. And Runcie wasn't spared: 'The cocky wee cratur,' as Buyers called him, seeing he wasn't there to defend himself. So you got real friendly with Buyers, and though you was only the loon about the place he was right glad to have you on his side (or so he believed) whatever the others thought, though one of them was your own father, hoeing at the other end of the squad. Head cattleman he was and you was second cattleman and orrabeaster (working the odd horse) besides looking after two colts and the shelt you drove for old Magnus and his mistress in the Governess cart, a small gig with rubber tyres and cushioned side seats, used by the gentry in the old days to drive their Governess around their estates with the bairns.

Tom Buyers was the first man you had ever seen smoking tea-leaves. His wife rationed him to two ounces of black twist (Bogie Roll) a week, and if this were exhausted before the grocer's vanman returned the following week he had to resort to the tea-caddy on the mantelshelf. It wasn't pleasant smoking: rather hot and tasteless, so that he slivered down his pipe stem and there was always a bead of moisture hanging from the bowl, and she raged at him for that, something he had to put up with from being hen-pecked.

Runcie Smart swore out that Buyers was afraid of his wife. She was a bit younger than Buyers and known as the Flower of Mullden, where she came from, though you couldn't say why they called her that. She was no special beauty, in fact the opposite, with moose-coloured hair and never a smile on her face; plain and childless and rather sulky, with little to say to her neighbours, which maybe wasn't a bad thing biding in a cottar hoose.

But she had bonnie legs, and all the men looked at them, with a wink to each other if Buyers wasn't aside, and they agreed you wouldn't see the likes of them on anybody but a film star.

Old Magnus engaged a single lad to take Runcie's place. His folk had a croft just across the parks on the moss road and he went home on his bicycle for all his food, so that he was no bother to Sally Birse or her serving quine.

The hyowe was finished and the hay in the cole and some of the peats home but Runcie Smart was still in his thackit biggin. Maybe Buyers had been right: that Runcie couldna get a job atween the Terms; but some said he wasn't looking for one, just sitting in his hovel to spite old Magnus. Nobody knew what he lived on though some said he had applied for Parish Relief. His wife had two bairns at her hip and one in her oxter; yet Runcie was no thief, nor was he much of a poacher. In fact the farming folk had nearly forgotten about Runcie Smart and his predicament when old Magnus gets a lawyer's letter sueing for a year's wages for Runcie, besides the cash value of his perquisites and the right to stay in his cottage until the next May Term. Furthermore, the letter said that he, Magnus Birse, had dismissed his worker without proper cause: that since there was no written agreement of policy there had been no breach of contract, or words to that effect, and that the alternative to the forgoing was to reinstate the said employee in his former employment, otherwise further proceedings would be taken in court.

It was a stamagaster for old Magnus, and when he showed the letter to his wife she pee-ed herself, never getting the length of the brander, but let it go on the flagstoned floor of the kitchen, where the quine had to dry it up with the sack cloth.

Magnus put on his spectacles again and came down the close with the letter to Buyers, like a squirrel with a nut, for he always trotted about like a beast on its hind legs, bent forward with his hands in front, palms inward, like paws, gnarled with rheumatism and grasping the letter. Buyers had been glad to get rid of Runcie, because you might say Runcie was undermining his authority as grieve about the place; the man not doing what he was told, which was an unwritten law of the farming hierarchy, that a worker must be disciplined, like he was in the army almost, or get out of his tied cottage. But the letter changed his tune and Magnus had an accusing look behind those thick glasses. Buyers could sense it even before the old man spoke: blaming him for picking a quarrel with Runcie over nothing and causing all this trouble with the man. Buyers had a look on his face like a ewe in a dipping trough and it looked like he would go into a sulk.

Magnus said they would just have to take Runcie back; that he had no choice, because he couldn't afford to pay a whole year's wages for nothing, besides the lad who was taking Runcie's place. They would just have to take Runcie back as orraman until the November Term, when they could get rid of the single man and Runcie could have his horses back, if he would agree to it. So old Magnus had to go crawling to Runcie's door telling him to come back, even to asking his favour to accept the job as orraman until the Term, when he could have his horse team again.

So Runcie came back with the buckles on his wall-tams shining like new silver and a gloss on his boots like newly ploughed lea, smoking a new Stonehaven pipe, and sets himself up on the cornkist again, like a dethroned monarch back in his royal chair, banging away with his heels to the tune of 'Drumdelgie'. Fair Cock o the Walk he was and like to rule the roost at Dockenbrae, watching the single billie taking in his dapple greys from the grass park before yoking time to have them harnessed on the dot, never letting on if he would have done the same, though it isn't likely when he had a lawyer at his back.

The corn was unsheathed, though still a bit green, expected to rax another six inches before it was fully ripe. The hay was all in the stack and forbyes a yoking in the horse-shim or a dab at the second-hoe you was mostly employed in the peat moss.

The chaumer at Dockenbrae had been burned in the fire two years earlier, and when they built the new steading they didn't plan for a new one, as there were plenty of cottar houses for married men on the place. When you came to Dockenbrae as a halflin it was agreed that you got your board and bed with your parents, seeing that your old man was cattleman. It had been a fine change from the chaumer life and you got a better diet from your ain mither than you was accustomed to in the fairm kitchies, though Magnus paid her only a shilling a day for your keep, besides extra milk, tatties and oatmeal, and a load or two of peat for fuel.

Now your old man always took in the kye for the milking, three or four milk cows with the bull, a big black brute of an Aberdeen-Angus that Magnus hired out to the crofters round about who couldn't afford to keep one to serve their cows. He charged them so much for every calf and they had to pay your old man a shilling for every service with the bull, though it was only to open the gate to let them into the park. So it was no shilling no service as far as the crofters and your old man was concerned, though most of them paid up, especially if it was in the evening when they had to get your old man away from the fireside. Sex has no trysts in the bovine world and has to be answered on call, and folk had never heard of Artificial Insemination or 'glass tube calves' as they are called nowadays. Like the tenant farmer who had engaged an ex-fisherman as stockman and one day he had to send him with a cow in season to the Home Farm for service where the bull was kept. So the fisherman took the cow in a halter to the Home Farm, and when he returned the farmer thought he'd better ask him what had taken place, seeing that the fisherman lacked experience in these affairs with cattle.

'And foo did ye get on than?' the farmer asked when the fisherman entered the farm close with the cow.

'Oh fine,' said the fisherman. 'The bull went up beside the cow and whispered something in her lug, and for fear that she forgot what it was he wrote it on to her arse with a red pencil!'

Another version of the story was that when the farmer asked what had happened the fisherman replied simply: 'Oh top hole sir!' without a smile on his face.

'Och,' said the farmer, less convinced: 'I thocht you wad mak an arse of it somewye!

But old Magnus Birse kept a bull himself, so that your old man didn't have to go stravagin over the countryside embarrassin folk with sex starved cows. But between times, to keep the bull content, besides having him near at hand, he went to pasture with the milk herd, and he stood in a stall in the byre while his wives were being milked; chained by the neck to the forestall, though he also had a brass ring in his nostrils for emergencies, fixed there by the blacksmith - if you could get hold of it in any tussle you was likely to have with a frisky bull. The done thing was to chain the bull first, maybe with a bit of cotton-cake in the trough to take up his attention, then tie up the cows, while they chewed the cud and flapped their big lugs in your face, and you whispered their pet names and anything else you was feared to mention to the kitchiedeem in a haystack.

Like the farm chiel who was a bit shy and rather slow in the uptak and didn't know what to say to his lass when he went courting. So he eavesdropped on a courting couple behind a hedge and listened to their conversation, especially concerning what the lad had to say. 'You have eyes like a dove,' says the lover, poetically, speaking in English to charm his lass, or to impress her with his refined vocabulary - 'You have eyes like a dove my dear; a breath like a thousand meadows . . . and you're a cupid!'

Next time our farming billy was out with his kitchie quine he sets her down in the hedge and says: 'Ye've een like a dog, a breath like a thoosand middens . . . and ye bugger ye're stupid!' And we can only guess the reaction of the offended maiden.

Ah well, one summer evening, when your old man bent down to pick up the bull's chain he turned on your father and threw him into the forestall, where he sat helpless in the cement trough while the great head of the bull played punch-ball with his knees, bashing them against the concrete, till his knee-caps seemed like egg-yolks with every yark from the muscled neck of the bull. It was a cat and mouse affair, the beast now roaring and foaming at the mouth, your old man at his mercy, while the great black mass of bone and muscle hurled itself against the figure jammed in the feed trough, crying for help, while the enraged bull, cheated of his fun of throwing him in the air, bellowed in his fury.

But wherever old Magnus was he heard the uproar, and he ran to the cow byre as fast as his tottering old legs would carry him. He opened the sliding door and saw what was happening, while your old man yelled from the forestall. Magnus grabbed a long-handled fork and jabbed at the bull. He was an old man over seventy, frail and bent with the years, but desperation gave him courage and he pricked at the tough hide of the sweating, bellowing animal; the warm smell of him strong in the byre, and the green skitter flying from the arse of him, his long tail lashing it all over the place. Magnus probed and stabbed at the black noisy brute till he fair danced in his frenzy, blowing and snorting from his brass-ringed nostrils, distended in rage, swack on his hoofs for his great size, till he pranced out of the stall and turned on his owner, while your old man crawled to the open door, through between the farmer's legs to safety, while Magnus held the beast at bay with the fork.

The cows stood around in wonder but never got in the way; perhaps a bit surprised at the onslaught of their chief on a human body. But Magnus stood his ground, prodding the sharp three-pronged fork at the bull, a valuable beast moneywise but a killer in his present mood; only the cold sharp steel held him off, or he would have crushed the old farmer as a fly against the wall. Magnus held the enraged beast at the end of his trident, like St George with the Dragon, his breath now coming in gasps from his efforts to defend himself. But he slipped and fell on the wet greep and the bull lowered his head to charge. He was a coward against the cold steel, but now that the fork was down he gave Magnus a buffet that sent him along the greep like a bairn's toboggan, right between the legs of Runcie Smart in the open door, where he had dropped his milk flagon when he heard the noise.

Runcie ran past the bull, picked up the fork and thrust it into the animal's ribs, the brute now roaring in pain and terror, while Runcie withdrew the fork and dodged behind him. The fork was tipped with blood and there was a red trickle from the bull's ribs. He turned on Runcie but shied at the fork, and with a final snort he ran to mingle with the cows. Runcie opened the barn door and chased him inside, where he charged at the straw and threw it over his back.

Old Magnus had struggled to his feet and was groping in the straw and sharn for his glasses, lost in his tussle with the bull. Runcie went to your old man in the passage, now moaning in his agony and hugging his bruised knees. Runcie lifted him on to his feet but he couldn't stand. Magnus found his splintered glasses and stuck them on his nose again, grumbling about Buyers not being at hand at a time like this. It was a wonder he hadn't heard the commotion he said, while Runcie now tied up the cows. The kitchie quine came in with her pails for the milking, fair surprised at the uproar and staring at your old man lying in the passage. Magnus asked her if she had seen Buyers and she said he was over at the kitchen door with his teem flagon, waiting for his milk.

Runcie told Magnus your old man was crippled and couldn't stand on his legs, so he went off to tell Buyers to yoke the shelt in the float and take your old man home. So they laid him on the float, on a cushion of straw, still trembling in his fright of the bull, and they drove him gently down the cart road to the cottar house, where your mither was watching anxiously from the door.

You was sent to the village on your bike for the doctor. He came quickly in his motor car and looked at your old man and said that no bones were broken but that one of his knee-caps was dislocated and the other grazed and inflamed, besides severe bruising on his legs and shock. He was put to bed and the doctor said he would have to rest for a week or two and then try walking on crutches, which he would loan him from the surgery.

Magnus had the bull destroyed. A motor float came and took the brute away, and a gey struggle the driver had loading him, with a spring-hook fastened to the ring in his nostrils, with a long rope down the length of the byre to the loading ramp, up the gangway of the float, and out through á slot at the side, where the driver could pull on the rope when Buyers and Runcie loosened the bull, prodding him from behind with forks. But the brute was thrawn and lay down on the rope, staring about him with his bloodshot eyes, blowing and snorting and the sharn all over his back from his swinging tail. Buyers shouted in his ears and they got him to rise, twisting his tail and prodding with the forks till they got him on the gangway, then into the float and a chain about his neck - away to the slaughterhouse, his wives grazing contentedly by the wayside.

Your old man was a long time or he recovered from his pounding, and sometimes you wondered if he did recover completely. Physically he wasn't bad, except for a jab of rheumatics in his knees, when he could tell you it was going to rain. But his nerves were shattered, and he sometimes sat up in the night with a great yowl, till he wakened himself, and everybody else in the hoose, unless your mither got a dig at him with her elbow when he started,

239

choking the scream in his throat, and when she asked what ailed him he said: 'It was that bull again wuman, he'll be the death o me yet!'

But as far as Magnus was concerned there wasn't a man about the place like Runcie Smart. After all he had probably saved the old man's life, for if he hadn't appeared when he did, and acted so gamely, there's no saying what the bull would have done to old Magnus.

When the hairst was bye it wasn't long or you could see that Buyers had watered all the corn rucks, seeing he had built them all himself and there was nobody else to blame. They were sprouting green round the shoulders by the middle of November, the sheaves all grown together so that they couldn't be thrashed and had to be thrown to the cattle as they were, a sore loss to old Magnus in his declining years. He was afraid to sack Buyers after what happened with Runcie Smart, but Buyers was that affronted he left of his own accord at the November Term. Runcie took his place and they kept on the single lad for the dapple greys. Runcie had full charge at Dockenbrae until the roup in May, when Magnus sold everything off and bought a house in the village, a house with a new-fangled bathroom, where he had more control of his wife when she went looking for a brander by the kitchen door.

Dockenbrae was sold to another farmer and he never asked any of the old servants to stay on - not even the kitchie quine. He would be bringing new workers of his own choice to carry on the place and everybody at Dockenbrae had to look for other jobs.

Runcie Smart went home to a place about a dozen miles from Dockenbrae, in the next parish but one, where everybody was a stranger to him, or so he thought - but who should be foreman there but his old arch-enemy Tom Buyers. Each had engaged to the farmer without the other's knowledge, which was common enough, and as each was fee-ed on a twelve-month basis they would have had to put up with each other's company again for another whole year - such was the irony of the cottar's life.

Runcie's only consolation was the prospect of further admiring the leg-stems on the Flower o Mullden, especially now that it was near the end of the nineteen-twenties and short skirts were the fashion with the women folk. And would you believe it - by the end of the twelve months Tom Buyers and Runcie Smart were as thick as fresh butter on oatcakes, each visiting the other, and Buyers' wife taking a great interest in Mrs Smart's bairns, maybe because she had none o her ain. And Runcie would be in bye at Buyers' house of an evening, listening to his gramophone records, sitting by the fireside smoking their pipes, and when Buyers reached up for the tea-caddy Runcie would produce his pouch and offer him a pipeful of tobacco, the price he had to pay for inspiration from the Flower o Mullden.

The Shearing

There was nothing extraordinary about the Monkshood place as a fairm toon; it looked like most of its neighbours in the Tullymarle countryside, hiding behind its muffler of trees, with only the lums of the dwallin hoose showing in summer, though you could see most of the steading in winter when the trees were bare.

What was uncommon about the Monkshood farm was the man who owned and worked it, a retired doctor from London, who had done well in practice among the gentry there and came up north to fulfil a life's desire - a passion for farming. All his working life as a medical practitioner Dr Leiper had read and dreamed about having a farm of his own. The depression of the 'thirties had made it possible, when he came on holiday up north and the Monkshood place came on the market and nobody wanted to buy it; the price just right for his bank account with enough to spare to give him a reasonable start. It was a good farm the doctor had chosen, though more by chance than foresight or good judgement; land with a mixture of clay in the brown soil, especially on the upland parks that carried grass and turnips well, and even corn or barley in an average year when the sun didn't scorch the braes. There was some peat in the howes that needed to be drained for better cropping, but once he had the ditches cleaned he soon had them flushed with grass. There was also a lot of fencing to be done for the sheep he kept, and he bought a lot of new posts and wire and told the grieve to spare no expense in having the place secure, every post the same height and the wires level with the ground. Nor was he far from the peat moss, where he could supply himself and his workers with ample fuel, and faith he thought it a blessing in the cold batter of the north wind that came over the knowes in winter, whipping out of a freezing sky that sent the old doctor to warm himself at the kitchen range.

Dr Leiper's wife had died before his retirement, poor soul, worn out with cancer, though some folk just called it decline, leaving the doctor and their son Kenneth in the care of the housekeeper, a Miss Biper, who had been in their service for a two three years. Young Kenneth was now nearing twenty-three and sitting for a degree in science at the college in Aberdeen. Miss Biper had moved up north with the doctor, complaining bitterly about the coldness of the weather and the infernal rain that was never far away; and the thick damp fog that came rolling up from the sea and hid everything for days on end, so that she couldn't see the wee cottar house at the end of the farm road where the grieve lived, nor any of her farming neighbours, whether they had a washing out or no, which was most unlikely in the seeping mist. Maybe she had been a bit sheltered down in London yonder and felt a bit cosier, and London fogs didn't isolate a body as they did up here; there was always the neighbours and the houses across the street, the odd bit of gossip at the shops and the bus stop. Nowadays Miss Biper had to rely on the local vanman for almost everything ᴊhe required, and any tittle-tattle that was going in the district. When she went to Aberdeen she had to take the country bus, a long weary lumbering journey with very seldom anybody to talk to that she knew, and very little in the scenery that inspired her urban mind. All this because the doctor didn't have a motor car, and hired a local taxi to take him about on his farming affairs.

And there was that domineering fog-horn on the coast that moaned most of the night, so that she couldn't go to sleep for its monotony, and the whole dark world seemed to be closing in upon her little bed. Of course the neighbours never believed this when the vanman told them, for they were sure she was more often in the doctor's double bed than she was in her own single one, creeping ben to him when he wanted her, the lamp in her hand, and if you was calving a cow about the place or lambing a ewe in the dark hours of spring you could see what you thought was going on, though up till now nobody had managed to prove it. Willie Bartok that was the grieve had the lambing in the springtime, sleeping time about with his assistant in the farm house, one relieving the other in the lambing buchts, and they said they heard the housekeeper talking in the doctor's room when she was supposed to be in her own. But Miss Biper was good to the men and they wouldn't breathe a word against her, unless it were behind their hand so to speak, or over a friendly pint at the Emporium; and if Willie Bartok reached the stage of blowing the froth from his tumbler he would tell you there was more in the bitch than anybody was aware of, except the doctor maybe who knew her better. Aye faith Willie said he had seen something uncanny at the Monkshood place; something that made him wonder, but the doctor was a gentleman and he wasn't saying another ill word on the pair of them.

Be all that as it may, in daylight hours you would never have suspected anything irregular between Dr George Leiper and his housekeeper, for he treated her with the utmost respect, always addressing her as 'Miss Biper', as if he had never been nearer to her than across the dinner table. Norma was her christian name but he was never heard to use it in such familiarity, and she always approached him as 'Mr Leiper', not 'Doctor' Leiper as you might have expected, him being a specialist and all that. But Bella the kitchie quine had sharp eyes and sharper ears, and as Miss Biper kept her pretty well in her place (mostly in the kitchen) she wasn't slack to find fault with her employers, or to slander them a bit if she got the least inkling of their intimacy.

But the doctor was well liked in the parish, especially by the crofters round about who borrowed some of his implements from time to time from the grieve, who first asked the doctor if so and so could have the Tumbling Tom for a turn at his hay, or the horse lorry for a load of straw? In the first years, before the doctor got to know his neighbours, he would ask his grieve what sort of chap this neighbour billy was, and would he bring the thing back unharmed? So Willie Bartok spoke for the crofter lads with the doctor, who had the best and newest implements in the parish, and so long as they brought them back clean and undamaged they could borrow what they wanted.

Though the doctor was well enough to do he never mixed with the bigger farmers or the gentry, always with the poorer folks (maybe because he had seen enough of the toffs in Harley Street) and some of the crofters and cottars would approach him with an ailment their own doctors couldn't cure. He would never visit a patient, in case he offended the local physician, but if a patient could be brought before him he would listen carefully to their symptoms and advise them on what they could do to help themselves. Some folk called him a 'Quack' for this while others he had helped said he could perform miracles, an allegation which brought him to the notice of the minister, the Rev. Pullock, down at the manse at Tullymarle, surrounded by his crows, where you couldn't get a shot at them so near the kirk and the gravestones, though they ravaged your tattie parks and sheltered in the manse trees. He was a bit like a crow himself the Rev. Pullock, dressed in his black surtoo coat and pedalling along on his bicycle, except for the dirty white collar round his neck. He paid the doctor a visit on his bicycle, not to bless him as a saint or for his powers of healing, but to see if he could get him to join his kirk, for the doctor would be a good source of revenue, especially if he could make him an elder. But the doctor was non-committal, merely indicating that he belonged to a brotherhood of his own choosing, and that most likely they would give him decent burial when the time came, though it wouldn't be in the kirkyard at Tullymarle.

The doctor kept a lot of sheep on the hill parks, a fine flock of Leicester Cheviots with a reputation for prize-taking and a pedigree for good breeding; strong heavy ewes that were a struggle when you compared them with the ewes of the neighbours who shared the doctor's dipping trough, because they couldn't afford one themselves, or hadn't taken the trouble to build one, what with the drainage problem and dripping slips and gathering pens and foot-rot troughs that were required to meet the new regulations demanded by the government. Of course they paid the doctor for the use of his trough and brought their own dip; even brought sticks and peat to heat the water to melt the pails of solid McDougal Sheep Dip, but for all the doctor charged them gave no inducement to have a dipping trough of their own.

The shearing was a bit late that year that young Kenneth Leiper was expected to pass his exams at the university. The doctor had spoken to his grieve about young Kenneth's homecoming, expressing a desire to see his son again and hoping that this time he would graduate and qualify for a teaching post in science, seeing he wasn't the least bit interested in agriculture.

Willie Bartok thought he knew young Kenneth fairly well, though he'd been grown up before his father came north. A studious chiel you would have thought and serious like when he came home for the holidays and sometimes worked with the men at the hay or in the peat moss, or hyowing the neeps or tatties. But Willie the grieve knew there was another side to young Kenneth, a side that his father knew little about, except for the debts he sometimes had to pay for him, mostly gambling debts, though he told his old man a different story. The glaring fact was that young Kenneth had no interest whatsoever in his education, and his passion in life was drink and gambling, all the time hoodwinking his father with his good intentions, and how far the old man suspected him was anybody's guess. He had a bit lass too that he sometimes brought home with him, a better quine than he deserved; but she hadn't been seen for a while and folk thought he had given her the slip, or maybe she had left him for his bad habits.

Kenneth had bad drinking bouts and he kept bad company. More than once the grieve had come upon him in the barn, sleeping it off where his cronies had left him from a passing motor car, or when he stepped off a bus, all boozed up and afraid to meet the housekeeper or his father; and Willie Bartok would take him up the road in the darkness of morning to the cottar house, where his wife would wash young Kenneth's face, brush his hair and his suit and give him breakfast to sober him up a bit before he met his father, sometimes keeping him at the fireside till nearly dinner time. And there was those strange tablets he carried in his pocket that he said were to help him through his exams, and to help him look his father in the face with another failure.

Willie Bartok gathered his sheep early on the morning of the shearing, as soon as the dew was off their backs, the collie dog swinging round the brae to gather them in, rounding up mothers and lambs without a bark, simply answering to Willie's whistle from the gate, where he stood ready to open it when the flock had been foregathered. He would do the same with every park, for there were several flocks scattered on the braes, and Willie liked to have a flock gathered and penned for the shearers before breakfast, when the lambs would be separated from their mothers, the ewes herded to the catching pens to be brought before the shearers.

You could hear the baa-ing of the ewes on the neighbouring farms, and the persistent bleating of the lambs, now they were denied their mothers' teats, and the folk would say 'Faith aye, the doctor's at the shearin!' A tarpaulin sheet was spread out upon the grass for the shearers to work on, mostly to keep the wool clean, while they sharpened their long shears on an oil-stone, their pipes lighted and ready for the fray. They were hired men, mostly two of them, who made their living at the shearing, going from farm to farm in the summer months, and when that was finished they took to ditching or working in the peat moss; then harvest, and draining and fencing in the spring, casual work they did in their spare time from working on their small crofts that couldn't earn them a living. Dick Sow and Harry Hemp were men who could clip a ewe in about three-and-a-half to four minutes at the height of the season, when the wool had risen nearly an inch from the skin, with only the merest threads holding it, where the shearers made a quick and easy entrance, flashing round the falling fleece like hand-made lightning; snaking round the body of the ewe in a growing curve, the rich white wool falling back before the incessant clisp of steel, the blue-bladed scissors slicing into the oily fleece while they held the ewe in the various positions that suited them, tilting their restive bodies this way and that, starting at the throat and finishing up at the tail, until they had them out of their coats and standing for a moment in the sun, breathing fast on a full stomach, and seemingly mesmerized in their nakedness, then leaping from the tarpaulin sheet with a new swiftness, bounding for their lambs and freedom. The ewes returned naked to the fold, so that the bairns scarcely knew their mothers, except for her baa and the feel of her teats, while they nosed her udder for suck, big growing lambs that were thirsty from the day's heat, bouncing their heads under the mother's flanks, lifting her nearly off her hind legs, a lamb at each side mostly, wagging their short tails gleefully, and the mothers sniffling over them in jollification that the worst was over and they were reunited with their bairns.

Two of the farm hands bundled up the fleeces, tying them separately for trampling into the woolsack, now slung from the rafters in the empty byre. Willie Bartok had a steady job driving away the shorn ewes and their lambs and bringing in another flock for clipping. The men who tied the fleeces took the ewes to the shearers, catching the ewes by the neck in the narrow pens with self-closing gates, worked with a thin rope and a weight over a post. They caught the struggling ewes and dragged them by the chin and flanks to the tarpaulin sheet, where they set them on their hurdies, each man a ewe at a time, and held them there until a shearer finished the ewe he was at and took over, splitting the wool at her throat and working down her belly, first round one side to her back and then the other side, peeling off her fleece like a jacket, even to the leg holes.

The shearers were paid for the number of ewes they clipped, each man counting his own by taking a penny from his pocket and dropping it into his cap on the grass, or by taking a match from one pocket and dropping it into another, each man using his own method. And there was no cheating, because the number of ewes they clipped had to correspond with the number of the flock, including bare-backs, ewes that had lost their wool on barbed wire fences or tufted over the whin bushes. But the shearers mostly snipped off the tufts that were left on their backs and counted her as a full fledged ewe they had clipped, helping themselves to a bonus they fully deserved. An average fleece weighed from five to seven pounds from the bigger ewes, and when trampled into the great woolsacks the total wool clip could reach up to nearly two tons.

The shearing lasted for three or four days, depending on the weather and how early in the forenoon the shearers could get started, sometimes waiting or the sun was hot, which brought out the oil on the wool, maybe giving you a bit more weight and making it easier to insert the shears between the wool and the skin of a ewe's back.

Now the kitchiedeem came over to the sheepfold with the piece basket, hot tea and scones with strawberry jam, biscuits and a bottle of beer for each man, thirsty at their work, tormented with heat and flies. So the shearers finished the ewe they were at and all work stopped for nearly half-an-hour, while the shepherds teased the quine about her lads and she poured their tea and took their banter in good spirit, sometimes returning it as good as she got. Even the bleating of the sheep died down, except for the occasional high-pitched baa from the grass pens where the lambs were still in orphanage. After tea the shepherds drank their beer and had their smoke and ground their shears on the oil-stone, counted their pennies or matchsticks and talked to Miss Biper, who had come over to see how the work was progressing, and maybe to crack a joke, even a blue one, for she wasn't above a hearty laugh was Miss Norma Biper, no matter what the cause of it. She had extra men to cook for during the shearing and she preferred doing it herself rather than leave it all to the kitchen lass.

After dinner the doctor appeared, a grey tweed hat on his head, a knee-length coat of mixed texture, even in the height of summer, breeches and topped socks and his walking cane, more out of habit than the need of one. He was clean shaven, rather puffy-faced with high colouring and a bee-stung underlip, his eyes slightly bloodshot while he gazed on the flashing shears of the clippers and the growing mound of newly fallen fleeces. Sheep fascinated him, and what he had read about them in books he now endeavoured to put into practice, the ambition of a lifetime; all the years of work in the medical profession merely a means to an end, the realization of a dream, and he counted himself fortunate that he had lived to achieve it. It was the same with cattle and he thought himself blessed with a man like Willie Bartok to look after them, a man whose work and knowledge of the breeds made his path easier.

Doctor Leiper had an instinct for having men like Willie Bartok about him. He was a shrewd judge of character and for two years after coming to the Monkshood farm he had waited an opportunity to engage Willie Bartok, watching his work on a neighbouring farm with patient admiration. When the time came he fee-ed Willie long before the roup at the place he was leaving, before anybody else had the chance, tempting the man with a wage he could hardly refuse without being downright bad mannered. It was enough to give a man conceit of himself, but Willie Bartok was not that sort, and his only concern was to make sure the doctor never regretted engaging him. Oh aye, Willie had his suspicions about the doctor and his housekeeper, a fine carry on they were having the two of them if all was known, but it was none of Willie's business and he wasn't going to concern himself; the doctor was a good master and that was all that mattered to Willie Bartok, except maybe when he had a drink with his cronies on a Saturday night at the Emporium, when Willie whiles said things about the ongoings at the Monkshood he didn't intend letting on about.

Meanwhile the shearing was in hand and the doctor had a word with Willie on how the work was progressing. A good clip Willie told him and the weight of wool would be well above average. Given an early start tomorrow he expected the shearers would be finished by dinner time. Today the sun burned from the heat-hazed sky like a brick furnace, with not a breath of wind to blow away the flies, now lively over the sheep pens, tormenting man and beast in the heat of labour. Willie added that they would maybe have to dip the sheep again soon against fly-strike, the lambs at least before weaning.

On the last day of the shearing Willie Bartok had his brose as usual and the morning promised well for the clippers, with very little dew on the grass and the sky not too bright at this early hour. Willie lit his pipe when he left his cottage and walked down to the farm to fetch the dog for the gathering, the last field for the season, and glad he would be when it was over, though the trauchle of hay and peat moss still awaited them. It was sore on his feet with all the walking, though he wouldn't have to go round his sheep so often after they were clipped, as there would be less danger of the ewes dying on their backs once the wool was off. He could reduce his rounds to the normal twice a day instead of three or four times before the clipping, when the ewes were heavy in wool.

Willie got the dog out of his kennel and slipped his leash, the dog leaping ahead of him through the stackyard, where some of last year's corn stacks were still standing, to be threshed by portable mill later in the summer. Willie heard the dog barking between the ricks, which was most unusual for Rover 'cause he seldom barked. He must have come upon a weasel or a hedgehog to disturb him so, or maybe a rat in the ruck foons. Willie followed the barking around the flat circles of loose stones that were the foundations for stack building when he tripped on something that nearly knocked him over in his stride. It was the feet of a man in grey trouser legs, and as he followed the line of the suit to the body and the face he could hardly believe his own eyesight. There was young Kenneth lying there behind a rick with his mouth wide open and staring up at the morning sky. But there was no light in those eyes and they gave no sign of recognition. God knows how long he had been there but probably most of the night. He was expected home this very day, most likely with flying colours from the university, or so his father hoped and would be waiting for him. Willie kneeled beside the young man and felt his pulse, the dog wagging his tail furiously, squeaking out his recognition and licking the cheeks of his young master. But there was no life in the cold wrist, the arm as limp and heavy as a piece of lead piping. Beyond the outstretched hand a small bottle lay amongst the stones. It was empty and Willie read poison on the label, then replaced it where it was lying. Willie had a twinge of conscience but he couldn't resist having a look at the envelope sticking out of the young man's breast pocket. It was an I.O.U. gambling debt of nearly £300, something his father would have to meet, and Willie slipped it back where he found it, besides a photograph of his girl friend that had fallen out with the envelope.

Willie was trembling when he stood up, for he had gotten a bit of a fright, but he gathered his wits about him and walked back to the farmhouse. He rapped on the housekeeper's window but got no answer. So he took a long binder whip from the gig shed and tapped on his master's window upstairs. It was the housekeeper who opened the sash and looked down sullenly at the grieve. 'What is it Willie?' she asked, little above a whisper, not to waken the doctor; 'so early in the morning - you'd think it was lambing time, never mind the shearing.'

'Would you come down Miss Biper,' Willie said quietly, just loud enough for her to hear, 'I've got something to tell you, quiet like, before the doctor hears it.'

Inwardly Willie was thankful she had answered his tapping. He didn't want to be the one to break the news of such a tragedy to the old man. By telling the housekeeper she would relieve him of the ordeal.

'I'll be down Willie,' she called softly, then pulled down the window and closed the curtain.

But she was sleeping with the doctor. There could be no denying it now. Willie had seen for himself and he was convinced. And those little bones he had dug up in the front garden - they were human after all. He had been sure of it but was afraid to mention it to anyone except his wife, least of all the housekeeper because of his suspicions. Now he was glad he hadn't. When Miss Biper fell with children the doctor would know how to get rid of them. Willie remembered those old days now and then when the housekeeper was indisposed, apparently with the influenza, and Bella was mistress in her absence. When Miss Biper recovered she would bury the evidence in the garden in the dead of night, deeper down than Willie was supposed to dig in his ordinary duties. Two or three nests of small bones he had dug up over the years and as quickly buried them again, afraid of what he had found. Willie knew fine it wasn't something the dog had buried. A pair of bloody butchers they were but you'd think they were saints. But with this new tragedy upon them he wouldn't tell a soul, except his wife, and maybe it would bring the pair of them to their senses.

And next time at the Emporium over his glass of beer Willie would tell his cronies that the doctor was a proper bloody gentleman, and he wouldn't be lying at that!

Two Men and a Boat

'The mere fact o bein alive wad kill ye come time!' Old Forbie Tait, farmer of Kingask, said this from time to time when some neighbour body died; whether he attended the funeral or no it was his stock phrase for the occasion, even though he knew fine that old Doolie Nash had drunk himself into his coffin, or that Waldie Podd had slaved himself to death for siller on that bit croft on the Windyhills above the kirk at Peatriggs, atween Slypigo there and Badengour. High on the face of the brae stood the kirk of Peatriggs, its bare stone spire polished by the wind and rain from the sea, a braw kirk and a fine monument to the devotion and industry of its congregation in the upkeep of such a place: an everlasting memorial to the indomitable spirit of man, far outlasting his brief span to grasp and spend, to lust and love, striving for a bite of meat and drink to keep him alive, with a vague promise of something better beyond the grave; something he didn't understand - clinging to a blind faith and a soulless purpose, nailed to the cross of life with no escape but death, and gathered at last to the cluster of gravestones that surrounded the kirk on the brae.

Always in your lug at Kingask was the growl and boom of the sea, swooshing over the rocks and boulders embedded on the beach; sometimes sullen and angry, tearing the seaweed from its roots and strewing it on the shore to the very edge of the road, where it rotted and stank in the summer sun and bred flies by the million. The next storm would submerge the dykes of rotting seaweed and reclaim it for the sea, the tang of fresh dulse strong in the wind, the undercurrent convulsing the water into monstrous waves, now careering ashore with their white manes rolling inwards, curving towards the beach, the white spume exploding over the rocks, drenching the road in lashings of spray. Next day, with a fall in the wind the sea would be quiet and peaceful, caressing the shore in gentle playfulness, all bubbles and sunshine, blown froth and flotsam, lapping the roadside at high tide.

Outbye Brochan was the lum of the gut factory, pointing out of the sea beyond the bents like a sore thumb, tall and gaunt and blackened with soot, the smoke curling out to sea in the herring season, or spreading over the land in a blue transparent haze, the smell of herring brine strong in the curing yards, your thoughts all pickle and trodden salt, like snow that had lain too long in a foul winter, giving a deeper boom to the growling of the sea, like a far off symphony on the waters.

When you left Brochan on the coast road to Candlebay, out by the gut factory, you could see the farmhouse at Kingask, like a beleaguered castle, with peep-hole dormers on the ark-shaped roof, gunloop windows on its steep harled walls, with small stubby chimneys crowded on its gables. If you was looking for a fee out bye on the Candlebay road the sight of this forbidding structure would have given you the shivers for a start, especially on a cold spring evening and the wind blowing through a harp of spray from the sea and the spindrift lashing the road. Kingask House stood apart from the village, just beyond the meal-mill, like a fortress of formidable strength, the steep roof covered in the small slates of a former century, surrounded by a curtain wall enclosing the gardens, its pigeon-hole windows peering out like searching eyes over the green parks, the front door studded and hinged like the clasps on a sealed bible, with a boar's head knocker of wrought iron high up from the bare stone step and the rusting grill over the cellar.

Nor were you ever likely to forget that coast road the first spring evening you clapped eyes on the grey fortress farm of Kingask, the sky all ragged and torn by the north-east wind whipping off the sea, the fitful shafts of sunlight glancing on the water, the giant waves careering ashore, their white beards crested in foam, cascading against the rocks in fountains of flying spume, spilling out in bubbles and blown froth on the road, littering the beach with rich smelling seaweed torn from the ocean bed.

About two miles out along the coast you could see the village of Candlebay, huddled on the bents 'like a painting on a wall', with net poles on the links and ship masts in the tiny harbour, the wind-chopped sea stretching to the grey horizon.

It looked as if the North Sea was heaving a lash at the stranded fishing drifters that littered the two-mile stretch of coast from Brochan to Candlebay and Spitullie. About a dozen wooden steam drifters had been abandoned here and cast ashore by their owners; stripped of all valuable material, so that only the hulls and decks remained, towed round from the breakers' yards in Brochan and cut loose to find their own graves on the rocks, lashed ashore by incoming tides, to die ignominiously by the roadside. The villagers picked their bones when the tide was out, carting off all that they could manage for firewood; hacking first at the pinewood decks, then the oak and ash of the hulls, sparing nothing that would burn in their iron-barred grates, though the wood was impregnated with thirty years of sea salt. A few of the villagers set themselves up as firewood merchants and stripped the boats professionally. With big hammers they drove out the iron spikes and nails that held the planking together, first the decks and then the hulls, prising the boards apart with crowbars, leaving only the ribs sticking up from the shingle, so that folks called it the Drifters' Graveyard, and as one old skeleton disappeared another hull was cast adrift on the tide.

Jock Webster was king of the timber wolves, beating all his rivals with a second-hand motor-lorry, driving the wood inland to the farmers and cottars, selling it by the load. You soon got to know him once you was fee-ed at Kingask, and the difference between deck planking and hull timbers, though he charged a higher price for the pinewood, saturated for years in tar preservative, like railway sleepers, first-class kindling in the morning to boil your kettle quickly for brose making, before you started work in the byres.

Nearing Candlebay you could see the fishermen's houses, solid little structures of stone and lime, roofed with slates or red pantiles, gable on to the sea and the road, maybe as a safeguard against the sea-spray that flew over the roofs in stormy weather. Some of them were harled and whitewashed, others with the stonework around the doors and windows painted in different colours; one house green, another blue, one brown or yellow, others black and red, a picturesque rivalry that was both quaint and cheerful and full of character. The 'room' end of every house boasted an aspidistra or a Lily of the Valley in a brass or porcelain pot on a fretwork or polished hall table in the window, shrouded in floor length curtains of heavy material that was the last word in respectability, and you could nearly be sure that the family bible and hymn book would be lying on a table in the centre of the room; on a round polished table with carved legs, covered with white silk embroidery as a sort of miniature tabernacle for the Lord's anointed.

The fear of the Lord was great upon the fishermen and their families; a fear of His wrath that held them secure in the narrow paths of righteousness; a fear of the Lord who moved upon the water, who could catch a waterspout in the cup of His hand, or harbour a boat to safety with the blow of His breath - He who tilted the mighty iceberg with His fingertip, who strove against Satan and evil continually, and gave everlasting life to the faithful; He whose word was like the sound of restless seas in stony places.

But there were some who had forsaken the Lord and the mission halls, and had succumbed to the demon drink, or the vice of gambling and betting on horses, and these were frowned upon by the respectable fraternity, while the Witnesses of Jehova sought to gather the wayward sheep back to the shelter of the fold. But money was scarce in the hungry 'thirties, and though drink was cheap it never produced the debauchery of more recent times, for in those days the harvest of the sea was as profitless as the harvest of the land; more so since the end of the herring boom between the wars.

The little motor yawls of the fishermen were hauled up on the pebbled beach, or tethered to the piers in Candlebay harbour, which had been built for bigger boats in the days of the herring bonanza, but now deserted save for the few motor boats that swung at the ropes from the painted capstans on the pierhead. When the tide was out you could see the wives and daughters of the fishermen gathering bait on the dark green slippery rocks out by the harbour mouth, while the men painted their yawls and net-floats that looked like a balloon festival in rainbow colours floating in the sunshine, and all the time the splash and swoosh of the waves and the cry of seagull and the rich tang of the sea.

There was even a boat-building yard at Candlebay, busy on the new seine-netters that were replacing the old steam drifters lying on the beach with their ribs in the sand. The new boats were also of wood, somewhat smaller than the old herring boats, and were propelled by the new diesel engines that were

251

replacing steam. These new wooden boats were shortly to prove a Godsend against the magnetic mines of Hitler's secret armoury, sweeping them from the water where ships of steel couldn't go near them.

But now you were in the village and heading up the brae to the meal-mill and the miller's dam, where you rounded the corner and got your first close-up of the great house of Kingask, dwarfing the steading behind it; surely built as a tower keep you thought, big for a farm house, and must have been there for more than two-hundred years, even before the Jacobite risings.

But old Forbie Tait was no Jacobite; he was far too cautious for that and never liked taking chances, and although he took a passing interest in Royalty it was a fair bet he would never have joined Prince Charlie and his rebels. He was the ca-canny Scot who never liked feeing a lad on his first interview, but merely sized you up, prying out all the particulars he could gather of your past experience, so that he could form some opinion of your character, and not having a telephone wherewith to get your qualifications from your last employer he was obliged to look at your references. In a day or two, when he had time to think it over he would write and let you know if you was getting the job, meanwhile interrogating any other chiels who looked in bye in answer to his appeal in the paper for a reliable cattleman, offering them the same terms of wait and see - while Forbie made his choice at leisure. But you told old Forbie you was having none of that palaver, because it was getting too near the Term and you wanted to know where you stood; if he wasn't going to give you the job right away you was going to look somewhere else. He looked a bit abashed at this but had another think, and as a special favour for the man who had recommended you in the first place, an old grieve who had once worked at Kingask - because of this Forbie decided to ignore precedent and take the risk of engaging you that very night while you sat in his kitchen at Kingask. You would get a pound-a-week in cash, which was £52 for the year, paid monthly, at the rate of £4 at the end of each month and the balance at the Martinmas and Whitsun Terms. This was a reduction of £2 over the year from what you was getting in your present employment as a dairy cattleman. But coming to beef cattle Forbie considered you would have an easier job and a Sunday off once a fortnight in winter (when the foreman would look after your nowt - once you had sorted them in the morning) and you wouldn't have to get up so early in the mornings as you did in the dairy byres; five-thirty would be early enough to be ready to start at six, after you had your breakfast, two hours later than you was in dairy work. And you would get the usual perquisites: coal, meal, milk and tatties, house and garden, and you would be allowed to keep about a dozen hens, provided you wired them in so that they couldn't scratch in the fields. So it was all settled and you got a cup of tea from the mistress at Kingask, a pleasant enough like woman with common-sense talk, and then it was time for you to take the coast road again on your bike, past the drifters' graveyard, this time in the dark with your new electric dynamo, which was attached to the rim of your rear wheel, heading for Brochan and the Bogside.

So here was you fee-ed to go to Kingask, where you would get away from

252

the skitter and chauve of the dairy byres, and you'd get a longer lie in the mornings and a Sunday off, which was something to crow about in those days of slavery. Wilberforce should have freed the slaves at home before he concerned himself with those in Africa and the southern states of America: the industrial workers, the miners and the farm servants; especially the farm workers, who in some instances had worse working and living conditions than the negroes he campaigned for. If ever there was a case for charity beginning at home this was it, where for several decades after Wilberforce, even to the end of the first quarter of the twentieth century, British farm workers were still working within sight of Uncle Tom's Cabin, and there were still quite a number of whip-cracking Simon Lagrees amongst our farming chiels - not all of them of course and some were gentlemen, but they were a minority.

But your new job with Forbie Tait gave you a feeling of confidence in those last few anxious weeks before the May Term, a period of grim uncertainty for the cottar, until the breadwinner had some prospect of a roof over his head and a bite for his family in the coming year, and when this had been attained a new sense of security and a feeling of renewed independence soon began to show. Now you could snap your fingers at folk who thought they had you in a corner - not having a house or a job (or so they thought, because you kept those things to yourself for a while) cowering under their authority, while all the time you was laughing up your sleeve, and now you could tell them to go to hell because you was going to Kingask. Trouble was that the same thing would likely happen again in a couple of years, when you'd be cursing Forbie Tait; but meantime you blessed him for what you thought was a new freedom, a new lease of life - and so it went on in the cottar's lot.

Forbie sent a motor lorry to flit you, not that you had much in the way of furniture, but a few bits of sticks and dishes and bedding and a crate of hens. In fact your kitchen dresser had cost you only four shillings and sixpence at a second-hand sale and was little better than a hen coop. But there you was with all you possessed in the world and you bundled Kathleen and the bairn into the lorry cab beside the driver and his second man and sat on the load yourself, clinging to the ropes while the cold wind whistled about your ears. The only thing you remembered about that flitting was the speed of the lorry, like you thought they'd have all your dishes broken and your furniture out of joint, tearing on like that, just to have their Saturday afternoon off, which was something you didn't get on the farms; like you was just cottar dirt and it didn't matter much for the bits of stick you had for furniture, so long as Forbie Tait paid for the flitting, and you felt like telling the driver this, for you was fell annoyed when you got off the load at the cottar houses at Kingask, high up on the hill above the sea and the parks.

Here then was the second cottar house Kathleen and you had flitted to, the first one with a young bairn between you. It was a double cottar house, with the chimneys from both sections on the middle of the slated roof, and stone porches at the gables. Badgie Summers that was foreman lived in the nearest half-house and you would have the end biggin furthest from the road. The porch was handy for a pram or a bicycle or such like; besides the pails of water you would have to carry up the brae from the tap at the farm. The back bedroom window looked down on the village and the sea, now deep blue and spume-flecked in the face of a stiff breeze coming off the land. Badgie Summers was home for his dinner and he gave you a carry inside with your furniture, no doubt casting a critical eye over your bits and pieces, thinking it was hard times for young folk setting up house, for no doubt being an older man he would have better furniture; the older, heavier stuff of solid mahogany, substantial compared with the flimsy material you was getting nowadays, and soon riddled with woodworm. But you had your bed, table, chairs and dresser; dressing-table with mirror (with two paintings by Constable on the sidewings) washstand, meal-girnal and your chaumer kist, about all you could afford in those hungry times, second-hand at that, besides your bedding and curtains, pots and pans and dishes. The only odd bit of furniture in your load was a glass case with a model ship in it, a cardboard cut-out of a steam cargo boat you had made in the evenings of your spare time; an unusual hobby for a farm Jock, and while Badgie carried it into the house he remarked that you had fairly come to the right place for makin boats, and you supposed that he meant the boat building yard down in the village. Of course you was just fair daft on boats at this time of your life and your daftness was expressed in your efforts with models, though you had no real desire to go to sea in any practical sense.

But it was good of Badgie to give you some assistance with your furniture, the first time you had seen the man: round-faced, high-coloured and beardless, not even a moustache, with keen blue eyes that shone like polished gig lamps, his cap on a slant on his short-cropped head, bull-necked with massive shoulders, wearing his kersey-tweed trousers and dark blue fisherman's ganzie, like the men wore in the village (but without the smell of herring about him) and you would have thought to look at him that he was a sort of crofter-fisherman who didn't know much about the bigger farms you had been accustomed to and their ways of working away inland from the coast, though he spoke in the doric tongue as broad as you'd hear many miles inland from the sea. His wife took Kathleen and the bairn inside until you had the furniture unloaded, then treated the pair of you to a bite of dinner and a cup of tea, real neighbourly folk, and then Kathleen put the bairn in the pram and Badgie's youngest quine diddled him about for most of the afternoon, while Kathleen helped you to lay the bit linoleum you had kept from the last place for your bedroom floor and gave you a hand to set up the bed. She then hung curtains on the windows, with white lace screens nearest the glass and placed her pot flowers on the sills. You left her to scrub the cement floor in the kitchen while you tidied up your odds and ends in the garden shed and fastened your hens into the ree.

Badgie Summers was a big hardy chiel who had survived the Kaiser's War and he called his medals 'badges', the medals he had won for his dour courage on the Western Front and he sometimes wore them on Remembrance Day at the kirk, so the folk just called him 'Badgie'. After the war he had married and cottared at Langstraik, one of Forbie's out-farms, but for the last twelve years he had worked full-time at Kingask. He worked three horses instead of the usual pair, 'cause Forbie Tait liked to have a spare horse resting in the stable, taking it in turns as a pair at the plough or harrows, mower or tattie-digger, and the only time he had the three yoked as a team was for the five-tyned grubber in spring or for the binder in hairst. Forbie had a great care for his horse beasts and never liked to see them tagged with wark or besotted in rain, their fetlocks matted in frosted mud and needing a wash with soft soap. Forbie never liked that, nor did he puddle his folk either, and if you was pulling wet turnips on the brae above the steading, or ploughing lea by the shore, at the first patter of rain Forbie or his son Tom would whistle you home, so you had no need of an oilskin suit and it was your own fault if you got wet through. The lad that was foreman before Badgie didn't always listen to Forbie's whistle, or pretended not to hear it and kept on ploughing in the rain, maybe because he didn't like cleaning harness or mixing hen feed up in the loft, which was the sort of job Forbie would have waiting for him under a roof. When he lowsed at last in a heavy downpour and came home with his pair Forbie was waiting for him in the stable. The lad was taking off the harness from the wet backs of his mares and hanging it on the pegs, his own jacket as wet as them, when Forbie says to him: 'By gum lad,' says he, 'ye can tak a spaad and gyang ootside an del neuks if ye like but ye're nae gaun tae puddle my horse!' But after sixteen years in Forbie's service Badgie knew the old man better than this and always lowsed his horse when the rain came on.

The beasts always came first on most farms. It was for the sake of the horses that you got two hours for your dinner; not so that the horseman could rest, for half the time he was supposed to be grooming and feeding them, and the two hours gave them plenty of time to chew and masticate their hay, though they never lay down in the stall at dinner time. It was the same with cattle: a stirk in a stall was always more important than the man who fed him; worth more commercially than a stockman who could be had for £1 a week in the glutted labour markets, while a nowt beast would be worth £20 to £25 once he was fattened for the butcher. But Forbie usually put human being before beast, which couldn't be said of most farmers in the days between the wars.

One of the pleasantries of your early days at Kingask was wakening up around six-o'clock on a Sunday morning in summer, getting up and going over to the bedroom window to see the foreman taking your three cows from pasture into the wee byre for milking. This happened once a fortnight in summer, on your Sunday off, a fine change from the dairy byre, where such indulgence was unheard of; when you had to be there yourself every morning, Sunday or week-day, at 4 am sharp, unless you were ill or had taken a moonlit flit, for sleepin-in wasn't allowed for and was liable to bring you the sack.

But here at Kingask you had a beef cattle herd that required no attention while on summer grazing, and with only three milk cows in your charge, milked by the kitchiedeem, you had much less responsibility. On the Sunday mornings that Badgie took in the kye he stood in the byre and smoked his pipe, leaning over a travis post while the lassie filled her pails from the warm bulging udders. When it was your Sunday on duty you milked the cows yourself, and the kitchie lassie got her full Sunday off, a relief service which had been performed previously by Edith, Forbie's younger daughter, until the women folk discovered that you was a practised hand milker, then wouldn't give you peace or you did it. Badgie couldn't milk and had no desire to learn (especially when he was a horseman) nor was he keen that you should do it either, because when it happened on week days it sometimes kept you from the field work, which didn't please Badgie if he thought he was getting too much to do on his own. Indeed there were surprisingly few menfolk who could milk a cow by hand, the good old-fashioned way, thinking maybe it was a bit below their dignity, especially if they were horsemen, and so they left it to the women, never realizing the finger cramping exercise it really was. But being a dairy cattleman you had learned this excruciating art, though in this case you got nothing extra from old Forbie for your pains; nothing beyond the knowledge that you was giving his daughter a longer lie in bed on Sunday mornings, besides the satisfaction that you was giving the homesick kitchiedeemie a longer day at home with her family; indeed her sweet smile of thankfulness made it seem worth your while.

On most of the beef farms it was also your duty to take a stroll through the pastures on Sunday mornings to check on the cattle: stots, heifers, stirks or yearlings, breeding cows and calves, counting their numbers in each park, to make sure none were ill, strayed or stolen, an exercise which might have taken you just over an hour, provided there wasn't water to be pumped somewhere to their watering troughs, which took a while longer of your time. But old Forbie liked to go through the cattle fields himself on Sundays (as he did on week days) maybe as a mode of exercise, but he wouldn't pump the water. So you looked from your other window at the front of the house (your kitchen window) and there was Forbie in his parks, clad in his usual brown suit and checked cap, pipe in mouth, the reek flying over his shoulder, one hand behind his back, the other waving his walking stick, slashing at the odd thistle or tanzy you had missed with your scythe.

Ah well, on Sunday mornings such as these, when you looked from your bedroom window and saw Badgie Summers taking in your kye - somebody else doing your work - you just smiled to yourself and crept back into bed with Kathleen, warm and cosy (provided the bairn wasn't standing up in his crib howling for his milk bottle) and you'd fair think you was King of the Castle. It was usually oatbread and cheese for breakfast, because Kathleen was an excellent baker of oatcakes, and as oatmeal was a perquisite it paid you to have a wife who could bake; especially if you could buy a kebbock of home-made cheese from the farm wife, or from one of the crofters, and with good strong tea to wash it down, with cream and sugar, and then some scones and marmalade - well, there wasn't much to complain about. And then you could light your pipe and sit down in your second-hand armchair and get stuck into the *Film Weekly* or the *Picturegoer* you had bought on the Saturday night when you was at the pictures in Brochan. Kathleen would be spoon-feeding the bairn on her knee at the table, a bib under his chin, while he mumbled some sort of mumbo-jumbo between the spoonfuls, kicking his mother's legs and reaching for anything on the table he could get his hands on, and sometimes toppling the sugar bowl.

But you was far away in Hollywood, reading all the gossip about the film stars: their marriages and divorces, their next starring roles, like Robert Donat in *The Ghost Goes West,* Shirley Temple in *Curly Top,* or Katherine Hepburn in *Mary of Scotland,* and there were whispers of a young crooner called Frank Sinatra. Then you read the film reviews, production news, etc., admiring all the exotic stills and bathing beauties, which would absorb you till nearly dinner time, and you could still jump on your bike and get the Sunday papers if you wished, 'cause you was a glutton for newsprint. After dinner you could hoe the tatties you had planted in the garden, now well above the ground, or weed your vegetables, then rig yourself in your marriage suit (the only one you possessed) and when Kathleen got dressed the pair of you would take the bairn in the pram to the village, round the closed shops and the deserted harbour, and two or three times you'd gone right into Brochan, on to the beach and the promenade, where you each had an ice-cream cone from the vendors, sometimes two, because the Italians in Brochan had awfully good ice-cream, and you'd give the bairn a lick at your cones in the bye-going, smiling up at you there so pleased like, despite the cold sea wind that whipped at the pram hood, even in the height of summer, for it was always cold in Brochan.

On the way back you'd wheel the pram up Mid Street, so that you could see the stills at the Picture House, black and white and glossy, and the hand-bills with all the particulars of next week's programmes, so that you could make a choice of at least one night's showing, though most likely you'd go yourself and Kathleen would have to stay at home with the bairn, unless it was a special programme you wanted her to see - pictures like *Mutiny on the Bounty,* with Clark Gable and Charles Laughton, *Under Two Flags,* with Ronald Colman and Claudette Colbert, *How Green Was My Vallay,* or *Back Street,* pictures with a romantic or feminine appeal you knew Kathleen would enjoy, for she was no addict of the cinema and you had to select her films. With you it was different and most of the run-of-the-mill pictures appealed to your infatuated imagination, and that to such an extent that you was almost incapable of criticism, a worshipper who could find no fault in his gods, or should you say goddesses, for it was the great days of Garbo, or Dietrich, or Barbara Stanwyck and Irene Dunn, those whose every gesture, every smile, every tear was watched and dreamed upon and cried over by millions in those days.

On such occasions when Kathleen accompanied you to the cinema Mrs Summers next door took in the bairn, little Brian. It didn't happen often but when it did Mrs Summers was delighted. She liked bairns, and so did her daughters, especially Esma, the one still at school, and between them they spoiled the brat, even to such an extent that he would hardly claim his mother when she came back, so that Esma had to come round with him in her arms and

257

lay him in his crib before he was content. As it was he sometimes crawled along to the Summers' doorstep, and later, when he got on his feet he ran round half-naked (when his mother had removed his pants for toilet) and when he saw Badgie and yourself coming up the road for dinner, he would come running down the road to meet you, running right between the pair of you with his bare bum, even on the coldest days, and Badgie would say: 'Man, that's the wye I like tae see a bairn brocht up; nae neen o yer coddelt bairns but hardy as they come!'

Then there was the time that Kathleen went down the close for water, and Mrs Summers and Esma saw her go past the window, and once she was well down the brae, Esma ran round and took little Brian out of his crib, still with his dumb-teat in his mouth, where Kathleen thought he would be safe or she returned, and Esma ran round with him in her arms and hid herself in her mother's bedroom. Kathleen had been gone about ten minutes, and the first thing she did on her return was to look in the crib, and when the bairn wasn't there she went in a state, wondering where he could be. She looked over all the house, even up the stairs, thinking she knew not what but nowhere could she find him; so she ran round to Mrs Summers and gasped out that the bairn had disappeared.

'Disappeared!' cried Mrs Summers, pretending shocked surprise.

'Aye,' said Kathleen, 'I went to the waal for watter and left him in his crib. When I cam back he wasna there and I've searched high and low for him!'

'Gweedsake,' said Mrs Summers, 'but he canna be far awa. Did ye leave the side o the crib doon?'

'No,' said Kathleen, 'I left it up, so that he couldna get oot; he could never climb owre the top o his crib. I jist canna think whaur he can be.'

Kathleen was beginning to get hysterical and Mrs Summers could hardly keep in her laugh, while all the time pretending to be serious.

But even with jam on the dumb-teat Esma couldn't keep the bairn quiet any longer in the back room, and he gave himself away with one of his little gurgles.

Esma emerged from the bedroom with the bairn in her arms and Kathleen took him from her a little angrily, for she had been on the verge of tears in her anxiety.

But it was soon forgotten and after school hours Esma would jab the back of their fireplace with the poker, and when Kathleen heard the dunts in the back of her grate she knew it was a signal to come round, mostly to play cards for an hour before she made the supper, with little Brian at her knee.

Another time Esma knocked in the evening, which wasn't usual for her; just before the lamp was lit and you could scarcely read the papers, and when Kathleen ran round Badgie was sitting reading the daily paper with a stump of candle burning on his head.

'See what the bitches have come till,' he cried to Kathleen, 'they wunna licht the bludy lamp tae lat me see tae read the papers.'

But after a month or two with Badgie Summers you soon learned that he knew a lot more about farming than his fisherman's jersey gave him credit for, especially at hoeing time when he could spot a charlock weed among the turnip plants before you could see it; particularly among the yellow turnips, which it most closely resembles, more so than swedes, because of its coarse leaf and lighter colouring, and with your untrained eye you would have singled out the charlock and left it for a healthy yellow turnip at the end of your hoe-blade, a useless weed that sprouted a yellow flower and podded seed but never grew a bulb to feed hungry cattle. This coastal strip of Pittentumb abounded in the yellow charlock weed, known all over the Bogside as the skellach, and the folks near the coast blamed their ancestors for bringing it on to the land with the seaweed, carting up the dykes of rotted dulse and tangleweed from the shores, using it on their crofts as fertilizer. Of course a body had no real proof of this; maybe it was that the richness of the dulse, impregnated with iron and iodine, encouraged the charlock to grow more profusely round the North Sea coast, where the grain and turnip fields were sometimes as yellow as though you had sown them with mustard seed, while on the inland farms of the Bogside the yellow menace was much less prevalent. It is an oily seed that grows only on the blackened furrow and is never seen on healthy grass, lying dormant in the under soil for a decade; perhaps for ever, but bursting into flower wherever the plough has broken the surface to give it air and life.

Coming from an inland fairm toon a body was much less accustomed to the charlock plant, especially in its younger stages in the turnip drills, when the leaves are the size of a 'moosie's lug', as they say in the Bogside, which is a good size for starting the hoe. Badgie had been brought up with the weed; well aware of its disguise in the seedling turnip drills. No wonder then at the end of your first hoeing season at Kingask that Badgie took you (literally by the lug) to the turnip park and pointed out your yellow drill alternately with his own that didn't have a yellow flower to be seen in them. All over the park every second drill blossomed its yellow flower; for now, about six weeks after hoeing, the charlock was in bloom, which of course it isn't at hoeing time, being then but an inconspicuous seedling of the 'moosie's lug' variety, but no damned use to anybody. Nor could you deny your incompetence, because there were only the two of you at the hoe, with nobody else to blame, so it was easy to pick out your yellow drill, beginning second from the dyke. No wonder that old Forbie himself had paid you a visit at the hoe (for maybe Badgie had been watching your drill from the corner of his eye and reported it - not caring to mention it himself) and Forbie had bent down and pulled out a charlock seedling you had left and asked if you knew what that was? Maybe they'd had this experience before with strangers. But of course you were so cocksure of yourself in those days you said 'Aye,' that it was a skellach; that you knew fine what it was, thinking they were taking the raise of you, while all the time they were merely biding their time to confirm their suspicions that you didn't know, or at least that your eye wasn't yet properly trained to spot the charlock weed in such profusion with the yellow turnip seedlings. In the maincrop swedes however you were more or less faultless; with a clean, well-dressed drill, and perhaps for this they overlooked your other failings.

259

All the same you had enjoyed hoeing that season with Badgie Summers, just the two of you in a fifteen acre field, up on the brae above the farm and the cottar houses, cold and windswept in winter but warm and sunny enough in the long days of summer. Badgie had a great hairst of war stories and a firm belief in the Tory Government, headed at that time by Stanley Baldwin, and later by Neville Chamberlain as Prime Minister. Of course you never adhered to any political party and simply declared yourself Independent, so that you had no political arguments with Badgie. If you had been a staunch Labour man, or even a Liberal, you would have been the odd man out in any case, because most of the farmers were Tories and they drove their workers to the polls in their own cars, throwing hints that they should vote Conservative, seeing they were getting a hurl, and this was the myth that kept Sir Robert Boothby so long in Parliament as their representative at Westminster. But sitting on the fence as an Independent they couldn't make head nor tail of you, and you escaped a lot of useless argument.

But you listened to Badgie's wartime exploits with great relish, especially about the huge skirling shells that the Germans sent over the Scottish trenches. The Scots called them 'coalboxes', because of their great size and black smoke in explosion, and they seemed to make a noise like 'Faur-ee-bidin? Faur-ee-bidin? Faur-ee-bidin?' which, translated from the doric simply means 'Where are you staying?' repeated several times very quickly as the shell hurtled overhead, searching out the kilted Scots, then made some attempt to answer its own question by crumping down with a tremendous explosion in some Scottish trench or supply line behind the front. Badgie took the mick out of the British army 'Bull' and spit-and-polish mania that existed during the First World War. He said the Germans were untidy in comparison and didn't have to wash and shave all the time; some of them even had beards, and though the British Tommies were allowed a moustache (neatly trimmed) they went about most of the time like scraped pigs. Badgie told the story of the sergeant in the Gordon Highlanders who was daft on discipline and square-bashing: how he gave the order 'Stack rifles,' then formed his platoon in a straight line the whole length of the barrack square, dressing from the right, and marched them to within a few inches of the stone wall. 'Halt!' he cried. 'Eyes front,' then 'At ease . . . sporrans aside . . . up kilts . . . down pants . . . out cocks . . . and . . . wait for it . . . wait for it . . . and . . . PISH!'

There was also the story of the Scottie home on leave, a postie from Candlebay, and when someone remarked to him that the Somme had been a terrible battle he replied: 'Och aye man, the human heids were comin stottin doon the hill like neeps and buggerin a' the wye!' 'I stood whaur thoosins fell,' said another, trying to go one better, though it wasn't a thing to brag about, nor to be laughed at. 'Aye Sandy,' said a cronie, who knew Sandy as a bit of a braggart, 'it had been whan ye changed yer sark ah doot !' Then there was the case of the discharged Highlander who married a dubious lady of the streets and on their bridal night she removed her wig, her glass eye, and then her false teeth, each time remarking: 'How do ye like to be done Jock?' By this time Jock was undressed so he pulled up his nightgown and cried: 'Shot off at Mons woman - foo div YE like tae be done?'

You had met only a very few of these men on the farms in your own lifetime who could fully grasp and discuss world politics with intelligence and Badgie was one of them. Some of them (excluding the war veterans) were almost totally unaware of the world and its ways beyond the parish boundaries, though they knew these boundaries extremely well, and most of the folks within them; all their faults and foibles, their varied characters and chitter-chatter, and whose intimate affairs occupied their ultimate perimeter of thought. The better informed on a wider scale were those who read their employer's newspapers, mostly one with a conservative slant, though that didn't matter; it was the information that was important, before the days when radio became popular on the farms - when you heard it only in the chip-shops or in the pubs when you went into the towns. Most of the cottars had gramophones, but these were for entertainment, not for political reform, but for Cornkisters and Hilly Billy singers of 'Old Faithful' and 'Home on the Range', or any song or instrumental item that was popular at the time, like Gene Autry with his guitar, George Formby with his ukelele, or Gracie Fields singing like a lintie.

But though Badgie was well informed from his master's newspaper he was by no means educated or cultured: it was merely a village pump, pub-crawl knowledge that he had of the world and it suited his purpose, and once he had filled and lighted his pipe at the end of a long and weary turnip drill you could enjoy his lively talk on world affairs right to the other end, forgetting your twisted neck and aching shoulder muscles in Badgie's rapporteur; in fact he lightened the work and shortened the time and the drills with his well-informed newsing. And Badgie wasn't a bore or a blabber-mouth and he was easy to listen to; and a good listener too when it was your turn. And there was plenty to talk about in the middle of the 'Hungry 'Thirties', or during the two years you was at Kingask: what with Mussolini's rape of the Abyssinians; General Franco and the Spanish Civil War; Japanese aggression in Manchuria; Hitler's expansion in Europe; the death of King George V; the abdication of Edward VIII, and the unsettled state of the monarchy at home - no end of subjects for discussion, and Badgie had a good smattering of knowledge and a strong opinion on most of them. In fact it could be added that Badgie's involvement in world politics was partly to blame for your detachment from removing the charlock weeds from the turnip plants; in that he was taking your mind off your work, but blissfully so.

And while the grey sea growled endlessly on the coast, and the cloud patterns changed in the sky, Badgie had his say, while you listened intently and drew on your pipe subconsciously. He told you how he was come of cottar folk, and that his father had been a grieve for most of his working life on the bigger farms further up the coast. His father had died of a festered throat he said, swallowing the poisonous pus in his sleep when the boil had burst, almost choking him when he awoke, and that the poison went all through his body and killed him, leaving his wife with a growing, school-age family, and nothing but parish relief to support them. All caused by working on the farms in the rain Badgie said, and catching a chill from his wet clothes. Badgie now had a wife and son and two fine daughters; the son married and cottared somewhere, the oldest quine fee-ed at a fairm toon, while Esma the youngest quine was still at the school in the village. His wife was a stoutish well-faced woman with a friendly smile and disposition, and as things turned out almost a mother to your Kathleen when your own little Winifred was born.

Forbie Tait himsel was a rigorous master, though not a hard one, but set in his ways and thrawn to change; eccentric almost in his conservative attitude to life and farming, and fortunate that he had lived a decade before the catastrophic upheaval of the second agricultural revolution. He was the lessee with the oldest tenancy on the estate; indeed he was born on it, though on a different farm, up at Langstraik there, which was farmed nowadays by his oldest son, Maxwell Tait. Forbie's long tenancy of Kingask was honoured by the Laird of Slypigo on reaching its fiftieth anniversary, when he and his family were entertained to a grand dinner and dance in the big hoose up at Boganchero, attended by all the swanks, lawyers, bankers, factors and contractors, and all the other tenant farmers on the estate and their wives and families, when Forbie was presented with the Laird's crest and insignia, with his own name engraved on it and the number of years he had faithfully paid his rent (though that wasn't mentioned) but it gave account of his long years of good husbandry on the farms of Kingask and Langstraik, though for his work on Kingask in particular. So you could say that Forbie Tait lived in a tied house, just like his cottars, under the jurisdiction of his Laird, in the same way as you was responsible to Forbie; the only real difference being that you paid a sub-let rent to Forbie with your labour, while he paid the Laird in cash, and any major neglect on Forbie's part was likely to land him out on the road with his flitting, all of which when you thought about it made the great tower house of Kingask seem less impressive or desirable.

Kingask lay on the north side of the Mattock Hill, though you couldn't see it from the farmhouse, only from the top of the brae above the cottar houses; a shapeless hillock hardly worthy of notice, grey and featureless in sun or shadow, the sky above it sometimes mitred into a dome of hammered lead, or the wispy clouds all corrugated and torn apart in the struggle between wind and rain in the elements of weather change; the hill shrouded in mist above the green parks that stretched all the way from above Peatriggs to Slypigo, over the Windyhills from Badengour, where the sea raged in a fury against the cliff face.

What with your literary turn of mind and your flair for the movies it could be said that at this stage of your life you imagined yourself as a sort of country bred Charles Dickens; just as in a later time in your rustic existence you associated yourself with Mark Twain, after you had seen his filmed biography, all of which may be a form of mild insanity, but also a source of inspiration which most artists experience in their desire to emulate their betters (hero-worship if you like) reaching for the star that shines at the top of the ladder they are scaling. In the present instance you had just seen David O. Selznick's version of *David Copperfield,* and you was reading a copy of *A Tale of Two Cities,* so the influence of the great novelist was strong upon you. But there was a cosiness in Selznick's production of the famous classic that you couldn't match in your spartan existence as a poor cottar in one of the most remote corners of our country's coastline; not even in pastoral style, because of the bleakness of the landscape and the withering climate. But in Kathleen at least you had all the beauty and warmth and sweetness of Maureen O'Sullivan, Selznick's choice of heroine, and in Kathleen also you had a competent cook and mother and housewife, far superior in health and spirit to the delicate, fragile, frivolous Dora, devoted to her wayward pomeranian poodle - and though Kathleen was fond of cats she would never fuss over them as Dora did or put them before her husband. Such was the conceit of your literary mind at the moment and the novel that was in you would have a long time to wait.

When the winter came on you was obliged to Badgie to supper your nowt in the evenings when you went to the pictures in Brochan, about once a week; feeding the cattle in the byres with fresh hay and shaking up their bedding with a fork, a service that old Forbie insisted upon, and had bargained for with you at feeing time. Badgie did the job when he suppered his horses, when Forbie and young Tom would be in the stable with him for a blether, taking the neighbours through hand or any political tittle-tattle that had been in the papers, like Baldwin's decision not to let King Edward VIII marry Mrs Simpson; or Hitler's march into Czechoslovakia, things like that, which did interest you to a certain extent, but not to the length of one whole hour and thirty minutes, which was the common length of their stable sessions, evening after evening, every night of the week, while you stood there with your flagon of milk, bored to silence on your wearied feet (after a hard day's work) because nobody sat on the cornkist, and you would have been considered lazy had you tried it. So you just stood there waiting patiently for the foreman to blow out the lantern and close the stable door, for to have left before him would have been considered the height of bad manners - even on the excuse that the bairn needed his milk before bedtime. Kathleen was wearied waiting for you and the bairn's milk, but when you whispered this to Badgie and said you would have to be home sooner he said you was hen-pecked and that he wouldn't put up with it, and that if it was the pub he was in he would stay as long as he liked and that no white-faced woman would stop him. Kathleen said he was a selfish brute for this and that you should come home sooner in spite of him, although of course you never did, in case you offended him, or that he thought you unmanly.

On your visits to the movies on winter evenings you escaped these stable gossip sessions, much obliged though you was to Badgie for attending to your cattle, especially as he seldom required you to do the same for him in the stable, supperin his horse, because the only time he went out was on Saturday night, down to the pub in the village with the blacksmith, and the two of them looked in by the stable on their way back after closing time. When you was away at the movies Badgie brought your flagon of milk home with his own and left it on your doorstep, rapping on the window to let Kathleen know it was there, and that she could get her bairn fed, and on these occasions Kathleen said he was usually earlier than other evenings when you was with him. And maybe you got your character in the stable behind your back when you wasn't there to defend yourself.

But sometimes there was a cow calving, not only the milch cows but maybe one of the sucklers, there being about a dozen of them on the farm, and as you couldn't ask Badgie to watch these as well you had to look in at the byre yourself on your way back from watching Dorothy Lamour as *The Jungle Princess,* or Ginger Rogers in *Don't Bet on Love,* and if Polly-Wolly Doodle was in labour, or Little Dolly Dander (for so you had them named) you had to take off the jacket of your marriage suit - the only one you had - put on an old waterproof and give such assistance as was necessary. On the night you saw *Rose Marie* Gorgonzola gave birth to a fine son. You called her this because of her mixed blue and white colouring, marbled like the famous cheese, a big-boned friendly animal, though most of the others were red shorthorns. So, with the Ave Marias of Jeanette Macdonald and Nelson Eddy still ringing in your ears you helped deliver Gorgonzola of a swarthy bullock, still with the chain about her neck, eager to lick him dry, so to please her you dragged him up beside her, and being a suckler she was allowed to mother him until his weaning. First thing in the morning you'd get a bucket of warm water from the farm kitchen, with a dash of oatmeal, and give it to Gorgonzola to drink, besides the first pailful of her own milk, after the calf had been fed, something that these old farmers insisted upon, and maybe that was why they had never heard of staggers or milk fever, because they were replacing a deficiency the natural way, or as they say - a gallon a day keeps the vet away.

The only time Badgie required your assistance was the night his roan mare gave birth to a foal, when you sat up all night with him in the loose box, where the mare had plenty of room to throw herself about, nickering to Badgie and staring at him when she felt the pains coming on. 'Hae patience lass,' Badgie would say. 'It's a lang time or mornin,' adding that she had herself to blame for taking up her time with that stallion in the springtime. Old Forbie had supplied you both with a bundle of Chamber's Journals as reading material, where you lay on the straw under the lantern, and about midnight young Tom came out with a cup of tea and shortbread. The mare foaled suddenly about four o'clock in the morning, without much help from either of you, a furry-like creature with a white spot on his forehead and legs like a giraffe, and after it was over Badgie said you'd better go home and get an hour's sleep before you started in the byre, that he would be in no hurry yoking up until well after breakfast when the foal would be footed and reaching for his mother's teats.

Having had considerable experience as a dairy cattleman you had some idea of how to produce milk from the three cows under your charge at Kingask. Not so much in summer of course when these things are governed by the weather and the state of the pasture; but during the winter months when the cows were hand fed you knew what to give them to encourage butter-fat in quantity as well as quality. It wasn't long or Deborah and Edith were expressing

264

their surprise at the thickness of the overnight cream on the milk basins and on their porridge bowls, which would nearly float a penny they said; enabling them to churn more butter and curd more cheese than they had ever done before from three cows, even with a separator. Even Mistress Tait herself commended you on the new richness of their milk yield and wondered what you could be feeding these cows on to give such cream. Of course old Forbie must have known that you was rather heavy on the bran supply, and the kitchiedeem knew that you came to the scullery every evening at tea time for a pail of warm water, and with this you mixed a sloppy bran mash for three dairy cows, adding a little crushed oats (besides draff when you could get it) and they licked it out clean from the feed troughs, when you would throw in a handful of oilcake as bonus (which was meant for fattening cattle) and even though one of the cows was almost dry - which nearly always happens pending a calving - and there had to be calvings, the increased rations of the other two soon made good the deficiency.

But it wasn't only in milk production that you was gradually gaining favour with old Forbie Tait of Kingask, for in your first winter on the place you had actually produced fat cattle for the Christmas sales while still carrying their first teeth, a feat young Tom or even Forbie himself had never seen in his life before. Neither had you for that matter, and if they had asked you how you had managed it you couldn't have told them. But to them it was an achievement worthy of discussion at the stable meetings, especially on the evenings that you wasn't there to hear it (but away at the pictures) except that Badgie told you the next day. So it was at least a credit to your efficiency and diligence in attending to these beasts during the long months of early winter. Of course they were a good class of bullocks before you ever saw them; Aberdeen-Angus mostly, for Forbie bought only the best in the store-cattle rings, paying such a price for them he said that they left only their dung as profit (after paying wages) there being such a small margin to work on between the store and fat cattle prices. But Forbie slivered down his pipe when he said this and spat in the close; the bigger the lie the bigger mouthful so to speak, like it was when he told you he had been farming out of capital since the Liberals went out, though he still voted for the Tories. But he took these bullocks off the waning pasture in early autumn, in the middle of harvest really, inside to tares and green corn in the byres, which gave you the long end of the year to finish them off with hay and early turnips (or what had been left of them after your dastardly hoeing), crushed corn and oilcake, ready for the Christmas sales.

All the same Forbie was delighted with your efforts in the byres, and although he didn't give you anything extra for your pains he rang your praises loudly to the neighbour folk, and when they weren't there to listen there was always Badgie Summers. Badgie would be ploughing in the muck you had spread out on the stubble, well up on the brae, when Forbie would take an afternoon dander to see how he was doing, or maybe just to pass the time and get away for a while from the women-folk, walking beside Badgie for a couple of rounds to stretch his legs, making good use of his staff, talking to his foreman, while Jug and Dandy strained at the yoke and swingletrees, snorting out their white breath in the mild frost that hung over the stubble fields, biting on the steel bits that held them so tightly to the reins in Badgie's hands; heads down, necks curved, plodding canny forwards, harness glinting in the weak sun over their backs, their tails tied up with tufts of straw, exposing the shorn rumps; their legs and bellies clipped bare to a straight line from breast to hind hip, Badgie walking behind the closing furrow, one foot in front of the other in the narrow trench, 'the ploughman's gait', as they called it, while he listened to his master and never slackened a step.

Now if there was one thing that Forbie hated the sight of it was tufts of straw and dung sticking up over the ploughing, and for this reason he liked to see it well spread, 'small as mice' feet', as the saying goes, so that the plough-tail could topple it into the furrow, buried from sight, humus and manure for next season's crops, breaking up and decomposing itself in the services of nature reclaiming her own. But there wasn't a tuft of sharn to be seen on Badgie's rigs, not even on the midses or shallow feerings, the seams where the plough-rigs are joined together, so that Forbie's profits from his cattle beasts was well hidden. But he wouldn't hear of you spreading the dung with a fork, which was lighter and easier on your back, with three or four sharp prongs that pierced the dung heaps easily, except when there had been a spell of frost, when you could scarcely mark the muck heaps with a shoulder pick. The first time Forbie saw you spreading dung with a fork he sent you home for a short handled byre graip, which made a better job he said, and wondered what you had learned at your last place. So you just humoured the old man and did what you was told, and apparently he was pleased with the result, your praises now ringing in Badgie's ears while he strode beside him at the plough.

Forbie liked to get a young man so that he could 'mould him to his wyes', as he told Badgie. The trouble was that the young lads never stayed long enough about the place to be 'moulded', but were up and away at the next May Term, twelve months being about the limit of their endurance of Forbie's 'auld farrant wyes o doin things', so that Forbie's purpose was continually being thwarted and the moulds wasted before the molten metal had solidified and taken shape to his satisfaction. So Forbie was forever casting new moulds for a cattleman to please him, and year in year out Badgie had a new neighbour next door to him at the cottar house. If you could stay for just two years as cattleman, that was the limit at Kingask, but really there were times when the old man tried your patience.

The only mould that had ever set to please Forbie Tait was the one he had cast for his foreman, Badgie Summers, who had been with him now for sixteen years, first at Langstraik and now twelve years at Kingask, and Forbie had so moulded Badgie that he couldn't put a foot in the wrong place; knew every move that the old man would make, and what would please him and what would not - in fact you could add that old Forbie had wound Badgie round his little finger and made him a farmer's man in every sense of the word. When the Term time came round feeing Badgie was only a formality, and when Forbie asked him to bide on for another year Badgie wouldn't say yea or nae the first time, usually waiting or Forbie tried him a second time, when Badgie would ask for an extra pound or two to his yearly wage, which mostly he got; or if the general trend was falling wages Badgie would hum and haw until Forbie agreed not to take him down in pay. So while others came and went for miles around Badgie stayed on year after year, secure in his job as foreman at Kingask, with a new stockman next door to him every second year or so, sometimes only a twelve-month if the new billy didn't suit old Forbie.

But now it looked as though you was going to stay longer than most with Forbie Tait, and more than a year next door to Badgie Summers, and at the end of your first year you was asked to bide on in good time before the cottar market, to make sure you didn't take a fancy to moving, and you got £2 more to your wage over the next year. Even your bad hoeing had been overlooked in view of your good husbandry in the byres. In all conscience you was really tidy at the hoe and next year you would be wary of the charlock weed.

But you had gone to the cottar market just the same, just to get the day off and maybe to meet some of your old cronies from the Bogside. You had come home early with the train, and after dinner, still in your marriage suit, you went a round or two with Badgie at the plough, telling him all the news of the market, the lads you had seen and where they were moving to, the things that interested Badgie, seeing you was so well in with him and settling in fine for a cottar life on the farms. About a quarter to four in the afternoon Badgie loosened his theets from the swingletrees and hooped them on the backbands of his pair and went down the brae to sort your nowt, past the cottar houses, sitting on Jug's back, the chains swinging by her sides under Badgie's tackety boots. After tea you was off to the pictures in Brochan, off to see Constance Bennett in *Topper,* with Roland Young; not by choice but because they had closed one of the picture houses and there was nothing else to see. This was another side of your life that Badgie nor anyone else could understand; except that you was 'picture daft', and any arty side of the business never entered their heads.

It was in the early summer of your second year at Kingask that you made your first real effort in journalism. Here for the first time in your strange incongruous life you was going to see yourself in print. You had been writing when you was at the school, and again when you was off work for a month when you was single, living with your parents after an attack of epilepsy. But these efforts never emerged from longhand, silly childish stories from the brain and hand of a schoolboy. This time you were to flourish in bold type in Forbie's daily paper. Of course you didn't know this yet and as it turned out to be abortive in relation to the rest of your career it wasn't all that important. But it was a start, a faint glimmer of the light that was to shine so brightly for you in much later years. It was so transient at this stage that dear Kathleen scarcely noticed it, though it did seem strange for her that her man should get a letter in the newspapers: a half column on the ethics of the bill newly introduced by Parliament to bring unemployment benefit to the farm workers. It was perhaps your one and only venture on the political spectrum and fair amazed the folk next door and the neighbours for miles around. To think that they lived next door to a chiel who got letters printed in the papers fair amazed them, and when a second epistle was printed they just couldn't get over it and you was the talk of the turnip fields for weeks on end.

Of course old Forbie had read your letters but made no comment about them; maybe thinking you was a bit touched in the head and would soon be standing for Parliament, in which case he would have to look for another cattleman, maybe one who didn't have his head so much in the clouds above the cottar house on the brae at Kingask. What was more important was that Forbie's daughter had read your letters in the press, especially Deborah, who (to your surprise) was herself something of a freelance journalist and had her weekly spot in a farming journal. She sought to encourage you and gave you books to read: *Blood Relations,* by Sir Phillip Gibbs, and a translation from the French on *The Life of Napoleon.* You became newspaper daft and read every article you could lay eyes on, mostly from Forbie's *Press & Journal,* which was a day old before you got it from Badgie, or Beaverbrook's *Daily Express,* which you could get in the village for a penny; two-pence for the weekly *Illustrated,* and fourpence for *Picture Post,* also the Sunday papers you could afford and your film weeklies, one or two of which you had read from boyhood. It was all grist for the mill and you just couldn't get enough of the stuff to keep you going, even though you worked a ten-hour-day six days a week and Sundays once a fortnight and had only the evenings to spare. To be in love with something like this is an experience you wouldn't like to have missed: this inner fire that burns you up with a delightful glow and devours slothful time with relish, bringing you alive to the fingertips. Strange that this hunger for the printed word should come upon you now - you that had been born and brought up in a home where not a book existed, scarcely even a bible; everything you had read had been borrowed or loaned, except for the occasional twopenny *Comic Cuts* or *Comic Chips* or the fourpenny Buffalo Bill novel, Sexton Blake or Dixon Hawke you had picked up at the bookstalls. Even yet, in the second year of your marriage there wasn't a book in the house longer than you had taken to read it, then returned to the source from which you had borrowed it.

But now you felt you had read enough to be able to write an article, even two articles; so with writing fire in your brain and red ink in your veins you set off on your bike to Brochan for foolscap (fool's cap - and now you know why they call it that) ink and pen-nibs, then sat down in all earnestness to write a fruitless essay for newsprint. Of course it was hopeless, even before you started, being in longhand for one thing. But you enclosed a spare envelope with stamp in case of rejection and waited, guarding your secret closely and telling Kathleen not to mention it to Mrs Summers, because Badgie and young Tom would likely laugh at you in the stable if they heard of such a thing. But just wait till they saw your name heading an article in the daily paper; not a letter mind you, but a full-grown article you would get paid for, then you could afford to let them laugh - all of them, old Forbie among them, laugh their fill. Maybe you had deceived yourself too long with the idea that you was meant to be a farm worker, while all the time you was a born journalist with ink in your veins - or so you deluded yourself; and now you found yourself on a road with no turning. Maybe the craze for cold print would ease off but in the meantime it burned with incandescent brilliance and brightened your dull skies for weeks on end.

The article came back with your first rejection slip, the first of nearly a hundred that were to follow, but as you were not aware of the prospect it didn't dampen the flame that burned within you; on the contrary the setback merely inspired you to write still further, another article; this time confiding in Deborah, the farmer's daughter, and she revised your work. It was a sort of documentary on the evolution or development in shipbuilding, particularly in Scotland, from the primitive hewn out tree-trunks of the early Picts to the launching of the Queen Mary on the Clyde, with most other things in between, from the Roman and Viking galleys to the Wooden Walls, China Clippers, Windjammers, the *Comet* , and paddle to screw-driven steamships. The idea had come to you from a picture on a calendar hanging in your mother's kitchen, depicting two cavemen in animal skins hacking out their boat from a fallen tree-trunk with their stone axes, tied to the shafts with hide thongs - an idea that kindled your imagination on how far shipbuilding had progressed from this primitive beginning to the mighty *Queen Mary.* The boat-building yard at Candlebay had also coloured your mind, besides your present nearness to the sea and passing ships; even battleships like the *Hood, Nelson* and *Rodney,* on their way from Rosyth to Scapa Flow, and you had started smoking Senior Service cigarettes to get pictures of the great Dreadnoughts. Your last article had been about the little fishing village of Spitullie along the coast and maybe it had little appeal for publication. This was a much wider canvas and with Deborah's revision you was convinced of acceptance, even in longhand - such are the vain hopes of the devoted scribe.

Of course you failed again and this your first real fling at journalism died the natural death it deserved. And never again did you ever ask anyone to revise your work. And what did you want to be a journalist for anyway? Surely you had seen enough of newspaper movies to show you the rat race it really was: American talkies like *Front Page, Scandal Sheet* and *Hi Nellie,* seen in your single days and not yet forgotten. First you had wanted to be a film projectionist; mad about the job you was but never got a start. And here you was cottared now with a wife and bairn and still mucking out byres and feeding nowt and dreaming about this never never world that still eluded you from far off. You didn't realize it then but you were actually on the threshold of a venture that was going to cost you forty years of struggle and frustration and heartbreak before the final joy of achievement. Now you have reached that goal you can look back with pride on your perseverance against all odds, with all the doors slammed in your face; with no education, no influence, no backing, no money, nothing but bare-fisted determination, yet with these handicaps you had literally battered down editors' doors and had their readers look at your hack - even beyond the first paragraph, right to the end, and then it reached the editor's desk. Eventually you had them print the stuff, in full detail, not a comma changed or

269

an exclamation mark - though spelling wasn't so good. When you read the galley proofs it was the greatest thrill of your life; like a young mother with her first baby . . . something else you wouldn't have missed for all the tears it cost you.

And now you can tell the world about these two men and their boat; those cavemen in their animal skins with their thonged axes, hulling out their canoe from a fallen tree . . . you can tell it after forty years of crying in the wilderness, and people can read about the inspiration for one of your very first unpublished articles; an article that never saw the light and couldn't be reconstructed because you have forgotten the details.

But old Forbie Tait never lived to see your success. 'The mere fact o being alive killed him in time,' just as he had said, and he was gathered at last with his brother farmers in the kirkyard at Peatriggs. But you knew what his comment would have been at the stable sessions in the evenings at Kingask, had he lived to see his old stockman in book form: 'By gum, them that lives langest sees the maist ferlies!'

Badgie Summers wasn't long after you at Kingask either, only two more years. When Forbie asked him to bide on the first time Badgie said he hadn't made up his mind, but Forbie didn't give him the usual second chance, and that was the end of Badgie at Kingask.

Dark Encounter

The old woman in the kitchen box-bed was in her eighty-ninth year and totally blind from cataract. Twenty years earlier, when the infection first troubled her, an operation could have saved her eyesight, but Liza Boad wouldn't hear of it, and lived out her life in total darkness. Worse still, she had lost the use of her legs, but for a few steps at a time, holding on to somebody for support, and now lay in bed day and night. She knew each member of her family by their voices, by the feel of their hands - even to biting into them gently to feel the knuckles on their fingers, and kissing and fondling each hand as a way of expressing her pleasure at having their presence by her bedside. The smaller, softer hands of her grandchildren were also familiar to her, and smaller still the hands of her great-grandchildren, presented to her from time to time over the bed, still in the arms of their mothers, Liza's grand-daughters, while her seeing hands caressed the baby's face and head, until she got the shape and size of it. 'So that's little Bella than,' she would habber, 'my but she's growin',' and the baby's cheek would be held up to her withered lips for a kiss.

Liza's own childbearing had extended over a period of some twenty years, which gave an extreme of ages, from the oldest to the very youngest of her offspring. Some of her family were dead, while others were abroad, and seldom home, and some of her grandchildren she had never seen. She had outlived her husband by nearly twenty years at Stonelairs, the small farm now worked by Sinclair Boad, her youngest son, the only one of her four sons still a bachelor, and he had been on the farm since the day of his birth nearly fifty years ago. It had even been settled by the family that Sinclair would get the farm when his mother died, since he had given most of his life in looking after her and keeping the home together, and maybe denied himself a wife in the process.

Since her husband died there had been only Liza and her son on the farm, Sinclair doing all he could for his failing mother, which hadn't been so bad so long as she had the use of her limbs, even in her semi-blindness, but had got steadily worse with her fading eyesight, and worse than ever now that she was bedridden. Sometimes Liza's married daughters spent their holidays at Stonelairs, which was a blessing for Liza and a godsend for Sinclair, since their menfolk helped him in the fields, while their wives caught up with the housework. In the long winters of their absence Sinclair managed on his own, even to dish-washing and laundry, besides cooking a spartan diet and carrying his mother to the earth-closet in the garden, all after a day's work in the fields and attending to the cattle in the byres, relieved at times by one or other of his

271

sisters or a niece who came at a week-end to tidy up and cook a proper meal.

The most frequent visitor was Thelma Rae, Sinclair's oldest sister, and sometimes she brought Effie with her, her eldest daughter and niece of Sinclair, relieving him from a lot of his household chores; and field and stable duties also when Effie was there, for she was a sonsie limmer and worked like a horse beast. And all because Liza said she couldn't afford a kitchen lass, though her real reason was that she was afraid Sinclair would take up with a serving quine; especially if she was a bonnie lassie, and since she couldn't be sure of engaging an ugly one in her blindness she wouldn't take the risk. Not that any woman is that ugly in the eye of the male, but that wasn't Liza's way of looking at things, and a word like 'unattractive' for her simply meant ugly.

But the day came eventually when Sinclair told his mother he simply couldn't go on doing a double job and she would just have to engage a servant lass for the kitchen work. He wasn't getting any younger he insisted and was sore tired out at the end of a day without having to do housework. His other complaint might have been that he had no relaxation, no social contacts; never a dance or a concert to break the monotony, where he might meet a woman he had a fancy for, who might become his wife, something his mother would just have to accept, though most of it had passed him bye and he thought less about it as he grew older. But Sinclair never discussed these things with his mother, though each suspected they knew each other's thoughts about it and left the fly on the wall. Not that Sinclair didn't have his feelings about sex, and his liking for a dram, which was mostly confined to market days, or the occasional Saturday night in town when he could leave his mother in the care of one of his visiting sisters; and these were the only occasions that Sinclair came home the worse of drink, raving a bit about his old mother being a tether about his neck and him not having a chance to look for a kitchie-deem, though he never went as far as calling her a wife. But as the effect of the drink wore off Sinclair settled down again to his old routine and listening to the wireless, which was about his only diversion from the grindstone in his daily life. But even his sisters had a soft spot for Sinclair in his dilemma, and not a little of their sympathy, in a quiet sort of way; never hostile in their mother's presence, especially Thelma, who had sons of her own she wouldn't like to see in the same position, tied to her mothering petticoats.

Liza pondered the problem and turned from one side to the other in the darkness of her prison bed. During the long lonely days when her son was in the fields, and the quiet sleepless nights that had no ending in light, Liza pondered, till finally she had the answer, and she told Sinclair he could fee a kitchen-maid on condition that she slept with her in the box-bed. It was a crafty thought, and the full force of it nearly knocked Sinclair sideways when she told him, for it had never dawned on him that she was afraid he would take up with any lass she fee-ed for kitchie-deem. But he raised no objection, glad of her consent, and at length between them a maid was engaged to look after her.

But it didn't last long, for Liza gave the quine such a heckling from the box-bed while Sinclair was in the fields, that she soon left them, scarcely leaving

272

her imprint in the box-bed. Another girl was found but again Liza harried her from daylight till dark, hounding her from chore to chore, and even in the box-bed, till the quine told Sinclair she couldn't put up with his mother and left them. They had no better results with a third maid, though she stayed a bit longer than the others, with some remonstration from Sinclair, reprimanding his mother for her behaviour in front of the girl, who was sometimes in tears, because she didn't like sleeping in the box-bed, and in her absence Liza said it wasn't like him to let a quine come between him and his poor blind mother, but that she knew all along this would happen. Sinclair began to wonder if he wasn't worse off with a serving quine than he had been without one, and in the solace of the thought he wasn't all that disappointed when the third lass never returned from her Sunday off to sleep in the box-bed.

There had been moments of bliss when Sinclair could whistle at the plough on the thought of it; the new freedom he could enjoy even though youth had left him, with a quine to look after his mother while he did a bit of galavanting - but the prospect was short-lived and he was soon back at his mother's bedside, never sure if he was taken with the quine that had just left, for they were never long enough about the premises to find out.

It was after the third quine had left Stonelairs that Thelma offered her daughter Effie to Liza her grandmother as kitchen help. Effie was out of service at the time and Thelma offered her with the best of intentions, not the least of them out of sympathy for her brother Sinclair, to relieve his dual responsibility, since the alternative of feeing a loon to help him on the grun would have added to their burden, providing bed and board, and was no real solution to the problem. But with Effie on the job Sinclair had a servant lass who stood up to Liza Boad and her blind bullying, and was still on the job at the end of a whole month, though she flatly refused to sleep in the box-bed, and just as well for Liza that she didn't, because for sheer bulk, lying at the back, she would have heaved her frail old grandmother on to the stone floor.

But strangely enough, when Effie Rae came to do the housework at Stonelairs the tyranny ceased, and old blind Liza left the quine alone to do almost as she pleased. Maybe this was what the old woman wanted, an ill-faured creature like her grand-daughter, Effie Rae, who would be no attraction for Sinclair, and being a close relative would also keep them apart. She remembered Effie from the days of her sight, but from time to time, maybe just to reassure herself, Liza would call the quine from her kitchen duties to kneel by the bed, and the old woman would caress her face fondly with her sensitive fingers, which gave the unsuspecting Effie the idea that her grandmother adored her, and she smiled and giggled while the soft feeling hands prodded over her face. Liza in her mind's eye shaped out Effie's big flat nose, wide cheek bones, broad protruding mouth and buck teeth, small piggish eye sockets and tiny ears close to the sides of her man-sized head, then ran her fingers through the floss of dry colourless hair, and over her haunched, masculine shoulders - thoroughly convinced there was nothing here for Sinclair, what though her eyes should gleam like diamonds, her teeth like pearl, because

273

colour was the only thing that baffled Liza. But she was sure there was no enticement for Sinclair her son in such a framework. Then Liza would withdraw her groping hands and the lively Effie would rise up and get back to her housework, her podgy face wrinkled in smiles.

But Effie was not illiterate, for she could read the newspapers, and sometimes read to her grandmother by the bedside in the evenings when the lamp was lit, a service for which Liza was extremely grateful, in that it passed the time for her, besides keeping her in touch with the outside world. Effie even suggested that her grandmother should take up the braille, but Liza said it was too late in life for her to be bothered with it. But Effie had a new portable radio, which she set by the bedside, and Liza could listen to it for hours while Effie busied herself in byre and kitchen.

But Liza had not reckoned with Effie's man hunger, nor her son's moral weakness, and within a few months Sinclair and her granddaughter, uncle and niece, were sleeping in the same bed and enjoying each other. Nor did Liza know of Effie's illegitimate child, born to her while in former service, now in the care of Thelma her mother, one of Liza's great-grand-daughters she had never caressed with her searching fingers. It was one of the skeletons in the family cupboard that had never rattled in Liza's hearing, nor had Thelma divulged the secret, fearing perhaps that her mother would have rejected Effie had she known of it, though the rest of the family, including Sinclair, had known since the child was born.

Effie wasn't an attractive woman by any standards; almost totally lacking in feminine qualities, with a dull-witted brain and an impudent tongue, thick muscular legs and arms, and yet some lad had thought fit to make her a mother, and a quite capable mother she had turned out to be, though the lad hadn't married her. Now in her thirties she had almost given up hope of getting a man, though her hunger for sex still whittled at her marrow, with any man who thought fit to give her a second look, or who came conveniently within her influence. But she was as strong as the proverbial ox and a willing worker in house or byre, and old blind Liza was satisfied that in her wisdom she had made a good choice with Effie Rae to assist her trauchled son.

Effie wasn't long before she was with child to her uncle, the wife-starved bachelor who had been a willing partner in her wiles of seduction, performed in the old woman's world of darkness. But Thelma's sharper eyes were quick enough to observe her daughter's stoutness, though the build of the quine made it easier for her to hide it from strangers.

'What's this ye've been up till?' Thelma asked her daughter, out of hearing of her own mother in the box-bed, 'Ye're gettin affa stoot!'

'Oh naething, mither,' Effie replied, trying to put her mother off, 'I'm jist puttin on a bit of weight; there isn't all that much tae do here and plenty of good meat.'

'Weel weel,' her mother retorted, not all that sure of her ground, 'ye're puttin it a' on in the same place, that's what puzzles me.'

But if Thelma had her suspicions she said nothing at the moment to her brother on the subject, though she might have noticed how he was trying to avoid her searching glances.

'My mither noticed my condition the day,' Effie told Sinclair in bed.

'What did she say?'

'Oh, jist that I was gettin fat in the wrang place, but she's nae sure yet ye see. And when she is sure she'll jist hae tae get used tae things as they are.'

'Couldn't ye get rid o't?' Sinclair enquired.

'No Sinclair, I've told ye that afore. I dinna want tae get rid o my bairn. Haein a bairn's nae a' that bother for me; it's easier and healthier than an abortion I shid think.'

'But the scandal quine: I'm nae yer proper man; I'm yer uncle.'

'Then what are ye doin in my bed Sinclair Boad? Ye ocht tae be ashamed o yersel, takin advantage o a poor innocent quine.'

'Look wha's speakin. Innocent did ye say? Ye dinna ken the meanin o the word. And what if something is wrang wi the bairn? Ower inbred or something, seein we're close related.'

'We'll jist hae tae tak that chance Sinclair my loon; there's naething we can do aboot it noo.'

'Wheest quine, mither will hear ye!'

'Lie doon and sleep than. Forget aboot the scandal till it comes.'

Effie covered herself to the ears with the blankets and was soon snoring. Sinclair lay awake until daybreak.

As time wore on, however, Effie's condition became so apparent that she couldn't hide it from anybody, except her blind grandmother, who had never thought of lowering her hands to Effie's breasts, and if she had Effie would have got on to her feet quick enough; but the fact was that Liza had long since ceased to caress her, convinced of her integrity as a trustworthy grand-daughter. And while others of the family were aware of what was happening a sort of conspiracy was contrived among themselves to hide it from the old woman. To keep the ageing Liza in ignorance of what was taking place under her very nose seemed the most important thing for all of them to do. After all she was still the mistress and Sinclair the heir apparent, and it wouldn't do to disillusion her about her supposedly dutiful son, especially when the will had to be considered, for they couldn't have her changing that. And besides, the shock of the thing might kill her prematurely.

Thelma Rae, Effie's mother, perhaps realising this, did her best as ringleader to get all the others sworn to secrecy, all of her brothers and sisters and in-laws when they came visiting, and their grown-up children besides, each confiding in the other, but mostly with Sinclair as the scapegoat and Effie the innocent victim of his lust. In fact some of them secretly scorned Sinclair as having taken advantage of his dull-witted niece, though they never said as much in his hearing. Sinclair avoided his older sister as much as he could, or stayed in the kitchen when she was about, where she couldn't accuse him in front of their mother. But eventually he had to face her and confess his guilt, with a good swig of whisky to make it easier, for Sinclair was finding solace in drink.

'My God Sinclair,' Thelma stormed, 'this is a hell of a state of affairs. Yer ain niece! I thocht ye wad of had mair sense, a grown man. If I'd kent this was goin tae happen I wad never hae latten the lassie come here in the first place. Good God, whatever cam ower ye man?'

But Sinclair wasn't totally unprepared for his sister's accusation. Worry and guilt and shame had sharpened his wit, and fortified with John Barleycorn he gave her an answer she never expected, nor would have given him credit for in his sober senses; an answer that stunned and surprised her, leaving her almost speechless with anger.

'Maybe ye're nae sae innocent as ye look,' Sinclair retorted. 'Ye've kent for years that I've been desperate for a wife, and when ye saw yer chance ye sent Effie here tae tempt me, and I can assure ye she was a willin partner, and she's jist as guilty as I am. In fact she led me on, and ye seem tae forget it's nae the first time she's had a bairn ahin the dyke, so she's got good experience. I think ye sent her here tae get her bairned tae gie ye mair say at Stonelairs than ye are entitled till; maybe even get oor mither tae change the will after ye've had me disgraced, and you bein the auldest o the family, if onything happened tae me, or if mither disowned me, ye could be the next in line, with family consent, and I ken that man o yours has had an eye on the place for years, thinkin maybe that though ye was a woman body ye was more entitled to it than me.'

'Weel weel,' Thelma reasoned, 'that's all the thanks I get for tryin tae shield ye. Ye ought tae think shame o yersel. How wad I want tae disgrace ye when I'm tryin hard tae keep a' thing secret frae oor mither . . . tell me that?'

'Maybe it suits yer purpose, or tae shield yer quine . . . bidin yer time. But whatever ye say it maks nae difference noo, the harm's done, and it canna be helped. But ye better haud yer tongue for Effie's sake, if ye want me tae treat her weel and bring up her bairn.'

Thelma almost spat at her brother, but for the sake of Effie, and perhaps to shield her own conscience, she said no more, but turned and left him, for maybe Sinclair, in his desperation had touched a guilty nerve.

Everybody seemed to hope that old Liza would die before the bastard child was born, or that Effie would somehow lose it beforehand and conceal the crime from her grandmother. It was easy enough to deceive her at the moment, but what would happen after the child was born? How could they stifle its cries at birth? What could they say to the family doctor when he came to deliver Effie? Could they shamelessly take him into their confidence and blame some innocent bystander as the guilty father, leaving Sinclair in the clear, for the doctor well knew they were not man and wife. He had brought Effie into the world from the womb of her mother. Maybe it would be better to hire a private doctor in the toon, who knew nothing about them, but then again he would have to be kept away from Liza in the kitchen bed - unless they used the front door, then he wouldn't have to pass through the kitchen. Still it would be better to take their own doctor into their confidence, by reason of not upsetting the old woman, which he would understand, who ever the father was.

276

Finally, on Thelma's advice, Sinclair agreed to plead ignorance with their own doctor, swearing blind they didn't know who the father was, Effie stubbornly refusing to divulge who the guilty party might be, even to the doctor - above all to the doctor, whatever his suspicions might be. Not that the doctor might ask, but better be prepared in case he should, for the whole thing was a blatant embarrassment to all of them except Effie, who didn't seem to care who was the father of her child, or what anybody thought about it; or maybe she just hadn't the sense to care, though she wasn't a fool either.

Meanwhile Liza was well content, for up to the very end of her pregnancy Effie had attended well to her grandmother, and the old woman had never seemed so pleased with herself in her blindness for years. The only thing that annoyed her was Effie's sudden craze for playing the wireless full blast in the ben-room, preparing for the day when it would have to be used to drown the cries of a howling infant, just to get Liza used to the occasional sound of it, despite her protests.

When Effie's time was come for delivery Thelma told her mother that Effie had the 'flu or something, and she would be attending to Liza's needs herself for a few days, an explanation that Liza accepted with some concern, enquiring daily at Thelma for Effie's welfare.

Effie's pregnancy was terminated behind closed doors, the family doctor complying with Thelma's earnest request not to disturb Liza in the kitchen, and a fire was lit in the ben-room to provide hot water, all with as little bustle as possible for Liza's sake. Effie stifled her moaning in the pillows when the pains seized her; not that it was all that difficult for Effie, seeing it wasn't her first child, and she had an animal's strength in childbearing, almost scorning the assistance of a doctor, but for the breaking of the umbilical cord, which she wasn't sure about, and the loudness of her mother's protests when she suggested self-delivery. But it was cheap at the price Effie considered secretly, in her craving for sex, and out of good manners or embarrassment the doctor never asked her who had taken advantage of her supposed maidenhood.

And when the bairn cried in the ben-room and Liza enquired about the noise Thelma told her it was a play on the wireless Effie wanted to listen to, and they kept the doors closed to deafen the sound. Within a few days Effie was up and about again and sniggering over her grandmother as if nothing unusual had taken place, while her infant daughter slept soundly in the ben-room.

Visitors were a problem, especially a neighbour body who wanted to see Sinclair about a stray stirk or the loan of a farm implement, and expecting to be asked inside to enquire for his ailing mother, for nowadays Sinclair held them at the back kitchen door or talked to them in the middle of the close, wondering how much they knew or suspected, or if their visit was merely curiosity. Effie had kept out of sight of most of the neighbours during the latter stages of her pregnancy, but sometimes when Sinclair wasn't about she had to go out to the vanman for groceries, bread or meat, and he was bound to notice her condition. There was also the postman on his bicycle, when she ran into him unexpectedly at the corner of the milkhouse; and what the vanmen and the

277

postie told them the neighbours tried to confirm, though they found it difficult to pierce the screen of secrecy surrounding Stonelairs. But whatever their suspicions it would be a long time or they saw Effie's bairn running about in the close, though the time would surely come when the little girl would reveal herself, though Effie considered there was little sense in worrying about that for the present. She would think of some likely story when the time came. Meanwhile she kept the infant securely in the ben-room, drowning her cries with the wireless, and dried her nappies at the peat fire, right in front of her grandmother's bed, though Liza was none the wiser; no more than the neighbours from what they spied on the clothes line.

But as the months flew by and the child grew bigger it wasn't so easy to deceive old Liza. When the creature wailed in the dead of night, cutting a tooth or because of a colic, too late for the wireless to be blamed, Sinclair held a pillow over its piteous little mouth, tempted to leave it there longer than was necessary, to stifle this awful spectre that now haunted his conscience day and night. He had no love for his child that was born of lust, and but for Effie's hysteria, and her powerful arms, he was sorely tempted to suffocate the child with the pillow. How could anybody know what had caused its death - or so he imagined - so long as he had the will to do it. But Effie got out of bed in the worst of cases and walked the floor with her bairn, soothing it with a dumb-tit, until the child fell asleep and lay quietly beside her.

Effie had registered the birth and gave the child her own maiden name of Rae, with Nina as a christian name, and soon they would have to get it vaccinated to comply with compulsory law. Secretly Sinclair wished it would die, for it gave him no pride as a father, rather the opposite and degraded him. But Nina was a hardy wee girl who took after her mother constitutionally; and not a little in looks, with strong mongolian features, and throve every day forthwith, sucking at her mother's breast, sometimes staring at her reluctant father with his own blue eyes in reflection, which sort of reconciled him to his fate and he smiled in spite of himself.

But Sinclair was restless in his sleep and brooded at his work over the evil that assailed him, indulging himself strongly in whisky to drown his sorrows. And all the time he felt that the eyes of his neighbours were upon him, wondering why both lums were now reeking at Stonelairs, both but-and-ben, kitchen and ben-room, when only one had smoked before, unless he had flitted his mother ben the hoose. But Effie insisted that she must still have a fire in the bedroom to keep the bairn warm, whatever the neighbours thought. What could the neighbours think of him having a bairn by his niece? Some of them were bound to suspect he was the guilty father. But he had been wrong about Thelma - presuming she had been hatching a plot to undermine him with his mother, and he could see now she had been doing her best to cover up for him, and maybe to protect Effie.

Sinclair tried sleeping in his own bedroom again, off the kitchen where his mother lay, but within a week of celibacy Effie was tempting him back to the ben-room, hungry for sex, for it was something you could hardly speak of as

278

love. He was torn between guilt and desire, good and evil, but between Effie's hips again he forgot the consequences, ecstasy stronger than will. For a time they practised evasion, but eventually in her passion Effie clung to him until he spent himself in her child-hungry womb. For Sinclair it was a glorious moment of forgetfulness, but in the aftermath he almost cried out in despair, his thoughts a pin-cushion of guilt and foreboding, blending his sleepless lids with the light of day, while Effie snored at his back.

Out in the lonely fields by day, with God as his witness, castigating his guilt, Sinclair would reform his principles, resolving that when bedtime came he would be steel-willed and unyielding; but as the hour approached, and his mother fell asleep, temptation seized him and he yielded, stealing along the passage to the ben-room, where the bed was warm and Effie was waiting for him, elation setting caution at defiance. She now had Nina in a crib, loaned by one of her sisters, which seemed more civilised and natural; more like man and wife Sinclair thought, mitigating his guilt and making his crime seem more legitimate, like God had winked almost, and turned his back on sin, a compromise with the devil. Now they had the bed to themselves again, and when Effie opened her great hips to him Sinclair was powerless to resist. For a glorious half-hour he enjoyed her amorous convulsions; oblivious to everything but the thrill of the rapturous present, and in the elation of the moment he spent himself in the heat of her desire. Even the aftermath seemed more congenial and he fell asleep delightfully exhausted; until the grey of morning brought the devil to his window, demanding the wages of sin, doused in the rim of the whisky glass or the day could be faced.

How long could it last? How long would it be or the devil had his soul completely? How long would it be before Effie was pregnant again? Oh God! And what would be the consequences this time? Thelma had made it clear that if it happened again she would take Effie away from Stonelairs, and but for her helpless mother would have done so in the first place. It wasn't a threat that worried Sinclair; rather the opposite if his sister was going to relieve him of a dual burden - temptation and its consequences, God and the devil at the keyhole of his soul.

But the problem was getting too big even for Thelma, for how could she harbour Effie and her two bairns by Sinclair - if there was another one - besides the one she had already? In which case Sinclair thought maybe he could defy his sister and claim his right to Effie as his wife; not lawfully of course, nor in the eyes of the neighbours - and then the fear of incest frightened him. Even the Law had business in what you did in your own home when it came to that, and there was also the thought of imprisonment. All of which made Sinclair reach more often for the whisky bottle, though it brought but temporary relief. Nearly a bottle a day he was now consuming and it wasn't enough, and even Effie was getting concerned over his drinking, perhaps without realising she was partly the cause of it.

But Sinclair reached a stage when he realised he couldn't exist without Effie; at once his torment and his salvation, even though her very presence overshadowed him with guilt. His life seemed worthless in either case, overwhelmed by sex and drink, and he was losing interest in the farm, neglecting the work that had formerly been a sense of pride in his life. And what if Nina should prove to be imbecilic? He had heard it said that even cousins could have bairns that were malformed or mentally defective, or both; too inbred, so what could he look for with his niece? Nina wasn't old enough yet to see what she was going to be like, but if she turned out to be a slivering idiot he would go for his gun.

Within nine months of her delivery Effie was pregnant again. She reasoned with Sinclair that they had managed last time and they would manage again. What the hell did it matter how many bairns they had, especially if they were all as healthy and sturdy as Nina was, and physically at least Sinclair was bound to agree with her on that score. Effie insisted that so long as she looked after her bairns properly it was nobody's business about Sinclair and her being uncle and niece. And besides, old Liza couldn't live all that much longer to know anything about her illegitimate grandchildren, though 'ill-gotten' was the hyphenated term that Effie used. She sometimes thought Liza was a bit dottled already, the things she spoke about, her thoughts far away in the past, and speaking in her sleep to folk that were dead. Effie was callous in her reasoning Sinclair thought, and the ethics of law never entered into it. Incest was a word she scarcely understood and when Sinclair spoke of going to prison she giggled in disbelief, merely asking what was going to happen to her and the bairns while he was away. But to be fair to Effie it must be said that she performed the role of wife and mother admirably, almost with grace and capability, belying her rough exterior, but she had got hold of the wrong end of the stick.

By the time old Liza died Effie was big with her second child to her uncle. And Sinclair couldn't face his sister in the open nowadays unless he was drunk, while Thelma and her man both stared at him speechless; merely shaking their heads and almost hissing in anger, while Sinclair hiccupped over his whisky bottle and leered at them from the armchair beside his mother's bed. They dare not say anything in the hearing of his mother, and Sinclair clung to her for protection, determined not to leave the kitchen while his sister and her man were in the house. The others he could abide once in a while, his brothers and sisters who came in bye to see their mother; none of them as brazen or outspoken as Thelma, and because the affair didn't concern them so closely they never mentioned it, whatever they said among themselves in Sinclair's absence. Nor could they afford to snub Effie, who now assumed the part of mistress at Stonelairs, none daring to challenge her flagrant authority; least of all her mother, who now fitted into the scene where Sinclair had imagined her to be, accusing her of usurping his claim as rightful heir to the farm, an insinuation she had denied bitterly. An atmosphere of tension pervaded in the family, a smouldering collaboration teetering on flame and fused with explosive, subdued in the presence of approaching death, when Liza had a stroke that robbed her of speech.

And while her great-grandmother-cum-grandmother lay in deathly silence

Nina began to lisp her first syllables of speech. Her blubbering efforts while she stood in her crib, her mongolian features strong in resemblance of her mother, were mistaken by Sinclair as the first symptoms of what he dreaded, that she would turn out to be a mumbling, half-witted monstrosity, a conjecture enlivened by his intake of alcohol and the inflamed condition of his thinking. Yet he had the sense not to mention his suspicions to Effie, perhaps fearing her reaction, if she understood the full implication of his fears. Strong though she was in her womanhood Sinclair reckoned that the shock might be too much for her while she was still carrying his second child, and whatever it might turn out to be there was no need for making matters worse. He would say nothing about it until after the birth, if even then, but perhaps would let her find out for herself, if Thelma didn't forestall him, for Sinclair felt certain his sister would notice it first. What his second child would be like worried him even more, raising his consumption of whisky to a full bottle a day, which kept him running back and forth on his bicycle to the emporium, and the way things were going the day would come when Effie would have to fetch it for him, to satisfy his craving, and even now she complained about his drunkenness, especially when he was in such a stupor that he couldn't perform at bedtime.

Sinclair found his mother stiff and cold in the box-bed when he came through one morning from the ben-room. She had died peacefully in her sleep it seemed, without fuss or mute farewell; her sightless eyes closed forever on his guilt, though Sinclair found no solace in the thought, rather the opposite when he visualised the funeral and all the staring eyes. His crime was getting out of doors, beyond his control, with little consolation in the thought that he wouldn't have to use a pillow to silence the second child of their lust; nor turn up the radio when it yelled in the evening, nor stop Nina from crawling through to the kitchen, dreading the day when he would have to pretend to his mother that it was the dog squeaking under the table. But still in the horrors of drink he dreaded the funeral, when he would have to face a barrage of relations; their searching eyes prying into his affairs and glowering at a tearful, bloated Effie, swollen with his sin, blubbering over her departed grandmother.

Sinclair took another look at his mother, all these thoughts struggling quickly through his fuddled brain, then staggered back to the ben-room to tell Effie what had happened. Effie raised herself from the bed that creaked when she left it and went hurriedly through the passage to look at her grandmother. Then she went into hysterics, falling with her great bulk by the bedside and sprawling her arms over the dead woman, weeping in supposedly uncontrollable grief, while she took one of her grandmother's lifeless hands and rubbed it against her own tearful face, biting into the fingers that felt no pain in death. Sinclair somehow knew she would act like this, and standing behind her he also knew she could just as easily be switched off, for her grief was superficial and not of the heart. He pulled her away from the bed and got her on her feet, then told her to dress and run for somebody to get the doctor, and while Effie sat on the room bed, pulling her Cashmere stockings up to her thick sturdy thighs, Sinclair poured himself a glass of whisky and dashed it against his aching

281

throat, the bite of it hitting his palate in a quenching shower, enabling him for a moment to think more clearly.

Effie flew for a doctor, her coat fastened loosely about her, a scarf round her head, in her bauchled shoes, scrambling over the frosted furrows, nearly a mile to the nearest neighbour who had a telephone. Then Sinclair knew that his hour of triumph had come, the final chance to free himself from his burden, once and for all. His last sane thoughts were for his mares in the stable and the cattle in the byres, all waiting patiently for breakfast, duties that he used to perform before touching his own. But what he had to do now was more urgent than anything he had ever done in his life before, and it had to be done quickly and correctly while Effie was scouring the hills for a doctor, before she could return to thwart his purpose. And it wouldn't take long for the sobbing Effie to raise the dire alarm.

Sinclair threw the cork in the window sill and poured himself another glass of neat whisky. It would be his last but it would steady his jaded nerves for the final achievement. And while he gulped it down his eye caught the infant Nina still asleep in her crib; her mother's heavy, almost mongolian features clearly evident in the relaxation of sleep. Then he remembered the pillow and how easy it would be to suffocate her now and save her from a lifetime of misery, besides rubbing out the surviving evidence of his crime; this helpless creature that would carry his guilt into another generation. With a sudden stride he reached the bed, grabbed a pillow and stared down at his sleeping daughter. But indecision stiffened him in the act, drink and the devil striving with reason, the pillow hovering an inch or two from the baby's mouth, trembling in his hands, awaiting the pressure of his mighty arms. It wouldn't take long. He reckoned about three minutes to be certain, for he couldn't have the child reviving after he had gone. A few moments of convulsive consciousness, a furtive bundle struggling in his hands, then all would be still at last, while the panting Effie came stumbling over the fields.

It would be so easy to take the child with him, into oblivion; away from prying eyes and incestuous tongues. Under the sod she would be out of sight, an insubstantial memory that would eventually die, whereas alive she would restore his posthumous guilt with every day that dawned. Then he remembered the other bairn still in Effie's womb, and the only way to destroy it was to destroy Effie and wipe the slate clean. It was the master plan. But why hadn't it occurred to him sooner? So much killing in so little time. It was more than he had intended; and even with the demon whisky dancing in his veins he shrank from the prospect, this working for the devil.

First he would have to choke Nina, then load the gun and wait for Effie at the gable of the milkhouse, where she sometimes ran into the postman, only this time it would be the postman from hell; and she would come upon him unawares, unexpectedly; with no time to think poor bitch, and he would fire both barrels into her heaving belly. The rest would be easy in comparison.

But it was too much in so short a time, and making up his mind was hindering him, wasting precious minutes. By now Effie would be on her way back and he would have to hurry. Maybe this was how the devil worked; in the heat of passion, coming upon you unawares, with little time to think before the deed was done. Then the child awoke and broke his resolve, brushing away the pillow with her little hand and smiling in his face. She smiled up at him with quite lovely blue eyes, almost like his own, and he just couldn't do it . . . not now. Nina stood up in her crib and reached out for him and he threw away the pillow. This time he tilted the whisky bottle into his mouth and poured the fiery liquid down his burning throat, then dropped the bottle and ran to the kitchen, Nina crying after him.

He took a last fond, yet almost careless look at his dead mother and then burst into his bedroom. He snatched the polished, double-barrelled gun from a corner and opened the breach, held the weapon in the crook of his arm, reached up to the shelf for a box of cartridges, inserted two in the barrels and slipped a few in his pocket - in case he should change his mind and wait for Effie - then closed the gun with a snap and bolted for the back kitchen door.

There was no sign of Effie, but he could picture her coming over the fields, panting, from the nearest neighbour, and he opened the safety catch on the gun and pulled back the dogheads. Back in the house he could hear Nina yelling from her crib, crying for her mother. It would be so easy to go back into the house and blow her into kingdom come, but those blue eyes deterred him.

The collie dog eyed him from his kennel and came whining to the full length of his chain, wagging his bushy tail, expecting that Sinclair would release him for a rabbit hunt when he saw the gun. Then he barked loudly, so Effie couldn't be far away. But he must not weaken, though looking at his mother had almost broken his resolve, until the thought of all those staring eyes at the funeral restored his will to die. It was better than a lifetime of shame and guilt.

The dog was still barking, Nina still screaming from the ben-room and Sinclair's heart was beating fast. He walked in the other direction from the milkhouse, towards the gig-shed at the other end of the steading. The farm close was full of singing hens, scraping at his feet, and the barn cock stood up in the midst of them, flapped his wings and crowed 'Cock-a-doodle-doo,' all looking for breakfast, and the cooing pigeons flapped up to roost on the byre tiles, afraid of the gun.

Sinclair swung the wooden bar from its catch on the tarred door of the gig-shed, opened one half of the door and walked inside. The stable was just through the stone wall and the horses nickered friendly-like at the sound of the creaking door. The light was poor inside, for there was no window in the building, only a small skylight curtained with cobwebs, and the old gig stood at the further wall, slung from the rafters by the shafts.

On the work-bench Sinclair cut a length of binder twine from a ball, tied it in a loop and hooked it on to the triggers of the gun, then made another and bigger loop on the string for his foot. He set the butt of the gun on the earthen floor and set his right foot in the loop. He tried it for tension, making sure that the gun would go off before his foot touched the ground. He balanced himself

283

on his left foot, holding on to the bench with his free hand for support, while he held the gun firmly upright with the other. The hens were squaking and scattering in the close, and from the corner of his eye Sinclair saw Effie running to the kitchen door, likely when she heard Nina screaming, a neighbour woman at her heels, which hadn't occurred to Sinclair, and would have blundered his other plan. He put the barrel of the gun securely in his mouth, biting into it with his teeth, held on to the bench, tramped down his foot and blew his brains into the cross-trees of the old tiled gig-shed.

Effie had scarcely reached the ben-room when she heard the shot, and snatching up her bairn she ran outside. The dog was barking and the hens were cackling and the cattle lowed in the byres. Effie knew it was past milking time, but the gig-shed door was open, and the two women looked at each other and ran towards it and peered inside, through the blue smoke.

'Oh Sinclair,' Effie cried, handing her bairn to the neighbour, 'what's this ye've done to yersel?' She threw out her arms and fell beside him, careless of the spattered blood, and sobbed her heart out on his slightly quivering body, until her neighbour bent down with her free hand and pulled her away, while the mares nickered again in the stable.

The doctor's car purred into the close and the neighbour woman took him to the gig-shed, old Liza quite forgotten in the excitement, though the doctor got round to her in time.

So they had a double funeral at Stonelairs, and they buried Sinclair with his mother over her husband in the same grave. And nobody pointed a finger nor ventured a stare upon poor Effie, everybody being too much appalled by the tragedy.

So maybe Sinclair hadn't died in vain.

The Windmill

When I was a loon in short breeks I often used to meet the Oyster King on the face of the brae under the cottar hoose. I might have been on the way to Scotstoun for messages with my hurlie, or I would be pulling grass by the roadside for my rabbits when I met Mr. Royston. But in Buchan you didn't bother with real names, for if you had mentioned 'Mr. Royston' to somebody they would have said 'Oh aye, the Eyster Keeng,' thinking that you were being pan-loaf and trying to imitate the gentry. In fact you would have been lucky if you weren't laughed at and taken the size of, ridiculed and intimidated.

Mr. Royston was a big broad shouldered man in a dark blue suit, grey hat, white shirt, tie, black boots and walking cane; always dressed the same, the only thing that was sometimes different was the tie, nothing else, and as he was never untidily dressed he must have had a stock of these dark blue suits, with accessories to match, except for gloves, for he was always bare-handed, his big knuckles sticking out when he closed his hands over his staff. Except for a slight grey moustache he was clean shaven, a man in his early sixties, with a large stern face, stone grey eyes, big ears, and always chewing black sugar, so that his strong teeth were always stained, his breath smelling of liquorice.

When you met Mr. Royston the first thing he did was to put his hand in the small left hand pocket inside his jacket and gave you a few lumps of black sugar; hard, strong stuff like coal, not the soft liquorice kind that you got in straps, or in sherbet bags at the shop, and it had a bittersweet pungent taste that hung about your mouth for nearly an hour afterwards. Some of the farm workers chewed tobacco, but mostly they spat out the bree; but Mr. Royston never spat, in fact he was a gentleman, clean, good-mannered and English spoken, though he was a Scotsman just the same.

But though Mr. Royston gave most of his acquaintances a lump or two of black sugar when he met them on the road, some of them would have gone across fields a mile out of their way to avoid him. Mostly he asked at the grown-ups if they wanted black sugar, but as most of them didn't like to refuse they put it in their mouths while they spoke to him, whether they liked it or no, man or woman, well aware of its potency as a gentle bowel laxative, and hoping they would be home before it took effect. Folk thought Mr. Royston must be bothered himself with the dry-darn when he chewed that stuff all the time. Others thought it was an antidote for smoking, for he never smoked, and never drank that was heard of, though it was whispered that he had an eye for the women, especially the cottar wives round about though he always left a half-crown on the mantelshelf when he visited them, mostly during the day when their menfolks were at work in the fields, and the bairns at school, the only thing that made it look suspicious. Otherwise the women swore out that he was a proper gentleman in *that* respect, and never laid a finger on them disrespectfully, but always left something for the bairns.

Those with a guilty conscience gave Mr. Royston a wide berth, because they were afraid of his staff, for he had already clobbered a few rascals of the parish, and those he spared from the rod got the sharp edge of his virulent tongue. Oh you didn't need a minister with Mr. Royston in the parish, nor a bobby either come to that; but those who behaved themselves had nothing to fear from meeting Mr. Royston on the road, except for the black sugar, though in time the most respectful of his neighbours learned to refuse it politely and Mr. Royston took no offence.

He was the equivalent of a laird in the parish, and since he owned and worked three farms and lived in the biggest one he was entitled to that distinction, though actually his neighbours were not his tenants, except for a couple of crofters on the fringe of his small estate. Most of his neighbours were owner-occupiers, while the rest of the farms were leased from a Landowners Syndicate down there in Edinburgh.

But though the Oyster King wasn't the recognised laird he dominated the community in baronial style, and farmed his own land with such proficiency and thoroughness as to set them all an example. Barrabrae was a laird's toon to perfection, even with a glass roof over the farm close and a clock tower on the steading; a walled garden in front of the farmhouse and a belt of trees encircling it, the farmyard laid with causey blocks, most of which had been supervised by Mr. Royston himself since he came home from abroad. There were even brass nameplates on the horse carts, polished by the grieve every Saturday, after he swept the close. Most farmers just had tin plates on their carts, with their name and address painted on to them in small lettering, and if a lad had fee-ed to a place in winter, and wasn't sure where it was, arriving in the dark he would crack a spunk to let him see to read the cart signs, as there were no signposts at the road-ends, and by this means he could make sure he had come to the right place, and then he would look for the chaumer. But the cart signs at Barrabrae were etched out on the brass, like the carat stamp engraved upon a wedding ring, and the flash of a match merely brightened it into a glitter, so that the lads couldn't read the name-plates on the carts at Barrabrae.

Mr. Royston also had first-class harness, and the lads took some pride in keeping it bright and shining, both for cart and plough, and their sturdy Clydesdales filled their collars and were well fed and groomed. Even the roots of the fencing posts were tarred or creosoted before they were driven into the ground, to preserve them against rot, and the heavy wooden gates into the parks were also painted regularly, and all the doors and windows about the house and steading, sometimes changing the colour from year to year. The copings on all the stone dykes round the fields were pointed with cement, to prevent the cattle from knocking them down, and every park had a watering trough, or one built

286

into the dyke that served two parks, and fitted with ball-cocks to save water, the one scarce commodity at Barrabrae.

Mr. Royston had been a man of the world, well travelled, and had brought back souvenirs from his journeys abroad: paintings and antiques, which were hung and displayed in the farmhouse, treasures from Australia, New Zealand and the East Indies, where Mr. Royston had amassed a fortune in pearl fishing, having been inspired as a boy by the voyages of Captain Cook, and that was why the folk called him the Oyster King. He had grown up as a barfit loon in Scotstoun, a whaling port on the north-east shoulder of Scotland, but instead of joining the whalers in Greenland waters the boy Royston sought the warmer climate of the South Seas, embarking on a China Clipper when he left school at fourteen. He learned the art of pearl-fishing and became one of the richest merchants in the trade. At one time he owned three luggers, manned by native pearl-divers, and a sixty-ton schooner, which he captained himself, for carrying stores. He lost the schooner when she hit the Pender Reef, when he and his crew just had time to clamber into the rigging before the boat was awash, and they later escaped in the small boat to Freemantle, on the mainland of Western Australia, where Mr. and Mrs. Royston resided at the time. When he retired from pearl fishing the Roystons returned to Scotstoun, when he bought the estate of Barrabrae, where he had herded cattle as a barfit loon, and was now the most respected farmer in the locality.

Folk in the Bogside said he whipped his native pearl-fishers when they refused to dive and fed them on handfuls of rice, and that was why they feared his cane when he settled at home, because he was an adept hand at using it, as Jock McGee could well testify, when Mr. Royston caught him leathering his mother. Jock couldn't sit down for days afterwards, and he hid himself under the straw in the barn when he saw the Oyster King coming to visit his mother. The croft was on the Barrabrae estate, and Jock and his mother carried it on after her husband's death. Jock was a 'Coon' to Mr. Royston, as was everybody else who offended him, and they said that was what he called his pearl-divers in the South Seas, 'Bluddy Coons'.

But for all that Mr. Royston was kind to his cottar folk, and anyone who called at the farmhouse never departed empty-handed, but was always treated to a bag of biscuits or sweeties from Mrs. Royston, herself a Bogside quine, and if you worked casual on the farm, like harvesting or gathering potatoes, after supper in the farmhouse Mr. Royston was always standing at the back kitchen door when you left and slipped a half-crown into your hand, over and above your wages.

Besides the farms Mr. Royston owned property in the town, and every year at Christmas time he sent a horseman with a cart loaded with a sack of potatoes and a chicken for each of his tenants. Now it so happened, in the year of which I write, Mr. Royston's potato crop was a failure, and he had to buy potatoes from one of his neighbours for his tenants in Scotstoun. He bought the potatoes from Geordie Sang, a bit of a scoundrel who farmed in the Reisk of Dams, and he told his foreman to weigh out some second-rate orra tatties for the toonsfolk, and he kept his better samples for a steeper price in a scarce market. Some of his tenants complained to Mr. Royston that their potatoes had been poor quality this year, and a great many of them rotten, and though it had been a poor year for the tubers Mr. Royston had paid for the best, and there were good fresh potatoes to be had if you paid for them. It was then he realised what Sang had been up to and he told Mrs. Royston he would thrash that coon within an inch of his life, and though the woman was worried she knew it was useless trying to stop him. So he went after his cheating neighbour in a great rage, his silver-mounted stick swinging in the air.

I met Mr. Royston on the brae at the Reisk, and that day he never offered me the customary lump of black sugar; in fact he hardly noticed me pulling clover for my rabbits, but walked straight past, slashing his stick on the long grass by the roadside, his face like the sky before a thunderstorm, his step brisk and lively.

He came upon Sang in the farm close and without question or parley he thrashed him to his knees, the great stick flicking the air in sword play over his victim, the chaumer chiels afraid to interfere, despite Sang's cries for help, and his wife wringing her hands in supplication for mercy on her offending husband. 'Treat my tenants like swine you would,' cried the pearl-fisher, 'and feed them rotten potatoes, while I pay you the market price for the best. You bluddy coon,' he cried, 'that'll teach you a lesson, and if you don't call off that dog this minute I'll smash his snout so bad he won't be able to eat or bite another living creature in his life. And furthermore,' he yelled, 'if you send for the police I'll have you to court as a swindler, and I've got plenty of witnesses in the toon, waiting with their sacks of rotting potatoes.' And then Mr. Royston straightened his hat and stamped out of the farm close, one of the workmen holding on to the dog, growling at his departure, while the rest of them ran to pick up their master, and his wife prepared a soft seat for him in the kitchen.

'My God he'll pay for this yet,' Sang muttered, as they helped him to the kitchen door; 'I wunna get the bobby but I'll hae my revenge some day!'

Now it was a fact that despite his wealth and great influence in the district, Royston was dependent on Sang for every drop of drinking water on the Home Farm. Maybe that was why, when he returned from thrashing Sang he stopped and looked at the windmill in Sang's field. Then it occurred to him that he should have thought of this before his onslaught on Sang, but in the heat of anger it had escaped him. Now the reality of the thought stopped him in his tracks and he stared at the windmill, revolving slowly on the face of the brae. But 'the mistakes of wilful men must be their schoolmasters,' as Shakespeare says, and Royston realised the truth of it, for he was now in a predicament that walled him in all round. What if Sang should stop the windmill and deprive him of his water supply? Royston was more afraid of this than he was of Sang going to the police, though even there Royston would have been punished for taking the law into his own hands. Yet this didn't worry him so much as what might happen with the windmill, and he cursed himself for his rashness and lack of foresight. But maybe it wouldn't occur to Sang that he had his enemy by the throat; that by putting the brake on the windmill he could have his revenge on Royston, thirsting him into submission, or at least an apology. Royston went home with his brain on overtime, striving for a solution to his problem.

A day or two passed, and as nothing happened to the water supply at Barrabrae, Royston realised that the vital stroke of genius hadn't yet occurred to Sang, nor apparently had anyone suggested it to him out of sympathy in his quarrel with the Oyster King; maybe because they feared Royston more than they disliked Sang, for Sang wasn't popular with his neighbours, and most of them would have given him his own way just to get him hanged, if he was foolish enough to put his head in a noose. Royston was respected, thereby gaining a point over his adversary. The neighbours knew that Royston was honest, upright and generous, whereas Sang was a cunning cheat, something that Royston had just discovered in his potato deal. Sang would have stoned you out of his parks looking for teuchats' eggs, or sent the dog at you, or he would have cheated your father out of a week's pay if he thought he could get away with it, especially if your father couldn't count money and your mother had stuck up for him and reminded Sang of the deficiency. On the other hand, if anybody was in serious trouble they consulted Mr. Royston; even running after him if they saw him on the road with his stick, when he would lean with both hands on the silver-mounted tip and listen to the tale of woe from crofter or cottar, and sometimes even by the bigger farmers, and then he would set his lawyer or an estate agent or whoever was required to deal with the problem, and in the worst cases paid the expenses from his own pocket. It wasn't unknown for him to send his horse carts to flit a poor cottar who was in straits and couldn't afford to pay for it, so the poorer folks had a lot to thank Mr. Royston for.

So you could say that Royston had more friends in the parish than Sang had, but though you listened to their talk about the potato affair in chaumer or at market, or even at the kirk on a Sunday, you couldn't really make out whose side they were on - but one thing was sure, nobody had mentioned the windmill. Maybe because they weren't dependent on it, or directly affected by its use, the thought had never entered their easy-going minds - a factor which gave Royston a breathing space to prepare for the day when it did, and whispered it in Sang's ear, if he didn't think on it first himself.

Royston looked a long time at the windmill that evening as he came down the road from Sang's place. It stood in the middle of Sang's park, a latticed structure of steel about twenty feet high, with a pump house at the base and a giant wheel on top, fitted with blades to catch the wind, and a huge tail to vary direction if the wind should change, like the vane on a weathercock, but much larger, with the name of SAMSON printed across it in great white letters. On windy days the bladed wheel spun rapidly, while the great tail darted back and forth like a kite on a string, vibration rocking the latticed pylon supporting the mechanism, the driving shaft down the centre working up and down feverishly, while in the shed at the bottom the pump churned the excess water to foam as it gushed down the overflow, and when the drain spilled over it flooded the pump-house floor and ran down the field, a fearful waste of precious water in a dry spell and a danger of wrecking the windmill. On windy days like this Royston walked up to the mill and applied the brake, tightening the rope on a wall bracket that slowed the wheel, or stopped it completely in extreme cases, reducing the risk of damage. Royston was so much concerned for the safety of the windmill that he looked after it himself, never trusting it to Sang, and this they had agreed upon when the structure was built.

Then there were days of calm when the windmill scarcely stirred; long hot days of summer sunshine that dried up the ground and drained the reserve cisterns so that everybody at Barrabrae had to save their water. At a lower elevation this never troubled Sang. He had the bottom half of the main cistern at his own steading and it was never empty, while Royston had the top half to give him gravitational flow. At the last gasp Royston would come storming up the brae and stare at the motionless windmill like the Ancient Mariner at the copper sea, then he would clamber over the dyke and walk up the footpath to the pump-shed. This year the field was in grass, but when corn or turnips were growing, Sang left a clear path for Royston. Inside Royston would stare at the stationary pumping-rod and the rusting pump into which it was inserted, and the oily, stagnant water dripping back into the main supply well under the building.

But for all his genius in planning and laying out the water scheme Royston wasn't a god; even though he was by now a town councillor where he had once run barefoot he couldn't bid the wind to rise or divert the supply of water. Years ago he had laid the supply pipe deep underfoot across a quarter of a mile on Sang's farmland, and there it must remain. He paid Sang a rent for the half-share on the stance on which the windmill stood, and the same for the site of the main cistern at the top of the brae, and for the pipeline, all settled in a land court and duly signed by both parties, and by witnesses at law, a contingency which might deter Sang from cutting off the water supply, or from interfering with the windmill, though Royston could by no means be sure of this. Now he realised fully how this incidence had placed him at Sang's mercy in a quarrel. Every time a cottar wife at Barrabrae filled her kettle; every time a cattle beast drank from a water trough; every time Royston himself took a glass of water from the kitchen tap, Sang was now staring at them all as from a mirror on the wall, his eyes hateful, his face set, licking his dry lips in a lust for revenge.

So far Royston had never found sufficient water on the Home Farm, only ditch water on a neighbour's boundary, which supplied some of his fields, and in dire straits he had been forced to cart water from one of his out-farms for his thirsting cattle beasts, though the thought of carting water for everybody about the place appalled him, and he searched his mind for some alternative.

Shortly after his quarrel with Sang, Royston kissed his wife on the cheek and said he was going for a long walk, though he didn't tell her where he was going, just as he had played down his report to her on how he had reprimanded Mr. Sang, not to give her concern, so she merely cautioned him, and told him to put on a cravat in the cold wind, though he refused to wear an overcoat. Then he took his hat and cane from the hall-rack, put a lump of black sugar in his mouth, and set off down the farm avenue.

It was mid-January and bitterly cold, but Royston was accustomed to having the elements about him and the wind in his face; good for the circulation he said and kept the blood going in a walk. Rich as he was, he never had a motor car, preferring rather the exercise that walking gave him, and he phoned the town for a horse-cab on longer journeys, though he frequently walked to Town Council meetings in Scotstoun. Sang had a motor car but Royston snubbed him on the subject and regarded it as an insubordination on Sang's part, muttering that the creature could ill afford it, adding under his breath that Sang had probably swindled somebody to get it, and after the potato affair he was more convinced of this than he had ever been.

He walked to Craigie Simpson's croft, on the edge of the heather on the Berryhill, the man who had divined for water the last time Royston had tried it. Craigie was owing payment to Royston for three loads of turnips he had bought the previous spring, and no doubt that's what he would think the big man was after, to settle the account. It was in Royston's mind, but when he saw the poverty of the place he decided he would settle it in a different manner; especially when the two urchins opened the door to his knocking, only half-clad they were and without shoes on their feet in mid-winter, and what Royston could see of the kitchen was bare and comfortless. If money was all he wanted here Royston felt he should turn on his heel and depart, for he remembered the days of his own poverty and his heart went out to the bairns. One of them said their parents were out in the byre and went over the close on her bare feet to fetch her dad. There was no smile on Craigie's face when he saw Royston, for he remembered his debt, until Royston told him he wanted him to divine for water again, and that he could forget about the price of the turnips before he even started. Craigie's face lit up. 'All right Sir,' he said, 'but as I told you last time it would be thirty feet down and under rock, you're better with the old windmill for all its bother.'

'Never mind about that,' Royston snapped, 'when can you start?'

'Tomorrow if you like.'

'Right, tomorrow then, and bring your assistant,' and Royston left five shillings for the bairns, for he knew there were more of them somewhere and departed.

Next day Craigie Simpson cut a fresh broom twig in the shape of an oversize catapult, and holding the twin ends in his hands, knuckles uppermost, the point of the stick before him, he walked slowly over the spot where he had formerly divined water at Barrabrae. As he approached the central area the point of the stick began to rise, and directly over the water vein the elevation was stronger, so that he couldn't force the stick down again, but yet it wouldn't rise to face level, as he had expected. He stopped and kicked a hole in the ground with his heel. 'There it is Mr. Royston,' he said, 'same as last time; the vein hasn't shifted, and we'll have to blast the rock to get the water.'

'This time we'll blast,' said Royston, remembering the last time he had refused, rather doubting Craigie's genius with the divining rod, though he believed what Moses had done for the Israelites.

Craigie and his assistant took off their jackets and with their spades they threw the earth aside from a wide area. They dug for days with pick and spade until they were underground below head level, then further and further until they had to shore up the crumbling walls, one of them filling the bucket at the bottom and the other pulling it up with a rope to empty it on the surface. At the end of the week they were down twenty feet in hard core but still no sign of water, and every day Royston paid them a visit to see how the work was going.

Twenty-five feet, thirty-five feet and still as dry as dust; not even moisture, a deep frightening hole where oxygen was getting thin and the men had to take shorter spells down in the well, scrambling up and down the ladders and criss-cross of planks supporting the walls. It was exhausting, nerve-wracking work, and even though Royston had given them one of his own men to help, Craigie and his man were tiring. Lack of oxygen was crippling them, now so scarce that a match wouldn't burn at the bottom of the hole. When they struck rock at last Royston lost patience however and cried out to Craigie: 'Damnit man, you'll have to give me stronger proof of water there before we blast; it doesn't look like it to me!'

Craigie came up the ladder, panting for air, and looked Mr. Royston straight in the eye. 'You want more proof, Mr. Royston?' he gasped.

'Aye,' said Royston, 'how can ye be so sure there's water down there in that dry hole?'

'Have he got an oil paintin Mr. Royston?'

'Aye, I've got a whole room hung with them man. Come to think of it I've got one of Moses striking the rock with his rod to provide water for the Israelites.'

'Then, Mr. Royston, tak that picture into another room where there are no other oil paintins and set it against the wall; then blindfold me, and give me my twig, and let me gyang into the room and I shall find the picture; and when I do, will ye be convinced there is water here?'

'We'll see,' said Royston, still doubtful, but after dinner that day, Craigie Simpson wiped his boots on the mats in the big hoose - he wouldn't take off his muddy boots because he said the ironwork on the soles had some attraction for the mineral he was looking for in the painting - and Mrs. Royston tied a thick cloth round his eyes and handed him the broom twig, which led him straight to the picture of Moses hanging on the wall.

'Now,' said Craigie, still blind-folded, 'lead me to the lawn, and throw a copper penny in the air; not a silver one, but a copper penny, and wherever it lands I shall find it.'

So they led Craigie through the front porch on to the lawn and Mrs. Royston threw a penny in the air and Craigie searched for it in the grass with his twig outstretched before him. In about three or four minutes Craigie found the coin and stood over it between his leather boots, the stick pointing up in his face. Mrs. Royston untied Craigie's blindfold and her husband picked up the penny.

'We'll blast the well,' was all he said.

The blasting had to be controlled, so as not to dislodge the scaffolding supporting the walls, yet strong enough to split the rock and release the water. Royston employed an explosives expert from the Department of Public Works, equipped with a compressor and pneumatic drills, and he supervised the blasting.

The first detonation was a sharp crack that awakened the district and threw stones a hundred feet out of the gaping well, but all the neighbours saw was a puff of brown smoke drifting over the field. News had got around though that Craigie Simpson was digging a new well for the Oyster King and they had a fairly good idea of what was going on.

Sang heard the bang and saw the puff of smoke and in a flash he realised what Royston was up to. He looked at the windmill on the face of the brae, and just as quick it came to him that this was the weapon with which to fight his enemy. Why hadn't he thought of it sooner? And yet if Royston didn't find water it could be his trump card after all. He didn't go to the police because he feared the scandal, but this was something that could be done on the quiet; on the sly, behind somebody's back, which suited Sang's nature, and he gloated over his brainwave. Immediately his own cistern was full he would stop the windmill, thus depriving Royston of a flow of water from a higher level. In this manner Sang imagined he could humiliate Royston and bring him begging for water; either that or it would develop into a war between them, Sang running to brake the windmill and Royston to release it, and likely they would clash and Sang remembered Royston's stick and the thrashing he had endured and decided he would be better prepared next time, armed with a knife, or maybe even the shot-gun; after all, the most they could charge him for would be manslaughter, and he would plead self-defence. Then he changed his mind about the shot-gun; at least for the present, for with that they could maybe charge him with murder.

The blast in Royston's well had not brought them water, so after the mess had been cleared up another charge was set for the following day, round about noon, when the horse beasts would be out of the plough, not to frighten them in the furrows. Meanwhile Sang had shut off the windmill and Royston's cistern was falling fast.

The second blast was no more successful than the first had been, and when the taps ran dry at Barrabrae Royston ran up the road to see what had happened to the windmill. He couldn't see it from the farm, only from the top of the road that ran over the hill, and by the time he reached the summit he was out of breath, his heart hammering and pulsing in his throat, wild with rage. The windmill was stationary, even with a fair breeze going, and Royston realised that Sang had turned it off; that the blasting had given him away, and that Sang had had the brainwave Royston suspected would come to him, sooner or later, only it was sooner than he would have hoped and their private war had begun.

Royston was not a young man, and he had another quarter of a mile to walk before he reached the windmill; yet he struggled on, his walking stick at a swift pace beside him, until he reached the small hinged door into the shed at the base of the windmill. Inside he released the rope from the pegs that held the wheel in check, and the great vane swung round until the wind caught the wheel and set it whirling, the interior shaft plunging up and down driving the pump, a small spurt of water escaping the valve at every thrust, the wooden shed trembling in the vibration set up by the mechanism. There was only one thing for it: stand guard over the windmill; at least until nightfall, when the cistern at Barrabrae would have gathered some water, and by heaven, if Sang appeared he would split his head open, and Royston fingered the silver-mounted end of his staff to reassure himself.

Mrs. Royston became aware of her husband's absence and sent her maid to look for him at the well. Craigie Simpson was hauling up pailfuls of shale and splintered rock, while two men filled the buckets in turn down in the well. He told the lassie her master had gone to look at the windmill, though he himself of course knew little of the feud that existed between Royston and Sang, except for the gossip he had heard about Sang getting a thrashing, and considering the reason for it Craigie thought he deserved it, though Royston shouldn't have flouted the law.

So Mrs. Royston got the grieve to send one of the farmhands to look for her husband at the windmill, where he found his master pacing round the structure like a Serjeant-at-arms. Royston thought of leaving the man on guard a while to relieve him, while he could nip home for a cup of tea; then changed his mind, because he didn't want to involve his men in a quarrel which was strictly his own, perhaps invoking strife and ill-will where it was quite unnecessary; and besides, he was doubtful whether the man would be a match for Sang if he appeared, for Sang would merely order the man to get off his land, and in all fairness he was quite entitled to do so. He sent the man home to tell his wife simply that the windmill needed attention and he would be home by nightfall.

Darkness fell, and Royston shivered in the cold another hour but Sang never appeared, so he left the windmill whirring merrily and set off for home. He had to confide in his wife at this stage and told her everything, and she cautioned him to be careful, and Royston said he wasn't so old but that he could still look after himself with that Damned Coon Sang, whatever his tricks. All the same, his wife said, Sang might have one of his men with him and maybe he should do the same, just in case, but Royston reasoned that this would only spread the quarrel, and he wouldn't involve the servants.

Sometime in the night or early morning Sang had stopped the windmill again and Royston set it going in the forenoon. All day he watched with a flask of tea and just about dinner time he heard another blast from the well, and saw the puff of smoke, hoping every minute to see Craigie or his assistant come running up the road to tell him they had struck water. But nobody came near him, and as darkness closed in again in the short winter day, he closed the shed door on the windmill and walked briskly home.

'You'll catch yer death of cold,' his wife warned him, pouring a hot toddy for her man before his evening meal. But Royston ignored her, merely to say he was sticking to his guns; that no bluddy coon of a rascal farmer was going to frighten him; he who had faced far greater dangers in foreign countries (which she well knew), and Royston resolved to get up earlier in the morning and maybe catch Sang at the windmill.

'But that won't be the end of it,' said his anxious wife, fearful for the consequences if there should be another confrontation with Sang.

Royston reassured her. 'All right woman, give me another couple of days, and if we don't strike water in the well by then I'll go to law. I'll promise you that, but in the meantime I've got to keep the windmill going for our own supply of water. There is no other way.'

But Sang wasn't to be seen in the morning, though the windmill had been stopped again, until Royston undid the rope. All day he sat or paced around the structure, just to let Sang see he was on the job, for he had no doubt the scoundrel would be watching him from a skylight somewhere, or from a tree about the steading. At noon again there was another blast from the well; muffled it seemed and deeper down, and surely this time they had loosed the spring of water. But as the afternoon wore on Royston stopped watching the road, and stuck another lump of black sugar in his hungry mouth.

On the morning of the fourth day of his vigil, while it was scarcely daylight, Royston caught Sang running away from the windmill. Royston waved his stick at him and gave chase, catching him a whack with his stick before he reached the field gate. Another blow crumpled Sang's right arm, and the long knife he was carrying slipped out of his hand. But he ran on and Royston still gave chase, until Sang turned suddenly at the gate and grabbed Royston's stick with both hands. Now it was a struggle for the stick, each wrestling with the other and trying with their feet to trip each other up. They twisted the stick this way and that, each trying to get possession of it, until Royston tripped and fell and Sang wrenched the dreaded stick from his hands. And then he laid on Royston, the older man rising to his feet against the onslaught, taking most of the blows on his arms, until he caught Sang by the jacket and threw him on the ground, the pair of them rolling over each other and Sang holding on to the staff. Each punched and struggled and rolled on the ground until the stick was lost and they went for each other with bare fists, wallop for wallop, wherever they could get a blow in, each trying to rise to his feet, until he was pulled down again by the other, both panting for breath, but Royston being the older man was likely to go out first. And even while they fought an early morning detonation from the well failed to distract them. They swore at each other with bated breath, and the blood flowed freely, and yet they tore at each other like wild beasts, each determined to last it out, and now that Sang had got started his cowardice left him, and he swung at Royston with renewed vigour. The older man was losing his strength, unable to stop Sang reaching for the stick, and in the final tussle Sang got hold of it again; then up on his feet, slashing at Royston, who rolled this way and that, avoiding the blows, and holding his hands over his head to protect his face. Sang's face flared with rage, his eyes bloodshot, saliva at his mouth, trying to crack Royston over the head with the silver end of the stick, until Royston caught his foot and threw him on the ground again.

Both men were now exhausted, their blows more feeble, their breath expiring, their wrestling a mere embrace, until they fell beside each other, nonplussed, their bodies heaving, gasping for air.

Craigie Simpson came upon them at this final moment of capitulation, jumping from his bicycle and running into the field, when both men sat up and stared at him. 'For God's sake, Mr. Royston, we've found water, gushing so fast the well is near half full . . .' But then he stopped and stared at the two figures on the ground, soaked in blood and their clothes torn, now staggering to their feet again, Royston laying first hands on his staff, then his hat, which had gone early in the fight, while Sang staggered about searching for his knife. When he found the knife he put it in an inside pocket and came back to the gate, intending to styter past the two men without a word, until Royston held out his hand. Sang stopped and looked at him in a softer gaze, the hate seemingly gone out of his eyes, then at Craigie, who was still puzzled by the pair of them, and their behaviour; and then Sang took a step slowly forward and held out his hand to Royston. The two men shook hands in a mutual clasp and parted, Sang going up the hill to his farm, while Craigie took his bicycle and walked down the brae with his master.

'Dammit, you were right, Craigie,' Royston was saying, 'we've got water you say.'

'Aye, we have that, Mr. Royston; that last bang broke the seam. But it won't run by gravitation to the fairmhoose; ye'll have tae get an engine tae pump it - far mair reliable than a windmill, always at the mercy o the weather.'

'But you were right Craigie after all, that's what puzzles me. You see, ' Royston gurgled, 'that wasn't a real oil painting; it was an imitation print, the only one I've got that isn't real. How the hell did you manage it man?'

'But there was water in it,' Craigie protested, 'and that was enough!'

'Aye,' Royston laughed, 'and holy water at that.' And he fair roared with laughter.

'But the penny was real, wasn't it?' Craigie persisted.

But Royston was still roaring with laughter. And normally he didn't often laugh.

One-Armed Bandit

Fergie Mann had filled his hoose with dothers trying to get a loon. You could remember a blacksmith who had fathered a football team trying to get a quine, and had managed it at the twelfth arrival; but Fergie wasn't so fortunate and his wife drew the line when the sixth quine made her appearance, for maybe she had had enough of her own sex and wouldn't risk another try. But though Fergie Mann was also a football fanatic he hadn't a loon of his ain to kick a football in the close, though that wasn't the proper reason why he wanted a loon at his heels. Quines could play football come to that, and all manner of ball games; in fact Fergie got great amusement watching his dothers stotting a ball at the kitchie gable, throwing it against the wall and kicking up a leg to catch the ball under it on the rebound. Some of his quines could even stot two balls, catching them alternately in perfect rhythm as they bounced off the wall, like a juggler on a stage, higher and higher and never missing a catch.

But Fergie Mann's desire for a loon in his family had a deeper purpose than playing football, for it was to help him with the wark at Kinsourie, the sixty acre place he owned and worked on the bents at Pittenheath, and maybe a loon could take over when he was too old for the chauve of the place, and maybe under the sod at Bourie kirk.

Aye faith, and that reminded him that next Sabbath was the autumn sacrament and he would have to attend, a bit of a scutter when he was haggled with the wark at the end o hairst, but he would just have to go for the look o the thing and to please the wife. He hadn't been to the spring communion and it wouldn't do to miss two of them, though the wife and one of the married quines had been at the last one. You never knew when you would need a minister and you had to keep in touch with the kirk for fear you offended him.

All of his six daughters had grown up now, four of them married, one in service in the toon, and Babee the eldest helping her mither with the hoose wark and sometimes on the grun, gaitherin tatties and sic like, that were a fair profit when ye could catch the early market, and they grew fine here in the sand aff the bents, better than the corn that was mostly strangled in knot-grass.

Babee would have been married too, but that she fell with a bairn to the son of a big farmer who had jilted her, maybe thinking she wasn't good enough for the likes of him, though she was good enough to take up with. So Fergie gave his quine shelter at home and in reward she had given him a grandson. A grandson! It was a Cup Final Day in Fergie's life when that loon was born. It was a blessing in disguise that wiped all the shame from his conscience of his

297

dother having an illegitimate bairn. What did that matter? He had been denied a son and heir to Kinsourie but now he had a grandson who would bear his name and serve the same purpose.

Fergie was cheerier at the marts and roups than the neighbours had seen him since the Dons Football Club won the Scottish Cup, beating Hibs by 2-1 in 1947. He was like a cock on the sharn midden after the moulting and had been crowing ever since the loon was born. And he diddled that bairn on his knee with an affection that made his other daughters jealous that he didn't take so much notice of their kids, his grand-children that had been born in honest wedlock. He had two loons among his town-bred grand-children, and they were all right for a game of football in the calfies' park, but they had no interest in the farm work and they were feart at the beasts and wouldn't go near a horse, or even a stirk that was chained in the byre. But he would bring up young Fergie differently, and as soon as he could speak he would teach him the farming ways.

Little Fergie he was called, after his grandfather, who insisted upon it, and as the father hadn't married Babee she had to give her son the family surname as well, which suited old Fergie just grand. He wasn't concerned about the father, so long as he paid for the upbringing of the loon. Babee could keep the money, it would make up for the wages he couldn't afford to pay her as a kitchie-deem. And if looks were anything to go by the father could have denied young Fergie on the spot, for by the time he went to school he was the spitting image of his old grandfather, and seeing that the chiel had married another deem by then he wasn't likely to be interested.

Babee's loon had no fear of the nowt beasts; a sturdy nickum who could corner a calf or hold a ewe in a pen or his grandfather got a look at her hoof growth. With every year that passed the loon became more and more interested, until he lived and breathed farming ways, and apart from his days at school he was always with the old man, even to sharing his football enthusiasm, and never missed a match at Pittodrie.

Mechanisation was beginning to bite in the Bogside, as it was all over the country, folk selling their work horses and buying a tractor, and the necessity caught up with Fergie Mann and he sold the pair of work beasts and bought a Massey-Ferguson, one that started on petrol with the gear handle but ran on paraffin once it was heated up. He sold the horses for dog meat because nobody wanted them. It was sad to part with the petted creatures but he didn't have much choice. All the farmers in the Bogside were doing the same thing and nobody wanted horses. They were sold cheaply for whatever use could be made of them, and it was mostly for tins of cat or dog food or as meat for the circus lions.

The sawmillers bought horses to drag fallen trees out of the forests, and that reprieved some of them, while others were sold in Europe for barge pulling, but it was all a mere drop in the ocean compared with horse redundancies over many years.

Fergie carted his harness down to the beach and threw it into the sea: saddles, collars, hames, britchens, backbands and theets and bridles, because nobody wanted that either, and but for the saddletrees and collar pegs still sticking out of the stable walls you would never have guessed there had been a horse beast at Kinsourie, and where there once had been the sweet scent of hay there was now a stink of paraffin.

He also got rid of most of his horse implements, mostly for scrap, but as some of it could be adapted for the tractor on a small place it wasn't such a loss, except that it broke your heart to see a fine longboard plough or a drill-moulder carted away to the scrapyard. Harrows, rollers, bone-davie, binder, reaper, and tattie-digger could be used with the tractor, once you had added a hitching-bar, and the same with the horse carts, fitted with motor tyres. Sparkie Lowe the blacksmith at Bourie did most of that sort of work, now that he had a welding plant; in fact he was almost obliged to do it, because in a year when he had shod about three-hundred horses he was now down to a mere dozen, and these also would soon be gone.

Without the horses Fergie had a surplus of hay, enough to keep a puckle extra stirks in the stable, which added to his income at the store cattle sales, and helped to pay the balance he was owing for the tractor. It was a handy little machine that could be whisked about anywhere without ill-usage, and could work for long hours on subsidised paraffin, which couldn't be said for the hay that fed the horses.

Things were looking up for Fergie Mann, especially since that loon of Babee's came on the go, and it wouldn't likely be long or you saw the scamp seated on the tractor thing, him that had cried all night when the horses were taken away, but now had forgotten about it with the sight of the tractor and all the things it could do on the croft and the hurls he got in the cart. It was plain to everybody that the loon had put new life into old Fergie; not that he was ever lacking in spirit, but he doted on the bairn like he was his own first-born, and his mother had a quiet safe seat in the leith of it, and had even gotten another lad, though that was nobody's business and the thought never troubled her father, so long as she left him with the loon. Babee had given her father something her mother had never given him, and though Fergie knew this wasn't his wife's fault and never hinted as much it was plain that Babee got her own way in everything, though she wasn't a quine to take advantage of her father's generosity.

But now it was the autumn sacrament at Bourie kirk and Fergie had scarcely a straw in his barn to bed the nowt. He should have thrashed on the Saturday but there had been a football match at Pittodrie and he couldn't have missed that for all your sacraments. He told his wife he couldn't go to the kirk because he would have to thrash a load of sheaves for the nowt. She said he had neglected this on purpose as an excuse for not going to the kirk; but he had managed to go to the football. But it didn't matter she said, Babee could take the car and drive her down; though folk would be wondering what had become of him, and so would the minister, seeing he hadn't been there last time, and if your tokens weren't handed in the elders knew you hadn't been there, and they stood in the porch to make sure that nobody else handed them in for you.

299

'It's your money they want woman, nae the tokens.'

'Aye, but ye're supposed to be there tae hand in the envelopes yersel!'

'Is ony o the quines comin oot frae the toon?' Fergie asked.

'No. Ye ken fine that was never arranged and it's owre late noo. You and I was to go and Babee would bide at hame wi the loon.'

'Ah weel wuman, but I'll hae tae thrash onywye. We canna hunger the beasts, kirk or no kirk!'

'Ye should hae thocht on that afore yer fitba.'

'But mighty, wuman, the Lord himsel stripped the ears o corn on Sunday tae feed his disciples.'

'That's nae excuse. Ye're a proper heathen. An fa will help ye tae thrash onywye? Ye canna manage yersel.'

'Och, the loonie will gie me a hand,' said Fergie, 'he's big enough noo tae throw inaboot a pucklie sheaves. Awa tae yer kirk wuman and we will see that the tatties are on the boil or ye come back.'

'See that ye put salt in them than,' and with that Mrs. Mann powdered her nose and got ready for the kirk with Babee.

'You and yer damned kirk,' Fergie taunted, though half in jest, 'If I had my wye I'd have the place burned doon!'

Now the mill was humming, but in his excitement Fergie hadn't left the heating lamp for long enough under the nose cone, so that the engine was back-firing like a regiment of Home Guards at rifle practice, the sky alive with croaking rooks, alarmed at the gunfire, and folk that were passing for the kirk thought that Fergie had gone fair starkers. But at length he had the engine heated up and chooking away right cheerily while he lashed the sheaves into the hungry stripper drum. But the loon wasn't fit to keep him going, struggling with every sheaf from the load that had been toppled on the barn floor. Fergie was in a bit of a fluster and excitement was one of his failings, impatient with any niggling thing that hampered his progress. The mill was whining in idleness between the mouthfuls of corn, impatient for the food that filled the riddles in its belly, for the straw that danced on its delivery shakers, the corn that spewed into the elevator cups speeding up to the grain loft, and the chaff that was blown into the cattle court; for though Kinsourie was a small place Fergie had kept abreast of modernisation.

Fergie came out of the feeder box once or twice to grab an oxterful of sheaves, the loon doing his best to supply him, when Fergie slipped and fell into the stripper drum, the ravenous mouth mincing off his left arm to the elbow, bones and all, spewing the wet red flesh and blood into the corn riddles, all in a flash, before Fergie even realised what had happened to him.

' Stop the engine!' he cried to the loon, and his grandchild sped to the engine hoose to stop its clamour, choking off the paraffin that was its life blood, for Fergie had taught him every move.

Old Fergie staggered from the barn and slouched round the corner to the kitchen door, the dog yelping at his heels, the blood from his elbow stump spouting in the air. 'My God,' he murmured, 'How long can I last?'

He collapsed on the kitchen floor, writhing in pain and shock, his warm blood squirting over the furniture, while he grasped the shattered stump in frustration. 'Give me a cushion, quick, Fergie loonie,' he cried. His grandson gave him a cushion from the settee and he thrust the raw stump into its folds on the linoleum, stifling the flow of blood from the severed artery. He calmed himself to give the loon instructions, flaying his excitement with pressure on the stump, while the oozing blood seeped into the cushion.

'Go to the phone loonie,' he cried, 'get Doctor Bilson's number in the book; ring him up and tell him it's urgent, that I've lost an arm in the mill. Hurry loonie, before I bleed tae death!'

'Loonie' was his pet name for his grandson, and now he used it with compelling urgency. 'Tell him to send an ambulance as weel,' he cried as an afterthought, while little Fergie thumbed through the leafy bulk of the directory.

It was a credit to Fergie's constitutional strength that he never lost consciousness, and he heard every word that his grandson told Doctor Bilson, or whoever was at the other end of the line, for maybe the doctor would be at the sacrament. He was seized with a violent trembling and he struggled to keep his throbbing stump on the cushion, now soaked with blood and spreading over the floor. When the full extent of his injury had filtered through to his shocked brain he was transfixed with a sudden fear. A fear of death. A fear of the Lord. 'Oh my God,' he muttered, 'I wish noo I had gone to the kirk.'

'Dinna leave me Loonie,' he cried in his vexation. 'Dinna leave me. Somebody will tell the folk at the kirk. Maybe you could 'phone the Mullart's folk, they're nearest the kirk, if they're nae a' at the sacrament.' Loonie complied, anxious for the safety of his grandfather, though the tears were running down his cheeks and he spluttered into the mouthpiece between the sobs in his throat.

Fergie was dazed by now and a thick glaur of blood had gathered round the beating stump, congealed on the cushion, and he dared not move it for starting the flow of blood again, an expediency that was saving his life. He just lay there, silent, staring at the walls, trembling, cold from loss of blood, the dog sniffing at the cushion, until little Fergie shooed him away. Then there was the noise of a car in the close and the loon ran to the door. Doctor Bilson was just getting out of his car, and further up the farm road an ambulance was approaching.

There had been no dinner for Babee Mann and her mother that fateful Sunday. They got the fright of their lives when the miller's housekeeper sneaked into the kirk during the sermon and told an elder what had happened, who whispered it to the minister, bending over the pulpit to hear it. The minister then came up the stairs in his long black robes and whispered softly to Mrs. Mann at the end of her pew. On returning to the rostrum the Rev. George Fiddes muttered a prayer for his wayward parishioner, beseeching the Lord to grant his safe return to the fold.

Meanwhile Mrs. Mann and her daughter were speeding on the road to hospital in Aberdeen. They had called in past at Kinsourie but found nobody there; only the dog in the close, wagging his tail furiously, and a blood-soaked cushion on the kitchen floor.

II

But now it was the autumn sacrament of the Lord's Supper again at Bourie kirk, almost a year to the day since Fergie Mann lost his arm in the threshing mill. And if you were sitting on the gentle slope of the gallery, behind Fergie and his family, you could see that his wife sat next to him, on his right side, ready to help him turn the pages of the hymn book she shared with him, while the sleeve on his left side sheathed an arm of shining steel. Babee and two of her sisters sat with their mother, their husbands on Fergie's left, out from the toon for the sacrament, though they didn't always come, but this was a special occasion - Fergie's first return visit to the kirk since his accident.

The family sat on one of the long varnished seats that stretched from the centre aisle to the ochred walls and the gothic window that looked over the fields and farmsteads. Kinsourie was about two miles away with its bourach of twisted trees, like withered arms in the raw dreich wind that swept up from the sea. The sunlight was fitful, darting shafts of light through the smudge of smoke cloud, spotlighting the barren fields with a deceitful glare, while the wind carried the rain squalls across the sky like quiffs of loosened hair. The congregation rose to sing 'Come, Ye Thankful People, Come,' and you couldn't say what Fergie's thoughts were: whether they were a torture of regret that he hadn't come to the kirk that fateful Sunday, or whether he was just thankful that the gluttonous mouth of the mill hadn't swallowed him completely, and that his minced remains weren't rotting under a tombstone beneath the window that looked out on his croft.

The thought of his wife as a widow brought tears to his eyes, though the hand that shared her hymn book was steady in her sight. 'You and yer kirk,' he had said jeeringly that Sunday, 'If I had my wye I wad burn it doon!' But she had never reproached him, or hinted that the Lord had punished him for his transgression. The only obvious difference was that she had to look up the place for him in the psalms and level out the pages, otherwise he brought up the steel shaft from his side, awkwardly at first, with a socket square in it that fitted the knob on the steering wheel of his car.

At work he fitted the robot arm with a sinister looking hook, or with a clamp attachment for the shaft of fork or hoe, or a pincer like contraption for picking up sheaves or holding out his newspaper, a mechanical existence that contrasted badly with his eager and compulsive nature, impatient with a handicap that distorted his anxious progress in the scheme of things. But his courage and cheerfulness in facing his deficiency had already earned him the nickname of the 'One-Armed Bandit', which was really a compliment to his indomitable spirit in facing his disablement. There were men in the parish who would have lost heart; who would have given up the struggle on a croft in the face of it, their spirit crushed in the effort to adapt themselves, but Fergie soldiered on with a smile, his bright eyes undimmed by fate, his thirst for life unabated.

Of course it was disheartening at first, especially when he got up in the morning and couldn't put on his clothes, the healing stump hanging uselessly by his side, throwing him off balance when he tried to hitch up his trousers; and it was nerve wracking trying to fasten shirt buttons with one hand and fumbling with his bootlaces. But he was a chiel of independent spirit and wanted to manage on his own; to carry on the work on the farm, but on those desolate mornings, with tears in his eyes, tears of desperation, his nerve-shocked body in a tremble, he was forced to turn to his wife for assistance. She was the only one who saw him on the floor like a frustrated child, struggling with his infirmity; to the outside world he was always on his feet and fighting. But he soon learned to leave his braces on his trousers and to sling them over his shoulders, and got a zipper on his flap for going to the bathroom.

But if you had expected any serious change in Fergie Mann that first Sunday back at the kirk you would have been surprised at his composure. His eager eyes were still as bright and cheery as windblown skies in harvest time, and men folks who enquired of his well-being were reassured that he was still his same old self. They got a poke in the belly with his steel encased limb that had them bowing before him as if they were doubled up with laughter, and for the women he held out the spike for a handshake, making the excuse that he had to use his right hand to remove his cap.

But sometimes in the kirk he felt the eye of God upon him, an apprehending eye, which hitherto he had scarcely been aware of on his conscience. Now in the face of the whole congregation he felt rebuked, and a fit of claustrophobia seized him, an urge to bolt for the door; that he was an outcast imprisoned with his guilt, much as he had repented his defamation of the kirk and wished to be back in the fold. His salvation was not to be found sitting brooding at home, however, torturing himself with regret; he had to be up and doing, and coming to the kirk he felt he was trying to make his peace with God. And if a tremble seized his body his wife would take his healthy hand in hers and squeeze it reassuringly, and a smile of relaxation would spread across his face.

But Fergie was an impatient Job, and his penance would be long before the Lord relented. He couldn't perceive that he was being tried in the fire, and that yet another sacrifice would be required of him in contrition for his waywardness, a parting that would bring more tears than he had yet shed; for the Isaac of this Abraham would yet be demanded of him before the Lord was satisfied.

In the meantime Fergie was thankful it was his left hand that had been severed, otherwise he would have been doubly smitten, for with his right hand he could still do many things, like holding a pen to fill in his football coupon, or spreading jam on a slice of bread; or even in turning the pages of the bible, wherein he sometimes found comfort in his distress.

But it was in the byres and fields where he felt his infirmity most keenly; stumbling like a bairn with a fork or a hoe, tethered to the shaft with the clamp on his steel arm, like a prisoner chained to a ball, tears of frustration welling in his eyes, while a rolling turnip evaded his capture, or a wisp of hay blew away in the wind. His working day was half as long again as it used to be and stretched into nightfall, when he fell exhausted into his armchair, which beforehand he had scarcely needed. Were it not for Babee and her help in the fields and byres, and little Fergie when he came home from school, his world would have been a shambles.

But he never lost interest in the Dons Football Club. Just as the kirk was a reassurance the football matches were an escape. Even before he got the knob for the steering wheel of his car he was at the road-end waiting for the bus, his grandson by his side, Babee left at home to feed the cattle. And when the Dons scored a goal he held up his steel arm and cheered them to victory. In the old days he held up both arms, but in the steel arm there was a defiance of fate, a challenge with adversity that kept him in the stream of life.

Little Fergie mastered the tractor before he left school, and while he ploughed and harrowed his grandfather stood in the field and gave directions, blowing on a whistle like a referee on a football pitch, and the loon learned the signals and obeyed like a sheepdog, on a code arranged between them, so many blasts for each command, and long into the twilight you could hear the shriek of Fergie's whistle.

From where Fergie sat in the gallery he could see everybody that came into the kirk from the door in the gable facing the road. They came in from the porch where two elders stood by the collection plate and took the token cards from the communicants. Except for those in the back seats everybody had to come up the centre aisle wherever they sat down, and those who came right under the gallery were in full view before they disappeared to take their accustomed seats. This being communion Sabbath the elders were gathered under the pulpit, in the very centre of the church, behind the lectern and in front of the organ, with the choir on either side, and such was the design of the building that this focal point could be observed from every angle, and today was a full house.

His sermon over the Rev. Fiddes came down the stair from his box and seated himself among the elders, where he partook of wine and bread with them as the Master with his disciples, and having blessed the trenchards of bread cubes and the glass thimblefuls of wine on the varnished trays, the elders would distribute themselves about the kirk, passing the victuals along the pews, each member taking a cube of bread and a thimbleful of wine, and when they had swallowed of the body and blood of the Saviour they deposited the tiny glass in a small bracket under the desk in front, where their bibles and psalm books rested.

This was Fergie's greatest embarrassment, when he couldn't pass the trenchard of breadcrumbs and the tray of wine glasses as formerly, and though he managed to put the cube of bread in his mouth, his hand trembled violently when he lifted the glass, while it rattled against his teeth, spilling the red liquid on his shirt front, the red blood of Christ. Worse still, while his wife took great care to place the silver handle of the tray securely in his hand, his neighbour on the other side, his son-in-law, had scarcely grasped it when Fergie in his excitement let go, and the tray and glasses splattered on the floor.

There was a great stir around Fergie, and the folk in front stood up when they felt the glasses birling round their heels, rolling down hill to the front of the gallery. But apart from the spilled wine it was quickly tidied up and another tray of wine was brought forth, though Fergie was flustered and went almost to pieces in his embarrassment. It was as if the blood of Christ had been denied him; as if he was unworthy at the table of our Lord, like an Escariot in the midst of the faithful, rebuked and ridiculed in the house of prayer. In one terrible moment he felt the presence of the Almighty.

But even as Fergie faltered on the steps of rightousness the eye of the Lord was upon him. For this prodigal son the fatted calf had yet to be slain for his homecoming. For this Doubting Thomas the Lord would yet stir up great waters, even as the commotion in parting the Red Sea; yea, even as great as the delivery of Jonah from the whale's belly would be the stirring of waters, and a strange new wonder would come up out of the sea for this present day Saint Fergus, which would bring him great riches and deliverance from evil, and would bring him forth among the Lord's annointed, in the way of the Lord, and he would go forth as Peter before him as a fisher of men. Thus, from the most unlikely sources, and by the most unusual circumstances, He chooses his disciples, even as fine metal that has been tempered in the forge of life. Then Fergie felt the comfort of his wife's hand in his own grasp and the strength of her body seemed to flow in his veins, and she soothed him into calm. The scene passed and the fluster on his face subsided, and the beating vein in his neck resumed its former normality.

There was a long interval while the elders continued their work, and Fergie watched and envied their fitness and capabilities in the face of his own disablement.

But when Benzie Wurrell of the Muckle Ward stood in the lower aisle with his tray a smile crossed Fergie's face. He remembered the story that had been told of Benzie when he picked up the prostitute in Aberdeen. He offered the randie quine thirty shillings for his fun but she would have nothing less than a fiver. But Benzie grudged a five-pound note that Friday in the toon and let her go. He wouldn't budge a penny, and when the quine left him she cried out: 'Ye wunna get muckle for thirty shillings!' Next week Benzie was back in the toon, but this time he had his wife by his side, her with her lang bit neb and her bleary een and her claes thrown on wi a graip. And they met this same quine in Union Street, and she glowered the pair of them up and down in passing, and over her shoulder she cried to Benzie: 'I tellt ye that ye wouldna get muckle for thirty shillings!' But of course Benzie's wife didna ken what the quine was havering about, or what she meant, and blissfully she was none the wiser.

It wasn't a thing to be thinking about in the kirk, but some of Fergie's rampant spirit returned with the thought of it and he almost laughed outright. At least it showed the colour of the elder's coat, and yet he was here unscathed regardless of his transgression. It made a bit of a sham of Christian justice Fergie thought, for his own desecration of the kirk had been no worse, and yet he had been maimed for it.

But from that day forth Fergie was a marked man, singled out from the multitude to carry the cross for Jesus. He was the chosen one of a hard Taskmaster who had tried him in the fire and found him worthy, and in the years to come the truant elder wouldn't be fit to untie the bootlaces of His disciple, so far would Fergus rise in favour with the Lord.

When all the elders had returned to the lectern with their trays and glasses the Rev. Fiddes went back up the steps to the pulpit and called the final hymn. After the singing he gave the benediction and everyone left the building and the fading organ music, and a lot of friendly folk crowded round Fergie and his wife to ask for his well-being.

III

The sacraments came and went and the years rolled on and things went well enough for Fergie Mann. During that time his daughter Babee got married and left the household, leaving her son with his grandparents. But to the neighbours Fergie had changed: gone was the rumbustuous extrovert, and in his place a serious minded gentleman of refinement; one who read books and studied theology and the lives of the Saints, spending hours in the town libraries and at college classes when he should have been at home helping young Fergie with the farm work. He had even stopped swearing and went to church every Sunday, and all you could get out of him was religion. He still went to the football matches occasionally, but not nearly so often, and lads like Benzie Wurrell said he was going clean off his head with religion, but if he didn't land in the asylum most likely he would be enrolled as an elder of the kirk; in fact he said it had already been suggested, and the minister had put forward his name, but that they thought he would be a bit awkward with the trays on Communion Sundays.

But Fergie was not dismayed by what the neighbours thought of his changing personality and his new outlook on life. Religion had added a new dimension to his perception of life; had given grace and beauty to what had formerly been mundane and commonplace, especially in nature and the changing seasons in relation to farming, something he had scarcely realised in his former existence. The Parable of the Sower had a new meaning for him, and he could identify with Joseph and his Brethren during the famine in Egypt, and what had previously been a boring sermon now transpired as almost an incantation on the elegance of Hebrew poetry. He had always loved the land and farming from a practical and commercial angle, but this new appreciation of scripture enriched his thoughts with something that went beyond physical cultivation; a soaring of the mind to meet the challenge of the infinite, to hold court with the unseen power of life, the spirit of growth, the unfathomable source and reason of being alive. Living by bread alone now seemed inadequate for Fergie, and seeking a fuller life became an inspiration, a mission that filled his thoughts with a divine purpose, that others might share his enlightenment. It was as if his physical disablement had been replaced with a mental faculty which had been repressed in his former masculine existence; a sort of staff to lean on which had become a torch in his hand.

Little Fergie had left school but still worked with his grandfather, ploughing with the tractor on neighbouring farms to make up his wages. He couldn't understand the change in his grandfather but accepted it as a sort of reaction to his accident in the threshing mill. And besides, his mind was on other things, like emigrating to Australia with one of his pals, but for the thought of leaving the old man on his own. But of course the neighbours had other ideas, and they said that Fergie had scunnered the loon with his religion. And who else would put up with Fergie saying grace at mealtimes and his bible readings in the evenings? If his ain loon had tired of it there wasn't much chance of a stranger putting up with it.

When Fergie heard of his grandson leaving, he thought of Abraham and Isaac, and that perhaps it was the will of God to do his bidding, to make it impossible for him to continue with the farm, and to embark upon the path of righteousness in a training for the clergy. There was one big snag - he couldn't afford it. Even though he sold Kinsourie at its present value it would scarcely keep him alive for the five years required for a scholarship in divinity, even with grants considered, and he would have to buy a house to live in.

Things were brought to a head in the hay time when Fergie lost his balance and fell off the horse rake that was yoked to the tractor. He fell in front of the long row of sharp prongs at the back, like a dancing portcullis between the wheels, and he was rolled forward on the hard ground like a wood log, while he yelled to the loon to stop the tractor. He was bruised and badly shaken when his grandson pulled him out, trembling all over, and he had to go home until he recovered.

The accident decided his wife that it was time she had her say. She insisted that they lease out the farm to someone else for cropping, on condition that they themselves remained in the farmhouse, though at the same time she knew that her man would eat his heart out with nothing to do. Nor would it bring in enough money to carry him through university, with enough to spare for their daily wants, for she knew what was in his mind and what he wanted to do, however daft it might seem to other folk.

All the same she had her way. Things couldn't go on as they were once young Fergie had left them, and they couldn't afford to pay for outside labour at the present high level of wages.

Then all of a sudden their grandson made up his mind finally to go abroad. He and his pal got a job with an Australian firm of earth-moving contractors, driving the big bulldozers on high bonus pay, far more than he could ever hope to earn with his grandfather, even on contracting work on outside farms.

Parting with his grandson was like the offering up of Isaac for Fergie Mann. He wept openly by the fireside, but the loon wouldn't be dissuaded. His passage was already booked and he was leaving with his friend in three months' time for Australia. Fergie lay awake at night wondering what he would do, and when he fell asleep he rolled onto his arm stump, which stung him wide awake again. His wife had little rest with him, and begged him to take her advice and leave farming, especially now that their grandson had gone.

It was eight years since Fergie lost his arm and he was now fifty-three; not too old yet for the ministry he considered - if he could afford it. Meanwhile they leased the land to a bigger farmer who also filled the steading with pigs, paying Fergie to look after them, and it looked like this was how he would end his farming days; a paid servant on his own premises, little better than the Prodigal Son of the bible.

He held a roup and sold off his livestock, tractor and implements and most of the hand tools, because it didn't seem likely he would have any further use for them, and the money would eke out his income.

But the fatted calf had yet to be slaughtered and there was a great stirring of the waters offshore from Pittenheath; a great commotion in the North Sea where oil and natural gas had been discovered, and the surveyors for British Gas and Total Marine were casting about on the coast for a suitable landfall for their product. One of them tripped over the steel crup of a saddle sticking out of the sand, where Fergie had thrown it all those years ago, and when he looked over the bents his eye lighted on Kinsourie, where Fergie was feeding his pigs, unaware that Divine Providence had relented and that his penance was about to be rewarded with a crown of gold, the Light of the Morning Star and the Keys of the Kingdom.

When the surveyor set up his direction finder he discovered that the saddle prow was in a direct line between Kinsourie and the Frigg gas field some two hundred miles north-east in the sea between the Shetland Isles and the coast of Norway. He called his companions in the search, and after some discussion they decided to put forward a suggestion that Pittenheath was the ideal place to bring the gas pipes ashore, with Fergie's farm bang in the centre, where they could install the thermal storage tanks and the buildings for processing plant and extraction of chemicals.

Fergie was glad he had always resisted his wife's persuasion to sell the farm, because the price he was now offered was far in excess of what the most enterprising farmer could have offered him. He told the Land Commissioners they could have the growthy bitch, and they assured him they could handle the couch grass, and when you saw these giant earth scoops sweeping up the dirt for the foundations of the gas buildings you could believe them. The sad thing about it was that Fergie's grandson had gone all the way to Australia for a job driving one of those bulldozers, tempted by the lucrative pay packets, when he could have started on the beach at home. But such are the ways of the Lord, Fergie concluded.

He got such a stunning price for Kinsourie that his neighbours called him the 'One-Armed Bandit' to his face, and said that he had hit the jackpot. But Fergie merely smiled and poked them in the belly with his fish-hook, which could have torn their ears off, had he not now been a man of God. Some of them who thought they knew him better said that the deil was aye guid tae his ain, but in this case they had hold of the wrong end of the stick, and they might have said that the sun always shines on the righteous.

308

Fergie bought a bungalow in Aberdeen, where his fellow elders said he would be much nearer the Dons and the football stadium at Pittodrie. He did attend a game or two but that was not his main purpose in the city, for he had already completed a two-year course on evening class bible study at King's College, and had graduated for a further full-time three-year training scholarship on theology and divinity studies. He matriculated as a Bachelor of Divinity, a licensed minister of the gospel, enabling him to preach in the parish churches, but until a charge could be found for him he became a sort of priest in limbo, standing in for ministers who had fallen by the wayside.

He eventually returned one Sunday to stand in for the Rev. Fiddes at Bourie, who was indisposed with pneumonia. It was standing room only to hear the Rev. Fergus Mann deliver his sermon, a bigger crowd than he had ever seen on Communion Sabbaths, with chairs brought in from the church hall for people in the aisles, while he stood there by the lectern in his long black robe, the steel arm of God hidden in its folds, gesticulating with his right hand, while he spoke in a hard clear voice that hushed the kirk to silence.

He lifted his text from the First Book of Corinthians, 15-50: 'Now this I say, brethren, that flesh and blood cannot inherit the Kingdom of God; neither doth corruption inherit incorruption. Behold, I shew you a mystery; We shall not all sleep, but we shall all be changed, in a moment, in the twinkling of an eye, at the last trump; for the trumpet shall sound, and the dead shall be raised incorruptible, and we shall be changed. For this corruptible must put on incorruption, and this mortal must put on immortality. So when this corruptible shall have put on incorruption, and this mortal shall have put on immortality, then shall be brought to pass the saying that is written, Death is swallowed up in victory.'

As a basis for his sermon he went back to Kinsourie, which no longer existed as a farm, but had been swept from the face of the earth by the will of God. He didn't speak of the loss of his arm or about his conversion; nor even of the couch grass which strangled his crops, even as the darnel in Palestine, but he dealt at length with another weed that had troubled him over the years as a farmer. He had ploughed it down every winter, hoping to get rid of it, but in the following summer it always appeared again, mostly in wet sour land; which was maybe how Kinsourie had got its name from our forefathers. In summer he attacked the weed with shim and hoe, at a time when it was mostly in flower, before it podded seed, and although he killed the parent plant there was always more to take its place. It was not a very troublesome weed but a very persistent one, determined to survive every form of persecution. Even weed-killers had not subdued it, for in the earth heaps thrown aside by the bulldozers he had seen it again in flower.

This plant was known as the Redshank, probably because of its pinkish flowers and sharing the habitat of these birds, and the botanical name *was polygonum persicaria*. It was also known as the 'Blood of Christ', because of one solitary crimson spot on each pointed leaf, like a spot of blood. Like the Passion Flower with its crown of thorns and its ring of crosses the Redshank was supposed to have been growing on Calvary, under the cross, and that the blood of the Saviour dropped on its leaves during the crucifixion. That may be hearsay, Fergie said, but what concerns us here is the virility of this persecuted plant, and its determination to survive in the most adverse conditions.

The Rev. Mann was not surprised that the couch grass survived, because it had roots everywhere in the soil, like the root of evil, but the Blood of Christ was an annual with an individual root and stem like any one of us in the wilderness of life. Each leaf had its spot of blood that signified this plant above all others in the field, just as each one of us has his spot of sin; and just as each generation is ploughed back into the earth another appears with its spots, for the process of life is eternal, and the presence of Christ immortal, and would remain with us like the spots on the leaves.

Now the Rose of Sharon, known to gardeners everywhere as *hypericum calycinum* is a plant of similar structure, with a lovely yellow flower which has earned for it this biblical name, like the lily growing on the banks of cool Siloam's shady rill, with visions of a land flowing in milk and honey. But not for the Rose of Sharon these spots of blood on the leaves, which you might say was an omission on Nature's part, because the *hypericum is* a domesticated plant growing in gardens, protected and nourished by garden lovers everywhere, which would have ensured a perpetual reminder of the crucifixion. But the wisdom of God shines through even in Nature, for garden cultivation is not the theme of Christianity; rather it is a fight for survival in the midst of persecution and anarchy, with the flower of the fields and boglands as its emblem, exposed to the elements and the plough and the hoe. Even the Passion Flower was denied this divine privilege, not so much because it was a hot-house plant, but because it blossomed but for a day and died with the sunset. Such an emblem was not for religion, which isn't for a day but for all time, though its life in bloom marks the duration of Christ's suffering on the cross.

The silence in the church was uncanny. Surely this was not the Fergie they had known in the past; the worthy who swore freely and cracked foul jokes at roups and mart; the football fanatic who waved a steel arm to cheer his favourite team to victory; the Peter Pan who went on the rampage with a tin-whistle in the gloamin, now in his flowing robes and decanting on the glories of Christ and religion. But their ears had not deceived them, and his strident voice kept them awake with an inspired urgency they dared not ignore.

The actual reappearance of the defiled Redshank plant did not really surprise him, Fergie said, because there were always some stray seeds left in the ground; what puzzled him most was what took place under the earth to make it sprout - this rejuvenation in the seed during the spring months that sent the plant forth again. This is an unseen resurrection that is almost spiritual in its infinite mystery. Science may try to explain it in botanical terms; they may even analyse it in a practical sense, but we remain mystified. The biological chemists will tell us that a teaspoonful of God's earth contains more organisms than the entire human race - but that does not explain the miracle of life.

This invisible transanimation is something of the spirit of nature and yet as tangible as the air we breathe, just as so many other things are hidden from us and yet we have to believe in them. It is a life force that even death cannot destroy, for it breathes life into death in perennial resuscitation, as witness the young tubers on the stem of the old rotting potato, for even as the old plant dies the younger is already alive. It is an inherent stimulus in disembodied nature, one of her hidden mysteries which science is at pains to describe for us. 'No human thought can imagine what is that transformation by which this corruptible shall inherit incorruption, and this mortal put on immortality. We sow a grain, we reap an ear, a corn. Likewise we bury a corruptible body; but it is not a corruptible body that we look for as the harvest.'

Fergie's voice showed not the least sign of self-consciousness, and he spoke with a conviction that compelled wrapt attention, even among the scoffers, dispelling doubt in the minds of those who wavered. Why then, he cried, if Nature can perform such miracles - why should we despair of our own spiritual resurrection? It is no more inconceivable than the infinity of space, which is without end or border line, and in this we believe, because we must, there is no alternative. Was it because of lack of evidence that we are sceptical of an afterlife? Nobody had come back to reassure us. Nobody but Christ, who had risen temporarily in the flesh for the benefit of the chosen few. In that assurance we must have faith; even though it be a blind faith, faith in the things which are hidden from us for a divine purpose we cannot understand, unless it be to give us a choice in dispelling evil to become Christians and achieve salvation, both in this world and the next which is to come.

There was a great sighing and coughing into handkerchiefs when Fergie had finished, and some were in tears, for they knew this man's background, and they just couldn't believe in the change that had been worked in him; a transformation which was even more striking than his theme on the Redshank plant, a weed in their fields that would now have their closer attention.

Fergie's wife didn't go back to her old seat in the gallery. On an occasion like this she felt that her rightful place was on the floor of the church with her husband, facing him from the front pews, where she sat with her daughter Babee and her man. They had come out from the city by way of encouragement for Fergie, but they were not long seated before they realised that he wouldn't require it. All the inspiration he needed was in the response of his congregation, in the earnest faces of the men and the tear-washed cheeks of the women. The reception overwhelmed him, for he had not sought to bring his old friends to tears. He had been apprehensive of his welcome but now he was almost ashamed of the composure their emotion had given him. After all, he had not dwelt on an emotional theme, but their hearts had gone out to him in his new found strength and faith; a man who had been struck down in their midst and was yet whole again, an encouragement to all who faltered on the treadmill of life.

And if his wife had felt embarrassment in their midst it soon slipped away in the encouraging smiles of her old neighbours, warming to her humility in the circumstances. Concern for her husband's welfare was nearer her heart than

311

any feeling of triumph or pride and her old friends acknowledged it. Babee choked back the tears of pride for her father and shyly avoided the assuring glances of her old acquaintances.

Fergie raised his arm of steel and called all to prayer, and with bowed heads they listened to him. He prayed for the sick and the weary and for those who were close to death; for the bereaved and those afflicted with sorrow, for those who were parted over long distances, and for those who were in distress over worldly affairs. He prayed for the welfare of our present Queen and her household, and for the divine guidance of our rulers in the affairs of state, and for the preservation of peace in the world. For the lonely and the weary he had a special word, and for the Rev. George Fiddes, that by the grace of God he would recover his health and rejoin his congregation.

But there was no mention of his own infirmity, or wherebye he had found his new strength to come amongst his old friends as an ambassador for the Most High and Mighty One.

'We plough the fields, and scatter the good seed on the land,' was the closing hymn and it filled the church like a crescendo. The average clergyman may have derided Fergie's sermon. But as a son of the soil he said what was in his heart among farming folk and they understood and were proud of him.

There may have been those who came to scoff but now they stayed behind to shake the hand of the One-Armed Bandit of Bourie.

Twilight Venus

It was four years since Jeck Knowles had come to work at Kinchurn, and now here he was sitting by the bedside of this dying woman. Tina had suffered a stroke, and now he watched over her unconscious body in the living room of the old farmhouse. The maid who was looking after her wouldn't stay the night when she thought her mistress was going to die, though she promised she would be back the next day.

It was a dark March evening and the window curtains were closed, and now that there was electric light on the place a white globe in the ceiling shone down on Christina Smith, known to almost everybody in the parish as Tina, spinster sister to Jason Smith, Jeck's employer. Jason had asked Jeck to look after her until midnight, when he himself would be free to come over from the Homefarm - or the 'Muckle Toon' - to relieve him.

Jeck Knowles was a youngish man and fairly good-looking, though a bit narrow in the shoulder blade to be much admired by women. When women looked at him he felt sure they felt as he did when he saw a woman with spindly legs - uninspired and emotionless. For all that he had got a bit wife and had three bairns and lived hardbye in the cottar hoose along the main road from the fairmtoon nearby.

Being an outfarm he worked mostly alone on the place, especially in the winter months, looking after the cattle in the byres, except when his barn was empty of straw, when the lads from the Muckle Toon would come across the parks and give him a bit bum of a thrash. Pulling turnips was his main job in the fields in winter. In the summer, when his cattle had been dispersed to pasture he joined with the squad in the orra wark, like hoe, hay and hairst and tattie liftin.

Tina had taken a dwam in the morning and the quine that was looking after her had found her mistress lying unconscious at the back of the bathroom door. She was only a temporary maid because Tina was an independent woman and managed on her own. But she hadn't been well this last fortnight and Jason had advised her to engage a maid to look after her. But when the quine found her mistress collapsed in the bathroom she ran to the byre for Jeck Knowles. She wouldn't have done this if the telephone had been working, when she could have 'phoned Jason, but there had been a batter of snow in the night and the wires were down, so she had to run for Jeck. Between them they managed to trail Tina through from the bathroom to the front room and laid her on the couch and happed her with blankets from her upstairs bed to keep her warm.

313

Syne Jeck put on his army greatcoat - the chiel had been in the Home Guard - and left his nowt howlin for mait and set off owre the parks for the Muckle Toon. It was still dark and the morning stars sparkled like golden pin-heids in the frosty sky, while the crunch of Jeck's welly boots broke the crust on the snow. It was heavy going and the wind whipped at his cheeks with an icy thong, while he snuggled his face deeper in the raised collar of his khaki coat.

There were lights at the Muckle Toon, winking through the naked trees, mostly from the byres, where the cattlemen were busy with the morning feed. Jeck knocked on the back kitchen door and the face of Jessie the maid keeked out at him in the mirk.

'What brings ye here Jeck at this time o mornin?' she speired him.

Jeck explained his urgent errand and the lassie ran upstairs to the bedroom of her mistress and Jason phoned the doctor from his bedside. Fortunately the phone wires to the main road were still intact and he got through.

That was nearly twelve hours ago and now there wasn't a mirror small enough in the room that Jeck could use to see if Tina was still alive, nor a feather that could be stirred with her breathing. But he thought he could just feel it on his cheek when he went close enough, so he refilled the hot-water bottle and replaced it at her feet. The doctor had said that the most important thing was to keep her warm, so he heaped more coal on the fire and soon had the place like a hot-house, despite the icy draughts from doors and windows.

Over the years Jeck had been quite a favourite with Tina, washing and polishing her car, cleaning her upstairs windows and looking after her garden in his spare time, and sometimes she'd take him into the house for a cup of tea and a blether, and maybe she'd give him the loan of a book to read, or play over the latest record she'd bought on her braw new radiogram. But there was nothing unusual about this, for there wasn't a tradesman working about the place, or a vanman who called, or a piano tuner who didn't have his cup of tea with her and a hearty chat in the living-room that had once been the kitchen in the old farmhouse.

Tina never tired of telling them the story about the time one of the old farm cottages was empty, and Jason her brother had decided he wouldn't use it again, because it had been condemned, and he would have it pulled down. For a time, however, Jason had allowed Tina to keep her hens in it, after the great gale when her two portable henhouses had been wrecked; collapsing like a pack of cards, her hens flying like birds to a far corner of the field, carried by the wind, and she herself had escaped serious injury, having left one of the sheds a moment beforehand.

So Tina filled the empty cottage with her laying hens and fed them twice daily, and Jason sent a man occasionally to clean it out. The cottage was close to the main road, and one day when Tina was in the cottage a gentleman came out of his posh car and tapped on the door, which was always closed to keep the hens inside. He wanted to know the road to some strange place, but Tina said you should have seen his face when she opened the door in her apron, with hens in the windows and standing on the shelves at her back, all clucking and singing away merrily as if poor Tina lived with them permanently. And she could hardly keep a solemn face to direct him on his way, far less explain her predicament; and she couldn't imagine what the poor man thought when he went back to his car, for he was off in a moment, no doubt in amazement, hardly believing the sight of his eyes.

Before that she had kept a tame pig that spent a lot of time in the farmhouse, lying on a rug in front of the fire, grunting away to itself when it wasn't asleep. One day a deaf mute selling books called at the door, gesticulating with his fingers. But before he really got started the pig sprang forth from the kitchen between his legs and down the farm close, and the poor man got such a fright Tina said, that if anything would ever make him talk that pig should have done it.

Meantime Jeck could hear the traffic faintly on the main road out at the front of the house, across the lawn, about thirty yards away, muffled in the snow that slowed their speed; and there was the occasional gust of wind at the windows, thudding the glass, a fresh wind that would soon dispel the snow. Otherwise the room was as quiet as a mausoleum, and Tina like an effigy under the woollen blankets, just as the nurse had left her.

Jeck lifted the lid of the piano and tinkled a few notes, not that he could play anything but he hoped forlornly that the familiar sound might waken Tina; that perhaps she would move her limbs under the blankets. After all, she was a music teacher and took in pupils for piano lessons to help out with the housekeeping money, for apart from the interest on her bank account she had no other income. People had lived for years after a stroke, Jeck reflected, and the doctor hadn't given up hope for her. He would be back in the morning as soon as it was light and the snow had cleared away on the roads.

Tina was a middle-aged, genteel woman, with a bit of refinement and culture, far above Jeck's standard of living, and yet he managed to talk to her in his own off-hand sort of way, with the little learning he had to keep up with her. She wasn't bad looking either, though getting a little plump and her hair was grey, with the slightest hint of a double chin. In the dark winter evenings she was all alone in the farmhouse. When the windows were in darkness and the garage door left open Jeck knew that she was away in the car. She would be off to play the piano at some local concert, or having a game of whist at the club; attending a sale of work or a guild meeting in the church hall, or at organ practice for the church on Sunday. She was always on the go, but always returned alone, put the car in the garage, closed the door and went up to the house in a brisk walk, fearless in the darkest night. But if Jeck came out of the byre about this time she would wait for him, and the two of them would walk up the brae together, talking about the stars, the weather, the phases of the moon, and what Jeck had missed not being at the concert. Sometimes they got on to politics and even religion and would stand half-an-hour together, especially if it were a clear calm night, and Jeck's patient wife would be wondering what had kept him so long in the byre, when he had only gone along to see that the cattle were safely bedded down for the night.

315

But besides being fearless in the dark Tina was also courageous in adversity, refusing to take life all that seriously, or even death itself come to that; joking with her doctors when they diagnosed her serious illness, holding death at arm's length; living for the present, one day at a time, heedless of tomorrow. Perhaps she knew instinctively that she didn't have long to live. But whatever her fear of death it never reached her lips. She was defiant and strangely insensitive to his presence over the years, and even as he cradled her now in his cold arms there was the shadow of a smile at her slightly twisted mouth.

Jeck put more coals on the fire and replaced the guard, while Tina's dead parents in their Edwardian clothes stared down at him from the papered wall, wondering what he had to do with their daughter. Another picture of Tina's that Jeck liked was the inside of a kirk with a young man playing at the organ and two angels looking in at the window and not a soul in the pews. Jeck thought the best time to look at this picture was in the early summer mornings when nobody was about, and he used to keek in at the window where it hung on the opposite wall before Tina was up, just as the angels were doing, spying on the young man at the organ, and the sight of it in the quiet secret light of the morning made him feel creepy all over.

Looking at it now wasn't quite the same. He wasn't spying any more, but the thought occurred to him that the angels might be keeking through the blinds at him now, watching him with Tina, before they came to take her away. He looked at Tina and he could have sworn her eyelids flickered. Maybe he just imagined it but he watched her intently for a while, then touched her cheek with the back of his hand, but she was still soft and warm.

He sat down in the armchair again and tried to read the daily paper but he couldn't anchor his thoughts. He got up again and took the blind aside but there was nobody there; nothing but the black sky and a white mantle of snow on the ground. Even the traffic had dwindled away and a sad moaning wind moved the naked arms of the trees. The mantel clock chimed ten and settled down again to its quiet ticking. Two hours yet before Jason would arrive.

Jeck was hungry. It was now over four hours since he had supper and Jason had told him to make himself at home. He could have helped himself to whisky from Tina's cabinet but he was not in the mood. Tea would be fine and he knew where Tina kept her caddy and her home-baked shortbread, scones and queencake. She did a lot of home baking and Jeck knew where she kept her tins in the pantry.

Jeck boiled the kettle on the cooker ring and brewed himself half-a-pot of tea. After tea he sat and smoked, helping himself from Tina's cigarettes on the mantelshelf. It was warm and cosy in such richly furnished surroundings, with a lush carpet on the floor, and after such a long day on his feet he felt drowsy, almost on the verge of sleep.

Jason had engaged Jeck Knowles as a stockman in this very room, after showing him round the premises and introducing him to Tina. She had lived here with her late mother since Jason took over the Homefarm. Formerly Jason

316

and his wife had lived here with their family, but when their father died Jason became manager of the family estates and moved to the Homefarm, changing places with Tina and their widowed mother, who had since died and Tina now lived here alone.

When Jeck first shook hands with Tina, Jason remarked to him that she had never been married - 'though she's had plenty of lads,' he added, jokingly: 'and if ever ye get tired o yer wife ye can come along and sleep wi her.'

Tina said nothing to this but smiled blandly, accustomed apparently to her brother's blustering jokes; perhaps half expecting that the chiel would accept them in a spirit of frivolity, though her white face coloured notably in the lamp light. But Jeck thought she must have turned forty and must by now have realised she was most likely to be left on the matrimonial shelf.

Over the last four years however, from occasional remarks by Jason, and some from the neighbours, a body could gather that in her youth the ebullient Tina had been something of a tomboy; more likely to be seen on the roof of the steading than in her father's parlour, or playing with the cottar loons in preference to the quines, and later with the chaumer chiels rather than with the females of her own age group. In fact Tina had established quite a reputation for herself with the youths of the parish, from farmers' sons and budding auctioneers to tradesmen and seedmen's agents, with the occasional bank clerk thrown in and the odd clergyman in passing.

But not one of them had managed to pin Tina down to domestic bliss, maybe because she was too particular in her choice of a husband - 'Owre ill tae please,' as Jason put it - or because she had always preferred her freedom to being tied up with a man and his bairns. By the time her father died Tina must have known she was at the end of her romantic tether, for her life was then devoted to looking after her ailing mother.

But Tina made no boast of her romantic conquests, nor explained to anyone why they hadn't led to marriage, and if she referred to the subject at all it was in a jocular manner. How she became a spinster was a topic enjoyed by Jason, who made a big joke of it and seemed to delight in making fun of her in front of strangers, a prerogative derived from the fact that he was himself happily married, as were their brothers and sisters, all except Tina, and she became the butt for his flagrant, boisterous, tantalising humour, which poor Tina, as the wayward black ewe of the family accepted without rancour.

Whatever the reason for her spinsterhood Tina still liked the company of menfolk, as Jeck could well testify, though he'd never breathed a word about it to anybody, not even to his wife, for fear he created ill feeling between her and Tina. Jeck minded on that time she had cornered him in the little milkhouse under the water cistern, across the driveway from the back kitchen door. He was filling the cottars' flagons just before supper time when she went in after him and closed the door at her back. There was barely room for the two of them standing between the shelves, and with Tina between him and the door Jeck had no escape. The window was a mere peephole in the gable, covered with gauze, so that nobody could see them, nor open the door while Tina stood behind it.

She had chosen the time and the place carefully, with about fifteen minutes to spare before the cottars collected their milk flagons. Jeck was defenceless, with a milk flagon in one hand and a measure jug in the other, so he just stood there while Tina kissed him softly on the cheek, her brown eyes searching his face for some reaction or response. But he just stood there, mystified, surprised and a little shocked that the sister of his employer could become so intimate with him. She was so tactful, so tempting, so bold; and though not really beautiful quite a woman in her way, with quite a lot to offer a lad of little means if he were anywise inclined to play the love game with her. With so rich a bait, so much to offer a poor cottar, Jeck was tempted for a moment to replace the utensils on the shelf and embrace her. Och it wouldn't matter for a bit kiss in the sly, nobody would know about it and her lips were rich and ripe, her eyes chasing his own in a futile orbit.

But where did these things end? This was how they began but the results could be wretched, and if Jason got wind of it he might sack him on the spot, in spite of all his buffoonery. And Jeck was a happily married man with little excuse for yielding to a lovelorn spinster, and though he tended Tina's garden he was no Lady Chatterly's Lover.

Tina was disappointed and her eyelashes fluttered in her displeasure. 'Are we too old for courting then?' she asked, her hands itching to lay hold on the tactful Jeck. 'I'm sure you're not amiss to a bit of love-making, even though you are married.' Jeck could have said he thought she might be past it, and how unfair it would be for his wife; but he just stood there, nonplussed, scarcely knowing what to say to appease her. 'Oh I suppose so,' he managed to say at last, thinking of the risk she was taking and rather sorry for her besides. Tina turned her back on him and opened the door, then stood for a moment watching him, perhaps hoping for a snap change of fortune, then left abruptly and skipped over to the house. Since then she had treated him more casually but things went on much as before. The odd cup of tea when Jeck was in the garden, a book to read, a chat on current affairs, the soft brown eyes watching him always; then a swish of skirts and she would leave him to his own torment and self discipline.

Since then Tina had been dogged by ill-health: first by a heart enlargement and the removal of two ribs to allow for expansion, and her only lament on this occasion, after extensive surgery, was that she now had a rib less than the menfolk, which hadn't happened since Adam and Eve, and she joked about the loss of her 'Woman's Rib,' which she said had formerly given her a feeling of superiority over the male sex.

She then developed an abdominal cyst which extended her girth prodigiously, when she joked with her friends about being 'in the family way,' and every male who had been enticed into her parlour was whimsically referred to as the father, though Jeck Knowles wasn't included in her catalogue. But those who paid a sympathy call, or out of curiosity, stayed to marvel at her courage in making fun of such a sinister misfortune.

By medical decree Tina was obliged to carry her growth for an allotted period, wherein the doctors deemed it ripe for surgery, a circumstance which enriched the humour of her pregnancy hoax, when Tina would hold her bulging waist line in both hands and laughingly predict the month of her delivery, saying she wouldn't have long to go now, and folk marvelled at her brazen stoicism and lively spirits.

When the surgeons removed the cyst at the infirmary they showed it to Tina and said it weighed twelve pounds, and she added relish to the story by saying it actually had hairs on it, and that she felt no pride in being the mother of this monstrosity - delivered, she joked, by Caeserian means. Fortunately her growth was not malignant and Tina came back from hospital slim as a teenage girl, boasting that the devil himself would be her next male conquest.

But Tina was laid low again, this time by cerebral haemorrhage, and the anxiety was that though she lived she would never be the same effervescent Tina, but more likely a liability to her family, and knowing Tina a body knew she would rather have died.

Again the clock chimed, eleven musical staves and Jeck got up from his chair once more to look at his charge. She still lay motionless in the single bed and the memory of his wife's dream came into his mind. Early that morning, while Jeck was at his brose, his wife told him the alarm clock had awakened her from a strange and rather embarrassing dream, and this would have been about the time that Tina collapsed in the bathroom. His wife said she had dreamed that she was in bed with the farmer, Jason Smith, and though the details were a bit hazy in her mind, she remembered that Jason had behaved in a most respectful and apologetic manner, the two of them trying to figure out how it was that they had come to be in the same bed; whereupon she was awakened by the clock, but determined to tell Jeck about her dream while it was still fresh in her mind. Jeck made fun of it at first and wondered he said what the devil would have got up to if the clock hadn't gone off.

But his wife didn't think it was funny, and neither did Jeck before the day was done, because Jason came to him in the byre just before dinner time and asked if he had a single bed to lend that would hold Tina in the living room, because the doctor didn't want her moved upstairs, and it would save them a lot of trouble in taking her own double bed downstairs.

Jeck went home to consult his wife and told her the riddle of her dream had been answered, and that it was a good thing she told him her dream beforehand or he wouldn't have believed her. He called her a witch, though a pretty one to humour her, and then the two of them set to thinking how they could lend Jason the single bed. Two of their loons had a bed each while the little nipper still slept in a crib, so they would put the two big loons in the double bed and Jason could have the single one, and Jeck said in fun that he didn't deserve it for sleeping with his wife. She slapped his lug for him and said if she had known he was going to make fun of her dream she wouldn't have told him about it, and she warned him not to tell Jason.

Jeck went back to the farm and told Jason he could have the bed and mattress, though he didn't tell him about his wife's dream. Jason went along to the cottar house to collect the single bed and mattress in the boot of his car, and when Jeck's wife saw him she could hardly look at him because of her embarrassing dream.

Jeck looked at the clock again and it was thirty minutes from midnight. He began to yawn from weariness waiting for Jason and sat down in the chair again. He had had a long day.

Then he must have dozed off in the armchair and the reality of the moment took the form of another drama. Somehow he knew Tina was dying and he had gone over to kiss her goodbye. Surely he thought in his dream there could be no harm in it for a dying woman. But it had become a kiss of life and she came alive in his arms, sitting up in bed and staring around her, whereupon Jeck ran to the phone and was reporting her progress to Jason. He was excited about her miraculous recovery, while he watched her from the hall, shouting into the phone:

'Now she has thrown off the blankets. She's coming out of the bed. She's on her feet, a bit shaky but she's holding on to the bed. She's coming over to the phone. You'll hear her in a moment. Here she is . . .'

Jason was shouting from the other end of the line. 'You've fallen asleep,' he cried, and he shook Jeck vigorously into wakefulness. 'It doesn't matter anyway, Tina's dead!'

'Poor Tina', was all that Jeck could say, and he got up and looked at her still in the bed, his mind jumbled between a dream and wakefulness.

'I was dreamin aboot 'er,' he told Jason, 'I could a sworn I saw her oot o the bed. It was so real like when ye woke me up.'

'Weel maybe she just got up tae go tae heaven, poor soul,' Jason said; 'she's just newly dead 'cause she's still warm. Ye havena neglected her and ye're fair done for want o sleep. Awa ye go hame tae yer bed. I'll tak owre noo but I couldna come sooner.'

Jeck took a last look at Tina, bade Jason goodnight and departed. Half-way along the avenue he glanced back in the darkness at the farmhouse, for he was now fully awake in the cold. Jason must have gone upstairs because there was a light in Tina's bedroom. Maybe he was replacing the blankets on Tina's own bed. She wouldn't need them now. Then he suddenly wondered: How close was a dream to the supernatural? Had he actually seen Tina's spirit leave her body in the minutes that he slept?

On his way home he had to pass the old cottage where Tina had kept her hens. It was empty now and the windows in darkness but a car was stopped on the road and a man was knocking on the cottage door, a loud hollow knocking that made Jeck's hair stand on end. In the darkness he looked like a man in black, with a Quaker's hat on his head, and long flowing robes like a priest.

But Jeck had seen enough, and he took to his heels and ran to the cottar house where his wife would be waiting. Should he tell her his own dream?

Naething in his Heid but Beasts!

'Naething in his heid but beasts!' That was what they said about Jason Smith, the farmer up at Bucklechnie, and they didn't mean lice, but that his thinking was all about cattle beasts, and a woman who had jilted him for that reason triggered off the aberration and it had stuck with Jason. But he had gotten another woman since then and was now settled down contentedly with a wife and twa bairns on the fairm.

But he certainly knew his cattle, and with a staff in his hand on the road, with fences at both sides, and the men herding the nowt for him, he wasn't long in selecting the fattest ones for the butcher on a sale day. To see them all in a bourach you wouldn't have seen the difference between one black stot and another, all Aberdeen-Angus breed and all so much alike, but when Jason had made his selection you had to admit he had separated the sheep from the goats so to speak. To say 'fattest' isn't exactly correct but cattle in prime condition would be nearer the mark. The unwanted bullocks were herded back into the field for further grazing, while those ripe for slaughter were herded to the loading ramp at the Home Farm, where a cattle float would be waiting to take them to the marts in Aberdeen.

Jason was kittle and short-tempered on these occasions, and would have sacked you on the spot if you had spoken back to him, or didn't jump to attention like a sodger when he cried on you to kep a beast that was likely to run away. He was an exciteable man, nervous and high-strung most of the time, but when working with cattle he bristled like a hedgehog, which seemed strange when cattle were his chief interest in life, and you thought he would be relaxed and confident in his judgement. But self-confidence was something he lacked, and he wouldn't even trust himself to buy store cattle in the sale ring, but had an agent do it for him on a small commission.

Jason didna like a dog amon the nowt, they waurna like sheep he said and had a mair defiant attitude; mair likely tae jump roon on a dog or kick 'im in the teeth than tae follow each ither like sheep. A dog upset the steers Jason said and the tyke was left at hame on a sale day. He had all the answers about cattle, nae only their beef potential but their behaviour as weel, what he called bovine psychology, by which he could predict how they would react in a tight corner or in front of an open gate when herding. He could foretell the weather by the way they capered and pranced about before a storm and he even spoke their language. He didn't require a dog to gather cattle in a field, he just stood at the gate with his hands to his mouth and mooed like one of themselves and in little over five minutes every stirk in the park was at the gate. They were less intelligent than a horse he said but not so stupid as sheep. A horse rose on his fore-legs first to see over the long grass; a coo rose on her hind legs, head on the ground and less aware of danger. According to Jason the ox was the most inquisitive mammal ashore or afloat. He swore by Taurus the Bull that if you lay down in the middle of a park of sheep they would ignore you, but if you lay down among oxen you would be surrounded in ten minutes, and if you lay long enough and still enough they would lick your face and go through your pockets and chew your hankie, but if you made a sudden movement they would panic and scatter. When a bairn was ill you looked to see if his tongue was coated; when a calf was off-colour you felt if his lugs were cold, and if they were it was a sure sign of ailment, or if he wasn't chewing the cud. When a stirk was standing all by himself in the corner of a park that was another sign of illness. And if you wanted to take his temperature you stuck the thermometer in his arse so's he couldn't chew it, even though he didn't have teeth in front on his upper mandible, like most other species of the cloven hoof.

But if Jason was well schooled in bovine behaviour he was less knowledgeable in human psychology, or perhaps he had less regard for humans than for cattle, or just didn't care about human reaction. But to give the man his due, if he had sacked you on the heat of the moment most likely the next day he would tell you to forget about it; that he was just upset at the time and anxious about getting the cattle away on time for the sales. He blustered his way through life and tidied up afterwards. His face twitched all the time from a nervous disorder and he was always scratching himself where you felt sure he wasn't yokie, and mostly chewing a straw because he didn't smoke, which might have eased him by way of a sedative. When he wasn't away in his posh car he swaggered about in corduroy trousers, his jacket swinging open and a watch and chain in his waistcoat pockets, a big man and his hat mostly tilted to the back of his head. He was a hard nut to crack before you got through to him, but after you had been in his service a year or two you found he wasn't all that bad and that he did have some good points. He criticised your faults but he also gave you praise if he thought you deserved it. 'Man, ye're makin a grand job o cleanin oot that ditch,' or 'That's the wye I like tae see a fence putten up, a' the posts the same heicht an level on the tap, the wires a' level wi the grun and a' the same distance atween them.' And then when you thought you were fairly in his favour and took a wee bit of liberty and was late in starting a job he would bark: 'If ye canna be here at yokin time ye'll nae be lang aboot the place!' So you had learned to ignore him and to trample most of the stite he said under your feet. He was a bit quick-tempered and kept a tight fist on his bawbees, but he always paid his servants regularly, and though they didn't get anything extra they got every penny they were entitled to. His wife made up the wage packets, your name and particulars written on the envelope in her neat lady-like hand-writing, the sum of money owing to you and the amount deducted for insurance.

She was a genteel body, the exact opposite of her man, the auburn-haired daughter of a Highland vet, and Jason had met her at a farmers' ball after some evening classes they had been attending. She was the stabilising influence behind Jason's bluster, smoothing troubled waters when he had had a row with the workmen, her sane quiet voice a balm to his agitated thoughts. Jason didn't like tea-breaks for instance, and he reckoned he lost ten minutes twice a day from each man who stopped for tea from his thermos flask. He declared that with a staff of six men this added up to a man's wages for a week, and that he would have to sack one of them to make up for it, and as nobody had taken the trouble to work it out mathematically he got his own way. But tea-breaks had become fashionable on the farms and he never managed to stop them. He tried it once in the hayfield and sacked one man as an example, but the rest all stuck together and defied him, and the new man appeared the first morning with a piece-bag on his shoulder and Jason gave up trying.

His wife was against him in this, and if any of the men were working in the garden or painting the doors and windows about the steading she took them inside and treated them to high tea. Jason would be looking at his paper in the kitchen but he never said a word and you couldn't make head nor tail of it between them. The mistress of Bucklechnie was an expert cook, trained in the School of Domestic Science, and her cusine was such that when the stem-mull was about the place she fed the working hands like they were at a Lord Mayor's banquet, so that they were hardly able to work, and lay down exhausted on the straw till yoking time.

The only time that Jason treated you was at Hogmanay. On New Year's morning he would come to the byres with a whisky bottle and glasses and he would pour you a good dram, wishing you 'A Happy New Year!' He probably did this because the stockmen were the only men working that day, while the tractormen were still in their beds. And he didn't mock you with a wee nip: oh no, you got a brimming tumblerful of Glenmorangie, and with nothing to dilute the stuff you was in high spirits by the time you'd finished your byre work, and went styterin home to breakfast like you had been a night on the binge. And if your cattle had sold well at the marts Jason would give you a pound note out of his wallet and a free week-end to spend it while your byre was empty. At the end of summer, before you was tied up for the winter, he would tell you to have a good week-end because it would be your last one free for seven months, until the end of the fattening season in May, when your byres were emptied of butcher cattle and the court stirks went out to grass. After Jason was sure that you would look after his cattle properly he began to put more trust in your endeavours and you would see less of him in the byres. Not that he interfered much; in fact you got more of your own way than you would have looked for with such a man.

'Man,' he would say, 'ye're the first cattleman I've ever seen feedin his nowt wi bruis't corn first thing in the mornin, maistly they aye gie them neeps first . . . but I'm nae gaun tae stop ye, yer beasts thrive owre weel for that.' You consider this a great compliment and you explain to him that the feed troughs are clean in the morning after you have scraped them out and are free of turnip smush and that the beasts are hungry then and lick up every oat-flake. Then he tells you he's going to have them try it at the Home Farm. But of course you was only at the oot-fairm of Kinchurn and not worth listening to.

There was that year that the straw was tasteless from a profusion of Day-nettle in the crop and the cattle at the Home Farm wouldn't eat it. But Jason noticed that the beasts on the oot-fairm were lapping it up and he wanted an explanation for this anomaly. So you took him to the shed outside and pointed to the treacle cask on its trestle in a corner. You were diluting the molassine treacle with water and spraying it on the straw in the wall racks. Another lesson for the folk at the Muckle Toon and they weren't going to like it.

Sometimes in winter the butcher selected his own choice of fat cattle from the byre stalls, a private sale that would save Jason commission fees at the marts and transport charges and he would be paid dead weight prices per hundred-weight with no overheads. Jason would warn you well in advance of the day that the butcher was coming, and he would tell you to hap up yer draff hurlie, 'cause he disna like beasts fed on draff; he says it gies the beef a yalla colour, like smoked haddock, and it's nae sae easy tae sell in the London market! So you would cover up the draff trolley with sacks in a corner of the turnip shed, and as you fed the stuff to the animals in the morning and the butcher wasn't coming until the afternoon he wouldn't know what you was giving them, unless he felt the smell of it. These visits were carefully timed by Jason to coincide with the feeding routine, when you had just finished giving the animals their turnips, and they were all munching heartily in the stalls, their flanks and bellies extended from muscular effort and the intake of food, rather than standing lank at the end of their chains with their hind hooves in the urine channel. Of course the butchers knew their trade and couldn't be easily deceived, but from where he saw them from the greep or passage down the centre of the byre, with a row of rounded buttocks on both sides and heads down in the troughs they made a fine picture of prime conditioned animals. It gave the impression of a lively appetite and healthy well-being compared with animals standing back from their empty troughs.

But the first thing the butcher did when he got out of his car he took off his heavy overcoat and threw it on the draff hurlie. It was a wonder you thought that he didn't feel the smell of it for it was like a distillery whenever you opened the door of the turnip shed. It was cheap at the time and when mixed with crushed oats the animals loved it and it bulked the feed. But the butcher said nothing and walked the full length of the byre, then made his selection, handling all the stots as he went along. Jason followed him with a scissors, taking a snip of hair from the beasts the butcher wanted, leaving a small mark of identification on their backs, just above the hind-quarters, but didn't spoil their appearance. 'I'll tak that ane!' the butcher would say, pointing to a glossy black two-year-old you had coddled and petted for nearly five months; 'and that ane!' after handling another, 'and that ane and that ane!' for it seemed he could tell lean meat from fat with his finger-tips, and he worked the length of the double byre with stalls at both sides. From a total of forty chained cattle he left a mere half-dozen, which was a pretty good average, even by Jason's standards. The butcher put on his coat and shook hands with Jason at the door. Then he turned and said: 'Ye needna bother tellin yer cattleman tae hap up that draff hurlie; it has a damned fine smell onywye, like a distillery - eh cattleman!' And then he was off.

Now here was a butcher selecting prime cattle from your byre for the posh hotels in London, where the gentry could afford to dine on silverside or sirloin steak, while at hame ye had tae be content wi a bittie beef tae stew or bile or a bone tae mak soup, or a dollop o fatty mince, all that your poor wife could afford to the vanman, even though ye was helpin tae produce the finest meat in the country, getting up before six in the morning on a bowl of oatmeal brose and working at week-ends for nothing, seven days a week for nearly eight months in the year. And it was no use complaining to Jason. He gave you everything you were entitled to as stipulated by the Wages Board. Jason blamed the butchers and the dealers for making the biggest profits. He said you never heard of a butcher going bankrupt while some poor farmer was calling in the receiver every week. His stock phrase was that after he had refilled his byre with young bullocks and paid his wage bill and overheads all that the cattle left him was their dung. 'A' that I'm left wi is their dirt an it dis help the corn crap a bittie!'

To make matters worse your good relationship with Jason over the years had aroused a bit of jealousy at the Muckle Toon owre the brae, especially with the grieve who liked to be furthest ben the lobby with the farmer. Too much of the oat crop was leaving the oot-fairm on the hoof, quite a profitable outlet for Jason in a subsidised meat market, but no credit for the grieve who liked to see it going into sacks in cereal returns, his main concern in the running of the place. But Jason had his priorities in proper perspective with the oat subsidy at a very low ebb, so that when the grieve complained that you was spending too much time in the byre and not enough on the outdoor work Jason ignored him, even told him to send someone over to help you out.

So the grieve hid your bruiser belt and you couldn't get oats crushed for your cattle. You searched for it a whole week in your spare time but couldn't find it. So you confided in the foreman tractor-man when he was coupin a load o neeps in your shed. He said he had seen the grieve hidin the belt the last thrashin day but he didna ken faur he put it. Maybe he did but was afraid to tell for getting himself into trouble with the grieve.

So you had to tell Jason what had happened, and at the same time you told him something else about the grieve, something you should have complained about months ago, or even longer, but that you were afraid of getting him into trouble with Jason. But by concealing your bruiser belt the grieve had forced your hand and you was tempted to have your revenge.

So next time Jason was in the byre you told him about the disappearance of your oat-crusher belt, and that without it your cattle were starved of oats. 'Ah weel,' says Jason, 'I'll seen sort 'at oot gin I gyang hame. I'll fin oot faur yer belt is or he'll gyang doon the road. Ye're sure it was the grieve that hid it?'

'Oh aye, the foreman says he saw him wi the belt the last time we thrashed.'

You then took Jason to the barn and told him to feel the ears of corn still on the straw that was supposed to have been threshed. Jason took a single straw in his hands and ran it through his fingers, where about half-a-dozen ears of corn were still on the stalk, and every straw was the same, clean conached.

'The grieve's thrashin that corn ower fast,' Jason says, 'he's nae gien the stripper drum time tae thrash the strae, nae eese ava.'

So you took Jason back to the byre and told him to look at the cattle dung in the urine channel, with the oats from the straw they had eaten still in their dung, without a tooth-mark, wasted. Oats have to be crushed or kibbled before cattle can digest them, otherwise the oat kernel comes through the beast whole and lands in the midden, worthless.

'That's done it!' Jason said and left the byre.

So he gave the grieve a month's notice to leave and he confessed he had hidden your pulley belt for the bruiser up the old chaumer lum where you had never thought of looking for it.

And Jason hadn't thought of it either, though there was naething in his heid but beasts. But he liked tae see his corn crap gyan oot aboot on the hoof, nae in bags, and it had cost the grieve his job.

Glossary

abeen: above
abody: everybody
affa: awful
agley: askew
agyaun: on the go, available
aince: once
airt: area, direction
aleen: alone
anaeth: underneath
anent: opposite
aneuch: enough, sufficient
antrin: occasional
athegither: altogether
ava: at all

backet: shaped wooden box, open at one
    end for carrying peat, potatoes etc.
back-speir: to talk back
bade: told, instructed
bailie: cattleman, stockman
baith: both
bannocks: pancakes
barfit: bare-foot
barra: barrow
bass: rug, mat
bawbees: money
beddies: a girl's game
bee-ruskie: bee-hive made of straw
ben: towards the other part of a two-
    roomed house
besom: broom
beuk: book
bicker: dish, helping of brose
bide: to stay, wait
bigg: to build
bigsie: proud, conceited
bing: heap, mound
bink: hob, small bank at side of grate
birn: heavy bundle tied with rope and
    carried on the back
birse: temper, anger
bizzin: buzzing
blate: ignorant
blibber: dribble, trickle

boll: ten stone of oat-meal
bone-davie: manure distributor, used
    originally for spreading ground bones
bool: a round marble used in schoolboy
    games
borealis: from aurora-borealis, northern
    lights or 'Merry Dancers'
bothie: apartment where farm workers
    lived, slept and cooked their own food
bourach: a small crowd
bowie: barrel
bozie: bosom, oxter
braw: grand, stylish
brazen: bold
bree: sauce, gravy, cooking stock
breeks: trousers
breet: opposite of brute, one deserving
    sympathy
breid: oat-oakes
breist: breast
brig: bridge
britchen: leather harness fitted over horse
    rump with chains for reversing or
    braking cart
brocht: brought
brose: oat-meal mixed with boiling water,
    salt and pepper
bubblie-jock: turkey-cock
bucht: shed, wooden building or lean-to
buckie: sea-shell
buggericks: slang or swear word
bummin: humming

ca: to call or drive
cairt: cart
canned: drunk
canny: careful to avoid risk, slowly
canty: cheery
caperin: clowning, acting the fool
carle or carlin: fellow of ill-repute, a
    schemer
casten or cas'en: cast off, changed or
    soiled
causey-steens: causeway-stones

chakie: haversack
chap: to knock, a hammer-blow
chaumer: chamber, sleeping apartment for
farm workers
chauve: to struggle
chiel: man
clacht: to grasp or clutch hold of, to snatch
claes: clothes
claik: gossip
clart: to smear, to soil
clipe: tell-tale, gossip-monger
clockers: broody hens
cloo or clew: ball of wool or straw rope
clyack: end of cutting in harvest
clyack sheaf: last bound sheaf in harvest
cogie: small wooden bucket for feeding
calves with milk
cole: haycock
conach: to waste
coonter-louper: shop-keeper or assistant
coordie lick: a challenging blow dealt out
amongst youngsters provoking a
response
coorse: wicked, spiteful, vulgar
corn-kist: large wooden chest or trunk for
holding corn in a stable
cottars: married farm workers
coup: to topple, empty, overturn
crabbit: short-tempered
craitur: creature
cronie: pal, chum, friend

dab-hand: expert
dackle: to hesitate, go slow, loiter
darg: to dig
daily darg: daily routine
daunder: to stroll, amble
daur: dare
daw: dad, father
deave: to deafen, a bore
deem: girl
ding: to knock, push over, thrust aside
dirl: to ring, vibrate
divot; sod, turf
dominie: schoolmaster
doo: dove, pigeon
dookit: dovecot
doot: doubt
dother: daughter
dottled: confused, senile

douce: quiet, sober
doup, buttocks
dour: sullen, sulky
dracht: draught, twin load or consignment.
Can also imply draught or wind.
dreel: drill, of turnips, potatoes etc.
dreich: dull, cold and wet
dresser: old-fashioned kitchen sideboard
with back and shelves
drizzen: dull, drizzly
drookit: soaking wet
droon: drown
dross or drush: peat crumbs
dry-darn: constipation
dry-piece: dry bread without liquid
dubs: mud
dumfoonert: dumfounded, surprised,
shocked

earth-closet: dry lavatory
eerie: weird, unearthly
eident: steady, consistent, reliable
eneuch: enough
ettlin: eager, impatient
eyen: eyes

farrier: veterinary surgeon
fash: to fuss, excite
faur?: where?
fecht: fight
fee-ed: engaged for employment
ferlies: strange happenings or noises
fern-tickles: freckles
fich!: an exclamation or cry of pain. A fich
is also the nipple on the bowl of a clay
pipe
firlet or firlit: from the English firlot
measuring 2.5 stones of oat-meal
fleer: floor
fleerish: flourish, steel knuckle-duster for
producing sparks from flintstone
flist: sudden blow, outburst of temper
fluffert: flurry of snow
foon: foundation for corn-stack
foonert: foundered, gone lame
fooshinless: lifeless, without substance
foostie: mildewed
forrit or forrard: forward, well advanced
fraik: to placate or pet, as with animals
frichen: to frighten

fule: dirty, unwashed
fung: lame
fusker: whisker, moustache
fut?: what?
futret: weasel

gaed: went
gaen: gone
garred or gart: made, forced
gaun: going
gawking: staring ignorantly
gear: goods, riches, possessions
geets: children
gelding: young castrated horse, clip or foal
genteel: gentle, refined, cultured
gentry: upper class
gie: to give
gig: small horse cart or car, usually with
    solid rubber tyres
gipe: fool, silly ass
gird: wheel-rim or spokeless hoop
girn: to complain
girse: grass
gite: mad
glaed: glad
glaiket: silly, ignorant
glaur: mud
glory-hole: lumber or junk repository
gock or gowk: idiot, fool
graip: short, cross-handled, four-pronged
    fork
grat: wept
gree: to agree
greep: byre or stable floor, cement or
    cobblestone
greet: to weep
grieve: foreman or man in charge of work
grippie: tight-fisted, mean
grouth: weed or couch grass, string-weed
grubber: horse-pulled, long-tyned
    cultivator
gyang: go

habber: stutter, stammer
hach: to clear the throat of glit or phlegm
hackin sticks: chopping firewood
haflin: young man, male teenager
haimes: steel frame fixed over horse
    shoulder-collar with hooks for drag-
    chains

hairst: harvest
hairy tatties: potatoes and dried fish
hake: wooden frame for drying fish or truss
    for holding straw
hame-ower: home-loving, plain,
    domesticated
hangman cheese: cheese curds pressed into
    guaze cloth and hung outside to drain
    and harden
hankering: longing, craving
hantle: large quantity
harn: rough sacking
harras: harrows
haud: hold
haugh: mud flats, river valley
haun: hand
haverin: talking nonsense
hefty: heavy, strong, powerful
hey: hay
hicht: height
hinna: have not
hinner: hinder, delay
hirple: to limp
hish: to shoo, herd, chase off
hist: a good number
hoast: to cough
hobble: crouching movement
hoch: animal hindquarters, below the
    buttocks
hoiter: to toddle like a toddler or to
    swagger
hooch: to shout or ejaculate from the throat
    while dancing a reel or jig
houdi: midwife
howes: valleys
hurdies: hips, thighs or animal hind-
    quarters
hyowe: hoe

ilk: kin, family
ilka: every
ill-faured: ill-featured, unattractive

jalouse: to suspect
jaud: jade, a woman of pernicious
    behaviour
jile: jail
joog: jug or cream stoup

kaim: comb

331

keek: to peep

kinch: to wind or tie up as with a rope or reins

kist: chest or trunk

kittle: to brighten up

kittlin: kitten; giving birth to kittens

knack: imitation noise of wooden cart wheel when sounded with hard k, as opposed to knack, meaning skilful, with soft k

knackery: animal offal factory

knowe: brae, mound, summit

kyard: woman with a sharp tongue

kyardin: verbal abuse, slander

lade: millrace

laft: loft, garret

lairy: soft, marshy (ground)

lames: fragments of broken crockery used in schoolgirl games

lauch or lach: to laugh

leal-loved: well-loved, sincerely

leather-jacket: larva or grub of the daddy-long-legs insect

leear: liar

leepy: small wooden box for feeding a measure of crushed oats to horses

let dab: reveal

limmer: girl of loose moral behaviour

littlin: baby or small child

loon: boy

loup: to leap

lour: to darken, cloud over, become sullen

lug: ear

lum: chimney

maet or mait: food, diet, menu, including red meat

mair: more

maitter: matter, something of consequence

marra: match, equal, similar in appearance

martingale: nickle-plated harness decoration, worn on a leather strap

mastitis: udder infection, sometimes referred to as udder-weed

maun: must

meck: half-penny

mere or meir: mare

midgicks: midgies

mirk: twilight, dusk

mishanter: mishap

moggan: hidden money-bag, sock or stocking, but can also indicate spats or leggings

mou: mouth

mouser: moustache

muckle: much, enormous

muffler: scarf or large 'kerchief worn round the throat

mull: mill

neep: turnip

neist: next

new-fangled: modern, up-to-date

nicked: pregnant

nickum: pet name for a boy

nicky-tams or waal-tams: leather straps with buckles worn below the knee by farm-workers

nieve: fist

nocht: nothing

nowt: cattle

onywye: anyway

ooball: woolball

oolit: owl

orra: odd, dirty, menial

orra-beast: odd or single horse

orra-man: odd man or casual farm-worker

ower: over

oxter: armpit

pap: teat, female breast

pech: to gasp

peewits: lapwings, teuchats

perquisites: provisions in lieu of wages

phaeton: four-wheeled horse-drawn vehicle

pickiesae: gaudy-coloured, soft tweed hat

piece: sandwich

pints: bootlaces

pirn: small wooden reel for holding thread

pleiter: to work in the rain

pleuch: plough

pleuch-stilts: plough-handles

ploy: antic, trick, stunt, gimmick

pooch: pocket

pooer: power

pooshin: poison

poother: powder

powin: the pound sterling

prig: to plead, beg, implore
puckle: small quantity
pucklie: very small quantity.
pun: the pound weight

quaik: heifer
queet: ankle
quine: girl
quirk: trickster, twister, con-man

rade: to be rid of
rael: real, realistic
randie: girl of dubious behaviour
rape: rope of straw or sprotts
rashes: bullrushes
ravel: ruffle, to entangle or entwine,
    confusion
rax: to stretch
reek: smoke
reeshle: rustle
reistit: roosted, rested
richt: right
rickle: heap, small cairn, ruin
rickling: stacking up wet peats on their
    ends to dry
rig: to fit out
rig or lea-rig: sections of a field in horse
    ploughing
riled: angered
rive: to tear, wrench or rend
rosette: a harness decoration
rottans: rats, vermin
roup: auction sale
rouse: to awaken or to anger
rowdy: troublesome, violent behaviour
rucks: corn, barley, wheat or hay stacks
ruggin: pulling
runt: stem, stalk

sab: to sob
sair: sore, painful
saps: milk and bread sops
sark: shirt
saut: salt
scrach, scraich or screich: scream or sharp,
    shrill cry
scrimp: to economise, cheat
scunner: to disgust
scutter: to delay, hinder or loiter
sech: to sigh

segs: rafia straw, can also imply reeds or
    bogland
sharn: cow dung
shelt: pony or light horse
shelvin: boards fitted on sides of horse cart
    to accommodate a bigger load
shie or shy: when a horse recoils or rears in
    fright
shim: light horse implement for removing
    weeds from between turnip or potato
    drills
shoudin-boats: fun-fair swing-boats
sic: such
sicht: sight
sieve: gauze strainer for milk
sieven: seven
siller: silver, money
simper: sigh or whimper, to utter a low
    whining tone of distress
skeely: skilful
skelp: to slap
skirl: to scream
skirlie: fried oatmeal and onions
skite: small quantity; to eject, squirt or
    spurt
skweel: school
slammach: fairy gossamer
sleekit: deceptive
slubberin: slavering, dribbling
smiler: large rake pulled by a rope from the
    shoulder
sneck: hasp or latch for fastening door
snib: small catch or door fastener
socht: sought
sort: to repair
sotter: mess
sough or souch: blast or force of wind
soun or soone: sound
sowens: form of gruel made from corn
    husk
speen: spoon
speir: to enquire
spleiter: splatter (of rain)
spoot: rone pipe or running well
spruce: tidy, neat, smart, clean
spunk: spirit, spark or match
spurtle: stick for stirring porridge
stamagaster: shock, surprise,
    disappointment
steen or stane: stone

steer: bullock, also stir or noise, upheaval

stem-mull: steam mill

stibble: stubble

stickit-nieve: clenched fist

stime: glimmer, infinitesimal patch of light

stirk: heifer, half-grown cow

stite: nonsense

stock: man, when mentioned favourably

stocket: stubborn

stot: castrated bullock

stoup: spout or cream jug

stracht-theets: drag chains at full stretch

straik: flat stick, used to whet a scythe or measure a bushel of grain

stramash: tumult, confusion

stravaig: to wander aimlessly

streikit oot: stretched out

stroop: spout, penis

stroud: screed, poem, song, monologue

strushle: rough, untidy, shabby, unclean

styter: to stagger

suppie: small drop, a trickle

surtoo: surtout coat, frockcoat, usually black

swack: swift, agile

swey: hinged or swivelled gantry over the fireplace

swick: to cheat

swines' hoose: pig sty

swuppert: fast, quick

syne: since

tanzy: ragwort, field weed with yellow poisonous flower

taraneezin: tormenting

tattie-boodie: scare-crow

teem: empty

teuch: tough

teuchat: lapwing or peewit

thackit: thatched

thackit-biggin: building with thatched roof

thocht: thought

thole: to endure

thoom: thumb

thrapple: throat; to choke or strangle

thraw-heuk: instrument for winding straw into ropes

thrawn: stubborn, unyielding

tig: mood or tantrum

timmer: timber

tint: lost

toshil: tassel

track: dress, usually untidy

trauchle: weary struggle

trig: tidy, respectable

troch or trochie: small trough of wood or stone

tryst: meeting place for lovers, a rendezvous, also to attempt, lure or persuade.

unca lookin: off colour, unwell

vricht: joiner, carpenter

vring: to wring, as in clothes washing

wall-tams: *see* nicky-tams

wannert: wandered

wark: work

wauken: to waken

weet: wet

weevil: worm or grub

whaup: curlew, snipe or pea-pod

whaur: where

wheedle: to entice or implore, to bargain

whirligig: merry-go-round, chair-o-planes

winna: will not

wizened: withered, dried up

wud: mad

wull: will

wye: way

wyte: fault, blame, guilt

yammer: to talk incessantly

yappin: chattering

yark: to rap or slam, a vigorous sudden movement

yaval broth: broth made the previous day

yaval crap: an oat-crop, two years running in the same field after lea

yerned milk: milk in the first stages of curdling

yett: gate

yird: earth, ground

yoke: wooden spar for pulling plough, also shoulder-yoke for carrying water

yokie: itchie

yokin: shift or period of work

yowl: howl, shout, cry out

yows: ewes